Praise for the novels of
JOE BUFF

"Joe Buff takes the reader through a labyrinth
of action and high adventure."
Clive Cussler

"Lots of action, lots of grit."
Dick Couch, Capt., USN (ret.),
author of *The Warrior Elite: The Forging of SEAL Class 228*

"A superb high-water mark in naval fiction."
Michael DiMercurio, author of *Emergency Deep*

"[Buff] delivers fascinating technical detail [and]
white-knuckle undersea action."
Patrick Robinson

"Buff makes for sleepless nights.
This man knows his stuff."
David E. Meadows, Capt., USN, author of the Joint Task Force series

"[Buff] will keep technothriller fans at
sea most of the night."
Booklist

"[Buff] out-Clancys Tom Clancy."
Kirkus Reviews

Books by Joe Buff

STRAITS OF POWER
TIDAL RIP
CRUSH DEPTH
THUNDER IN THE DEEP
DEEP SOUND CHANNEL

And coming soon in hardcover
from William Morrow

SEAS OF CRISIS

JOE BUFF

STRAITS OF POWER

HarperTorch
An Imprint of HarperCollinsPublishers

This is a work of fiction. Names, characters, places, and incidents are products of the author's imagination or are used fictitiously and are not to be construed as real. Any resemblance to actual events, locales, organizations, or persons, living or dead, is entirely coincidental.

HARPERTORCH
An Imprint of HarperCollins*Publishers*
10 East 53rd Street
New York, New York 10022-5299

Copyright © 2004 by Joe Buff
Excerpt from *Seas of Crisis* copyright © 2005 by Joe Buff
ISBN-13: 978-0-06-059470-1
ISBN-10: 0-06-059470-5

First HarperTorch paperback printing: September 2005
First William Morrow hardcover printing: December 2004

HarperCollins®, HarperTorch™, and ❦™ are trademarks of Harper-Collins Publishers Inc.

Printed in the United States of America

Visit HarperTorch on the World Wide Web at www.harpercollins.com

10   9   8   7   6   5   4   3   2   1

"Sir, when the love of peace degenerates into fear of war, it becomes of all passions the most despicable."

—Senator Giles of Virginia,
to President Thomas Jefferson,
before the War of 1812

The enemy you don't see coming, because of your own blind spots and preconceived notions, is the one who'll get you every time—and the enemy knows it too.

NOTE FROM THE AUTHOR

Submarines rank among the most sophisticated weapons systems, and the most impressive benchmarks of technology and engineering, ever achieved by the human race. Stunning feats of courage by their crews, of sacrifice and endurance, loom large on the pages of history. Since the end of the Cold War, a whole new generation of submarine classes, with astonishing sensors, weapons, off-board vehicles, and stealth, was conceived and is under construction by the United States Navy.

The world's oceans are the world's highways for the transport of goods and the conduct of commerce. Continued mastery of undersea warfare is vital, because whoever controls the ocean's depths controls its surface, and thus protects much of the world. Seapower, strongly employed, is key to upholding peaceful societies everywhere.

But do America and our Allies take our free access through international waters too much for granted? Advanced submarine technology is proliferating among countries who haven't always been our friends. Nuclear weapons are also spreading at an alarming pace, with transnational conspiracies, shrewdly hidden for years, only recently being unmasked. What mortal threats to freedom still remain hidden?

The enemy you don't see coming, because of your own

blind spots and preconceived notions, is the one who'll get you every time—and the enemy knows it too. The 9/11 Commission Report warned us all of "failures of imagination" and "unprepared mindsets." Beyond the global war on terror, what shape might the twenty-first century's almost inevitable, eventual, major worldwide armed conflict take? When faced with so many dangerous future unknowns, the Navy wargames worst-case scenarios to learn everything it can. As a professional writer and seasoned risk analyst, my extreme action-adventure novels aim to do the same thing, based on a firm foundation of extensive, constant non-fiction research. Perhaps the only certainty is that heroic submariners and special operations forces will play a key role in deterring that next big war, or in winning it.

Joe Buff
March 2005
Dutchess County, New York

STRAITS
OF
POWER

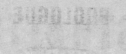

PROLOGUE

B y the middle of 2011, the global war on terror had flared up and died down repeatedly, with serious losses in treasure and blood. Personal freedoms in many countries had also been eroded, while international friendships more and more were a thing of the past. Third World economies teetered on the edge of ruin, even as some long-standing major players thrived; the divide between the haves and the have-nots gaped like an open, festering wound. Whole peoples turned inward, or turned against themselves, as ideologies became dogmas and moderation was crushed under cynical rhetoric. All this was the cost, and the legacy, inflicted or triggered by those whose highest goals were senseless destruction and death. Then, just as the worst of the terrorism seemed to have finally been contained, that struggle was eclipsed by a shocking new conflict of much greater magnitude.

In July 2011, Boer-led reactionaries seized control of the government in South Africa, which was in the midst of social chaos, and restored apartheid. In response to a UN trade embargo, the Boer regime began sinking American and British merchant ships. U.S.-led coalition forces mobilized, with only Germany and Russia holding back. Troops and tanks drained from the rest of Europe and North America, and a joint task force set sail for Africa—and into a giant, coordinated trap.

Then there was another coup, this one in Berlin, and Kaiser Wilhelm's great-grandson was crowned, the Hohenzollern throne restored after almost a century. Ultranationalists, exploiting American unpreparedness for such all-out war, would give Germany her "place in the sun" at last. A secret military-industrial conspiracy had planned it all for years, brutal opportunists who hated the unfettered cross-border mixing of the European Union as much as they resented what to them was seen as America's arrogance and bullying. Big off-the-books loans from major Swiss and German banks, collateralized by booty to be plundered from the losers, funded the stealthy buildup. The kaiser was the German shadow oligarchy's figurehead to legitimize their new order. Coercion by the noose won over citizens not swayed by patriotism or the sheer onrush of events.

This Berlin-Boer Axis had covertly built small, tactical atomic weapons, the great equalizers in what would otherwise have been a most uneven fight—and once again America's CIA was clueless. South Africa, during "old" apartheid, ran a successful nuclear arms program, canceled around 1990 because of international pressure. Preparing for the new apartheid, and working in secret with German support, the conspirators assembled many new fission devices; compact, energy-efficient, very low signature dual-laser isotope separation techniques let them purify uranium into weapons-grade quality in total privacy.

The new Axis, seeking a global empire all their own, used these low-yield A-bombs to ambush the Allied naval task force under way, then destroyed Warsaw and Tripoli. France, stunned, surrendered at once, and continental Europe was overrun. Germany won a strong beachhead in North Africa, while the South African army drove hard toward them to link up. The battered Allied task force put ashore near the Congo Basin, in a last-ditch attempt to hold the Germans and well-equipped Boers apart. In both Europe and Africa, the fascist conquest trapped countless Allied civilians: traveling businesspeople, vacationing families, student groups on summer tours. American and British citizens were herded into internment camps next to major Axis bases, factories, and transport nodes, and were held as hostages and human shields.

It was unthinkable that the Allies retaliate against Axis tactical nuclear weapons, used primarily at sea, by launching ICBMs loaded with hydrogen bombs into the heart of Western Europe—especially when the massive, murderous fallout of H-bombs dropped on land obeyed no nation's overflight restrictions. The Axis intentionally, shrewdly, avoided acquiring any hydrogen bombs of their own. Thus the U.S. and the UK were handcuffed, forced to fight on Axis terms on ground of Axis choosing: the mid-ocean, with A-bomb-tipped cruise missiles and torpedoes. Information-warfare hacking of the Global Positioning System satellite signals, and ingenious jamming of smart-bomb homing sensors, made the Allies' vaunted precision-guided high-explosive munitions much less precise. Advanced radar methods in the FM radio band—pioneered by Russia—removed the invisibility of America's finest stealth aircraft.

Thoroughly relentless, Germany grabbed nuclear subs from the French, and advanced diesel subs that Germany herself had exported to other countries—these ultraquiet diesels with fuel-cell, air-independent propulsion needn't surface or even raise a snorkel for weeks or months at a time. Some were shared with the Boers, whose conventional heavy-armaments industry—a world leader under the old apartheid system—had been revived openly during the heightened global military tensions of the early twenty-first century. A financially supine Russia, supposedly neutral yet long a believer in the practicality of limited tactical nuclear war, sold weapons as well as oil and natural gas to the Axis for hard cash. Most of the rest of the world stayed on the sidelines, biding their time out of fear or greed or both.

American convoys to starving Great Britain are being decimated by the modern U-boat threat, in another bloody Battle of the Atlantic. Tens of thousands of merchant seamen died in the Second World War, and Allied casualty lists grow very long this time too.

Almost a year into the war, in late spring of 2012, America is still recovering from serious setbacks in the Indian Ocean theater. The vital Central Africa pocket, composed of surviving U.S./coalition forces and friendly local African troops, is temporarily in less danger of being enveloped by the Axis—maybe. In a frightening new thrust from which the whole world is still reeling, Axis agents made serious trouble in Brazil and Argentina; key U.S. resource supplies and America's southern flank were suddenly put in jeopardy.

Now, the Germans plan a fresh campaign of astonishing daring and callousness, based on a hair's-breadth margin between success and utter catastrophe. This new Axis land offensive could topple an already unstable global geopolitical balance: Japan recently announced that it was a nuclear power, but insisted on staying neutral. Then the Israelis revealed that early in the global war on terror, they used supposed cooperation with German authorities to smuggle in and hide on German soil a dozen Hiroshima-yield atom bombs. The bombs would be set off by Mossad sleeper agents in Germany if Israel's survival was threatened by any Axis assault. The U.S. was given no notice of this in advance, and, from America's diplomatic and military perspective, Israel made the shocking announcement at the worst possible time. Relations between the U.S. and Israel are sundered by bitter mistrust. Most ominous of all, American and British intelligence see signs that the latest German attack somehow involves the Middle East.

If the situation deteriorates much further, and reckless Axis risk taking brings everyone involved too close to the brink—with Allied forces badly overstretched as it is—the U.S. will have no choice but to recognize German and Boer territorial gains. With so many atom bombs set off at sea by both sides, and the oil slicks from many wrecked ships, oceanic environmental damage has already been severe. Presented with everything short of outright invasion, and nuclear weapons not used against the United States homeland quite yet, the U.S. may be forced to sue for an armistice: a de facto Axis victory. A new evil empire would threaten the world, and a new Iron Curtain would fall.

America and Great Britain each own one state-of-the-art ceramic-composite-hulled fast-attack submarine—such as USS *Challenger,* capable of tremendous depths—and the Axis own such advanced vessels too. But there is a dangerous wild card, beyond the impending German land offensive. Unrecognized by the Allies for what role she'll really play, the first in a whole new class of nuclear subs has been custom built in secret in Russia, exclusively for German use: The ultrafast and remarkably stealthy *Grand Admiral Doenitz* is armed to the teeth and about to set sail. This tremendous covert increase in the level of Russian support for the Axis might disrupt Allied operations decisively. The U.S. is on the defensive as it is, and democracy has never been more threatened. In this terrible new war, with the mid-ocean's surface a killing zone, America's last, best hope for enduring freedom lies with a special breed of fearless undersea warriors. . . .

CHAPTER 1

May 2012

Commander Jeffrey Fuller stood waiting in the warmth on the concrete tarmac at a small corner of the sprawling U.S. Navy base in Norfolk, Virginia. He looked up at the very blue sky, telling himself that today was a good day for flying: sunny, with almost no haze; easterly breeze at maybe ten knots; and a scattering of high, whispy, bright-white clouds. Noise from helicopters taking off and landing assaulted his ears. Another helo sat on a pad in front of him, as its powerful twin turbine engines idled. The main rotors above the Seahawk's fuselage, over the passenger compartment, turned just fast enough to be hypnotic. Jeffrey had been badly overworked for much too long. He fought to not stare at those blades, and abandon himself to being mesmerized, and letting his mind go blank and drift away. But the intoxicating stink of sweet-yet-choking helo exhaust fumes, mixed with the subtler smell of the seashore wafting from the mouth of the Chesapeake Bay, stirred his combat instincts, helping him stay alert and on his toes.

Jeffrey glanced at his watch, then at the cockpit of the matte gray Seahawk. The pilot and copilot sat side by side, running through their checklists. The helo should be ready for boarding soon.

Jeffrey was glad. Ever since he'd woken up before dawn this morning, for some reason he felt the loneliness and burdens of command with added poignancy. This seemed a warning of bad things to come, things he knew in his bones would happen soon—Jeffrey had learned to trust his sixth sense for danger and crisis through unforgiving, unforgettable experience. The ceramic-composite-hulled nuclear submarine of which he was captain, USS *Challenger,* sat in a heavily defended, covered dry dock at the Northrop Grumman Newport News Shipbuilding yards not far from here, northwest across the James River. For several weeks now she'd been laid up and vulnerable, undergoing repairs and systems upgrades after Jeffrey's latest hard-fought battle, thousands of miles away, deep under the sea.

His rather young and clean-cut crew were working on *Challenger* around the clock, side by side with the shipyard's gruff and gritty men and women who applied their skills to Jeffrey's ship with a vengeance. Vengeance of a different sort was on everyone's mind, because this terrible war against the Berlin-Boer Axis was by no stretch of the imagination close to being won. Atomic explosions were devastating the Atlantic Ocean ecosystem, and stale fallout from the small warheads being used sometimes drift to settle in local hot spots even well inland. Gas-mask satchels were mandatory for all persons east of the Mississippi; radiation detectors were everywhere. Some reservoirs, too contaminated, were closed until further notice; entire industries, including East Coast beach resorts, were wiped out, even as other industries thrived because of the war. Only price controls, and price supports, prevented rampant hyperinflation or a regional real estate market crash.

A messenger had arrived, just as Jeffrey sat down to go over today's main progress goals with his officers. And now here he was, thanks to that message, not in the wardroom on *Challenger* but waiting for a helo shuttle at barely 0800—

eight A.M. Taken from his ship and crew on short notice, and ordered at once to the Pentagon without even the slightest hint as to why, left Jeffrey distracted and concerned. He was a man who liked control of his destiny, and was addicted to adrenaline: *Deny me these and I'm almost half empty inside.* The ribbons on Jeffrey's khaki short-sleeved uniform shirt did little to console him.

Even thoughts of his recent Medal of Honor, and his brand-new Defense Distinguished Service Medal, couldn't disperse Jeffrey's mental unease. Strong as they were in traditions and symbolism, the ribbons were merely small strips of metal and cloth. They paled compared to the draining things he'd gone through, and the awful things he'd had to do, to earn these highest awards from a thankful nation. The medals grated on Jeffrey's conscience too, because they made him be a hero and a national celebrity, but said nothing of those who'd been killed under his leadership. Jeffrey sometimes felt haunted by the faces of the dead; he had a keen sense of cause and effect, of the link between his actions and their consequences, and he remembered clearly every person who died while doing what he as captain had told them to do.

Jeffrey perked up when a crew chief came out of the back of the Seahawk carrying a bundle of head-protection gear with built-in sound-suppression earcups, and inflatable life jackets. Jeffrey put on all the safety equipment, donning the big, padded eye goggles last. He picked up his briefcase and his gas-mask bag.

Conversation was impossible now. The crew chief told his passengers what to do by using hand signals. The other passengers, junior officers and chiefs who were strangers to Jeffrey, seemed to know the routine. By privilege of rank and standard navy etiquette, Jeffrey got in last. He took the place reserved for him, among several running down the center of the fuselage and facing sideways, so he could look out a window. He buckled in, then shifted to get more comfortable on the black vinyl sheets of his seat.

The crew chief stowed the luggage; his assistant slid the

door closed. The crew chief came around and quickly checked everyone very carefully. He pulled Jeffrey's seat-harness shoulder straps uncomfortably tight, then gave a firm tug to the chin strap of his helmet. Jeffrey and the crew chief made eye contact. The navy didn't salute indoors, but the chief had seen Jeffrey's ribbons. The chief gave Jeffrey a look of acknowledgment, and extra respect. Jeffrey, never more rank conscious than he needed to be, returned the look and gave a quick nod. The chief's eyes showed a special hardness that couldn't be faked, and the gauntness of prema-ture aging that no one could hide, which proved he'd been in combat in this war. In comparison, the other passengers looked too fresh faced, their eyes in an indefinable way much too naive for them to be combat veterans.

Couriers, perhaps, Jeffrey thought, *or some other essential administrative jobs.*

He felt heavy vibrations through the deck and through his backside. The muffled noises getting through his hearing protection grew louder and deeper in pitch. Outside the win-dows the ground receded, then the Seahawk put its nose down so the main rotors could dig into the air and grab more speed. The helo turned west, inland.

Immediately, two other helos closed in on the Seahawk, one from port and one from starboard. Jeffrey knew these were the shuttle's armed escorts. They were Apache Long-bows, two-man army combat choppers. Jeffrey saw the clus-ters of air-to-ground rockets in big pods on both sides of each Apache. He watched the chin-mounted Gatling gun each Apache also bore, as the 30-millimeter barrels swiveled around, slaved to sights on the helmets worn by the gunners.

These escorted shuttle flights were necessary. The Axis had assassination squads operating inside the U.S., targeting military personnel with high-level expertise or information. They'd almost certainly been pre-positioned and pre-equipped secretly, during the long-term conspiracy that had led to the war. Some of the teams were former Russian spe-cial forces, Spetznaz, now in the pay of the Germans and willing to die to accomplish their tasks. The schedule of the helo shuttles varied randomly, and their flight paths varied as well, to stay unpredictable.

Jeffrey forced himself to relax. He was well protected now.

The passenger compartment smelled of lubricants, plastic, and warm electronics; there was no solid bulkhead between the passengers and where the pilot and copilot sat, and Jeffrey could see the backs of their heads if he craned his neck to the right. The compartment was stuffy from the aircraft having sat in the sun before, so the crew chief's assistant slid open a couple of windows. A pleasant, slightly humid breeze came in.

Built-up urban and then suburban areas petered out, and the land below was more forested, the road net thinner. The helos descended to just above the treetops without slowing, and the tips of southern pines tore by in an exhilarating blur. The Apaches both wore camouflage paint with blotches of green and black and brown, so they became harder to see against the foliage. Jeffrey's helo, with its plain gray paint job, would blend in much better against the sky for anyone looking at it from the ground. He assumed this tactic was intentional.

He folded his arms across his chest, lulled into a semi-doze by the Seahawk's steady, reassuring rotor and transmission vibrations and engine roar. He still felt pangs of regret for finally ending his on-again, off-again relationship with Ilse Reebeck, a Boer freedom fighter who'd joined him on several classified missions. Once, Ilse had broken up with Jeffrey, saying they came from different cultures on separate continents, and with his seeming death wish in battle, Jeffrey could never be Ilse's choice for a lifelong mate, someone to father her children. But then she'd wanted to get back together again, and Jeffrey had been more than willing. The passion that resumed, whenever they were on leave together, quickly became as stormy and edgy as ever—and eventually Jeffrey had simply had enough. He realized that the two of them were in an emotional co-dependency, that the same things that drew them together also triggered deep-seated resentments.

Jeffrey was startled when the helo suddenly banked

sharply into a very tight right turn. The power-train vibrations grew harder and rougher as the helo's deck tilted steeply to starboard. The g-force pressed Jeffrey into his seat; outside, the world slid down away from view and he could see only the sky. Jeffrey's gut tightened. He grabbed wildly for armrests that weren't there and felt afraid and didn't know what to do with his hands. The others in the compartment also showed worry . . . except for the crew chief and his assistant, who were amused. The Seahawk leveled off and everything returned to normal.

Jeffrey realized that this was simply a course change. The crew chief pointed out the starboard side of the aircraft; Jeffrey turned his head as far as he could. Through a window, he barely made out a city on the horizon. He concluded that the helos had passed well south of Richmond, and now were flying northeast, toward Washington. Below Jeffrey, the trees sometimes gave way to open, rolling fields, many recently plowed and planted—with food in short supply nationwide and the transportation infrastructure overstrained, every spare acre of available soil was farmed.

Sitting back again, and looking out the port side, Jeffrey noticed hints of the Blue Ridge Mountains in the distance, paralleling his flight path. Both army Apache gunships flew near the Seahawk in a loose formation.

Jeffrey began to think about what sort of meeting awaited him at the Pentagon. He assumed he hadn't been told anything for security reasons. He took for granted that the meeting was vital, or he wouldn't have been torn away from supervising the work on his ship. He guessed it had something to do with another combat mission. Jeffrey dearly hoped this was so. He ached to get back in the thick of it, to defend American interests and give the Axis one more bloody nose—or maybe in this round knock their teeth out.

Through his earcups, and above the noises of flight, Jeffrey noticed a strange new sound. He lifted one earcup, and even over the deafening turbine engines mounted not far above his head, he heard a nerve-jarring siren noise in the cockpit. The crew chief and the assistant, whose flight helmets—unlike the passengers'—were equipped with intercoms, seemed agitated. They began to stare very nervously out both sides of the aircraft.

The Seahawk banked hard left and almost stood on its side, buffeting Jeffrey in his harness. The helo leveled off but kept turning and stood on its other side, wrenching his neck so he almost got whiplash. Both engines were straining now, and the siren noise continued. Jeffrey was afraid they'd had a control failure and would crash. Then Jeffrey heard thumps, and felt bangs. *Oh God. We're disintegrating in midair.*

The Seahawk turned hard left, again. It fought for altitude. Through the window Jeffrey saw multiple suns, hot and almost blinding. Then he saw something much worse.

Two black dots approached the Seahawk, fast, riding bright-red rocket plumes that left billowing trails of brownish smoke. Jeffrey understood now: Those little suns were infrared decoy flares. The Seahawk was under attack from shoulder-fired antiaircraft missiles. There were Axis assassination teams at work somewhere on the ground.

Either they somehow learned my helo's flight plan, which wasn't set till the last minute, or they were camped there for a while, knowing they'd have a shuttle pass within range eventually—and today they got lucky.

Jeffrey felt more thumps and bangs. His heart was pounding and his hands shook badly, even though his mind was crystal clear. The crew chief and his assistant gestured for everyone to grab the straps of their shoulder harnesses—to steady themselves and avoid arms flailing everywhere—as the pilot and copilot pulled more violent evasive maneuvers. Jeffrey did what he was told, and it helped, but not a lot.

He hated feeling so defenseless. Any second a missile could strike the Seahawk, or its proximity fuse could detonate. The helo's tail could be blown off or its fuel tanks be hit and explode or shrapnel could shred the unarmored cockpit. Shattered and burning, pilotless, the Seahawk would plunge into the earth.

There was a sharp blast somewhere close, but the Seahawk kept flying. It made another hard turn, and Jeffrey saw that one of the missiles had been fooled by the decoy flares. A ragged cloud of black smoke mingled with the heat flares floating on small parachutes.

The other missile was rushing off into the distance, with a perfectly straight red beam from nearby seeming to shove it away, like a rod of something solid. Jeffrey realized this was an antimissile laser, designed to confuse the heat-seeker head and homing software of the inbound enemy weapon. What Jeffrey perceived as a magic rod was the nonlethal laser beam lighting up fine dust and traces of smoke in the air. The laser came from one of the Apaches.

The Seahawk jinked, and he caught a glimpse of an Apache unloading a rippling salvo of rockets at the spot where a missile plume still lingered, rising from its launch point on the ground. The rockets streaked like meteors and pulverized an area of trees in a series of flashes and spouts of dirt. But Jeffrey saw no secondary explosions—he was sure the attackers would have more missiles, and they'd relocate themselves quickly after making that initial telltale launch. They probably even had all-terrain trucks, disguised with freshly cut greenery so they'd be mobile and harder to see.

The other Apache emitted a different-looking solid red rod from its chin. This, Jeffrey knew, was a burst of cannon tracer rounds from its multibarreled Gatling gun. The thing could fire three thousand rounds per minute. The gunner and pilot were after something. The Gatling gun fired again, and this time there was a brilliant, heaving eruption on the ground. Flames and debris shot high into the air.

Scratch one group of bad guys.

But how many other groups are there?

Jeffrey heard the siren alarm again. More missile launches had been detected by the Seahawk's warning radar.

The view outside was confusing. Missile trails and rocket trails and laser beams intertwined in the sky, and fires burned in several places on the ground—including ones from the infrared flares. Jeffrey knew now why the shuttle's flight path was set to avoid populated areas. Every piece of ordnance fired had to land somewhere or other, and civilians on the ground could be injured or killed.

There was another hard blast from outside, much closer. The Seahawk shuddered, but continued to fly.

The whole thing started to seem unreal. Jeffrey knew this sensation: It was panic taking hold. There was nothing he could do but stay imprisoned in his flight harness, and everyone in the passenger compartment exchanged increasingly desperate looks. Jeffrey felt like he was in some battle simulator gone wild, or immersed in a demonic video game. The Seahawk pulled hard up and went for more altitude. Jeffrey saw an antiaircraft missile coming at them from the side, rising fast enough to stay aimed at the helo.

At the last possible second, the pilot rolled the Seahawk so that its bottom faced the missile. The sickening roll continued, until the helo was upside down. The helo dropped like a stone, the heat of its engines shielded from the missile by the bulk of the fuselage. The missile streaked by harmlessly above them, through the spot where the helo had flown moments before.

The falling helo finished the other half of the barrel roll. Jeffrey was completely disoriented. He looked out the window to try to regain situational awareness. At first he was looking straight down at the ground—more treetops, very close—and then the Seahawk leveled off, regaining speed.

There was another large explosion on the ground. The air was an even more confusing tangle of tracer rounds and laser beams and heat decoys and smoke trails coming up and going down. The ground now had the beginnings of a serious forest fire.

Another missile was coming right at the Seahawk. The Apaches did what they could to divert it with their spoofing lasers. The Seahawk popped two more heat flares, but then ran out. It had lost too much altitude to maneuver aggressively now, and the enemy missile still bore in.

The missile warhead detonated. Jeffrey felt its radiant heat through the windows a split second before the shrapnel from the warhead battered the helo. He was sprayed by a liquid, and was terrified that it was high-octane fuel or flammable hydraulic fluid. But the color made him recognize it as arterial blood. The crew chief's head had been nearly severed by something that punched through the fuselage wall. Jeffrey watched the assistant crew chief look on, horrified, as his boss died quickly; the young and inexperienced kid went into a trance from mental trauma. Some of the other passengers were bleeding from wounds—Jeffrey wasn't sure how bad. Pieces of smashed window Plexiglas covered everyone and everything. The Seahawk kept on flying, but the vibrations were much rougher and more ragged. Jeffrey had to do something.

He unbuckled and grabbed fittings to steady himself. He worked hand over hand the few feet toward the rear of the aircraft. He pulled off the assistant crew chief's helmet, with its intercom headset, placing his own on the kid's head as best he could. He put on the better-equipped one and spoke into the intercom mike.

"Pilot, your senior passenger. Crew chief dead, and wounded men back here. What are your intentions?"

"AWACS has vectored us north to a well-patrolled area. Ground-attack fast movers inbound." Fighter-bomber jets, for extra support. "ETA fast movers fifteen minutes." An eternity. "Apaches both still with us, sir."

"Can your ship make it to Washington?"

"I might need to put down in the next field we come to."

"That would make us sitting ducks if there are more bad guys out there."

The pilot hesitated. "Er, understood, sir. . . . How bad are the wounded?"

The wounded were another good reason to not land in the middle of nowhere. "Wait one. Where's the first-aid kit?"

The pilot told him, and Jeffrey spotted the big white box with the red cross on the cover. *What's left of it,* he thought. The first-aid kit had taken a direct hit from behind from a fragment of shrapnel, which went straight through and embedded itself in the opposite fuselage wall. The visible edge of the shrapnel was shiny metal, razor sharp. The first-aid kit was useless, with most of its contents either broken or torn to shreds.

The deck of the helo was becoming slippery, with blood. The wounded sat in pools of it. "We need a hospital, fast," Jeffrey said into the intercom. "It's a disaster back here." He took off his life vest; it would just get in the way as he worked.

Three of the other passengers looked very pale and sweaty, and their unfocused gazes kept flitting around, definite signs that they were going into deep shock from their wounds. One suffered ever-worsening respiratory distress. A chief, unharmed like Jeffrey, also got up to help the other passengers. Together, he and Jeffrey searched for sites of bleeding. They bandaged limbs, abdomens, punctured chests as best they could. The overhead was so low they had to move around stooped over. Pieces of loose bandage, and shreds of fuselage insulation, flapped and blew in the wind coming through the open or smashed windows. Sunlight shone through holes that hadn't been there before the attack. The coppery smell of blood was growing thicker.

Up close, Jeffrey caught the stench of other men's raw fear. Even though they were strangers, his being so close to them—watching their faces while he worked, offering words of comfort—created a bond. Pleading, agony, stoic resignation, despair and then renewed hope roller-coastered through the passenger compartment, dragging Jeffrey each inch of the way.

When will the next missile finish us? How long until the transmission quits, or a big rotor piece comes off, or one of the engines catches fire?

He stumbled as the helo tilted.

"Uh," the copilot's voice came over the intercom, "we've been vectored to a hospital with a helipad. Local fire department is rolling to meet us. Our ETA is six minutes."

Jeffrey glanced forward into the cockpit. Many panel

lights glowed yellow or red, which couldn't be good news. Jeffrey had visions again of the helo crashing.

"Can you stay in the air for another six minutes?"

"Keep your fingers crossed, sir."

As he bandaged serious shrapnel wounds, Jeffrey tried to think only positive thoughts. He noticed that his uniform ribbons were thoroughly soaked in other peoples' blood.

CHAPTER 2

Thanks to some heroic and desperate flying, Jeffrey's helicopter barely landed safely at the hospital in Virginia. He helped off-load the wounded onto gurneys already waiting. While the Apaches circled overhead to stand guard, the casualties were rushed into the emergency room. Firefighters foamed down the damaged Seahawk, just in case. The dead crew chief was put into a body bag; his assistant, still dazed from the whole ordeal and barely coherent, was walked inside the hospital by two nurses. Jeffrey was vaguely aware of someone holding a video camera.

Inside, at the nuclear-biological-chemical decontamination point federal law required all hospitals to have, Jeffrey stripped and took a thorough shower. Blood had soaked through to his skin, and only as he scrubbed himself did he realize that some was his own. His cuts and scrapes were minor, but needed attention nonetheless. Then a doctor made sure Jeffrey rehydrated; the energy drink was exactly what he needed.

The next problem was clothing. Jeffrey's uniform was useless, stiff from caked and drying gore. Even his shoes and socks were ruined. Someone thought to get him a hospital janitor's clean beige coveralls; beige was close enough to khaki to look military, and the jumpsuit was much like the one-piece outfits submariners wore on patrol. The repeatedly laundered cotton was comfortable, considering that Jeffrey lacked underwear. The local fire chief gave him a spare pair of boots.

Jeffrey retrieved his wallet, with his smart identification cards; he took his rank insignia from the collars of his uniform, washed the silver oak leaves, and pinned them to the collars of his coveralls. *Much better.* He heard the noise of an arriving helicopter and went outside. He'd been told this replacement aircraft would take him the rest of the way. With the damaged Seahawk sitting on the helipad, the new one landed in the parking lot.

The ride to Washington was routine. Jeffrey saw all the usual sights. They put down at the Pentagon. Federal Protective Service agents, brandishing submachine guns, hustled Jeffrey into one of the gigantic building's entrances.

Jeffrey was surprised to see his squadron commander standing in the lobby, waiting for him. *Challenger* was home-ported at the New London Naval Submarine Base, on the Thames River in Groton, Connecticut. The ship belonged to Submarine Development Squadron TWELVE. Captain Wilson—a full captain by rank, not by job description like Jeffrey—as the squadron's commander was addressed as "Commodore."

Wilson watched Jeffrey approach, and frowned. "You're one hell of a sight, as usual."

Jeffrey winced. Wilson, a tall and muscular black man, was a tough and demanding leader, especially when dealing with Jeffrey one-on-one. Last autumn, when Lieutenant Commander Jeffrey Fuller had joined *Challenger* as her exec, Wilson—a full commander then—had been her skipper. Both men were promoted in February, to their present ranks and jobs, as part of a wider shake-up of military personnel because the war wasn't going well.

"Did you fly down today, sir?" Jeffrey asked. Wilson's regular office was on the base in Groton.

Wilson gave Jeffrey a sidelong glance. "Unlike you, I managed to not get shot at."

Jeffrey recovered from the gibe much faster this time. Wilson was always doing this to him, because he'd spotted Jeffrey's impetuous, rebellious streak practically the moment Jeffrey had reported aboard *Challenger*. Wilson beat him up about it, hard. The dynamic worked for both of them: Jeffrey knew he needed such mentoring, and felt tremendous respect for Wilson.

"Do they know yet if my trip was compromised, sir?"

"So far, the FBI thinks not. None was taken alive. Search dogs found their field latrines. The aggressors had been hiding in that area for several days."

"I suppose there's some comfort in knowing we're secure, Commodore."

Wilson made a face. "Captain, you don't know the least of it. Come with me."

The two of them walked down a long hallway and passed increasingly stringent security checkpoints. At one, Jeffrey was made to hand over his briefcase, to be retrieved later. Both men were scanned carefully for recording or camera devices. They were clean, and allowed to move on. Jeffrey's borrowed firefighter boots were a size too large. They clumped as he walked. The boots were heavy, and hot.

They approached an anteroom, and Jeffrey saw another senior officer waiting. This was Admiral Hodgkiss, the four-star admiral who was Commander, U.S. Atlantic Fleet. A former submariner himself, Hodgkiss now was in charge of all American naval assets in the North and South Atlantic. Hodgkiss was short and wiry, with an almost birdlike build, but he was the smartest man Jeffrey had ever met. He possessed a nasty temper that kept his subordinates sharp—or got them transferred.

Hodgkiss liked results, and Jeffrey produced results, so Hodgkiss liked Jeffrey.

Hodgkiss shook Jeffrey's hand warmly, then squeezed so hard it hurt and didn't let go. He looked Jeffrey right in the eye with a piercing glare.

"You started the day off with a bang, didn't you, Captain?"

"Yes, sir," Jeffrey said politely; Hodgkiss released his grip. Hodgkiss had a reputation for being able to read peoples' minds. Jeffrey kept his mind studiously blank. He wondered what was going on. Hodgkiss's headquarters was in Norfolk. If he was here, with Wilson and Jeffrey, something big was happening.

"Come into the chamber of dark secrets," Hodgkiss said. "We'll fill you in, believe me."

They went through a heavy door, guarded by two marines in full battle dress, with pistol holsters. Jeffrey felt uneasy, in a different way from during his helo flight.

So far in this war, every time I've been ordered to a meeting with top officials like this, it ends up with me going out to sea and getting almost blown up by atom bombs.

The room they entered was completely empty, with another heavy door on its far side.

Hodgkiss stopped and turned to Jeffrey. "You know you'll be on the news tonight."

"Admiral?"

"A cameraman got footage of your Seahawk landing and the rest of it after that. The censors made them delete any views of the aircraft and the body bag, and told them to run it only in black and white. It seems that so much blood in full color would be bad for home-front morale."

"Understood, Admiral."

"But the point is, your helo made it, and the two badly wounded are stabilized now. That sort of thing's good for morale. The regional chapter of the Red Cross wants to award you and that chief lifesaving medals. They say that without the first aid you did, both men would've died." Hodgkiss gave Jeffrey a crooked grin. "I believe some folks

down Virginia way know a good photo op when they see it."
Hodgkiss waited for Jeffrey to say something. The admiral
was skilled at using silence as a tool in conversations.

*He forces you to fill the awkward silence . . . and God help
you if you respond with something awkward, in any sense of
the word.*

"I'll do whatever I'm ordered to do, sir."

As Wilson stood by and listened, Hodgkiss chuckled. He
patted Jeffrey on the arm; six inches shorter than Jeffrey,
Hodgkiss had such presence and charisma that the man
seemed larger than life. Hodgkiss's touch was electrifying.
"After the war, you ought to go into politics. The media love
you, Captain, but then they always love a winner while he's
still winning. . . . But right now you have more pressing business."

As Hodgkiss reached to open the inner door, he glanced up
at the ceiling and rolled his eyes. He said, mostly to himself,
"If they only knew."

Through the door was a windowless conference room,
with very thick walls and a low ceiling. The furnishings were
comfortable but spare. There was only one occupant, a trim
man wearing a blue pin-striped business suit. He sat in the
middle of the far side of the conference-room table, going
through papers. A laptop lay on the table, unopened. The
man looked up when he heard the door, then stood.

Hodgkiss made the introductions. "Gerald Parker, meet
Captain Jeffrey Fuller. Captain, our friend Mr. Parker here is
from Langley." Jeffrey tried to hide his surprise and mounting concern, but a poker face wasn't one of his strong points.
Langley was Central Intelligence Agency headquarters.

"Good to meet you, Captain," Parker said. "I recognize
you from your pictures." Jeffrey fought off a grimace that
wasn't Parker's fault. As a submariner, Jeffrey craved stealth
above all else. Being so well known made him uncomfortable. His job was to hide, silent and out of sight. The two men
shook hands.

"Sit, everybody," Hodgkiss said, taking the head of the

table. Jeffrey and Wilson sat down facing Parker. No one had even told Jeffrey what the agenda was. A briefing?

Hodgkiss glanced at Parker. "It's your show."

Parker sighed. "Where to begin?" Jeffrey judged him to be in his late thirties—roughly Jeffrey's age. He spoke with a polished, upper-class manner that made Jeffrey think of Harvard degrees, or cocktails at the Yale Club, or a leading investment bank. Parker came across as outgoing, yet reserved at the same time. Jeffrey sensed the man projected a well-honed persona. He kept an invisible wall around himself that held everyone, and everything, at a distance emotionally.

There's a level at which this guy can't be touched. . . . His eyes are very arrogant. . . . The curl of his lips is too unforgiving. . . . I really don't like him at all.

"Captain," Parker said, "since our success in reinforcing the Central African pocket, indications and warnings have intensified that the Axis plan a different aggressive move soon."

"We'd have to expect that," Jeffrey responded, trying to offer something noncommittal but informed. "They need to regain the initiative, militarily. And quickly, or the putsch leaders in charge in Berlin will be publicly undermined, their power weakened."

"The problem for them, the big question for us, is where they can most effectively engage the Allies next. Militarily."

Parker said that last word with the slightest hint of a sneer, then waited. Jeffrey tried not to react. He decided to learn from Hodgkiss and didn't say anything, to let someone else fill the void that Parker had created by his pause.

Parker filled it himself, assertively. "Signals intercepts and code breaking, thanks to our chums at the NSA, are giving us conflicting signs." The NSA was the National Security Agency. "Human intelligence, what we have of it, isn't helping to clarify things much." He let that hang in the air, like bait, looking right at Jeffrey.

He's playing my game back at me already. . . . Careful, this guy's an old pro from the infamous "Company." A corporate survivor when other heads rolled, or he wouldn't be here now.

A veteran of inside-the-Beltway battles, in an outfit that doesn't take prisoners.... But he doesn't come across like your typical intell analyst. Too worldly wise a manner, and traces of well-traveled earthiness.

A spy handler, then? That's wicked, dirty, Byzantine stuff.

Jeffrey decided to go with his own strengths, and be entirely straightforward and simply take Parker's bait. "What sort of conflicting signs?"

"Satellite photos show there's a buildup of forces in occupied Norway. The threat there would be a move against the UK, or, more likely, Iceland, to outflank the UK."

"I could see that that would be a priority," Jeffrey conceded. "It'd give the Germans much better access to the North Atlantic.... And their not-so-neutral helpers, the Russian Federation, would probably love to see something precisely like that."

The Greenland-Iceland-UK Gap was a well-placed nautical choke point, an accident of geography that during the Cold War had helped block Soviet subs from reaching the open ocean easily. Now, with the G-I-UK Gap under Allied control, it did the same to modern German U-boats.

This was why the coup leaders knew they had to conquer France. They gained hundreds of miles of coastline that let out on the ocean directly, with near-indestructible U-boat pens still standing from World War II.

"We can't tell how many of the assets we're seeing in Norway are genuine," Parker went on. "We know the Swedish arms industry is working under contract with Berlin to mass-produce and export dummy replicas of the Germans' Leopard III tanks. Perfect for using as decoys. A fiberglass-variant body that on radar looks like ceramic-composite armor. Natural-gas burners to mimic engine heat, the works." Sweden was neutral, assertively so, and shared a long border with Norway. "That's just FYI.... Then there's the North African front."

"North Africa? But our pocket's too strong for another

Axis offensive.... Strike east instead of south? A push through Egypt and Israel? I don't think so. Not with those dozen nukes Israel planted in Germany."

"So you think North Africa's a diversion, a bluff?"

Jeffrey hesitated. "That makes the most sense."

"How do you know the alleged Israeli nukes in German cities aren't the bluff?"

"They told the Germans where they'd hidden one, and they found it and disarmed it. It was real. That's public info."

"So maybe there was only the one, not twelve."

Jeffrey blushed. *Ouch.... This is frightening.* "Does anyone know the truth then, besides Israel? If the Germans even suspect they're bluffing, the deterrent effect would be lost."

Parker smiled, though it didn't seem to Jeffrey like anything to smile about. "After a couple of months of, shall we say, rather extreme search efforts, the Germans found another bomb."

Jesus. "So it isn't a bluff."

"We do know the Germans are moving their tanks and dummy tanks all over the place like crazy.... And I want you all to see something." Parker turned his laptop on. He activated a flat display screen mounted on the wall.

Wilson and Hodgkiss leaned closer.

An image appeared on the screen. Jeffrey could tell right away that it was a very-high-definition satellite photo. It showed two dozen airplanes, in formation, over water.

Jeffrey peered at the screen. With no visual cues in the picture, he couldn't tell how big the planes were. "They look funny." Their wings were too stubby compared to the fuselage bodies. "Where is that?"

"Black Sea," Parker said. "And they are funny.... The following capability is highly classified, Captain. You're seeing it on a need-to-know basis."

"I understand." Submariners had to be very good at keeping secrets.

"The actual image resolution is much finer than this display screen can reproduce. I do not exaggerate to say that on the original, with proper equipment, you can watch one of the copilots picking his nose. I could tell you exactly how long his fingernails are, but I won't." Parker tapped a few keys. The frozen still image, in shades of gray, suddenly changed to full-color movement in video—without losing any sharpness at all. The satellite camera followed the planes. The angle of the picture slowly shifted as the satellite orbited.

A pretty high orbit, maybe a thousand miles, to have such good dwell time.... I had no idea you could watch things, live, in color, from outer space so perfectly like this.

Now Jeffrey could see that the aircraft were flying right over the water: Backwash from multiple jet engines mounted on each fuselage—not on those stubby wings—created rooster tails on the sea. As the planes moved, and the amazingly powerful camera tracked them, a coastline entered the picture.

An inlet or bay.

The aircraft slowed and formed in single file. Jeffrey noticed ships, then buildings and vehicles on land. These established a sense of scale.

Jeffrey finally realized what he was seeing.

Holy crap, that's the Bosporus Strait! That's Istanbul! Those planes must be gigantic.

"Wing-in-ground-effect aircraft," Jeffrey said aloud.

Parker cleared his throat. "We know the Soviets experimented with these things as far back as the 1960s. One project was called the ekranoplan. It actually flew. Flew very well, thank you. The Sovs canceled the program, even before the Berlin Wall came down. At least, we thought they did. We don't know when they restarted, or how they hid it till now."

Wiggies, as the U.S. Air Force called the basic concept, relied on a cushion of air trapped between the bottom of the wings and any smooth surface, such as water or a flat beach. This gave them vastly greater aerodynamic lift than airplanes flying higher up. In theory there was no limit to their dimensions—the bigger, the better. For short spurts, they could gain enough altitude to clear bridges—something Khrushchev had mysteriously boasted about, but the claim had been dismissed at first as Communist disinformation. Then an early American spy satellite caught a blurry, grainy picture of one at a pier—wiggies were basically seaplanes. Using pier-side objects of known size for comparison, that ekranoplan was, to this day, one of the largest flying machines ever built.

Jeffrey was rattled. He knew some U.S. companies sold much smaller wiggies for civilian use—including as water taxies—but nothing in the Allied inventory, including the biggest military-transport aircraft America had, came even close to what he was seeing now.

The Russian wiggies were intended as the ultimate amphibious invasion platforms. Coming at you from way out at sea. Low and under your radar. Moving at hundreds of knots. Each of them carrying troops and tanks and the whole rest of an army—with cargo capacity per plane so big it was scary.

"Where did they go?" Jeffrey asked.

"Watch," Parker told him.

Turkey was neutral, so the modern Russian ekranoplans were exercising their right of military passage after prior notice. They quickly left Istanbul behind, transited the Sea of Marmara, and then went through Turkey's other tight spot between the Black Sea and the Mediterranean: the Dardanelles Strait. As the satellite began to lose a good angle, the mass of aircraft aimed southwest, to cross the Aegean Sea between Turkey and Greece.

The picture went blank, then resumed, a different satellite pass.

Now the planes were in the Ionian Sea, well within the Med, between Greece and the boot of Italy. Both countries were occupied by the Germans. With the Axis also control-

ling Spain and North Africa and the Strait of Gibraltar between them, large parts of the Med amounted to an Axis lake.

The Russian wiggies moored at a port between the heel
and toe of Italy. Jeffrey guessed this was the major harbor,
Taranto, outside the range of Allied cruise-missile strikes
from the Atlantic, or from Israeli waters too.

The video stopped.

"What was their cargo?" Commodore Wilson asked.

"That's the whole point," Parker said. "They carried no
cargo. The wiggies themselves were the delivery."

Jeffrey was shocked. "Russia sold them to Germany? In
plain view, just like that?"

Parker nodded expressionless. "We estimate each has a lift
capacity of over five hundred tons."

Jeffrey grimaced—that was even more than he'd thought,
five times what the air force's huge C5-Bs could carry. "But
if they're German flagged now, or whatever you call it, can't
we take them out with B-Fifty-twos or B-Ones and B-Twos
or something?" B-1s were supersonic strategic bombers.
B-2s were subsonic stealth bombers. Like the others, B-52s
had global reach from U.S. bases, with tanker planes refueling them in flight.

Hodgkiss shook his head impatiently. "They'd never make
it there, let alone come back, going that far inside Axis-
controlled and defended airspace. The air force already went
through this with me. The anti-stealth radar the Russians invented works too well. And the Germans have surveillance
assets concealed in satellites they built for Third World countries before the war, launched by the ArianeSpace consor-
tium. They can watch us multispectrally and there's nothing
we can do about it. So forget about a surprise air attack."

Jeffrey nodded reluctantly. "These ekranoplans give Germany substantial new options in the Med."

"Got it in one," Admiral Hodgkiss said. "But it gets a lot
worse. Mr. Parker?"

"We need to shift gears. New topic. With everyone eavesdropping on everyone else's transmissions, and cryptography now amounting to an entire classified body of work in math and computer science, it's difficult to be positive that any message has not been compromised."

"Granted," Jeffrey said. This was nothing new. With the outbreak of the war, the World Wide Web had collapsed into disjointed fragments as countries made impenetrable firewalls against external intrusion—by disconnecting their pieces of the Internet from the outside world altogether. In the U.S. and UK, and over the protest of many, cell phones had been banned except for persons with special licenses: Their signals were too easy to intercept and amplify billions of times from orbit. Massive parallel processing would give the enemy valuable knowledge from hearing loads of civilian chitchat and analyzing voice content in bulk. As a consequence of this real threat, everything that could be done was done by fiber-optic cable or wire; home-front propaganda stressed "Is this e-mail or phone call necessary?," and people paid attention; in the U.S., sending spam was a federal offense with stiff prison penalties; government bailouts kept the most-affected telecom companies going.

"The result," Parker went on, "besides the downer effect on civilian morale, and rampant paranoia, is to force us back to using early Cold War–era espionage trade craft sometimes. Human couriers, dead drops, that sort of thing. Well-proven things, from before the Internet or minicomputers were even invented. Which of course degrades the amount of information our surviving agents can convey, and badly slows how quickly they convey it."

Jeffrey digested all this. "You're implying that it's all become polarized. Either a cyberspace and electronic warfare arms race at the very high-tech end, or Mata Hari cloak-and-dagger stuff at the very low-tech end."

"That's exactly right," Parker answered. "Except, you should say *and,* not *or.* It's both at once, Captain.... One technique for maintaining covert broadband is to embed the message, encoded, in a seemingly harmless broadcast, but disguise it as underlying noise. It's an old idea. I can't say too much, except that all the major powers these days watch for such enemy messages, and use the same technique sometimes to send messages of their own. Again, there are top-secret math theorems about how to study noise and tell if it's too patterned to be harmless random static. People with Ph.D.s at Fort Meade do this for a living."

"Okay." Fort Meade was the NSA's headquarters. "With all due respect, what has this got to do with me?"

Jeffrey caught Hodgkiss and Wilson give each other meaningful looks, then they both turned to Parker.

"You're attending this meeting now, Captain Fuller, because several ominous things are converging fast."

"I'm listening."

"Again, without the details, the NSA can read pieces of some German military signals traffic."

"I'm sure they do the same thing to us."

"You don't know the least of it. . . . The NSA began, a few weeks ago, to pick up references to something their linguists translate as 'Plan Pandora.' "

"Like in Pandora's box?"

"It's a long-standing part of German war-fighting culture that they like to choose operational plan names that carry some meaning or aspect of the plan. We do that too, in peacetime, for public relations, but never in a major shooting war like this."

"Plan Pandora," Jeffrey repeated. "Open her box, unleash unspeakable horrors on the world."

"That's why I said it was ominous. There have also been repeated reference to 'Zeno,' which appears to be related to this Pandora plan. From the context, the NSA thinks Zeno is actually a code name for a person. And again, the specific code name chosen probably tells us something."

"Zeno as in Zeno's paradox? The ancient Greek guy?"

Parker nodded.

Jeffrey recited the paradox to himself, to try to see what was going on: *You can't walk across a room, 'cause first you have to go halfway there, then a quarter, then an eighth, blah blah, so you never get the whole way there.... Except Zeno wasn't an idiot. He knew people walked across rooms. That's what made for the paradox.*

Yeah, but this brain teaser is simple to solve nowadays. The ancient Greeks didn't understand how to sum a converging infinite series. A half plus a quarter plus an eighth and so on adds up to one, not infinity.

"It hasn't been a paradox for centuries."

"Precisely," Parker said, as if he'd let Jeffrey talk so he could pounce as soon as Jeffrey finished. "Paradoxes are solved by major breakthroughs in the conceptual framework through which the problem can be viewed. That's the part that's ominous."

"Zeno. This suggests the Germans have made some sort of new major breakthrough?"

"And I'm not finished."

"Keep going," Jeffrey said. "Please. You definitely have my attention."

"The NSA also intercepted a German message hidden in a Turkish TV station's signals."

"Did they break any of it?"

"They broke *all* of it. The message was sent encrypted, but using two different American codes, one within the other."

"What?"

"The outer code, once the NSA cryptanalysts recognized what it was, was easy to undo by using certain approaches and pieces of data. The outer code was something teams of hackers—'crackers' is the proper nomenclature when they're malicious—have failed to penetrate for years."

"What is it?"

"The computer algorithm used by New York's subway system to prevent counterfeiting their magnetic-strip fare cards."

"Huh? But mass transit's all been free since the war started."

"The latest algorithm from before the war, and the proper key prime numbers."

"Is this some sort of *joke*?"

"At first our NSA compatriots did think it was a hoax. But then they recognized the second code, the underlying one that carried the message."

"And . . . ?"

"It was another one of our codes."

"Don't tell me," Jeffrey said sarcastically. "The secret formula to a top brand of soda pop?"

"This isn't funny."

"Sorry."

"The second code was one of our highest-level navy command-and-control encryption routines. With number keys that were two or three weeks stale. . . . That's to be expected, if for whatever reason the sender had to work with a time delay at his end. . . . But our encryption routines were so well mastered that whoever did send the message was able to properly encode entire lengthy documents. I'm not saying fragments, I'm saying entire documents. And not *our* documents. . . . If they were our documents, it could just mean they intercepted what to them was gibberish and beamed it back at us to confuse us. . . . The documents are German documents. Needless to say, the broken navy code was discontinued immediately."

Jeffrey sat there stunned. "Wait a minute." He glanced at Wilson.

"Take your time," Wilson said.

" 'Someone'—you're sure they're German?"

"We think so," Parker replied. "We need you to help us verify that."

"How?"

"Step by step," Parker said dryly.

Jeffrey pondered this. "A German sent a message encrypted in two American codes, one inside the other. He sent us German documents using our own supposedly unbreakable codes.... These documents would be classified, to the Axis? Not just last month's newspaper from Leipzig or something?"

"Absolutely these would be classified documents."

"He's acting like a friend. He's done us two huge favors, right? He sent us secret German materials, and he warned us that they compromised one of our most important crypto protocols."

Parker nodded.

"But why *two* codes? And the New York City *subway*?... Wait, I think I see why. He had to keep the Germans from knowing what he was doing, right? Otherwise, they'd pick up exactly what we picked up from Turkey, and know they had a traitor, and they'd track him down and string him up. So, the outer code is one he broke on his own, moonlighting, so to speak, knowing that no other German could read it, but we could, once we recognized it."

"Got it in one again," Hodgkiss said. "But our concern is that the guy is not for real, not what he seems, a red herring or a double agent. He appears to have some access to extremely close-held German naval information. Access that might be authorized to him, or unauthorized, we don't know. Since there seems no limit to what this guy can do, it's possible he isn't Imperial German Navy at all. It's possible he cracked his own country's security, and sent these particular documents to really, *really* hold our interest."

"As a point of caution," Parker warned, "we also need to step back and ask ourselves, hard, if any single human being could do all the different things this unknown person seems to be able to do.... That's one strong cause for suspicion right there. This looks too much like something concocted by a team, not an individual. Another long-term trait of German martial practices is that the deception schemes they hatch get overinvolved, overembellished."

"Concur," Hodgkiss said coldly. "And if indeed done by a team, this gets a lot lower probability rating of being sincere, and a vastly higher likelihood of being some sort of trap. A trap that by the sheer vastness and complexity of the scheme must promise tremendous fruits for the Axis, at a terrible cost to us." Hodgkiss turned to Jeffrey. "Captain, you're the only man alive who can take us to the next stage in understanding this."

Parker handed Jeffrey a stack of forms. "You're cleared for TOUCHSTONE Alfa. Sign these." Jeffrey signed.

Parker slid a thick manila envelope across the table. It was sealed, and marked TOP SECRET and NOFORN, in big red letters; NOFORN meant no non–U.S. citizens could know anything about it. It was stamped USE EYES ONLY, which meant it mustn't be read out loud or talked about in specific detail—this to defeat any enemy bugging devices even in areas that were supposed to be swept.

The envelope was also marked, oddly enough, "Task Group 47.2," which, if this was navy parlance, had to be a small unit of ships that Jeffrey had never heard of.

"These are the documents?" Jeffrey said. "In English?"

"See that door?" Hodgkiss pointed.

"Yes, Admiral." It wasn't the door they'd come through.

"Take the envelope and open it in there," Parker said. "Here's a pencil. Make notes if you want, but only in the margins of the documents themselves. When you're done, leave everything and come back out. Spend as long as you need, but remember, every minute counts."

"What exactly are you looking for from me?"

Parker deferred to Hodgkiss, who made one of his trademark intimidating eye locks with Jeffrey.

"Captain, tell us if these documents are real."

CHAPTER 3

The door into the small workroom was surprisingly thick and heavy, and the furnishings were sparse and drab: a card table and a plastic office chair. Jeffrey was startled to see a burly African-American standing against one wall. The man wore a sports jacket, with a bulge at his left armpit that Jeffrey knew must be a shoulder holster.

"Have a seat, sir," he said politely. His voice was strong and resonating, but his eyes were hooded.

"You've been here the whole time?"

"Yes, sir." He double-checked that the door was firmly shut, then turned hasps at the top and bottom. Bolts slid closed with a thunk. "This room is now ultrasecure."

Jeffrey opened the envelope. He spread the contents before him on the table. There was a cover memo from Commodore Wilson, verifying in writing his basic instructions on what to do. There were also the two documents, each in a white ring binder whose cover and spine said TOP SECRET NOFORN in bright red. The beginning of each translated document included a date: mid-January 2012, and late April 2012. Jeffrey started to read, the earlier first. Footnotes by the NSA's

German-language linguist specialists explained nuances of phrasing that didn't carry over well from German to English.

Jeffrey tapped his pencil's eraser end on the table. He read further. His heart began to pound. Despite the steady air-conditioning, the room felt much too warm. Jeffrey read more, at first in disbelief, then in utter fascination. He forgot the attendant watching him, he forgot his own fatigue. He began to have flashbacks. Sometimes, when he came across especially revealing passages, he nodded to himself while he read.

The documents were written in a direct and pithy style, as a linguist's notation had said they would be. The wording was formal, official, but the more of it Jeffrey consumed, the more the person who wrote it came alive. He could feel the writer's passion for his subject, and his pride, and caught hints of brilliant insights, and lasting regrets.

Feelings and sensations flooded Jeffrey now. The scream of torpedo-engine sounds, the deafening noise and pummeling of tactical nuclear warheads sending shock waves through the sea. The shouted reports of Jeffrey's crew in his control room, the orders he snapped out hoarsely in response. The hours of silence, waiting on nail-biting tenterhooks. The seconds of sheer panic and physical pain. The biting stench of smoke, and the rubbery taste of his emergency air-breathing mask.

With the second report, Jeffrey relived another recent battle. It was as if he watched over someone else's shoulder, seeing things as that person did, and getting inside his mind.

It was a formidable mind. It belonged to someone Jeffrey couldn't help but admire, and whom he feared encountering ever again. Yet such an encounter appeared inevitable, and the information laid before Jeffrey, sent by whoever had sent it, could make the difference the next time between survival and death.

The documents were postaction patrol reports, filed by an Imperial German Navy nuclear submariner. The documents had to be real. They *had* to be legitimate. Far too much conformed exactly to Jeffrey's own memory of the seemingly endless running battles. Too many open questions in Jeffrey's mind were being answered—with what seemed to be utter credibility. The writer knew things that only someone who'd *been there* every moment, *in command,* could possibly know. And Jeffrey was, indeed, the only person alive on the Allied side who could testify for sure that these documents weren't fake.

Jeffrey lost all track of time, devouring more and more. At last he finished reading. He looked again at the first pages, with the name of the German captain who'd prepared them. Jeffrey needed to stare at the name in print, to try to assure himself that he wasn't dreaming. He knew the man's face already, from an old file photo. He knew the warrior in the man, from mortal combat. Twice he and Jeffrey had clashed at close quarters, in a viciously personal way, in some of the most significant naval engagements of the war. And twice both men had survived when others had not.

Jeffrey fought to regain his equilibrium. He clawed his way back to the here and now. Yet still he stared at that name.

Ernst Beck. Prematurely balding, not handsome, known to be Jeffrey's age but happily married, with twin ten-year-old boys. Son of a dairy farmer outside Munich, in Germany's Bavarian south, where he'd grown up in good sight on a clear day of the towering snow-capped Alps. A modest man, even shy, judging from his file photo—a photo that Jeffrey kept windowed on his console screen while leading *Challenger*'s crew to the ends of the earth and the bottom of the sea, to try to kill Ernst Beck.

What are you planning next, Captain Beck? How does your role fit into Plan Pandora? . . . And who in the name of God sent me your patrol reports?

———

Back in the larger conference room, Jeffrey finished a penetrating debrief from Wilson and Hodgkiss while Parker listened.

Satisfied, Hodgkiss grabbed a secure house phone and dialed an extension. He said, "Admiral Hodgkiss. It's affirmative," and put down the phone.

Hodgkiss stood. "From here it all gets harder with every step. . . . Now that we know what we know, we're ready for the next meeting. This time, Captain Fuller, don't speak unless you're spoken to."

———————

A few minutes later the foursome sat in the enclosed vestibule outside a different conference room. The vestibule itself was highly secure. An aide manning a small desk told Admiral Hodgkiss it would be a while before the meeting was ready for him and his group. Hodgkiss nodded as if he'd already expected this.

Hodgkiss and Wilson took seats on leather easy chairs in one corner and murmured together out of Jeffrey's earshot. Jeffrey and Mr. Parker sat at opposite ends of a couch by a glass coffee table. A large and very high-ranking assemblage began to show up and go through the inner door, between two more guards. These marines wore full dress uniforms, crisply starched, not combat fatigues—and held rifles with fixed bayonets. They snapped to attention each time a dignitary passed. So did Jeffrey. Hodgkiss, Wilson, and Parker also stood.

The chief of naval operations arrived, the four-star admiral who was the most senior active-duty person in the navy. The director of naval intelligence was with him, a vice admiral, a three-star. They were trailed by aides and staffers. The admirals stopped to shake hands with Hodgkiss and Wilson and Jeffrey. It was military etiquette for a senior to always salute a junior who'd won the Medal of Honor, but the navy—unlike the army—didn't salute indoors. The CNO and his retinue went inside.

The director of the Central Intelligence Agency got there

next; he nodded at Mr. Parker and Parker nodded back—the man was Parker's ultimate boss, yet Jeffrey sensed there was more to those nods, some sort of question and answer being passed. The DCI was a quiet man, though well-spoken, with a background in high-power Washington think tanks. The DCI's posture was slightly stooped, yet his gaze was alert and alive; like Parker, he wore a business suit.

Then the army chief of staff went in, the four-star general who headed the active-duty army. An army one-star accompanied him, along with more aides and staff. They all ignored Jeffrey's group, which seemed very rude behavior. The army chief of staff was known to be well practiced at being hard to read, opaque.

The director of the FBI appeared, gave Jeffrey a dirty look, and went into the conference room. The FBI man projected a thinly veiled mean streak, almost sadistic, and Jeffrey smelled trouble ahead, though he had no idea what might be brewing.

Hodgkiss and Wilson went back to talking privately in their easy chairs. To Jeffrey, judging from their stern expressions and stiff body language, the dialogue wasn't relaxed.

On the couch, Parker slid over to Jeffrey. "That aide and the guards are cleared for anything they might overhear. That's why they draw this duty."

"Makes sense."

"I am now going to brief you on something else you need to know. It will come up in this meeting and you wouldn't want to look completely out of the loop."

Jeffrey had to bite his tongue. "I'm listening."

Parker spoke to Jeffrey in an undertone. His manner was condescending, impatient, as if he resented needing to fill in a tyro on something in which he possessed vast expertise. The gist was that a German in the enemy's consulate in Istanbul wanted to defect to America. The German, assigned the code name "Peapod" by the CIA, was a bureaucrat in his country's trade mission to Turkey. Peapod claimed to have vital information about impending dire German intentions in the Middle East, and he asked to be extracted immediately, but refused to give more details on whatever information he had.

"How did he make contact?"

"We initiated it. Through someone who works for us at a brothel."

"Prostitute?"

Parker nodded.

"How did you know he wanted to defect?"

"We didn't. We sometimes recruit married men by extortion, after illicit sex. We wanted more knowledge on Turkish industrial dealings with Germany. Thought we'd made a mildly useful catch, but this guy held out a whole new game plan."

Jeffrey thought about this. "In Istanbul?"

Parker nodded again.

"Are you trying to say that Peapod originated the other items we just looked at?" Beck's reports.

"We don't know. That's part of what this next meeting is about. If the subjects under discussion are in fact that closely related, Peapod has to tantalize us while being very careful to keep his HumInt contact via the prostitute, and the TOUCH-STONE Alfa SigInt transmission, looking totally separate to save his neck at his end. The Germans stationed numerous seasoned espionage men in Turkey before the war. A lot of that strength is ex-Stasi."

"Former East German secret police?"

"Very nasty people. They've been rolling up our network of in-country agents as if it were child's play. Peapod will *not* want to get nabbed because Berlin realizes too much is suddenly coming our way out of Istanbul, and he won't want to leave an obvious big finger pointing straight back at him. Then, when we're ready, assuming we're interested enough to act at all, he and we will have to move rather rapidly on his extraction."

"How could a trade attaché have all that other expertise and access?"

"His job at the consulate might be a cover for entirely different work the Germans have him doing there."

"This is what you meant before about the Mata Hari stuff?"

Parker glanced at his watch. "We'll see how much longer before they call us in." He gestured at the conference-room door. "The more you know, the more you can help assess the situation. . . . Istanbul is a big seaport. Neutral merchant-ship crews get ashore, then soon sail away somewhere else. Good business for the legal red-light district. That's how our agent in the brothel relays short messages from Peapod to us."

"Microdots?"

"Too easy to detect. Peapod pays her in cash, in many small bills, with pen and pencil marks and stains in particular places in the stack to indicate particular words. The seamen in our employ get the money from her as change, and then at their next port of call they phone home, or to a friend in Russia, Yemen, wherever. Relayed on, using different people as cutouts, more phones, it gets to the U.S. roundabout, by word of mouth in cipher phrases."

"Clever."

"Necessary. With Germans on one border and Russia in their rear, Turkey has to make a big show of preserving her neutrality. Our operatives with diplomatic cover, when the Turks have the least suspicion they're CIA, are expelled as personae non grata. Then Turkey refuses to accept credentials of any replacements. That's another reason we're so thin on the ground over there, and our agent's comm links need to be transient sailors."

Jeffrey thought about this unpleasantness, digesting it.

Zeno was a German code name intercepted by the Allies. The fact that the U.S. even know of that name was top secret. And Peapod was the CIA's internal code name for a German who wanted to defect. The name Peapod, and his desires, were also top secret. TOUCHSTONE Alfa was the CIA's code name for material someone in Istanbul sent the U.S. . . . . If Peapod had sent TOUCHSTONE Alfa, and a whiff of this leaked to the Axis, America could lose a golden opportunity to shorten the war.

And if Peapod could do all the technical things involved in obtaining and transmitting the TOUCHSTONE Alfa documents, then was Peapod the same as this mysterious Zeno person?

Jeffrey's head was spinning. "If Peapod is for real, why won't he give us more of what he knows?"

"To make us come and get him."

Jeffrey frowned. "I don't like where this is leading."

"Nobody does."

The CNO's aide came out and asked Hodgkiss's group to go into the conference room; they entered. The head of the table held two empty chairs. One long side was occupied by the army people and the dour FBI director. The other side was taken by the navy and the CIA director. Parker sat next to his boss. Hodgkiss, Wilson, and Jeffrey took seats farther down the same side. Aides and staffers sat on less opulent chairs against the walls, behind the top brass they supported. Since the foot of the table was also empty, the whole thing looked to Jeffrey like a face-off between two adversarial parties. The atmosphere in the room reinforced this impression.

Everyone rose when the president of the United States walked in, followed by the national security advisor. Jeffrey had had a back-channel private talk with the president before his most recent undersea mission, the one for which he'd gotten the Defense Distinguished Service Medal; the commander in chief was a retired army general who'd presented Jeffrey's Medal of Honor at a ceremony in the Rose Garden of the White House—for the mission previous to that. The national security advisor, Jeffrey knew, was a retired U.S. Air Force four-star general. She'd been the most senior woman in the armed forces, and had a severe and no-nonsense manner. The president was more laid back, most of the time, and his smile was warm when he did smile. But now he looked tired.

An aide checked names on a personal-data assistant, then turned to the director of the CIA. "Everyone present is cleared for Peapod and TOUCHSTONE Alfa, sir."

The meeting resumed. Hodgkiss gave a summary of Jeffrey's assessment of the two documents. The president peered at Jeffrey from far across the table. "Are you *absolutely* positive, Captain?"

"Yes, sir. Those have to be Beck's own reports."

"No doubts in your mind whatsoever?"

"None, Mr. President. They were definitely written by someone who was there."

The FBI director butted in at once. "I take strong exception to that."

The president furrowed his eyebrows, but gestured to go on.

"Is it not true, Captain Fuller, that that 'someone,' as you put it, might have 'been there' by being on *your* ship repeatedly, knowing *you* extremely well?"

Jeffrey was staggered, and speechless.

"Well?" The FBI head was very hostile.

"You mean someone who was in battles on *Challenger,* as some sort of spy, and helped the Germans reverse-engineer reports that were the mirror image of what I saw and did? So that the reports would be believable to me?"

"Yes, that's what I mean."

"My crew are loyal. We've been in nuclear combat together. They all passed thorough security checks."

"Answer my question. Is it not possible those reports were prepared as counterfeits of Beck's real ideas and tactical style and the lessons he learned, with help from a well-informed plant on the Allied side?"

"I *suppose* in theory it's possible.... But only in theory."

The FBI man was visibly exasperated. "I'll take a tack you're more familiar with.... What do you think of mutineers, Captain?"

"Not counting refusal to obey an illegal order?" Illegal or-

ders included being told to violate important safety procedures unnecessarily, or to massacre civilians. "Real mutineers are traitors."

"And are not defectors traitors too?"

"I—"

"Forget your sympathy because they come from the other
side over to us. Are they not traitors to their country?"

"Yes. But—"

"And are you not aware that many defectors turn out to be
double agents, really working for our enemies all along? Or
change their minds and want to go home? Or are actually
working both sides against each other for their own selfish
interests?"

"Counterespionage is outside my expertise, sir."

"Well, it's not outside the FBI's expertise. So, now that I
have opened your eyes to the reality that lies *beyond* your
expertise, Captain Fuller, is there not a traitor among your
people?"

Jeffrey shook his head. "It's impossible."

"You forgot something. I'm not surprised, considering."

"Sir?"

"I'm glad to see you've distanced yourself from her lately.
The situation was becoming outrageous enough as it was."

Hodgkiss jumped in. "That's unfair, Director, and frankly,
I think it's in bad taste."

"There's nothing fair about spy hunting, Admiral. Every
angle must be examined with a complete lack of emotion.
Ilse Reebeck is a defector to the Allies. Therefore, to the Axis
she is a traitor. Traitors are traitors, period. She had a close
personal relationship with you, an intimate one, which *you*
ended, did you not, Captain?"

"Yes." Jeffrey was getting angry.

"Can you prove that Ilse Reebeck has not changed loyal-
ties again, or that she was not a double agent all along?"

"But she helped the Allies in ways that no one else could.
She risked her life for us."

"Spies risk their lives every day. That proves nothing. Those previous missions of yours could have gone ahead had she never existed. They would probably have been successful too, by reaching deeper into *American* personnel resources to assist you and your SEALs."

"I can't deny that possibility."

"I consider Reebeck hopelessly compromised. We've had mounting suspicions about her the past few weeks. Odd messages being left for her on the phone. Brush bys from strangers who then evade our best trackers."

"You've had Ilse under *surveillance*?"

"As I said, she's a turncoat. We're narrowing in now on solid evidence that she works for the enemy."

"I can't believe it. It must be some sort of Axis scheme to discredit her, ruin her usefulness to us."

"That's what they'd want us to think, *isn't it*? So they can work her hard as a source for them while we dismiss it as a ruse?"

"Er—"

"This ridiculous transmission from Istanbul only reemphasizes our doubts. It gives us a concrete thing she's done to help the other side." The FBI director turned to the president. "It is my categorical recommendation that Reebeck's security clearance be pulled, and that these patrol reports from Beck be dismissed as frauds sent by the Axis as part of some monumental deception gambit."

"But you weren't *there*," Jeffrey said. "You don't know what she did for us. And with all due respect, you're not a submariner, sir. Those reports read like the real thing. I *was* there."

"No, Captain. I was given clearance to read your most recent reports. I do know what went on. The Germans have plenty of cause to feed you phony information, to fool you about a particular adversary's thought processes."

"You mean give me the wrong impression of Ernst Beck? But he's in South Africa now. His ship is undergoing repairs in the hardened underground dry dock in Durban."

"Just so. His superiors thus have a paramount motive for misleading you."

Yeah, it makes it easier for Beck to break out past the Allied naval cordon there. That would strongly motivate anyone, Jeffrey thought.

Jeffrey was positive Ilse wasn't a spy. But he barely had a chance to open his mouth.

"And don't stick up for your ex-lover. You let her get much too close to you, you let her get into *your* mind to learn all your preconceptions and blind spots and other vulnerabilities. She knows exactly what things you're willing to risk your life for, and what you'd fall for in falsified reports. She fed that to the Axis, and they're feeding it back and you swallowed it whole."

Jeffrey sat there, confused.

The chief of naval operations spoke up. "Director, you've laid out one scenario. Everything you say is circumstantial. Ilse Reebeck was very thoroughly vetted in the beginning. At the moment she's an indispensable member of Admiral Hodgkiss's staff. Her whole family was executed on TV for resisting the Boer coup, for God's sake."

"Peoples' feelings and allegiances change," the FBI director retorted. "For all we know, deep down, she hated her family, and was glad to see them hang. Many agents are borderline sociopaths. Do you have any incontrovertible proof that she hasn't turned, or been turned, since you cleared her?"

"No. Do you have any incontrovertible proof she's a spy?"

"Not yet. Soon. And in the meantime, circumstantial is good enough for me. In counterespionage, circumstantial is sometimes all you get."

The president cleared his throat. "Miss Reebeck's current security status is not the main focus today, nor are Captain Fuller's dating habits decisive to the agenda. His opinion that those two transmitted documents are real can't just be ignored. . . . However, I emphasize that stronger verification is needed before any action would be justified."

"The clincher," the CNO said, "is that they were sent to us in one of our own most important naval codes. That was an invaluable tip-off for us, completely separate from the issue of Beck's reports and Reebeck's loyalty."

The FBI director shook his head vehemently. "The Germans might have suspected that we'd soon realize the code was broken. They might fear we have moles planted in their intelligence apparatus. They could easily have passed on something seemingly priceless to us, which from their own point of view they believed we'd find out about quickly in any case." He turned to the head of the CIA. "Am I not right?"

"Well, hypothetically. I can't say too much about who we do or don't have working for us where, for very obvious reasons. But we definitely have to remember that the Germans are seeing everything from a perspective that differs from ours. So yes, it's possible that the feeding back of one of our own codes, to warn us it had been broken, could be a red herring."

"In that case," the FBI head declared, "the *entire* transmission is valueless."

This point hung heavily in the air.

The president leaned forward. Everyone was immediately attentive. "To my mind, the scenario that the message is valid has still been neither proved nor disproved. What we've achieved is to put the different scenarios clearly out on the table."

Everybody nodded, including the FBI director.

"All right," the president said. "Let's move on. The question of Peapod."

The FBI director started in again, aggressively. "Wannabe defectors in time of war are a dime a dozen. All we really know about this guy is that he goes with whores."

"He would still be useful to us," the CIA director said. "We like to have our agents by the short hairs."

The president chuckled at the unintentional play on words—sex and short hairs—and everyone else laughed. Jeffrey thought some of it sounded forced.

The national security advisor talked for the first time during the meeting—she was well regarded as a woman of few words. "I'm going to pose the question that has begged to be asked and answered since we came into this room. Is Peapod the same person who sent that transmission?... This then raises another question. Is Peapod then so priceless that, whatever it takes, we have to extract him, or is the transmission bait to help the Germans place a double agent in our midst?"

At first no one spoke. *Those are the two big questions, all right,* Jeffrey told himself.

"If he did have such high access," the CNO thought out loud, "we'd want to keep him in place so he could give us even more. He says he knows important things about the upcoming German offensive, but insists on telling us in person. Only in person. That *does* seem a little odd."

"What else do we know about Peapod?" the president asked the CIA director.

The DCI glanced at the people seated away from the table. "Aides, staffers, all of you out of here please." The junior men and women left; the inner door was locked behind them.

"To answer your question, Mr. President, not much, except by logical inference and informed speculation. That plus the age-old spy-craft rule that it's safest to assume things that seem connected aren't coincidence.... If Peapod, who, on the understanding that this *stays* inside this room, uses the name Klaus Mohr, has truly done everything he seems to have done, he's an exquisitely talented technologist. Klaus Mohr might not be his original name."

"Even so," the army chief of staff said, "our prewar files on persons who might pose cyberwarfare threats should contain *something.*"

"People like this Peapod, this Klaus Mohr, might have been identified, searched for, early on by the coup planners, and whisked into an underground where they could continue their work, almost as a form of national treasure."

"You're trying to say that their best technical minds were drafted into the conspiracy and hidden away, even given new lives?"

The national security advisor pursed her lips. "So it's plausible, or at least conceivable, that Klaus Mohr, trade attaché, is in fact someone else, and his job at the consulate is his disguise."

The CIA director nodded. "That's a good assessment, ma'am. Educated guesswork, intuition, hunches, lateral thinking, plain common sense, they're squishy means of deduction but they're effective tools in the hands of our capable analysts."

The president spoke again. "Mohr's presence in Istanbul, instead of somewhere else such as safe in Berlin, suggests he needs to be forward-deployed for a purpose."

"Yes," the CIA head replied. "Istanbul is potentially fatal ground. We know the Mossad is murdering people from the German consulate there."

"Not at the embassy in Ankara too?" Ankara was the capital of Turkey, almost two hundred miles east and well inland.

"No, not in Ankara. Which says something, Mr. President. Istanbul is definitely Israel's focus for their hit teams."

"How's Turkey taking all this?"

"They appear to not be reacting, and we can't find out a thing about this from their government. . . . They've always had friendly relations with Israel. . . . Also, our brothel contact relayed that most of the people the Mossad killed were Peapod-Mohr's subordinates."

"You're suggesting the Israelis have launched a campaign against whatever it is the Germans are up to?"

"That does appear to be the case, Mr. President. Even the Mossad would not be so aggressive on neutral soil without good reason. Or what seemed to *them* good reason."

"Have we asked them?"

"Yes. They refuse to comment."

The president grunted. "Not surprising. Israel always does look out for number one.... But you *are* telling us that the Mossad's behavior seems to confirm that Mohr's actual activities, behind his cover story, are perceived as a serious threat to them?"

"Yes."

"Which seems to further validate Mohr as someone with crucial expertise, who needs to be close to Israel, on neutral turf, to do what the Germans want him to do."

"Yes. At least, so the Israelis think. They've made mistakes before, though, killed innocent people before."

There was another long and uncomfortable silence.

The FBI head broke it. "This is all so *circumstantial.* Whorehouses, maybe-misguided Mossad assassins, a trade attaché who might or might not be a trade attaché, who might or might not have sent us a weird transmission, which might or might not be a fake, and who might or might not sincerely want to betray his own country...."

The CIA director stared across the table and told him, "In the spy-versus-spy business, circumstantial is often all you get. You said it yourself."

"It's not symmetric, as you're perfectly well aware. Circumstantial evidence is enough to yank Reebeck's clearance. It's *not* enough to mount a big extraction job that could be a waste of time and lives, or a trap.... The Mossad activity, to me, is a throwaway. They could've been fooled by part of the same stratagem Mohr's aiming to pull against us, his pretending to be so valuable. He might be in Istanbul, *forward-deployed,* because it makes him just accessible enough for the snare he's setting to catch something juicy."

Jeffrey had to admit that the FBI director had done his homework. *Everything we know could be taken two ways. Everything. The CIA and FBI are deadlocked here.*

The president shifted in his seat, to announce a change in subject. "Let's tackle another wild card, the one that I don't mind saying really scares me. The Israeli atom bombs planted in Germany. They've become severely relevant. Peapod claims he knows about German intentions in the Middle East, and Istanbul is on one doorstep to the Middle East. What's the latest you've got on Israel's rules of engagement for setting off those bombs? Their prime minister clams up every time I prod him for answers, then turns around and demands more arms, aid money, and loan guarantees. Same old same old, Israel's stated official policy of nuclear ambiguity."

"Nothing new to report, Mr. President," the CIA director said. "The bombs are there as a deterrent. A deterrent is only effective if the other side knows you have the will to use it."

The national security advisor corrected him. "Effective if the other side *thinks* you have the will to use it. There's a difference between deterrence and retaliation. If Israel were really going down for the count, from a conventional or nuclear Axis assault, would they blow the bombs in Germany just for spite? Or would they fold, make peace, to prevent their own complete annihilation? Remember, Germany is a much bigger and more populated country than Israel, and this new regime is *not* anti-Semitic.... Germany would be hurt bad if ten tactical nuclear warheads went off, but their forces and command and control are dispersed throughout the occupied territories for exactly that reason. Israel, on the other hand, is the size of New Jersey. They haven't much room to disperse. Hit a handful of cities and there'd be nothing left of the place."

"That's true, ma'am," the CIA director said. "The problem is, this war is so different from the Cold War that all our old thinking and intell on Soviet thinking just don't apply. We don't know for sure if the Mossad sleeper agents in Germany who'd be told to set off the hidden bombs need a positive, specific, verifiable order to do so, or if they're also held under a sort of dead-man's switch. By the latter I mean that they need periodic 'all's well' messages, and if those stop for too long, their prestanding instructions are to yank the triggers. Kablooey."

The national security advisor looked dismayed. "With reliable covert comms from Israel to agents in Germany being so difficult, given German jamming and signals manipulation, an Israeli dead-man switch seems horribly reckless."

"Yes, ma'am. But remember, this was all arranged before the war, as a sort of ultimate fail-safe against another Jewish Holocaust, using supposed cooperation with German authorities in the war on terror as camouflage. Israel naturally felt they could rely on their fighter-bombers with tactical nukes to take care of the Arab countries. Their Jericho ballistic missiles and submarine-launched Harpoon cruise missiles are also more than adequate for that, but only local in range. Our assessment is that with the bombs sequestered in Germany, predelivered, so to speak, over intercontinental distances, the Israelis might not have fully considered the specific conflict situation we find ourselves in now . . . and independent of *that* factor, they might really be that reckless, or paranoid, or vindictive, or whatever you want to call it. The bombs quite possibly *are* on a dead-man's switch, with the Israelis locked into preexisting ROEs."

"How? Why? This sounds insane."

"Because any supposed change to the ROEs might've been defined as a sign of German tampering, and thus as a reason to detonate before the deterrent power was lost."

"Jesus."

"This raises the stakes to a whole new level," the president said. "It seems to me it's bad all ways, whatever Israeli A-bomb ROEs apply inside Germany. And it's bad all ways if the Germans' next move is attacking through Israel. Either nuclear detonations do break out, starting in the buffer zones of Libya's and Egypt's deserts, and ending in the middle of major population centers like Cairo and Tel Aviv and Frankfurt. Or the fighting stays nonnuclear, and if Germany wins, they impress and intimidate the neutral Muslim nations and we lose the Persian Gulf oil. Lose the oil and our war effort is crippled."

"If Plan Pandora has something to do with attacking Israel," the CNO said, "as combined Allied intelligence strongly does seem to suggest, then it's aptly named. The Germans are taking a mind-boggling gamble, whatever they do."

"I'd have to concur," the army chief of staff said. "Our own read on signals intercepts and satellite recon is that the Afrika Korps is building up for a major strike eastward soon."

"The NSA's best interpretation," the DCI added, "is that Plan Pandora is somehow wrapped up in German designs on conquering Israel by a modern blitzkrieg that isn't far off on the calendar. Pandora appears to not mean the entire offensive, but something unconventional that would aid or assist it. We warned Israel, of course, and they said contemptuously that they're way ahead of us, they're digging in, and their ambassador plans to squeeze us for stepped-up shipments of fighter jets and fuel."

"You didn't mention Peapod?"

"Of course not. There's proven lethal distrust between Israel and any purported German defectors. We do know they kill them on sight, on the presumption that it's safest to assume they're always double agents, or the contact meet is a lure to abduct or murder Mossad people. We're sure that's why Klaus Mohr went through all this rigamarole to contact *us,* when Israel is geographically much closer. We also know better than to try to convince Israel of Mohr's sincerity, given Israel's posture plus the fact that we aren't convinced about him ourselves."

"Okay. But if you're right about German intentions," the president said, "the wider implications are even worse. If the Persian Gulf states and Turkey stay aggressively neutral or go fully Axis, we haven't got a prayer of invading Germany on a broad land front. Lose that land bridge up through the Balkans into Europe's underbelly, and our one survivable way to topple the Berlin regime without resorting to nuclear arms would be hopeless. . . ."

The president sat back and stared at the ceiling for a minute. Still looking upward, he said to the room at large,

"I'm beginning to think the only way to find out what's really going on and what to do about it would be to extract Klaus Mohr and see what happens and what he tells us, ASAP."

"We've already considered that option," the army chief of staff said, jumping in at once, as if he'd been waiting for this opening all along. "We propose sending a Delta Force team cross-country. Make contact with Mr. Peapod-Mohr, liberate him from the clutches of his employers with as little fuss as possible. Wangle our way past Turkey's high-tech counterinfiltration and refugee snaggers with tech of our own, and bring him out."

"Staging from where?" the president asked.

"We have assets in Saudi Arabia and Kuwait."

"What are the odds of success?"

"Hard to quantify, Mr. President. It's about three thousand miles, round-trip."

The chief of naval operations harrumphed. "And that's just from Riyadh to Istanbul and back to Riyadh."

The army chief of staff's response was icy. "With no available bases or overflight rights, with Turkish airports under relentless surveillance, and with travel-documentation checking and fingerprinting so rigorous, we can't exactly take a scheduled airliner to Istanbul, or send Nighthawk choppers to whisk Mohr away. He'd be much too closely watched by his own people for him to hop on a plane, with or without our help."

The CNO made no attempt to conceal his skepticism. "Overland? Crossing Turkey's frontier through the most chaotic parts of Syria, Iraq, *and* Iran? Hidden in hay wagons or decrepit pickup trucks, disguised in Bedouin robes on camels, bribing smugglers and checkpoint guards, that sort of crap? Getting past separatist ethnic factions and drug lords and fundamentalist militias who'd slit a stranger's throat as soon as look at him? That plus a stretch of Turkey that's longer than from New York to Atlanta, and almost as heavily policed and defended, *each way*?"

"You have a better idea?"

"Yes, in fact I do. We'd get him via submarine."

Oh boy, Jeffrey told himself. *I knew this was coming.*

"With all due respect, Admiral," the general said, "are you crazy? Look at a map! The only way in or out of the Med is past Gibraltar or using the Suez Canal. You'd have to run a sub on the surface through the canal, in plain sight for a hundred miles. The Gibraltar choke point's even worse! You *might* get a submarine in, but you'd never get it out again!"

"Oh, I don't know," the CNO shot back. "We have some pretty stealthy submarines, and some aces up our sleeve. We didn't start thinking about Peapod just this morning either, you know."

"I can send in twelve guys! You're talking about a two-billion-dollar submarine with a hundred and fifty people aboard!"

"Not necessarily *one* sub. Maybe two." The CNO shrugged with theatrical nonchalance.

"That's even worse! It's double the risk, and the whole damn thing could still be a trap! *I can do it with twelve low-profile expendable guys!*"

"Enough," the president said.

Someone knocked on the door, then entered. The staffer handed a message to the director of central intelligence. He studied it. "We have another communication from Peapod."

"Enlighten us," the national security advisor told him.

"The message is forty-five hours old, that's how long it took to get here from there. It's been deciphered already from the code words actually passed. Part was added by Peapod's contact. She says Israelis tried to assassinate Peapod, right in the brothel, and killed both his German bodyguards, but he was able to barely escape." The DCI let that sink in, then continued. "She was able to verify that he made it back to his consulate safely, then she used her Ukrainian passport to catch the next plane home to Odessa." He turned to the CNO. "I think you should see this first." The CNO read the message silently, then it passed along the table to

Hodgkiss, then Wilson, then Jeffrey. The army generals and FBI director were annoyed by being kept waiting.

When Wilson handed the message to Jeffrey, the CNO said, "You better read the part from Peapod aloud, Captain."

Jeffrey saw that every eye in the room was on him. He read the message to himself first. He felt like he was suffocating, and elated, at the same time.

He cleared his throat, then had to clear it again.

" 'Captain Fuller: I, Klaus Mohr, sender of Beck's reports, am Zeno. I own the key to halting Plan Pandora. There is very little time left. Only you can get me out.' " Jeffrey had to clear his throat a third time. " 'Endless darkness if we fail.' "

The FBI director sputtered; he was brimming with piss and vinegar now. "What does some computer geek know about defector extraction? The fact that Peapod's asking for *Challenger* specifically only makes it look more like a trap!"

The FBI director keeps pounding on that. He's so fixated he missed the vital fresh clue, that Peapod mentioned Pandora and Zeno. Jeffrey was disturbed that someone at so high a level could commit such a glaring oversight. *Well, it sure wouldn't be the first time a ranking official screwed the pooch.*

"It could very well be a trap," the president said, "nested within a much bigger, less visible trap. I'm sure Peapod's message was worded by design. 'Pandora.' 'Zeno.' " The president spat out the code words. "They're attention getters, teasers, hooks. The fate of Israel, our Middle East oil, and our entire grand strategy to liberate Europe, even atomic warfare on land and the lives of maybe ten million people, hinge on whatever the Germans are up to." The president became grim. "It might not stop at the first ten million, either. Every country on the planet with A-bombs or H-bombs is already balanced too close to the edge, especially pro-Axis Russia. The wrong sort of initial spark to this tinderbox, with so many nations then getting more panicked or confused by the second, and things could escalate irrationally, spread wildly out of control. We could all get sucked into a black hole of thermonuclear annihilation, where everybody rushes to push the button before someone else does. Zeno's reference to 'endless darkness' might mean exactly this, a nuclear winter. . . . And the Axis are ruthless enough to try to use the mere *threat* of that happening, embodied in the potential for a first new mushroom cloud erupting near the Nile or in Germany to ignite the global tinderbox, to force an armistice where we cede them all of Europe and Africa." The president grew bitter. "This Israel-to-Berlin atomic trip wire, instead of a deterrent by the Israelis, becomes a lever with which the Axis propagandist bastards want to break the American public's will to resist by inflicting sheer terror."

The national security advisor gave her assessment, coldly and tersely. "The Axis aren't the types to blink first in that sort of all-or-nothing quick-draw showdown, which means in the worst case, we could be forced to accommodate them fast or be incinerated slightly less fast. Either way, we lose the war."

A collective shudder went through the group. No one spoke.

Jeffrey had been feeling a conceptual insight sneak up on him during the past few minutes, as he struggled to mentally integrate everything he'd heard and learned; now the intuitive leap burst fully formed, like a tsunami, inside his brain.

I suspect how the Germans intend the brinkmanship to work. It's the ultimate act of can't-lose aggression, if everything goes just right for them. . . . If something goes wrong at their end, it is wholesale Armageddon.

The bleak mood in the room had reached a crisis point. Jeffrey began to wonder if his well-honed ability to think on his feet during combat, further primed that very morning, let him form a conjecture that his superiors, all desk jockeys, just couldn't see. He opened his mouth, and Hodgkiss frowned at him instantly, but the national security advisor gestured for him to continue.

"Ma'am, the point is, the Germans are *not* insane. They wouldn't attack through Egypt and Israel unless Berlin really believed they had a way to keep their homeland, the sacred German fatherland, safe. Suppose that Zeno is a great computer genius after all, and he did make some kind of breakthrough. And I mean a really *huge* breakthrough, maybe with some strange new logic algorithm, or hardware a decade ahead of its time, I don't know. Then Plan Pandora could be to somehow neutralize Israel's ability to blow their bombs in Germany, at just the proper moment for the Afrika Korps to assault to the east. Peapod mentioning Zeno and Pandora by name in this message from the brothel might be his way of establishing bona fides to us. And if he is for real, he might be so appalled by what he knows and what he created that that's the reason he wants to defect, to help stop Pandora."

Everyone stared at Jeffrey, then turned to the president. Once voiced like this, it all fit too well for even the FBI director to object. The president looked up at the ceiling again, considering things very carefully. He took a deep breath, and let it out slowly, an exhalation that seemed to Jeffrey to be driven out of the man by the weight of the world.

At last the president nodded decisively. "There's no way in hell we buckle under to Axis intimidation or trickery without first putting up a damned good fight. We take the risk and take Mohr at his word. . . . Much as I've always thought some interservice rivalry is a healthy thing, we can't have separate teams competing and tripping over each other on this. . . . General, sorry, your Delta guys have to sit this one out." The president glanced at Jeffrey and winked, then turned to the CNO. "Admiral, activate Undersea Task Group 47.2 immediately. For now, we're in the body-snatching business, and Zeno is our prize."

CHAPTER 4

At the Severodvinsk shipyard complex, on the White Sea in bleak northwestern Russia, just south of the Arctic Circle, Egon Schneider was very annoyed. He had a stack of papers to sign on behalf of his government, taking official possession as captain of the latest piece of military hardware that Russia was selling to Germany. Schneider paused to rub his palms against his thighs for warmth; the yard office he was borrowing in this awful place was chilly. He flexed his cramping right hand, picked up the pen, and went back to work. Each form had to be done in triplicate, in each of two languages, with Schneider's original signature or initials in multiple places on every page—but hard copy, delivered by trustworthy couriers, defeated electronic eavesdropping.

It seems fitting somehow for it all to end like this, with drudgery rather than ceremony. But the entire process was a closely guarded secret, even in a New Russia that was openly aiding the Axis for selfish reasons of its own. *One of which is to have someone else cut America down to size.*

The Allies surely knew that the vessel existed. In today's world such things were impossible to hide. The U.S. and UK were meant to believe that this lead ship in a new class was destined for Russia's own Northern Fleet. They had no idea she'd been christened *Grand Admiral Doenitz*, in honor of the leader of Germany's U-boats in World War II. To the latest coalition of so-called Allies, *Doenitz* was known only as the first of Russia's Project 868U *Malakhit-B*-class fast-attack submarines.

She was the absolute best of everything that Germany and Russia could produce, enhanced by whatever else worthwhile their spies had stolen from the U.S. and UK: Twin liquid-metal-cooled reactors that provided tremendous power for their size, with all-electric drive to big DC motors that turned the pump-jet propulsor shaft—so *Doenitz* had no noisy reduction gears. A titanium inner hull, much stronger than steel, was surrounded by a thinner titanium outer hull, with a free-flooding space in between, giving the boat a crush depth of better than 1,200 meters—4,000 feet. The titanium double-hull arrangement aided quieting, was immune to magnetic anomaly detectors, and gave tremendous protection against incoming fire.

But it didn't stop there.

Liquid-metal reactor coolant, unlike the pressurized water used by the Allies, could be circulated by electromagnetic pumps. Since such pumps had no moving parts, they never made a sound, even when running at full power. The reactors were temperamental in other ways, but worth it: The coolant was radioactive, and would solidify if the reactors were ever shut down at sea for too long.

The outsides of the ship were made of a new composite layered material. One layer held grids of electrodes, and the substance flexed in response to impulses sent through these electrodes; the sonar men could use this to cancel sounds from inside the ship, and suppress any echo from hostile active sonars. The outermost permanent coating was made of artificial proteins and long-chain polymers, which were incredibly slippery, increasing speed through the water for a given power output, and further improving quiet by reducing the hull's flow noise.

Schneider smiled to himself. The portion of this outer coating on *Doenitz*'s upper works was one of the sub's most intriguing parts. Other electrodes made the special material there responsive optically—it could change color in small patches, and even alter its reflectivity. The ship could thus defeat LIDAR, a form of optical radar that used blue-green lasers to search for suspicious objects in the sea. *Doenitz* could also beat LASH, which, ironically, the Americans had perfected but not fully classified. LASH—littoral airborne sensor hyperspectral—used the backscatter of illumination from sunlight, caught via special sensors and then processed by computer, to locate anomalous color gradations and shapes, even deep under water that was dirty; the anti-LASH coating let Schneider's ship blend in perfectly.

But his favorite thing of all was in the engineering compartments. Another composite material, this one developed first by Hong Kong scientists, but foolishly not exploited by the American military, consisted of a rubber-and-epoxy matrix embedded with tiny lead balls. The size of the balls tuned slabs of this rubber to a specific frequency. The breakthrough by the scientists had been to show how a sheet less than 2.5 centimeters—an inch—thick could completely block sound at that frequency.

This didn't seem very practical to the U.S. Navy, because any submarine gives off sounds at a number of different frequencies—called tonals—and some of these varied widely up and down the scale even on a single ship as it altered its speed.

Schneider smiled again. The answer, like most great ideas, was obvious when you saw it, and German naval architects had seen it. *Use a sheet for each tonal that the sub gave off when making flank speed with both reactors pushed to the max.* Flank speed meant as fast as a vessel could go. Coat the inside of the machinery spaces and pump-jet cowling with the proper sets of slabs, and the submarine, once she accelerated to flank speed, would suddenly become very quiet. Normally, flank speed made any sub horribly loud. *Doenitz,* instead, would suddenly vanish from any Allied platform's sonar screens; Schneider looked forward with predatory relish to exploiting this secret weapon.

And the new ship was staggeringly fast. *Doenitz* did sixty-three knots on sea trials, ten knots better than the U.S. or Royal Navy's speediest submarines. Schneider intended to use his full complement of fifty atomic torpedoes well.

Someone knocked on the door of the windowless, guarded yard office he was using.

"Come!"

Manfred Knipp entered. "Excuse me, Captain."

"Yes?"

Knipp snapped to attention and clicked the heels of his boots. "Ship is ready for sea in all respects, sir."

"Jawohl, Einzvo. I'll be down." Schneider gestured at the papers piled on the desk. "Tell the tugs I need fifteen more minutes." Einzvo was German navy slang for 1WO, first watch officer, who was actually Erster Wachoffizier. Knipp was Schneider's executive officer.

"Jawohl." Knipp did a smart about-face and left.

A corner of Schneider's mouth curled up in a sneer once Knipp was gone.

He and Knipp were opposites; both had grown up in East Germany's stark and badly polluted Dresden, where traumatic memories of the World War II firebombing still lingered. But they'd met only after joining the navy when Germany reunified in 1991, trying to forget their impoverished youth under dreary Soviet domination. Both encountered prejudice because they came from the supposedly backward East, but reacted, compensated, in different ways. Knipp loved spit-and-polish, and took the glamour and glitter of court in this new Imperial Germany much too seriously for Schneider's tastes. The restored Hohenzollern kaiser was just for show. *Anyone with good sense knows that. The real decisions are made by the general staff, guided by an oligarchy of very rich and well-connected business executives. Acting by secret committee,* they're *the true heads of state.* It was with these oligarchs that Schneider identified, they whom he strove to emulate and intended to someday join. Invisible but lethal power, wealth so immense it need not be measured, privilege taken for granted, these were what drove Schneider's ruthless ambition.

Knipp was into meticulous procedures and rigorous checklists. Schneider went much more for the big picture. Knipp was married, with children; Schneider was single. Knipp believed in God, while Schneider was an avowed atheist. Knipp was tall and fit and handsome. Schneider stood at only average height, and was almost fifteen kilos—thirty pounds—overweight. Knipp had good empathy with other people, and a warm, approachable personality. Schneider was a loner in any crowd, distant and aloof by choice and by nature, but a polished mingler whenever it suited his purposes—and he aimed his networking high. Knipp was patient and happy to have this prestigious assignment on *Doenitz.* Schneider was always in a hurry and never satisfied, least of all now. But Knipp was a very good einzvo, and Schneider intended to take him along when he made his next big move.

This was the other thing that annoyed Schneider every time it crossed his mind.

I'm a full-rank senior to Ernst Beck, and a better submarine commander. I should have gotten the ceramic-hulled von Scheer *when her original captain was killed. Instead Berlin gave her to Beck, her einzvo . . . and then look what happened. He's holed up ten thousand sea miles south of me, undergoing repairs, and I'm supposed to head down there and bail him out like some sort of nursemaid.*

Schneider knew it was his own bad luck to be stuck in this

drab and filthy deep freeze, beating endlessly on the Russians to get *Doenitz* finished to proper German standards of exacting quality control. It took years of painstaking construction work, hounding the yard supervisors and foremen mercilessly, and he was indescribably glad that at last it was done. He thought the Russians were pigs, slobs, idiots. The food they ate was crap, and for years he'd lived on the same crap. They were all alcoholics and Schneider didn't drink. They were dreadful company.

But now it's time to get out of this place, forever.

Schneider took another quick break to rest his writing hand and try to get warmer.

For now, Beck is like flypaper. The Allies would have to keep him bottled up, blockaded. They knew that, some week soon, *von Scheer* would come out. By then USS *Challenger* was expected by Axis naval intelligence to be on the scene, waiting near Durban. She was the fly that Schneider intended to catch. She was the only submarine that could take on *von Scheer* head-to-head and have a chance to win.

Except for one thing. In water less that 1,200 meters deep, *Challenger*'s crush depth of four times that was irrelevant. *Doenitz* held every advantage.

And more 868Us were coming. A second one was almost ready for commissioning and then her shakedown cruise.

By the time the Allies realized these warships were owned and operated by the Imperial German Navy, it would be too late. In the meantime, acting as if they were Russian was Schneider's ideal disguise. He could hide in plain sight, and as a neutral the British and Americans had to leave him alone.

Until I surprise and sink Challenger, *and help Beck break out, and then apply my achievements in battle and my contacts in Berlin to have Beck relieved so I can take over* Admiral von Scheer. *The things I could do with her!* A ceramic-composite hull's crush depth, dozens of advanced torpedoes, a hundred-plus Mach 2.5 antiship cruise missiles, and her two Mach 8 anti-carrier-battle-group unstoppable scram-jet missiles—all armed with tactical nuclear warheads.

Schneider finished signing the forms. He got up from the desk. The yardmaster had left him a bottle of excellent vodka, as a parting gift. It sat on the desk unopened, and Schneider left it there. *Fuck the yardmaster.*

Schneider pulled on his parka and gloves, raised his fur-lined hood, and went outside.

It was almost midnight, yet the sun was barely below the horizon. *It's unnatural.* The yard complex was brightly lit. *No blackout precautions needed here in neutral Russia.* The sky above was overcast and had a yellow tinge; the air held the bite of coal smoke. As Schneider trudged down to the pier, through slush and scattered trash, the din of the giant shipyard surrounded him. Welding torches sparkled, cranes turned while their hydraulics whined, flatbed trucks rumbled by. He heard a locomotive whistle somewhere in the distance, high pitched and plaintive.

By the time he reached the pier where *Doenitz* sat low in the water, tied up, it had begun to snow. He cursed. *It's May already, and this close to the Arctic Circle it snows.* He went through the motions of saluting the Russian flag that flew from a gaff by the cockpit atop *Doenitz*'s broad, squat, streamlined sail. A handful of Russian submariners were already in position there. *Have to keep up appearances, in case of prying eyes.* Behind those men, the sail's roof bristled with raised photonics masts—the modern version of periscopes—and radio and radar antennas, and passive electronic counter-measures masts.

The Russians would remain aboard once under way, to help in the further training of Schneider's well-practiced crew, and to assist in fixing anything that broke. They'd also be there to play-act if human interface was needed with the outside world. Schneider intended to hold them at arm's length and let Knipp be his liaison.

Two weather-beaten tugs were already coming alongside,

to help the 868U maneuver away from the pier. Then they'd escort her out to deep water, common Russian practice. Black diesel soot belched from their funnels, and white water gushed at their sterns as the tug captains put their screw props into reverse.

Hit my ship too hard, you lousy Russian sorry excuses for sailors, and I'll personally have you shot.

Schneider used the removable metal walkway—the brow—from the pier onto his ship. The narrow strip of broken ice and seawater in between was oily, and it stank. He climbed through an open forward hatch, down into his submarine. Waiting there were two crewmen, as he expected, ready to thoroughly inspect the hatch and dog it shut for a very long time.

Schneider thought ahead as he walked a narrow, red-lit passageway. The overhead was low. Bundles of pipes and cables made the headroom even tighter, but Schneider wasn't tall enough to care.

Once they submerged he'd get some sleep. He wanted to be wide awake when *Doenitz* transited the Greenland-Iceland-UK Gap. He'd sound his active sonar as he approached, just like the Allied notice to mariners said to do, to show himself as neutral. Then he'd pause, submerged at thirty meters, while antisubmarine forces looked *Doenitz* over to verify that she was Russian, not Axis. Schneider was sure they'd pay close attention to the first 868U they'd have a chance to see and listen to from so nearby. He wouldn't turn on his anti-LIDAR and anti-LASH capabilities. They were top secret and there'd be no reason to use them. . . . But the joke would be on the Allies.

He'd probably pick up a tail right away, a conventional fast-attack sub. Schneider was sure he would lose it easily. If he was doubly lucky, he'd be able to draw a bead on the Royal Navy's HMS *Dreadnought,* their only ceramic-hulled sub, and put her on the bottom without the Allies ever knowing he was involved.

Schneider strode into his control room. Crewmen sat, intent on their instruments and console screens. None looked up, but he easily noticed how the men became more alert with him present, and he sensed their thinly suppressed camaraderie and pride.

They're following in their forefathers' footsteps, and they know it and they're glad. For the third war in a century, another German submarine puts to sea and steers into battle.

Manfred Knipp approached, respectfully awaiting orders.

"Einzvo, take the conn. Call up to the bridge and tell the Ivans to start moving. Let's get the hell out of here."

CHAPTER 5

After the meeting broke up late that day, Wilson and Hodgkiss told Jeffrey he'd be briefed on his mission soon—at least on those specifics that anyone could possibly plan in advance, under the circumstances. Wilson returned to New London; Hodgkiss and Jeffrey took separate shuttle helos back to Norfolk that evening. Jeffrey grabbed some fitful sleep in the transient bachelor-officer quarters on the base. He mostly lay awake in the dark, behind the black-out curtains of his room, his mind racing.

Long before dawn Jeffrey caught a courier helo across the James River to the Newport News shipyard. Beneath an infrared-proof cover the size of a gigantic hangar, the dry-dock slip was flooded, allegedly for engineering tests. *Challenger* floated beautifully in a surfaced condition, riding on the buoyancy from her air-filled ballast tanks. She was freed now from the rows of blocks that supported her weight when the caisson at the river end of the slip had been positioned and the water inside the dock pumped out. Instead, yellow nylon ropes—called lines—and portable rubber bumpers—

called fenders—held her 8,000 tons of streamlined bulk in place.

Aluminum brows provided access onto the curving black hull. Cables and piping for shore electrical power, fresh water, and other needs connected *Challenger* to housings on the indoor pier, which stretched farther than the length of a football field. Scaffolding surrounded the top of her sail, and Jeffrey saw sparks from a noisy grinding wheel where someone wearing a face shield smoothed the seam of a newly made weld. *That scaffolding goes pretty soon.*

Jeffrey went aboard and climbed down inside without formalities. Each time he met one of his ten officers or sixteen chiefs, he said a quick hello but told them not to let him distract them. Some of them looked like they hadn't slept in two days—and they probably hadn't. Jeffrey did a painstaking walk-through of his ship, wriggling deftly past crewmen and contractors who were hastily wrapping up whatever tasks they could finish before the end of the day. The excuse they'd been given yesterday was a fact-finding visit from someone rather senior at the Pentagon, the VIP's identity not disclosed yet for security reasons.

The reality, as only Jeffrey knew, was that his ship would put to sea tonight, and whatever wasn't finished would stay unfinished for some time. The inspectors from Naval Reactors had already been by while he was in Washington the day before. *Challenger* had passed, which was never guaranteed, and reflected credit on Jeffrey's crew. The nuclear-reactor safety inspectors always worked at arm's length, caring nothing for the careers—or operational schedules—of whom and what they examined.

Jeffrey spent hours going over the status of things on his ship, to make sure that all vital systems would be available when needed. Jeffrey's crew had been rotating through the various ultrarealistic team-training simulators available at the Norfolk base, to keep up their submariner skills. Otherwise they would have grown stale from weeks immobilized in dry dock, doing nothing but nonstop maintenance and repairs. On a laptop, alone in his stateroom, Jeffrey read through summaries of these simulator drills—everything from fighting fires to solving firing solutions and launching weapons—to double-check that there were no deficiencies since his last look.

Satisfied, Jeffrey made a final quick pass through his control room, now a pandemonium of focused activity. Toolboxes lay open on the deck, and tools were wielded everywhere by practiced hands. People—standing, kneeling, crawling under things—talked back and forth incessantly. The compartment was a mess of dismantled equipment, half-assembled display consoles, and dangling fiber-optic cables and wires; other cables in all different colors crisscrossed along the deck. Red DO NOT OPERATE and DO NOT ROTATE tags hung by the dozens. Jeffrey had to practically climb over folks to get through the narrow aisles. The crewmen and the yard employees, toiling side by side as usual during dockyard stays, scrunched to give him space to move.

Everyone seemed pleased by Jeffrey's attention and encouraging words, then quickly and intently went back to work. There was an underlying sense of collective urgency, that this effort was a contest in deadly earnest, not merely against a schedule but against a hated enemy. Relations with the contractors had been unusually smooth, and their labors during *Challenger*'s stay were virtually flawless on the first try. Almost nothing had to be redone, and complaints from the crew—whose lives depended on quality product—continued to be surprisingly rare. This was a pleasant change from what Jeffrey had gotten used to in peacetime, when periods spent in a shipyard could be rife with tension and arguments between dockworkers and ship's force.

As Jeffrey got set to leave to catch a helo back to Norfolk, he told his executive officer to have the propulsion plant in operation by nightfall; this was part of impressing the unnamed VIP. But Jeffrey's exec—XO—Lieutenant Commander Jackson Jefferson Bell, had been with him in every battle *Challenger* had fought. Bell sensed something was up, way beyond a VIP visit, but knew better than to ask unwelcome questions. He was two years younger than Jeffrey, and two inches taller, but had a less muscular build. He was married, and his wife had given birth to their first child, a boy, at the very start of the year. Bell was Jeffrey's interface with the rest of the crew on morale and discipline, on training and readiness—and what Jeffrey had seen this morning confirmed how increasingly effective Bell was becoming. He constantly exuded positive vibes.

"Expect a capacity load of ship's stores to start arriving any minute," Jeffrey told him. "Food, spare parts, everything. . . . At some point you'll have to stop all hot work. We'll be loading our torpedoes, missiles, mines, the works, right here. We've been given special clearance." Hot work meant welding and cutting—much too dangerous when explosive ordnance was being handled. "Juggle how you think best, XO, but every last item has to be properly stowed by the end of nautical twilight."

"Tight timing, Captain, on top of everything else that needs getting done." This wasn't a complaint. Bell was probing to learn the real deal.

"It's a full-scale preparedness exercise. We're supposed to get a SEAL team too. At least they can help on moving heavy objects around. The consequences if any aspect of the exercise fails will be . . . well . . . you don't even want to know."

Bell stood up straighter. "Understood, sir. I'll have the weapons-loading ramp rigged out, soon as we get the pathway clear of work obstructions. That's a top priority." The hydraulically retractable ramp ran from a forward hatch, through removable interior deck plates, down into the torpedo room. Food and parts were stowed through other hatches, farther aft, to avoid conflicting traffic paths both outside and inside the ship. *"Challenger* will be ready for anything by the time the stars come out. Depend on it, sir." Bell emphasized the word "anything," and stifled a knowing grin.

Jeffrey firmly gripped Bell's upper arm. An approaching enlisted man saw this, and promptly turned around and used a ladder to the deck below. "The crew and every witness *has* to think it's an exercise. If there's a security leak, that's the story we want leaking.... And the less time the Axis have to react, to get a U-boat close and try to hit us with cruise missiles while we're coming down the river...."

The muscles in Bell's face tightened. "Understood, Captain." Supplies could be sneaked in through tunnels and covered truck ways from nearby underground dumps.

But the moment the enemy notices too much odd activity, the clock starts ticking on Challenger's *life.*

Jeffrey shook Bell's hand. "See you late afternoon."

On the short helo hop back to Norfolk—above bridges snarled with Interstate traffic and rail yards bustling with rolling stock—one thing caught Jeffrey's eye. On the jutting Virginia Peninsula that shielded the shipyard from the sea, a large group of heavy earth-moving vehicles, painted olive drab, were lined up in rows as if at a depot. He didn't remember them being there this morning.

CHAPTER 6

Lieutenant Felix Estabo walked out of the hospital with a feeling of immense relief. The sun, nearing noon, glared hot, and the air along the Elizabeth River was humid—just the way Felix liked things. He'd grown up in Miami, the firstborn son of Brazilian immigrants, and Miami summers were baking and steamy. Pausing on the sidewalk twenty yards from the busy entrance, Felix took a few deep breaths to clear his lungs. The odor of wounds and antiseptic inside the tall, white building had been strong.

It still hurt, in his sides and around the left side of his collarbone, when he inhaled all the way. But Felix was very accustomed to intense and prolonged physical pain; it came with the exertions of his job as a U.S. Navy SEAL.

Telling lies was something he was much less used to. He'd been a good enough liar to convince the doctors that he had recovered from his broken ribs and bayonet wound and was fit for unrestricted duty. Felix patted the pocket of his crisply starched uniform shirt where he'd put the paperwork. His guilt at lying—about anything, to anyone—was more than offset by his excitement at being ready for action again.

Clearing his mind of the hospital visit was more difficult than clearing his lungs, because while here Felix had visited those of his men who were still confined to inpatient care. Virginia's Naval Medical Center Portsmouth was a gruesome place to walk through, heavy with the sights and sounds of the human cost of war. Lost limbs in the orthopedic ward, serious head and spine injuries in the neurology department, the constant agony of treatments for third-degree burns, or of bone-marrow transplants for radiation sickness. Felix had forced a smile for each of his men, and offered encouraging words, but was totally drained in the process.

What do you say to a kid who was a Navy SEAL a month ago, and lost both legs at the knees? What do you tell another kid, still undergoing skin grafts, who'll never want to be seen in public in short sleeves and shorts, let alone at the beach wearing nothing but swim trunks? And what do you do for a guy on life support, with grenade fragments through his skull and into his brain? How do you make it up to that guy's parents, keeping a vigil for him to wake from a coma that'll probably never end?

Felix turned and morosely looked back up at the building. *They're in there because they took orders from me.*

Felix tried not to notice the steady flow of civilian visitors into and out of the hospital. Those entering would try to be brave, the fathers especially. Family groups would leave, huddled together, dabbing their eyes, walking toward the covered short-term parking garage in a daze. Felix understood their torment, their helplessness, their rage.

Two months ago Felix had been a master chief in the SEALs, and was satisfied to remain so forever. U.S. Navy master chiefs, as a group, were the best social club in the world. They'd risen as far as an enlisted man could go, through years of hard work and tough hands-on experience, and even admirals paid attention when they had something important to say. Then Felix's CO announced what to Felix seemed terrible news: a promotion to commissioned officer,

with the rank of lieutenant. Felix tried to refuse—he loathed
the make-or-break fitness reports and political crap that came
with being an officer. His CO made it quite clear that a refusal would not be tolerated. With Felix's proven field-craft
skills and leadership ability, the promotion was thoroughly
deserved. More to the point, it was necessary, because Felix
had to be an officer to command an urgent mission. . . .

The memories of that mission were still as painful as
Felix's wounds, inflicted by a German Kampfschwimmer
commando who died with Felix's dive knife deep in his guts.
The memories haunted his dreams.

*I got the Medal of Honor, doing what needed to be done,
and I made my wife and kids and parents proud. I'd give it
away in a heartbeat if it could bring my dead men back to life
and restore my maimed teammates to health.*

Felix had another knife scar, on his face, a jagged line
from below his left eye down to the jaw—but that was from
twenty years before, when he was a teenager and had gotten
jumped by some punks from a gang in Miami. That old scar
made Felix stand out in a crowd, and made him look much
meaner than he was. Felix could be mean, but only when
forced to be or provoked; he thought of himself as the arche-
typal happy warrior. He loved being in the SEAL teams almost as much as he loved his family or God.

"Excuse please," someone said to Felix in a thick accent
he didn't recognize. "Is this for shuttle van to navy base?"

Felix nodded. He too was waiting for the van. The Norfolk
base was eastward, across the river from the hospital. Felix
usually lived and worked at the separate amphibious warfare
base, but had business now at the main navy base, where big
ships including cruisers and supercarriers tied up, some nuclear subs were home-ported—and major command headquarters was located.

The foreigner, in casual civilian clothes, was Felix's
height, five feet five, not tall. Unlike Felix, built like a tree
trunk, muscled as heavily as ever thanks to physical therapy

plus hard daily workouts he did on his own, this stranger was skinny, almost malnourished looking. He sported a black mustache so bushy it looked as if it needed a serious trim.

The man opened his mouth to start to say something.

Felix didn't feel like idle chitchat. He turned halfway away and tried to scowl.

The white navy shuttle van pulled up, and Felix boarded. He flashed his ID to the marine who was riding shotgun. Felix worked his way to the back of the van and sat in the far corner of the last bench seat.

The foreigner was the only other passenger, and he followed Felix and sat right next to him. The van drove away from the curb.

"I know your face," the other man said. "I bet you not know mine." The man caressed his own chin. "A nice new face, no?"

Felix sighed distractedly; the guy was talking nonsense. *This comes with the publicity of being a Medal of Honor winner who didn't get the thing posthumously.* "Please don't ask for my autograph. Not today. Please." But then his radar went off. *Who the hell is this person?*

The other man laughed, and his laugh was infectious. He winked at Felix. "If you knew things what I do, you want my autograph too, maybe."

The man reached for his wallet and showed Felix a smart ID card, bright blue with a gold stripe down the middle. It showed the man's recent digital photo, not as a still but a video that panned from full face to profile and back again while Felix watched. This ID verified its owner as a U.S. government employee with a very high security clearance. The man's name was listed as "XXXX" and the card gave little further information—at least without being plugged into a computer reader.

Very few people have such cards. Only very special *people.*

"You can call me Mr. Smith, or Mr. Brown, or Johnny Appleseed."

"Johnny Appleseed doesn't fit you, somehow." Felix was already engaged by the man's irresistible charm. He seemed only slightly older than Felix, who was in his mid-thirties, but he moved and talked with an assurance that normally came with many more years.

The man leaned close to Felix. "I think, you, me, we go to same meeting now."

Felix was suddenly cautious again. He didn't comment.

"I know another name. Friend of yours. He's a good friend of mine also." The man leaned close and whispered in Felix's ear, "Jeffrey Fuller." Then he started rolling up his shirt-sleeve. Felix expected him to show off a tattoo.

Felix was unimpressed, and impatient. Everyone knew the name Jeffrey Fuller. And it was an occupational hazard, being a Navy SEAL, to be accosted by people who wanted to either adore or impress you, or buy you a beer, or sometimes—foolishly—pick a fight. The gold officer's Special Warfare qualification badge on Felix's khaki uniform, centered above his spread of colorful ribbons, was enough to guarantee that much.

Then Felix saw the man's bare arm. There was no tattoo, but the scars from shrapnel and a bullet wound. They looked about six months old, judging by the state of healing.

The man stared Felix right in the eyes, and suddenly the stranger's eyes were hard, cold, killer's eyes. "Our mutual friend will be at the meeting. I got these standing next to him. Other good men died." The man rolled down his sleeve. For a moment his gaze was a thousand miles away.

Felix was able to place the man's accent now. He was a Turk, definitely, yet his speech bore hints of a German up-bringing too. *I don't like where this is going.*

The Turk whispered in Felix's ear again, and used a hand to mask his mouth. "We all three go on big trip soon. You'll enjoy." The man gave Felix a puckish grin, and his eyes were softer now. Then he flashed that harder look, as if flaunting the fact that he could turn it on and off at will.

Ilse Reebeck was pissed off. She sat in a small, windowless meeting room, at Headquarters, Commander, U.S. Atlantic Fleet, where she served now on Admiral Hodgkiss's staff as a combat oceanographer. She wore her workaday blue uniform as a lieutenant in the Free South African Navy, including the ribbon for her Legion of Merit, awarded by her country's grateful government-in-exile.

Across the little table from Ilse, near enough to be in her face, sat a pair of male FBI agents. They called themselves special agents. The only things special Ilse saw about these two was their pushy arrogance, and their eagerness to invade her privacy. Ilse had gotten her Ph.D. from Scripps, outside San Diego; she knew a lot about American culture and conversational idiom.

One of the men leaned forward, even closer. "When did you first start having sex with Jeffrey Fuller?"

Ilse was outraged. "That's none of your damned business."

The FBI agent didn't blink. His partner sat there, silent. In their dark gray business suits, clean shaven, tall and fit and earnest, the pair of them might as well have come from a cookie cutter. *Close my eyes,* Ilse thought, *and switch the two, and I don't think I'd notice a difference. Except, the silent one keeps fiddling with his suit jacket, and he's too careful about how he sits. He's probably the one wearing the recording device.*

"Commander Fuller was your commanding officer at the time."

"Only nominally," Ilse shot back. "He was acting captain, and I was a civilian then."

"So you do admit to having sex."

The agents had asked for this interview, claiming it involved routine inquiries on something in which Ilse was only tangentially involved. She'd told them she'd be glad to help.

They'd said they'd explain more in person. Obviously, they'd lied.

"This is absurd. I'm not answering any more personal questions."

The agent who'd been doing the talking was undeterred. He reached into his briefcase and triumphantly pulled out a sheaf of papers.

"We have it all logged."

"You have *what* logged?"

"Phone messages left for you at your quarters from numbers that can't be traced. 'Don't overfeed your cat. He's getting pudgy.' We know you don't have a cat. . . . Here's another. 'The full moon looks beautiful tonight,' on a night when the moon was just a thin crescent."

"I thought they were wrong numbers or something. Everybody gets strange things on their voice mail now and then."

"Who's your control? When did they turn you?"

"I have no idea who left those messages! I ignored them!"

"*Ignored* them? Shouldn't you have *reported* them?"

"I work twenty-hour days, sometimes seven days a week. When I get back to my quarters, I'm zonked. Voice mails that don't make sense I delete. Come on."

"How did they first recruit you? Was it with money?"

"Look. All phone usage is monitored by base security anyway. Artificial intelligence, expert-systems programs, *I* don't know. Why should I report what's being screened and archived already? That's where your so-called *log* comes from, isn't it?"

"Hiding in plain sight. Plausibly deniable. Clever, but we're on to it."

"Jesus."

The agent pulled photos out of his briefcase. They were pictures of Ilse, shopping, running errands, as other people in the crowd of a sidewalk or mall bumped into her. "Explain these. What did you hand off to them?"

"And you've been *following* me?" Strange men *had* been

brushing past Ilse, or walking into her, more than seemed normal recently. She'd sometimes wondered if they were pickpockets, or gropers.

"Why do you buy things off base when the exchange and commissary have everything at better prices?"

"I like brands they don't carry here, okay? I like to get away from the job now and then. So what?"

The special agent pointed to the message log and the photos. "Who taught you tradecraft? How did they get you the comm plan?"

"You can't possibly be serious.... Wait, are you two trainees? Using me for practice in some kind of exercise? You think you can get away with it because I'm a foreign citizen? Get lost. Go back to Quantico. I'm much too busy for this. And I intend to file a complaint."

"Oh no, young lady. This is not an exercise."

The two men stood abruptly, as if on cue. "Subject remains evasive and hostile. Interview terminated at eleven forty-three A.M." The FBI agent spoke as if to the air. *Getting it on the recording. Not even making a pretense now.* The pair of them gathered the papers and photos and walked out the door.

Alone, Ilse almost laughed. She'd been in vicious firefights against seasoned Boer and German troops, on missions deploying from *Challenger.* She'd even been involved in conducting nuclear demolitions.

The FBI would have to work a lot harder than those two weenies to intimidate me.

Wait a minute ... Tradecraft? Controls?

Fuming, Ilse went to see Captain Johansen, Admiral Hodgkiss's senior aide.

Five minutes later, Ilse was standing in Hodgkiss's austere, immaculate office. Johansen, blond, prematurely balding, a gruff man with no sense of humor at all, sat unobtrusively in a corner.

At Johansen's insistence, Ilse had just given Hodgkiss a summary of her interview with the FBI.

Make that an interrogation, not an interview. Interviews are supposed to be benign.

Hodgkiss was frowning. "Lord, they don't know when to quit."

"I thought I should tell someone, Admiral, right away." Ilse sensed that Hodgkiss hadn't expected the blatant confrontation either, but knew more about whatever it meant than she did.

Before she could ask him for details, Hodgkiss turned to Johansen. "Get the CO of the marine battalion guarding the base. Tell him I need a platoon for special duty till further notice. I want to see the platoon LT right now, with a squad in full battle gear."

"Yes, sir." Johansen reached for a phone. A marine infantry battalion held up to 1,000 men; a platoon, part of a company, would be about fifty.

Hodgkiss reached for his own phone. "It's Hodgkiss.... Yes, put me through."

Ilse stayed standing, taking everything in.

Hodgkiss spoke into the phone. "No FBI allowed on the base, on my orders."

He paused. Ilse assumed the base commander, a two-star rear admiral, was at the other end of the call.

"Correct. All gate personnel are to turn them away."

He listened.

"Tell them all objections are to come to *me,* personally, through the FBI director *only.* I'll speak to no one else."

He listened again.

"Good. Thanks. You too." Hodgkiss hung up.

Someone knocked on the door of the office.

Hodgkiss projected his reedy voice. "Come in!"

Ilse's eyes popped. A dozen marines, in black-and-white-on-gray urban-warfare camouflage, with helmets and body armor and heavy weapons, came into the office. They braced to attention in front of the admiral; their leader was a lanky

African-American with an all-business attitude that was only heightened by the thick-framed eyeglasses he wore.

"At ease," Hodgkiss ordered. "Lieutenant, see this woman?"

"Yes, *sir!*" Some of the younger marines tried not to gape, with mixed success. Ilse was used to this from men.

"This is Lieutenant Reebeck, an important member of my staff. I want you to rotate your squads, and provide her with twenty-four-hour protection."

"Sir, yes, *sir!* Sir, what is the *threat,* sir?"

"Some jokers from the FBI may try to have her arrested. I wouldn't put it past them to go tactical and sneak on the base, use disguises or subterfuge. Anything."

"Understood, *sir.*"

"Don't let her out of your sight. Roving perimeter security, the war room, her sleeping quarters, wherever. When she needs to use the ladies' room, I want two of you outside the door, and two more outside the windows. Nobody lays their hands on Lieutenant Reebeck without my permission."

"Understood, *sir.*"

"Work with my aide on the details. Dismissed."

The marines snapped to attention again, then filed out of the office after Johansen. The regular guard in the anteroom pulled the door shut behind them.

Hodgkiss smiled to himself, and murmured, "I love marines. They all have so much *energy.*"

Hodgkiss glanced at Ilse, still standing in front of his desk. That was the first time she'd ever seen him smile; already he was sour again.

"Just what we need. Now of all times. War with the FBI. Not surprising, after yesterday."

"Er, not understood, sir."

"Don't worry, Lieutenant. This goes way, *way* above your pay grade." Hodgkiss rolled his eyes. "They think you're a spy, and I think their director needs a very long vacation. The stress is affecting his mind."

"Um, thank you, Admiral."

"Don't thank me. The director can always try to go above *my* head. For a couple of weeks, at least, you better not leave the base."

"No problem, Admiral."

"If the Axis is trying to frame you, the FBI ought to focus on *that*."

Before Ilse could react to this, Hodgkiss had an afterthought and picked up his phone again. "Set up a call for me with the judge advocate general, at 1630." He paused. "Herself, yes. . . . Say I need her best read on jurisdiction, clearances for foreign nationals working on my staff. . . . South African, ethnic Boer." He hung up.

Hodgkiss glanced at his wristwatch, then at Ilse. "Let's move, we're both late for a rather important meeting."

CHAPTER 7

Back in Norfolk, Jeffrey wasn't surprised when he was led deep underground at Headquarters, Commander, U.S. Atlantic Fleet. Admiral Hodgkiss had a large conference room right off his big war room, on an upper level, but everything going on so far used the highest security possible.

An enlisted attendant showed him to the meeting room. "Go right inside, please, sir."

Just like the special meeting rooms at the Pentagon, this one had two marine guards, and two thick doors with an empty vestibule between them. Jeffrey was first to arrive.

A minute later Admiral Hodgkiss and Ilse showed up. Jeffrey was surprised to see them accompanied by two more marines, who scanned the room with their eyes and checked under the table.

Jeffrey and Ilse said hello, while Hodgkiss watched, unamused. Their breakup had been amicable, they'd met a few times since on navy business, and Jeffrey had far too much on his mind to feel emotional now. But Ilse was angry.

"Wait outside," Hodgkiss told the marines. "The meeting is classified. Lieutenant Reebeck will be safe enough."

What gives? Jeffrey thought better of asking. He didn't know who was cleared for what, and he had to avoid giving something away by an inadvertent question.

Hodgkiss took the head of the table. "Sit anywhere. This is an informal working session."

Two more people walked in. Felix Estabo was one of them.

Jeffrey came around the conference table and shook Felix's hand, a broad grin on his face. "It's good to see you again. All recovered?" Jeffrey had commanded the mission on which Felix had been wounded.

"I got the forms that say so." Felix turned to the civilian who'd arrived with him. "This gentleman tells me he knows you, Captain."

Jeffrey was puzzled. The man peered at Jeffrey, obviously enjoying the moment. There *was* something familiar about his eyes. Jeffrey never forgot a face, but he drew a blank on this guy. Then the man spoke.

"We killed many Germans together, you and Ilse and I."

The voice was the giveaway. "Gamal? Gamal Salih?"

"In the flesh. Except last time we met you were a mere lieutenant commander, and I don't recall all those fancy medals on your chest."

Ilse came over and embraced Salih, who wasn't the least bit shy in hugging her back.

Jeffrey and Ilse looked at Salih up close. "Plastic surgery?" Jeffrey asked.

"Yes. They did a good job, no?"

"A *very* good job. But why?"

"Since I spoke before the UN, the whole world knows my face. Or *knew it,* I should say."

Jeffrey and Ilse nodded.

"Not that it made any difference in the end," Salih said. "Lies, lies, so many lies. You know Churchill said that 'in wartime, the truth must be hidden behind a bodyguard of lies'? The problem now is, nobody knows when you're honest."

"Too true," Jeffrey said.

"But your government, at least, did keep their promise, the

promise you made when you convinced me to come back with you." He was referring to a mission to northern Germany, before Christmas the previous year.

"That you could return behind enemy lines?" Ilse asked. She'd been right there at the time, as heavy machine guns and main battle-tank fire poured in at the team, and their position had seemed hopeless.

"For that, I need a new face, and I've learned to alter my voice a little, and I've polished up my Turkish a lot."

Gerald Parker arrived. Introductions were made as needed.

"Mr. Parker is my teacher," Salih said to Jeffrey and Ilse. "At the farm."

"Got it," Jeffrey responded. The "farm" was a secret installation where the CIA trained their field operatives.

"Your English is a lot better than when we talked in the van," Felix said, half accusingly.

Salih's dark eyes sparkled. He stroked his mustache, for effect. "In the land of spies, nothing is what it seems at first, my friend."

Others came into the room.

Jeffrey recognized Commander Ralph Parcelli, CO of the Gold crew of USS *Ohio*. Jeffrey was impressed: Parcelli had been a commander for more than three years, and his ship was a very prestigious assignment. He'd probably make the rank of captain soon, and the grapevine had it that he'd already been tagged for early selection to rear admiral after that.

The *Ohio* was an old SSBN, a boomer sub, one of four converted to a new hybrid configuration. The *Ohio* had started life with two dozen big vertical missile tubes behind her sail; those tubes were her raison d'être, the reason she and her seventeen sister ships had been built. Each tube originally held a long-range Trident C-4 ballistic missile, with multiple hydrogen-bomb warheads on each missile, as the ultimate survivable strategic deterrent. To maximize their deployment availability at sea, each *Ohio* sub had two captains and two crews, Blue and Gold, so one could rest and train on land while the other hid beneath the waves for ten weeks at a time. After the Cold War, when the world situation changed and the funding from Congress came through, *Ohio* and three others of her class were refurbished. Now each tube could hold a canister of seven Tactical Tomahawk cruise missiles, for high-explosive land-attack missions. Two of her tubes were altered to become SEAL lock-out chambers. Space was made for sixty-six SEALs to sleep comfortably, and also keep fit in an extensive physical-training area. Other spaces held their special ops equipment and mission planning facilities—now that the Trident support systems and special navigation center weren't needed. Some of that SEAL gear could be stored in up to eight of her tubes, and the reborn *Ohio,* now designated an SSGN, could carry two Advanced SEAL Delivery System minisubs on her back. Each of these battery-powered minis could transport a team of eight SEALs to a hostile beach or underwater work site, in a warm and dry shirtsleeve environment.

Jeffrey assumed *Ohio* was nearby, at sea, submerged for stealth, and Parcelli had sneaked into harbor via minisub for the meeting.

Parcelli and Jeffrey shook hands. Jeffrey felt a bit self-conscious. He was wearing his workaday khakis, while Parcelli had come in dress blues.

With Parcelli was another commander, in khakis like Jeffrey. He wore the Special Warfare qualification badge—a Navy SEAL, like Felix.

"This is Commander McCollough," Felix said to Jeffrey. "Commander McCollough leads the SEAL complement on *Ohio.*"

Jeffrey and McCollough shook hands warmly. They had never met face-to-face, although *Ohio* and *Challenger* had worked together briefly. Felix and his team had come over from *Ohio* to *Challenger* in an ASDS, during a covert underwater rendezvous in the Caribbean.

"I'm honored, Captain Fuller," McCollough said. "I've been hearing a lot of good things about you and your ship."

"Thank you," Jeffrey said slightly awkwardly. Praise always embarrassed him, especially when delivered in McCollough's powerful voice and in front of so many senior people. McCollough was very tall, six-four easily, and his accent immediately gave him away as a Boston-area Irishman.

One more person showed up, slightly breathless. "Sorry I'm late." The newcomer was also a commander, but he was wearing combat fatigues. With practiced military eyes, he looked around, taking in ranks and subtly scanning shirts and jackets for ribbons. He saw Felix's Medal of Honor and said hello and shook hands.

Then he recognized Jeffrey's face. "Captain Fuller, this *is* a privilege. Commander Kwan, Naval Special Mobile Construction Battalion Sixty-six." Kwan was a Seabee—though strictly speaking, as an officer he belonged to the navy's Civil Engineer Corps.

"Where you in from?" Jeffrey asked.

"I move around a lot." Kwan seemed evasive, and Jeffrey guessed that his unit's real purpose was something hush-hush.

Hodgkiss did a head count. "Let's get down to business. This is a final informational briefing. Certain details will be withheld, to compartmentalize for security reasons. But you need the big picture of what's going on. Commander Kwan, thank you for attending."

"Of course, Admiral. Any way we can help."

"I'll have to ask you to leave fairly soon."

"Good, sir. My men have a lot to do." Kwan did look rather harried, but Jeffrey could tell he enjoyed his work and took satisfaction in what his Seabee battalion could do—whatever exactly that was.

People took seats, except for Hodgkiss, who remained standing at the head of the table. Behind him was a large flatscreen display. His senior aide—whom Jeffrey hadn't even noticed until now, so good was Captain Johansen at staying invisible within a group—connected a laptop to the screen.

Since not everyone had been at the Pentagon conference yesterday, Hodgkiss first quickly brought them up to speed on things they all were cleared for.

"New material," he said. "Step one is getting *Challenger* to sea. The Axis are expecting this pretty soon; they're keeping as careful an eye on her as we are on the *von Scheer.* Their own and Russian spy satellites, signals intercepts, pseudo-neutral observer informants, the works. *Seawolf* and *Connecticut,* our fastest and quietest steel-hulled fast attacks, have been pulled off other duty to sanitize the area well outside the Chesapeake Bay. Surface ships and seafloor hydrophones are helping too, and divers and robotic probes have checked the James River and Hampton Roads for mines or other enemy weapons and sensors. All this, however, still gives no guarantee that a class 212 U-boat might not sneak in range, and sacrifice itself to destroy *Challenger.* It would be a very good tradeoff from the enemy's perspective."

Everyone nodded.

"As some of you know, the 212s can launch subsonic cruise missiles with a range of a thousand miles. As many as a dozen missiles per U-boat, if they leave all torpedoes behind. The farther out they launch, the safer *they* are. To our disadvantage there's an unavoidable flip side: *Challenger* is most vulnerable while in dry dock and as she gets under way. She'll need several hours to reach water deep enough to submerge."

"Sir," Jeffrey said, "just out of curiosity, why haven't the Axis taken a shot at my ship already?"

"We suspect they're saving their worst for when they're sure your reactor is critical and well into the power range. And under that infrared-proof shelter, they won't know it until you come out. *Or,* until they get word from a mole inside, if there is a mole. They can always rationalize that you're a legitimate military target. Our problem is, you'd also be one giant floating dirty bomb, if they could seriously breach your reactor compartment using high-explosive warheads while *Challenger* is still near land. At the rate they've been escalating, nothing would surprise me. Their propaganda machine is already poised, we expect, to blame the U.S. for basing nuclear subs in a populated area." Hodgkiss turned to Parker. "Isn't that right?"

"That's our assessment, Admiral. They know it's been a hot button with some Americans for years."

Jeffrey pressed. "Then why haven't they gone after one of our nuclear carriers when she's been in port? You can't possibly hide a carrier, sir, and at the pier they're sitting ducks."

"Because they're *too* big. Their reactors are too well protected."

"Then what about the steel-hulled subs based here?"

"We *have* been taking careful precautions, Captain," Hodgkiss said. "Some of that you've seen yourself, in New London."

"Understood."

"However," Hodgkiss went on, "we do believe that this time it's different. The Axis very badly want to disable *Challenger* once and for all." Hodgkiss gave Jeffrey a wry smile. "You're just too big a thorn in their side. Sink you, Captain, and *von Scheer* has a much easier job breaking out."

"Understood." *So* that's *the next layer of cover story! I'm supposedly heading southeast, toward South Africa, to mix it up with* von Scheer....*And one reason Peapod-Zeno sent Beck's reports was so we'd all make a fuss over Beck, and distract pro-Axis spies in Norfolk or Washington from considering any other place as my target—like Istanbul. Klaus Mohr, you're one clever bastard.*

"Unfortunately, the Axis have had a month to anticipate and get ready for Captain Fuller's next sortie. We need to thoroughly spoof and decoy any cruise missiles that come in at *Challenger* tonight. A number of technical means will be used, just like when *Challenger* left from New London in the past. But because the terrain is so different here, flat and with no bedrock bluffs, Norfolk presents special problems. This is where the Seabees come in."

Kwan was very determined now to get his job done well.

Apparently he wasn't briefed on all this stuff before, Jeffrey thought.

"All right," Hodgkiss said, "let's keep going." He nodded at Johansen, and an image came on the screen showing dramatized pictures of how different warhead homing sensors worked. "The warhead terminal-guidance modes we need to worry about the most tonight are twofold. First, look-down radar that maps the terrain directly beneath the incoming missile, and compares it to prestored topographical contour data in the warhead's computer memory. Such radar is difficult to jam reliably, since it has such a narrowly focused beam and receiver.... The other method is visual and/or infrared-target picture matching. The missile is preprogrammed to know what the precision target looks like. Software uses key appearance and shape parameters to be able to spot the target from any angle or altitude of approach, even if the target is moving.... The missiles may also loiter in midair, watching a particular spot for a target to emerge or pass by, *if* they can get themselves oriented on recognizable landmarks.... The local streams and riverbanks we can't hide much, though we'll try, but that's where our ack-ack batteries are most concentrated. The Axis know this, so it's the landward final approaches they're more likely to use that most concern me. Commander Kwan, I think you can see now what your men and their equipment need to do."

Kwan gave a toothy grin. "Our excavators and bulldozers reshape the earth contours between the shipyard and the sea. We keep making changes till we get the all clear, to keep the Germans guessing constantly. Make hills and hollows where there didn't used to be any, move existing rises and dips by a hundred yards, pile up huge sand berms and dunes on the beaches.... And the fleet of heavy dump trucks full of gravel and coal off the hopper cars in the rail yards, we unload those to make instant ridges where there aren't ridges now. It's fiendishly clever, Admiral."

"The bridges across the James River will be closed to traffic, just in case. They'll be draped from above with radar-absorbing blanket material, unrolled from the cranes on the Seabees' barges, again to prevent a missile getting a navigational fix that way. The blankets will have dazzle patterns already painted on, to further confuse any visual homing sensors.... Which leads to my last point here. *Challenger* herself will have to be thoroughly camouflaged. Details on that await the Seabees assigned to the dry dock itself. Plans and supplies will arrive there for them soon. And, Captain Fuller, I warn *you,* be prepared for anything in that respect. You'll see other strange sights too, quaint or bizarre, before this is over. Mental flexibility is crucial."

"Er, yes, sir."

Hodgkiss raised a finger for emphasis. "None of this visible work begins until my say-so. Right now, those earth movers could simply be parked, awaiting transshipment by rail or truck to anywhere. The crane barges could be there to do routine bridge maintenance. The essential thing is to catch the enemy by complete surprise, start our terrain and visual spoofing from well inside their own decision loops. Act faster than they can react, change faster than they can adjust to or compensate for."

People nodded.

"Commander Kwan, now you understand what's really involved. Tell your people nothing they don't need to know, but get them motivated. What they'll be ordered to do will seem weird. That's the leadership task you face. Work your people and machines very hard."

"We won't disappoint you, Admiral. Nor you, Captain Fuller. There's a reason the Seabee motto is 'Can do.'"

"Thanks," Jeffrey said. He couldn't help but like Kwan, a construction-worker supervisor whose job sites were battlefields.

"One other thing before you go," Hodgkiss said to Kwan. "The threat of incoming missiles is real. Our land antiaircraft batteries and some antiaircraft warships in the bay will be on highest alert. Missiles, or parts of them and burning fuel, could hit anywhere. The same thing goes for antiaircraft ordnance. Whatever goes up must come down."

"We're used to being in combat, sir."

"Have some of your excavators ready to dig instant slit trenches if required. Tell your men to not take any dumb chances. However, since it's likely there'll be more than one wave of missiles, they are to continue working as long as possible. And they are not, repeat *not,* to provide humanitarian aid to injured civilians no matter how pressing that need might be. I know this will be difficult for them."

"It will, sir. Humanitarian aid is one of our long-standing traditions."

"Leave it to the local first responders and the National Guard. That's *their* job, tonight. Police and ambulances and firefighters are all plugged into the standing air-raid alarm communications grid. Your unit's sole responsibility is protecting USS *Challenger* by diverting Axis missiles from that dry dock and the water right outside, and from the ship once she's under way."

"Understood, sir."

"Very well. Thank you. Dismissed."

Commander Kwan left the room. Johansen followed him out, then locked the two thick doors as he came back in. "Room is secure."

"Next topic," Hodgkiss stated. He gestured with his chin, and Johansen projected a map on the screen. The map showed a stretch of the Atlantic Ocean, leading to the Strait of Gibraltar and then the Mediterranean Sea, plus the other straits that led to Istanbul, plus the Suez Canal, the Red Sea, and the Gulf of Aden—leading past more choke points to the Arabian Sea and then the Indian Ocean.

"This is the theater of operations for Task Group 47.2."

Everyone studied the map, which was generally familiar to most of those present.

"As you can all tell for yourselves, entry and exit to the Med will be extremely tricky. Certain diversions and subterfuges are planned. These will not be discussed here, because there is not a need for everyone here to know. Captain Parcelli, both you and Captain Fuller will be given sealed orders, to be opened only when in your staterooms on your respective ships."

Parcelli nodded.

"I'll go over only the bare bones now. Mr. Parker is to accompany Captain Fuller, to serve as debriefer and agent control once the person we want to extract is extracted. The extraction itself will be made via *Challenger*'s minisub, given the restricted waters involved. *Challenger* holds in her in-hull hangar a captured German minisub. Using hydrogen peroxide fuel, its speed and range are superior to our own ASDS design. High-test peroxide is extremely corrosive and flammable, but Imperial German Navy practice has been to run the risk. Because of the geography, we must run the same risk. However, as should be clear, this will aid mission stealth, using a German vessel near Axis-owned waters. The extraction team will be led by Lieutenant Estabo. His job is to covertly render ineffective the defector's bodyguards. Mr. Salih will accompany Lieutenant Estabo's team in the minisub, then work in plain sight as a Turk among Turks to make the personal connection with the defector himself once the groundwork is laid. Mr. Parker informs me that Mr. Salih has received extensive training for such a task. Mr. Parker also tells me that in the meantime, new communications will be established with the person seeking extraction, since the original on-scene contact quickly relocated for their own safety."

"This all sounds good," Parcelli said. He gave Parker a sidelong glance.

Seems he's glad to not get stuck with the CIA spook on this deployment. . . . And I can't exactly say I blame him, Jeffrey thought.

"Admiral," Jeffrey asked, "what about German computer security? How does this defector get out any software or data we need?"

"Presumably the same way he already sent us what he sent us. Or maybe by another way. We expect he'll make arrangements. It's the first thing he'd attend to, if he's genuine and thinking of crossing over at all."

Jeffrey nodded.

"Next, the command structure of Task Group 47.2, which will consist of *Ohio* and *Challenger*."

Captain Parcelli leaned forward to speak.

"No, Captain. You have more time in grade, but given the nature of the mission, Captain Fuller is designated Commander, Task Group 47.2. Captain Fuller has more experience in infiltrating constricted enemy waters with his ship, emplacing SEALs and freedom fighters clandestinely, and defeating enemy vessels head-to-head."

Parcelli sat back in a huff, obviously displeased.

Hodgkiss cleared his throat. "Captain Parcelli, while under way you will, at Captain Fuller's discretion, meet in person for orders and intentions that cannot be conveyed by him effectively via secure covert undersea acoustic link. Such meetings will take place submerged on the task group flagship, *Challenger.* You will attend such meetings by using one of your minisubs to move between *Ohio* and *Challenger.* Clear?"

Parcelli nodded, still not happy.

Trouble ahead, I think, Jeffrey told himself. *I've never led a task group before, let alone on a mission as important and hard as this one.*

"Part of your orders, both of you, regard emission control. While in the Med you are to maintain absolute radio silence. For optimized stealth, all communication will be one way, from Norfolk to you. Confirmation or cancellation of the mission will be broadcast at the time you're expected to be approaching the point of no return, the Gibraltar Strait. Given *Ohio*'s best silent speed with the hydrodynamic drag of two minisubs as loads on her back, that should be in eight days."

Eight days, plus maybe four more to sneak past Gibraltar, through the Med and to Istanbul....Lord, we're cutting it close. I remember what Mohr's last message said, about having so little time: "Endless darkness if we fail."

"Captain Fuller," Hodgkiss snapped, "do I have your attention?"

"Yes, Admiral."

"Good. For your information, *Ohio* retains good passive radio-receiver floating-wire antenna equipment from her days as a boomer. She has also been fitted with a new and stealthy towed raft-sled, to be used while well submerged. The raft bears a super-high-frequency dish to capture high-baud-rate satellite data, other antennas for enemy radar and signals intercepts, and a photonics mast to serve as a periscope."

"The raft is that new British design?"

"Exactly. *Ohio*, in short, will be the eyes and ears above the surface for both ships. *Ohio* will relay to *Challenger* by acoustic link all necessary data and information obtained by such means. This will include as near as possible to real-time oceanographic and weather data. Lieutenant Reebeck will be responsible for helping provide these analyses, to aid the task group in choosing the stealthiest path through the maze of islands and choke points and shallows within the Med."

Jeffrey glanced at Ilse.

"Like last time," Ilse said, deadpan.

"It worked well last time," Jeffrey said.

"To summarize for everyone present, *Challenger*'s flank speed is more than twice *Ohio*'s, and her crush depth is ten times greater. But moving slowly and not too deep for *Ohio*'s hull, even though the latter ship is half again as long, both vessels have fairly comparable stealth; as an ex-boomer, *Ohio* is superbly quiet. *Challenger* has eight torpedo tubes and her torpedo room holds almost sixty weapons. *Ohio* has room for only a dozen torpedoes and decoys, with four torpedo tubes. But *Challenger* holds only twelve Tactical Tomahawks in her vertical launching system, compared to over a hundred on *Ohio* even with her large SEAL complement comfortably housed. Furthermore, *Challenger* has little room for SEALs, and can only take one eight-man team, led by Lieutenant Estabo. Commander McCollough, on *Ohio,* will command the much larger SEAL company there. Both, and I stress both, ships' SEALs are under Captain Fuller's overall command."

Commander McCollough and Felix both said, "Understood." Parcelli seemed more irritated than ever. Hodgkiss continued, his voice clipped and all business.

"Challenger will serve as fast-attack sub protection for *Ohio* while transiting the Atlantic to the area of operations, and also after completing the mission. Once in the Med, however, *Ohio* will serve as an arsenal ship for *Challenger.* If despite all your precautions the task group *is* detected and attacked while in the Med, *Ohio*'s missiles and SEAL teams will provide essential heavy-fire support. Captain Fuller, for your information all of *Ohio*'s Tactical Tomahawks have the new high-explosive multivalent warhead and sensor package. Each can attack a ship or a moderately hardened target on land with equally high kill probability. One of *Ohio*'s silos is sleeved with a canister holding forty-two Polyphem antiaircraft missiles as well." Subsonic, and launched from underwater, Polyphems could knock down antisubmarine helicopters and maritime patrol planes.

That does give us a lot of punch, though I'd hate to have to start shooting missiles. They'd give us away in an instant, acoustically and visually. But like Hodgkiss said, the missiles are a last resort.

"What loadout will *Challenger* get, sir?"

"I'm afraid supplies of the multivalent Tomahawks are limited. This afternoon you'll receive six antiship and six land-attack high-explosive types. Your torpedo room is reserved for torpedoes, decoys, a handful of Polyphems, and off-board probes." A torpedo tube could hold four Polyphems at once.

"Understood. What torpedoes?"

Hodgkiss became more serious, as if he himself was worried. "This ties in with the rules of engagement for Task Group 47.2. Notice that in the Mediterranean, every point of the sea is within two hundred nautical miles of part of the land."

People knew this, implicitly, but even so a ripple of concern went around the room—not the least from Jeffrey. It meant that by the Joint Chiefs of Staff global ROEs for employing tactical atomic weapons at sea—as approved in advance by the president—inside the Med *Challenger* and *Ohio* could use no nuclear warheads even to defend themselves.

"I see you've figured it out," Hodgkiss said. "I'm sorry, but this is how it has to be."

The Axis won't be so reluctant to go nuclear, especially near occupied North Africa, especially against Challenger *and especially with their intentions for Plan Pandora.*

"Because *Ohio*'s prime purpose is to serve as *Challenger*'s escort while in the Med, and, as I say, she can only carry twelve units in her small torpedo room, *Ohio*'s fish will remain as they are, all conventional high-explosive Improved Mark 48 ADCAPs."

Parcelli seemed less and less pleased by the minute to have drawn this assignment.

"*Challenger,* however, will receive a mix of high-explosive ADCAPs and tactical-nuclear deep-capable Mark Eighty-eights."

"Sir?" Jeffrey asked.

"You have to cross the entire Atlantic from west to east, and later get your prize defector safely back to the States. Out in blue water, we don't know what you'll face, right? You might need to use nukes there. This way you will have the nukes."

"I run defense for *Ohio* outside the Med."

Parcelli snorted, as if to advertise that he was perfectly able to take care of himself.

Great, Jeffrey thought. *This guy'll be a joy to work with.*

"There is one other thing, I'm afraid, Captain Fuller.

Ohio's salvage by the enemy, once scuttled, is deemed acceptable by the Pentagon. Provided of course that all crypto gear and classified sonar software are destroyed, and the crew follow the code of conduct for being taken prisoner of war. *Ohio*'s basic construction and hardware are old, or were made public several years ago, or are already known to the Axis through spies who worked for the Soviet Union and then Russia during the 1980s and later, after *Ohio* was built and then converted. If the task group gets in serious trouble inside the Med, *Ohio*'s purpose is to act aggressively, salvo her weapons at worthwhile targets as rapidly as possible, to hurt the enemy as much as we can and draw attention and fire away from *Challenger,* improving the latter's chances of escaping and completing the defector extraction alone."

"We're counting on the enemy not expecting a *pair* of our nuclear boats to be working in partnership inside the Med? If they do detect one sub, they'll prosecute the contact but it won't occur to them to look for another sub in tandem right there?"

Parcelli sat stone-faced. Admiral Hodgkiss pressed on.

"*Challenger* is at all cost to avoid capture intact or nearly intact in the Med. Nor are any of her crew to be taken alive for interrogation, including as internees in neutral countries. Your state-of-the-art technology and capabilities are simply too valuable to be allowed to fall into enemy hands."

Jeffrey waited. He knew he wouldn't like what came next.

"The president has approved a modification to the ROEs, for this mission alone. There is one place, *here.*" Hodgkiss nodded to Johansen, who typed, and a red dot appeared on the map. "Here, essentially at the middle of a line from the southeastern tip of Sicily cutting across and down to the northeastern tip of Libya, separation from land is at its maximum in all directions, *almost* two hundred nautical miles. The water there, at twelve thousand feet, is also one of the deepest parts of the Med. Your orders, Captain Fuller, are that if in the last extreme your ship becomes trapped in the Med and is in immediate danger of capture or of being sunk, you are to make your best efforts to transfer your special new passenger, if extracted, to *Ohio* if the tactical situation permits, and then proceed to this point. Dive to the bottom and self-destruct with your own atomic torpedoes."

CHAPTER 8

Jeffrey caught a courier helo to the shipyard, with a heavy packet of sealed orders in his locked briefcase. He wasn't happy. A low-pressure system was forming somewhere west; high winds from the edge of a distant storm could ruin the infrared-opaque smoke screens intended for tonight, and enemy surveillance would be harder to mislead. The storm itself was forecast to pass through Norfolk during the daytime tomorrow, after *Challenger* was gone—the sky Jeffrey saw overhead from the helo was much too clear, almost cloudless. But Hodgkiss had said the mission couldn't lose half a day or more to wait for the storm and use it as cover, and he'd hinted there'd be other problems if *Challenger* sailed in broad daylight—which Jeffrey would understand when he got to his ship and got under way.

After landing, Jeffrey caught the next shipyard shuttle van, and under an awning entered the covered dry dock. Power saws and drills, and loud hammering, battered his ears. On the concrete pier on the far side of the dry dock, a structure was being built from two-by-fours and thicker beams, and big sheets of a stiff but lightweight material, not plywood but something synthetic. Men and women in combat fatigues were climbing all over this structure, strengthening the framing of raw lumber, fastening the sheets to the frame. The thing was almost as long as *Challenger*, and some of Jeffrey's crew kept glancing at it skeptically.

Jeffrey spotted his chief of the boat, whom everyone called COB. COB was a salty bulldog of Latino ancestry, from Jersey City. He was a master chief, the most senior enlisted person in Jeffrey's crew, responsible for many aspects of keeping *Challenger* and her people in fighting form. Now COB was keeping a seasoned eye on loading, as weapons went through one hatch from a special crane, food went across from a truck to the ship on a conveyor belt next to another hatch, and spare parts went down a third hatch into the engineering compartment farthest aft. Crewmen stood on the pier, on the hull, and moved up and down the ladders inside the hatches, passing things and scurrying like ants.

"Hello, Skipper," COB said. "Wel—"

COB was cut off by another power saw, whose screeching echoed inside the dry-dock hangar after it stopped.

"Welcome aboard, sir!" COB had to raise his voice above the hammering that didn't stop.

"Who *are* those people?" Jeffrey pointed across the dock to the opposite pier, some eighty feet away.

"Seabees, they said."

"What in tarnation is that *monstrosity* supposed to be?"

COB shrugged. "Looks like a cockamamie barn or something, sir. They wouldn't tell me, so I let them alone." COB had a sly sense of humor—in his early forties, he was the oldest man on *Challenger*. By age and title he held special privileges, and had repeatedly proven himself under fire in Jeffrey's control room. COB was a plank owner too; he'd been involved in *Challenger* while she was still under construction. This implicitly gave him even higher status. "If it's a barn, Captain, maybe it's for target practice. Get it?"

Jeffrey groaned at COB's awful pun.

COB joined Jeffrey in staring at the structure the Seabees

were building. Enough of the near side was done that Jeffrey could see that those large, rectangular sheets came pre-painted in different colors, mostly red or blue or green.

Jeffrey walked along the brow onto his ship, stood forward of the sail, and grabbed a bullhorn from one of his junior officers. The young man had been supervising the shutting of the vertical launch-system hatches, now that the dozen Tomahawks were stowed.

Jeffrey saw a master chief among the Seabees, talking to some of the workers.

"What *is* that?" Jeffrey projected his voice with the bullhorn.

No one across the dock reacted.

Jeffrey cursed under his breath.

"Master Chief! This is Captain Fuller of USS *Challenger*! What are you doing?"

The master chief turned and aimed a bullhorn at Jeffrey.

"Camouflage, Captain."

"Camouflage for *what*?"

"For *you*, sir."

Jeffrey went below and sat at the little fold-down desk in his stateroom. He read the portion of his orders he was supposed to know before getting under way. Further instructions, to be opened only later and in two stages, were contained in an inner, sealed pouch warning that its contents included incendiary self-destruct antitamper devices. Jeffrey was to now memorize the authorization codes he'd need to disarm these devices, then swallow the edible paper on which the codes were typed. One code was labeled for use as soon as convenient after submerging. A second was intended for after "Peapod occurred" or Jeffrey knew "Peapod would never occur." Cagey wording, presumably the postextraction egress plan out of the Med. He duly memorized and swallowed, alarmed that small firebombs would be in his safe.

The immediate-action items were his required time of departure, 2200—ten P.M.—and the point for joining *Ohio* underwater. The rendezvous was southwest of Virginia Beach, down the coast and well out to sea. But the specified place was on the shallow continental shelf, which extended much farther out before dropping off suddenly to thousands of feet. *Challenger* would have to dive in water less deep than her length—which was 360 feet from bow dome to pump-jet cowling. This was usually forbidden during peacetime. It gave scant room for the slightest error: The ship might crunch into the seafloor, or be rammed by a deep-draft merchant ship. Both were nightmarish outcomes, but now, submerging early was a necessity. Caution had to be traded for strategic and tactical stealth. The sooner *Challenger* dived, the safer, in the larger sense, she'd be.

And the calmer the surface, the shallower the place where I can first dare diving at all, and the less we'll be slowed getting there by having to fight the swells of a storm-tossed sea. Good reasons to leave in front of the bad weather.

Jeffrey grabbed his phone and called the control room.

"Control," responded the lieutenant (j.g.) who was the in-port duty officer.

"Control, Captain. Find the XO and have him report to my stateroom."

"Aye aye, sir." The lieutenant (j.g.) hung up. Jeffrey locked his orders in his safe. A moment later, the 1MC, the ship-wide public-address system, blared, "XO, please report to captain's stateroom." Jeffrey shook his head in disapproval.

Bell arrived in a minute, very concerned.

"What's the matter, Captain?"

"Nothing in that sense, XO. Get that kid's head straightened out, will you? We have messengers for finding people. The 1MC is *not* a paging system."

"Yes, sir," Bell said sheepishly. He took full responsibility for the violation of standard procedure. "We've gotten a little sloppy, sir, spending so long in port."

"Have the crew lose the sloppiness, smartly." The XO was responsible for crew training and discipline.

"Yes, sir." Bell was contrite.

"Lock the door." Jeffrey asked Bell for a general status report. The reactor was critical in the power range and carrying ship's loads, as ordered earlier.

"Excellent work, XO. Outstanding job. Give Willey and his department my compliments too. You might see him before me." Lieutenant Willey was the ship's engineer, a lanky and straight-talking man; Jeffrey had been an engineer himself, on his own department-head tour. He liked Willey and understood his perpetual air of intensity and his all-important fine attention to detail.

"Yes, sir."

"Mr. Parker and the SEALs all squared away?"

Bell explained the arrangements. Since he'd been sharing his XO stateroom, which had a fold-down VIP guest rack, with the ship's sonar officer—Lieutenant Kathy Milgrom, on exchange from the Royal Navy—complicated sleep schedules were needed to accommodate another rider and an eight-man SEAL team. Some junior officers, like the most junior enlisted men, had to hot rack—share bunks—which was rather unpopular, but *Challenger* had done this before. There was no room for people to sleep in the torpedo room; the huge compartment was crammed to the gills with weapons.

Next, Bell overviewed with Jeffrey the ship's other major systems and inventories, using Jeffrey's laptop hooked up to the onboard fiber-optic local-area network.

"Good. Now, be careful how you act. I'm sure the enlisted people and junior officers got the feeling that something is up. I don't want imaginations running wild, or a morale crash either. It's bad enough they can't know where we're going till we get there."

"Where *are* we going, sir?"

"After we submerge. We get under way at 2200. Pretend that's when our nonexistent dignitary from Washington is due for his alleged inspection. Get done whatever needs getting done before then. Secure shore power and other shore connections *now,* except the telephone. A readiness drill, remember, and absolute radio silence....Don't let me keep you further. Thanks."

Bell left quickly.

Satisfied so far, Jeffrey walked the few feet forward of his cabin to his control room. The change since this morning was astonishing. Almost everything was back in place, reassembled and tested. He kept going and took a steep ladder up one deck, and reached the bottom of the watertight trunk that led farther up through the sail. Both the upper and lower hatches were open. Jeffrey decided to climb, to eye everything from the vantage point of the bridge cockpit atop the sail. This ladder was perfectly vertical, with a tricky offset halfway to the top.

Jeffrey clambered up with practiced skill. He knew all experienced crewmen could make the thirty-foot climb one-handed; their other hand would often clutch a cup of coffee.

When Jeffrey got there, the wooden scaffold around the top of the sail was gone, so the crew and yard workers wore safety harnesses. They were doing the final checking to see that all of *Challenger*'s photonics masts and antennas, and her emergency ventilating snorkel, raised and lowered and rotated properly.

Weapons loading was finished, and that hatch had been returned to use by personnel; it gave convenient access forward, and its ladder was the least steep. Jeffrey glanced at his watch: 2000, 8 P.M., right on schedule so far.

Jeffrey turned to look at that barn the Seabees were building, along the pier on *Challenger*'s starboard side. *Well, they're as busy as bees, that's for sure.* Jeffrey thought for a second.

Eh, what the heck.

He verified that power was on to the bridge console. He palmed the mike for the ship's loud hailer. He turned the volume all the way up. *Someone has to test it, right?*

"Master Chief Seabees, ahoy." Jeffrey's voice boomed almost deafeningly.

That got the man's attention. He looked up, and saw Jeffrey leaning over the top of *Challenger*'s bridge.

He aimed his bullhorn at Jeffrey. "Captain?" The battery-powered bullhorn couldn't compete with *Challenger*'s loud hailer, backed by a 250-megawatt nuclear reactor plant.

"Explain what that thing does."

"It's a big cover." The Seabee chief gestured at the overhead traveling crane that straddled the dry dock. The chief tapped the side of the cover. "On crude visual, and radar, it makes you look like a smallish container ship. It rests on your hull on padded feet, held in place by ropes tied to your retractable deck cleats."

"How do I get the danged thing off?"

"It floats. Untie it when the moment comes, then sink straight down."

"Submarines don't 'sink,' Chief. They submerge." Jeffrey understood more now about why he had to leave in the dark and before the storm; in decent light this cover would fool no one, and in high winds with breaking waves it would be a liability—assuming the structure didn't fail altogether, leaving *Challenger* badly exposed at the very worst time, with its wreckage hitting her stern planes and rudder and pump jet.

"Uh, sorry, Captain. Submerge."

"Is it ready?"

"Almost. From up there I think you can see the opening for where you'll be standing on the conning tower, like now." The chief pointed at a spot on the roof of the barnlike thing. There was indeed an opening there; Jeffrey had thought before that it was just an unfinished portion.

"Test it."

"Sir?"

"Test it." Jeffrey pointed at the traveling crane. "Lift it, then drop it."

"It's not designed for *that,* Captain."

"No, no. I don't mean drop it on the concrete. I mean lift it up, let it drop ten feet in free fall, and brake the crane. Stress the frame. I want to see that it doesn't fly to pieces."

"Yes, sir!"

The master chief turned with his bullhorn and started issuing orders. The traveling crane moved. Men atop the camouflage cover rigged cables to the built-in lifting eyes on the cover's roof. They scrambled off using tall extension ladders, then removed the ladders.

"Lift it," Jeffrey said through the loud hailer.

"Wait," someone yelled.

Jeffrey turned. On the near-side pier, where the crew from *Challenger* labored at loading supplies, Jeffrey spotted Commander Kwan.

He palmed the mike. "Hello, Commander. What do you want?"

Kwan cupped his lips to his mouth. "To watch. This is what I came for. The bounce test."

"Oh. . . . Sorry to step on your toes."

"No problem, Captain. She's your ship!"

"You take over. I'll watch."

Kwan had shouted across the water to where *Challenger* lay. Jeffrey was impressed—the man could project a very strong voice.

Needs it, in his line of work.

"Captain!" someone else shouted. Jeffrey looked around, confused.

"Captain! Sir!" Jeffrey glanced straight down. Through the grating he was standing on, way underneath him on the deck below the bottom of the sail trunk, he saw the in-port duty officer staring up at him.

"What is it? Can't you use the intercom?" Jeffrey heard telephones ringing, on the piers on both sides of the dry dock.

The lieutenant (j.g.) filled his lungs and bellowed up the sail trunk.

"Vampires, vampires, vampires inbound!"

Jeffrey gripped the side of the bridge cockpit with both hands. Vampires meant antiship missiles.

"Are you *sure*?"

"Confirmed. *Confirmed*. Inbound, Mach 0.7, launch point bears zero-five-zero true." Roughly northeast. "Range less than two hundred miles and closing."

"What?" It didn't make sense. That was much too close. Jeffrey could hear other shouting on the piers now.

"Confirmed. ETA enemy missiles less than thirty minutes! Two separate launch points, sir, simultaneous launches."

That means there must be two U-boats.

"How many missiles?"

"Six, they think, sir."

Six so far out of maybe two dozen.

"Get back to the control room! Have COB sound battle stations!" That would at least have damage-control parties assemble with their gear—including a handful of radiation suits.

Jeffrey glanced at his wristwatch. It was barely 8:30 P.M. He heard the battle-stations alarm ringing raucously inside *Challenger*. Torn, Jeffrey made the only choice he could: He'd put to sea early and hope for the best.

A moving target is always harder to hit. And every ounce of spoofing and diversion has to help.

Jeffrey used the loud hailer.

"Commander Kwan, commence all deception measures."

Kwan held up a phone handset and nodded that he already had. He hung up the phone, gave Jeffrey a thumbs-up and a wave farewell, and jumped into a waiting Humvee. The driver floored the accelerator and the Humvee roared along the pier. It tore right through the blackout curtain of the vehicle entryway at the rear of the dry dock.

Jeffrey held the loud-hailer mike in one hand and grabbed the intercom mike in the other. He dialed the ship's internal 1MC. His voice sounded everywhere now.

"This is the captain. I have the conn. Station the maneuvering watch, smartly. Vampires inbound, this is *not* a drill. XO, take the deck in Control." Jeffrey glanced over the port side of the bridge. "You men there, cease all loading. Single up all lines. *Challenger* people get onboard. Everyone else get off. Retract the brows and the loading conveyors. Remove the handrails and toss them onto the pier." There was no time for such niceties as stowing those dozens of heavy handrails below. Jeffrey turned the other way. "Seabees, get the camouflage cover positioned and cleated down *now.* . . . Maneuvering, Bridge, stand by to answer all bells. Helm, Bridge, stand by on the auxiliary maneuvering units. We don't have time for tugs. . . . Shore party, get the forward dry-dock blackout doors and caisson gate open *smartly.*"

Jeffrey's world darkened for a moment as the long Seabee's camouflage box loomed overhead, then was lowered into place. Now Jeffrey could see why the thing's forward and aft roofs sloped: to give him better visibility. Its many weight-bearing feet and pads, both fore and aft, held it high enough over the top of the hull to leave some room for cascading water as *Challenger* cut through the seas.

The lighting inside the dry dock dimmed to dull red. As the covered dry dock's forward doors retracted to full open, Jeffrey heard air-raid sirens in the distance outside. He felt dull thuds in his gut, from heavy antiaircraft guns far off.

Two lookouts and a phone talker began to quickly climb the ladder through the sail trunk. All three wore night-vision goggles and battle helmets. The phone talker was already wearing his bulky sound-powered backup intercom rig, and trailing its wire; the lookouts had on flak jackets, and nighttime image-intensified binoculars swayed from straps around their necks. As he climbed, the phone talker held an extra helmet with night-vision goggles in one hand, for Jeffrey. These were some of the newest junior enlisted men on the ship, but they seemed eager, ready for anything, and proud to do their part.

Bell's voice crackled on the intercom speaker. "Bridge, Control. Ready to maneuver in all respects." Bell added that twelve Axis missiles were now in the air.

"Very well, Control. Helm, move us ten feet rightward, on bow and stern auxiliary maneuvering units."

Lieutenant (j.g.) David Meltzer, the ship's battle-stations helmsman, acknowledged. His familiar rough Bronx accent made Jeffrey feel better amid the crisis, but not for long.

How did the Axis know we were sailing tonight?

Why did the U-boats sneak in so close?

And why did they launch their missiles so early?

What did these tactics mean? Was there a spy?

Without any visible churning from the small auxiliary propulsors on the lower parts of the hull, *Challenger* slowly slid sideways to gain some room from the nearer dry-dock wall. Jeffrey put on his helmet, lowered the night-vision goggles, and adjusted the focus and brightness settings.

"Chief of the Watch, Bridge."

"Chief o' the Watch," COB's calm voice answered. He manned the ballast and hydraulics panel, next to Meltzer.

"Raise all masts except the snorkel mast."

COB acknowledged. The masts, retracted as part of the engineering tests, rose silently out of the top of the sail.

Behind Jeffrey, the lookouts clipped their safety harnesses into the fittings and then stood atop the roof of the sail, forward of the masts. Jeffrey pulled on his intercom headset and plugged in the wire. This cut off the loudspeaker and handheld mike.

He did a mental calculation.

This'll be tricky. The tide's still coming in.

"Helm, Bridge, rudder amidships. Ahead one third."

The water at the back of the dry dock churned madly. *Challenger* began to move.

"Bridge, Navigator," Lieutenant Richard Sessions's matter-of-fact voice sounded in Jeffrey's headphones. "First leg down the channel is course one-five-zero, sir." Sessions, not known for a neat appearance but admired for his high-precision work, came from a small town in Nebraska. He'd been *Challenger*'s sonar officer when Jeffrey was XO, until Kathy Milgrom was transferred with her valuable battle experience on HMS *Dreadnought;* then Jeffrey promoted Sessions to navigator, a department head's job. He'd never once regretted either personnel decision.

"Nav, Bridge, aye." As backup for the bridge's computer display screen, Jeffrey wrote with an erasable marker pen on the Plexiglas cockpit windscreen. With the night-vision goggles, he could read in the dark.

Challenger came out of the covered dry dock, and her bow began to swing to the right—upstream, north, the wrong way, with the tide. The wind came from the west, and caught the boxy camouflage cover, dragging the bow around more. The sky overhead was crystal clear; there was no sign of any smoke screen, just sheet lightning in the distance, to the southwest.

"Helm, Bridge, left twenty degrees rudder, make your course one-five-zero." South-southeast, into the oncoming tide.

"Left twenty degrees rudder, aye," Meltzer acknowledged. "Make my course one-five-zero, aye." The young man always sounded cocky, and owned a walk to match. He liked being given difficult things to do, flawlessly executing unique maneuvers Jeffrey would invent on the spot when in harm's way—or when piloting *Challenger*'s minisub to even more dangerous places. Meltzer had the bravery of a lion.

He'll need it, steering my ship through a cruise-missile air raid with us as the obvious target.

Jeffrey turned his head this way and that, assessing everything as *Challenger* swung leftward compared to the opposite bank of the river. The rate of the turn was uneven, and the ship rolled heavily too, because of the wind and the ungainly camouflage cover. *Challenger*'s wake curved back behind her, into the dry dock.

Jeffrey cursed. *That wake is a dead giveaway, as long as it persists, if the Axis target sensors are smart enough.*

There was something wrong with his night-vision goggles. When he glanced in the direction of the huge outdoor traveling crane, at the part of the Northrop Grumman shipyard that worked on aircraft carriers—a crane that could lift nine hundred tons, the tallest thing in the area—he saw multiple images. He also saw flashes along the horizon, toward the Atlantic. These might be artifacts of faulty goggles too. He took them off, but the flashes continued, yellow to the naked eye, backlighting the crane. *Make that cranes. I see . . . seven of them?*

Six of them swayed in the wind, their top cross beams making bouncing jerks as they stopped short against their guy wires. Jeffrey realized that these were inflatable replicas of something impossible to hide from either visual or radar. He was impressed by this other method of disorienting the target seekers.

The first concussions from the flashes, after a lengthy delay, reached Jeffrey's body.

More antiaircraft guns, or hits on missiles, or missiles scoring what their software thinks are hits.

Jeffrey estimated that the guns were thirty miles away, on the Delmarva Peninsula that separated the Chesapeake Bay from the sea. With rocket-assisted projectiles, they could reach out forty miles or more at faster than Mach 3.

Even so, we need to make tracks, and fast.

"Lookouts, conflicting traffic?"

"Negative, Captain. Nothing in sight in the channel."

Jeffrey ordered Meltzer to increase speed. With no radar and no tugs and not even any running lights, this dash through narrow waters was very chancy. "Control, Bridge."

"Control," Bell answered immediately, like the others all business now.

Jeffrey smiled. *Danger makes them come alive. I feel* Challenger's *soul stirring too, as if she's throwing off the torpor of her long sleep in dry dock.*

"XO, are we getting the navy air-defense command grid?"

"Affirmative, sir. Five by five in the radio room."

"Patch it into my intercom headset, left ear only. Normal ship circuit, right ear only."

"Bridge, acknowledged. Wait one."

"Bridge, Nav, two miles to next waypoint," Richard Sessions's voice sounded in both ears. "New course will be left turn onto zero-three-five, Captain." Slightly north of northeast, rounding the sharp corner of the Virginia Peninsula, leaving the waterfront of the shipyard stretching behind.

"Nav, Bridge, aye." Jeffrey jotted on the Plexiglas.

What the . . .

Dead ahead lay the I-664 crossing, near the mouth of the James River. Most of it was a causeway bridge, but part was a tunnel—so warships could pass with no fear that bridge debris would ever block the channel. At the north end of the bridge, U.S. Coast Guard buoy tenders and a cutter were at work. They had almost finished unrolling gigantic sheets of floating material, like a sports stadium ground cloth only much larger. The sheets were anchored to the riverbank and to the bridge, and were supported against wave action on their outer edges by buoys . . . and pulled into place against wind drag by the cutter.

They're changing the shoreline, literally. I'll bet those sheets will look like land on radar, optical, or infrared. They're shifting the end of the peninsula a quarter mile southeast.

Analyze that, Axis missiles.

In a few seconds Jeffrey's left ear registered crackling voices with different call signs announcing vectors and ranges and air speeds, and giving orders to more and more units to open fire. Antiaircraft missiles began to ripple-fire from ships farther out in the bay, or from batteries on land. Launch flashes pulsated rhythmically, and missile after missile rose on white-hot rocket-motor points of light, gained speed and broke the sound barrier, and raced out to sea. Their smoke trails began to obscure the northeastern horizon. The roars and thuds and booms were closer now, and louder, and overlapped. The latest strobing flashes seemed to freeze, as halting snapshots, a group of rotating, waving, thrashing excavator arms.

Kwan's people and their machines are busy.

But the jet engines of those Axis cruise missiles bring them almost ten miles closer for every minute that goes by.

And the barge cranes disguising the long south part of the bridge have barely started.

"Helm, Bridge." Jeffrey tested his new intercom setup.

"Bridge, Helm, aye," sounded at once in his right ear.

At the same time, in Jeffrey's left ear, another salvo of six Axis missiles was detected, and plotted, and tracked. The wind in Jeffrey's face, the rolling of his ship on the surface—at its worst on top of the sail—and the ever-increasing danger gave Jeffrey a strong emotional high.

Okay, Challenger. *Show me your warrior's heart.*

"Helm, ahead flank."

CHAPTER 9

Challenger made faster progress at flank speed. Soon she reached the I-64 bridge, designed like the I-664 bridge. From the control room, Sessions fed Jeffrey the next course change, to cross over the tunnel portion of the bridge. Jeffrey relayed the helm orders to Meltzer. The visible causeway parts of the bridge seemed to rotate slightly left as Challenger turned a few degrees to the right.

Jeffrey had a better view across the lower Chesapeake Bay, to the sea. A blinding flash erupted in the distance, and Jeffrey could see the low-lying Delmarva Peninsula in outline on the northeast horizon. There were cargo ships moored farther up the bay, lit for a moment as if by a flashbulb.

"Splash one!" someone shouted in Jeffrey's left earcup. The defenses had hit an inbound missile.

"Bridge, Control," Bell's voice said in Jeffrey's right ear. In the background, over Bell's mike, Jeffrey heard people in the control room cheering.

"Control, Bridge. XO, quiet in Control. One down means at least eleven are flying."

"Bridge, Control, aye."

I don't like playing the heavy, but it's my job.

There was another blinding flash, then two more.

"Splash another three!" a different voice said on the air-defense grid. Sharp, harsh rumbles arrived seconds later through the air.

The bridge console computer display said the time was 2024.

The first wave of missiles will get here any moment. We won't know if they're nuclear until they start going off.

"Radio Room, Bridge. Can you pick up the data link and feed me the air situation display?"

"Bridge, Radio, aye. Wait one, sir."

Overlaid on Jeffrey's navigational chart, there suddenly appeared icons for hostile inbound missiles. Outbound antimissile missiles showed too. Little lines from each icon plotted their courses and speeds. The Axis missiles were coming in Jeffrey's general direction. The friendly defensive missiles were going the other way, moving much faster, converging on the enemy weapons.

Two icons appeared to merge.

There was another blinding flash. The deep, rumbling concussion arrived much sooner than before. Jeffrey saw flames rain onto the sea—burning missile fuel.

Then things became so hectic, the battle was hard to follow.

Antiaircraft guns on the Hampton shore joined those on the outer peninsula. Missile batteries near the Norfolk navy base commenced firing. The Axis missiles were caught in a pincers. Icons moved fast on the bridge console screen. The noise from all around in the distance was loud even through Jeffrey's headphones. The flames and flashes were so constant he raised his night-vision goggles; he could see more easily without them.

A missile streaked overhead from Norfolk, its motor bright but with no sound. Then the sonic boom punched Jeffrey hard, followed by a tearing roar. To the left, over the bay, the missile detonated. An instant later there was a tremendous explosion in the air, and the radiant heat was searing— an inbound German missile destroyed by a defensive missile's proximity fuse. Jeffrey ducked instinctively. Smoldering shrapnel and debris pelted *Challenger*'s special camouflage cover. More missile and antimissile parts splashed into the water all around. Burning pools of fuel were floating too close for comfort off *Challenger*'s port side. The air was filled with smoke and an acrid, choking stench.

"Lookouts below!" Jeffrey ordered hoarsely. It was getting too dangerous up here.

The two men slid down off the roof of the sail, shimmied past Jeffrey and the phone talker, and descended the sail-trunk ladder. Jeffrey thought they looked disappointed. But they were much too exposed on the roof. At least the cockpit sides were armored.

Jeffrey turned to the phone talker. "Keep your head down!"

Jeffrey shut one half of the streamlining clamshells, which closed off the top of the cockpit whenever the ship was submerged. This gave the phone talker protection from above—Jeffrey had realized that his ship could be badly hurt as collateral damage, even if no inbound missiles scored direct hits.

There was an awful detonation behind Jeffrey, on the land. One from the first wave of missiles had gotten through, and been shot down or homed on something.

The Virginia Peninsula. A 1,000 pound warhead. People may have just been killed.

Jeffrey's deepest regret was that civilians might die so his ship could escape. He looked back as flames rose higher and higher on the land. He gritted his teeth till his jaw hurt.

God help them, those poor people, because I can't.

Jeffrey's latest lesson in military necessity was no less painful than his many earlier ones had been. He hoped the diversion measures had lured the missiles to crash in parks and not on dwellings—but from the size of the spreading fires, and the countless secondary explosions, it didn't look that way.

Gas tanks in cars. Oil tanks by houses, and oil in electric transformers on poles. Natural-gas supply pipes, and propane tanks in backyards, and hydrogen in anything equipped with fuel-cell drive.

Pandora's cost is already high.

Jeffrey almost jumped out of his skin as another enemy missile detonated in the sky while a different one hit land near the shipyard, simultaneously. The rumbles reached Jeffrey ten seconds apart, because the first missile had been closer. There was more fire on the water, and on the land. The fires lit up the sky. Fresh and stale smoke trails intertwined like strands of fluffy spaghetti. The constant glare and flashes drowned out the stars.

Sessions called again with a slight course correction. Jeffrey passed orders to Meltzer. Ahead of *Challenger* now lay the famous Lucius Kellam, Jr. Bridge-Tunnel. It ran for seventeen miles from near Norfolk to the south tip of the Delmarva Peninsula, carrying U.S. Route 13 across the whole mouth of the Chesapeake Bay. This bridge had two tunnel sections, each about one mile long, that ran between manmade islands. *Challenger* would use the southern tunnel channel, to round the point of Virginia Beach as rapidly as possible.

As they drew close, Jeffrey saw that the ten-acre islands at each end of the tunnel were surrounded by lines of tethered barrage balloons. Between the thick tethers of the helium-filled balloons were suspended meshes of thinner, lighter wires, like hurricane fencing.

Probably spun monofilament fibers. The mesh would stop an incoming cruise missile cold. . . . A warhead down the throat of a tunnel would sever the vital logistics artery—all seventeen miles of it—for much longer than just knocking out a prefab bridge section would.

Out beyond this final barrier lay the open Atlantic Ocean. The water was still much too shallow to dive.

————————

Challenger continued racing seaward on the surface of the water. Ten minutes later, as the antiaircraft cacophony diminished behind Jeffrey but fires still lit the sky, he wondered why the U-boats hadn't launched another salvo yet. Between them, they could have up to twelve more missiles.

Had they been sunk? Or had they used the first few missile launches to make the U.S. reveal the deception schemes and give away the antiaircraft ships' and defensive batteries' positions to spy satellites?

They would need time for such data to get to Moscow and be transmitted to the submerged U-boats by the Kremlin's extremely-low-frequency antenna. Then the U-boat captains would have to work out their next moves. Jeffrey wondered if this was why there was a delay. He asked himself if it might explain why the U-boats didn't shoot two dozen missiles as fast as they could, to try to swamp American defenses and overwhelm their target all at once—but have no second attack wave remaining.

Jeffrey's left earcup crackled. There were no kills claimed on the U-boats yet. They kept avoiding maritime patrol aircraft and helicopters that aggressively dropped depth charges and lightweight homing torpedoes near where the missiles had first risen from the sea. The U-boats used noise-makers to divert all the torpedoes, and applied skillful tactics to evade the depth-charge drops. Jeffrey could hear frustration rise in the voices on the radio circuit.

As the undersea noise and reverb from wasted torpedoes and depth bombs diminished, fresh sonobuoys seemed to show that the U-boats had spread farther apart—to make the antisubmarine forces cover a wider search area and split their efforts in two.

A new report came in. Jeffrey was electrified. Four more cruise missiles had just taken off, two from each of two places. The U-boats were definitely alive, definitely still fighting.

Once again the American antisubmarine aircraft closed in. This time the U-boats stung back. They launched Polyphems. The airplanes and helos scattered, using defensive countermeasures and escape tactics of their own.

Jeffrey was angry. *If* Challenger *was there, those U-boats would be dead by now.*

Then another call sign spoke, one that Jeffrey had figured out was from an air force AWACS plane, patched into the navy command circuit, overseeing the whole battle with its powerful radar dome atop the fuselage.

The latest salvo of Axis missiles was aimed in a different direction, more to the south, staying over the sea.

Jeffrey watched the new icons on the bridge-console computer display. They were on a collision course with his ship.

The air force joined the battle in earnest now: The AWACS vectored a squadron of F-22 Raptors, state-of-the-art supersonic fighters, to try to shoot the cruise missiles out of the sky.

There'll be around a dozen planes in that squadron.

"Bridge, Control."

"Control, Bridge, aye."

"Captain," Bell reported, "four vampires inbound, bearing zero-three-two, range one seven zero miles, approach speed five hundred knots. ETA twenty minutes."

"Very well, Control."

Jeffrey could see this for himself on the bridge computer, and he'd already heard it over the radio link, but it was Bell's job to tell him anyway, for redundancy and clarity.

Jeffrey watched the newest icons, for the Raptors from Andrews Air Force Base, near Washington. Their speed vectors were long, suggesting they were on afterburner. Their course arrows pointed southeast.

Someone very senior decided to leave the capital less pro-

tected, to try to aid my ship.... But it's touch and go as to whether the Raptor icons will get to the cruise-missile icons and stop them in time.

As if the U-boat captains were reading Jeffrey's mind and wanted to shake his confidence, the radio reported that four more cruise missiles had been launched. Jeffrey watched his screen. Their course was the same as the previous four, as if they too were chasing *Challenger.*

"Nav, Bridge."

"Bridge, Nav, aye," Sessions answered.

"Give me a course to the deepest water we can reach in ten minutes at present speed." On the surface, at flank speed, *Challenger* did over twenty knots—but energy wasted by wave making kept her from going nearly as fast as when submerged.

Jeffrey lifted his left earcup and strained to listen to the open air. He heard the sound of water churning up and over *Challenger*'s forward hull, hitting the support legs of the camouflage cover and swirling past the base of the sail. He heard the whistling of the wind over the Plexiglas windscreen and also through holes in the camouflage cover; panels knocked loose on the cover banged as *Challenger* rolled. The entire cover made a constant wooden creaking noise. But no guns fired, no antimissile missiles launched. Jeffrey knew that cruise missiles and Raptors were in a race beyond the horizon. He asked himself over and over if those missiles were aimed at what the enemy now knew to be *Challenger,* or if they followed a different approach course to have a better chance of clobbering the dry dock they didn't realize he'd left.

"Bridge, Nav."

"Nav, Bridge, aye."

"Course to deepest location is zero-nine-zero, Captain." Due east. "Be advised that that is close to the previous rendezvous point between *Ohio* and her captain's minisub."

"Understood. *Ohio* should be well south now, near her rendezvous with *us*. I see no added hazard of proceeding on zero-nine-zero."

"Bridge, Control, concur," Bell said. He'd been listening in; his station at the command console was only a few feet forward of Sessions's digital plotting table.

"Helm, Bridge, left five degrees rudder, make your course zero-nine-zero."

Meltzer acknowledged, from down in the control room with everyone else.

Even with the gentle rudder turn, at high speed and with her camouflage cover *Challenger* heeled dizzyingly.

Crap. My speed. Small container ships don't move this fast. If the Axis know anything, they know I'm not what I seem.

"Control, Bridge, prepare to submerge the ship." Bell acknowledged. "Phone talker," Jeffrey said to the youngster crouched beside him under the clamshell half, "when I order all stop, go below." The enlisted phone talker nodded.

"Control, Bridge, have men standing by at all hull hatches. When I order all stop and our way comes off, have them come up fast and uncleat the camouflage cover. Once they retract the cleats, they go below and dog the hatches."

"Bridge, Control, when our way off, uncleat the cover, go below, and dog hatches, aye."

Jeffrey watched his console. Raptors were picking off the Axis cruise missiles, but there were still too many missiles in the air. The missiles had not changed course. *Challenger* would be well inside the search cones of their sensors soon. *They'll come in right above the wave tops, straight at me at five hundred knots. I won't even see them till the final seconds of my life.*

Jeffrey had no weapons for defending against threats that moved so fast. *Challenger* reached the place Sessions had chosen for diving.

The seafloor's barely deeper than my ship is tall. Let's pray the Axis warheads aren't designed to go off underwater.

"Helm, all stop. Back two thirds until our way comes off,

then all stop." Backing—throwing the pump jet into reverse—halted the ship more quickly, since her hull had great momentum.

Meltzer acknowledged. The phone talker rushed below. The pump-jet wash churned forward from the stern, then ceased.

Challenger was a stationary target, with a radar cross section larger than a barn.

Jeffrey heard hull hatches popping open, and unseen crewmen raced to unfasten the camouflage cover. He heard wet ropes being cut with axes. The men went below and the hatches slammed shut.

"Chief of the Watch, Bridge, submerge the ship! *Dive, dive!*"

COB warned that the bridge hatch was still open. Jeffrey overrode the rules—this was an emergency crash dive. He heard air start to rush through the open ballast tank vents atop the hull, fore and aft. He could also hear, below, the electronic diving klaxon, and COB's voice announcing the dive on the 1MC.

Jeffrey locked the clamshells closed above his head. He detached the bridge display screen, cradling it under one arm. He clambered through the upper sail-trunk hatch. He could feel that the ship was taking forever to start to submerge. He dogged the hatch, then hurried down the ladder to the lower hatch. He pictured the inbound missiles, each a hungry, flying shark.

CHAPTER 10

Jeffrey took his place at the control-room command console. The control-room lighting was red, standard at night. The ship at last was submerged, with the Seabees' cover jettisoned. Bell sat next to Jeffrey, and assumed the XO's usual role as battle stations fire control coordinator. A lieutenant (j.g.) took over as officer of the deck; he was responsible for machinery status inside the ship, so Jeffrey and Bell could concentrate on the picture outside, and tactics.

COB and Meltzer sat side by side at the ship control console on the forward bulkhead of the control room. Jeffrey had Meltzer steer *Challenger* north at five knots, to put distance between the ship and the now-conspicuous floating camouflage cover—but without raising an obvious surface hump or wake turbulence that the enemy could home on. With the ship's hull so near the swells and the sky, this was a real possibility.

Jeffrey glanced at a chronometer, then at the vertical large-screen tactical plot on the forward bulkhead. The cruise missiles had been thinned out by the Raptors, but a small group was barely two minutes away.

We need to hunker down. It's just too shallow here.

"Helm," Jeffrey ordered, "all stop."

"All stop, aye, sir." Meltzer turned the engine order tele-graph, a four-inch dial on his console. A pointer on the dial responded. "Maneuvering answers, all stop!"

"Chief of the Watch," Jeffrey said, "on the sound-powered phones, rig for depth charge."

COB acknowledged. The word would pass quickly and quietly through the whole ship this way in a matter of mo-ments. "Rig for depth charge," as a modern expression, was used to warn the crew to hold on tight and be prepared for in-coming fire.

Jeffrey needed to do something to steady his nerves in the few endless seconds remaining until the missile impact on or near the camouflage cover. He felt his heart pounding, and could just imagine what some of the others were going through right now—especially the new people. His impor-tant passengers weren't in sight: Felix and the SEALs were assigned to damage-control parties forward. Gamal Salih and Gerald Parker waited in the wardroom farther aft, to help as first-aid orderlies. *They could all be too busy, soon.*

Jeffrey stood to make himself more visible, and peered around to inspect his control-room crew. They'd been reas-sured when he returned from the bridge in one piece, and they'd gotten themselves submerged okay, and now he was there with them as protector and authority figure.

The starboard side of the control room held a line of weap-ons and fire-control consoles. Since *Challenger* was much too close to shore to use her nuclear torpedoes, the weapons offi-cer, Lieutenant Bud Torelli, supervised the weapon-systems technicians in person. Torelli had a special-weapons console outside the torpedo room, for positive control when nukes would be fired.

The port side of the compartment held a line of seven sonar consoles. Royal Navy Lieutenant Kathy Milgrom sat at the head of the line. Neither tall nor slim, she spoke with a

Liverpool accent that Jeffrey enjoyed hearing. Like many of *Challenger*'s crew of 120, Milgrom wore eyeglasses—submariner eyeglasses, with narrow frames and small lenses, designed to fit under an emergency air-breathing mask. Jeffrey thought the eyeglasses combined with her build made Milgrom look owlish. As Jeffrey always reminded—corrected—himself, owls were birds of prey who hunted by night. Lieutenant Milgrom was extremely good at her job.

The thing that was missing from the newest control rooms were periscopes; instead, photonics mast imagery would be displayed on high-definition full-color monitors around the compartment.

"New passive sonar contact," Milgrom called out. "Airborne, short range, closing fast on bearing—"

A punishing *crack* hammered the hull. It hurt Jeffrey's ears and almost knocked him from his feet. The crew all braced themselves. Aftershocks and reverberation made *Challenger* shake, as remnants of the airborne blast force echoed through the shallow water between the bottom and the surface and then back again. Mike cords hanging from the overhead jiggled; the fluorescent light fixtures, suspended from spring-loaded fittings, swayed and cast moving red shadows. Construction dirt and dust—missed by the harried cleanup workers—were thrown into the air. Jeffrey grabbed a stanchion by the overhead and held on tight. *Times like this, I miss old-fashioned periscopes. They were great for grabbing.* He tried not to cough from the dust.

As the reverbing thunder from outside continued, a terrifying *kaboom* battered the ship and everyone and everything inside. The pain in Jeffrey's eardrums was intense. The surrounding sea was so disturbed by the nearby airborne detonation that *Challenger* lurched this way and that as the ocean around her sloshed. Jeffrey's hand, from gripping the overhead fitting, felt pins and needles—even though the entire compartment was shock isolated from the hull by rubber pads and oil-filled cushions and mechanical pivots, for quieting.

Once more echoes and aftershocks banged away at the hull. COB and Meltzer struggled at their controls, to keep *Challenger* from hitting the bottom or broaching. But there wasn't much they could do rapidly when the ship wasn't moving; she lacked any lift on her bow planes or stern planes.

Jeffrey waited for the next eruption. In these conditions, *Challenger*'s powerful sonars were no use in giving any warning.

Nothing more happened. Now Jeffrey noticed that the deck, and console screens and keyboards, and peoples' hair, were covered with bits of colored plastic.

Leftover crimped insulation from a month's work on the electrical wires. Hidden behind or under things, hurled up by the bashing we took.

More time passed. It was possible that some missiles had taken a dogleg course, so they wouldn't all arrive together.

Still nothing happened.

"Captain," Milgrom reported, "acoustic sea state diminishing." The noise outside was dying away. "New passive sonar contact on the port wide-aperture array. Assess as multiple fighter aircraft flying in formation. Contact fading rapidly." Milgrom gave the bearing, and Bell gave the contact's estimated course. Appropriate icons appeared on the tactical plot—the Raptor squadron, flying back to Washington together.

"I think that's that," Jeffrey said. "Chief of the Watch, on the sound-powered phones, maintain battle stations. Specify battle stations antisubmarine." The 1MC wasn't used submerged, in wartime conditions, for quieting. Jeffrey turned to Bell. "Fire Control, I smell something fishy."

Before Bell could open his mouth, Milgrom broke in.

"Captain, new passive sonar contact on starboard wide-aperture array." The wide-aperture arrays were sets of three rectangular hydrophone complexes, mounted along the ship's hull, one set each on her port and starboard sides. Because they were two-dimensional and rigid, unlike a towed array, and their spacing gave a much broader maw to catch sound waves than *Challenger*'s bow sphere, the wide-aperture arrays were extremely sensitive. Special signal-processing algorithms could use their data to do an extremely powerful surveillance of the seas outside.

"Sir," Milgrom said, "contact is signal from a friendly, disposable acoustic-link modem." A small, programmable, underwater buoy, which repeatedly transmitted a message by secure, covert, extremely high-frequency sound. The sound was low power, and shifted around many times per second in the two thousand kilohertz band—a hundred times above the limit of human hearing. Despite this, modems could have ranges of tens of miles. The frequency-agile design made it almost impossible for an enemy not possessing the proper specifications to even detect the transmission: It jumped much faster than the minimum time interval over which an enemy sonar system had to hear a steady tone before calling it signal rather than noise without overwhelming false-alarm rates. Decoding the transmission was a separate problem, assuming a hostile detection could ever be made.

"Message decrypted by radio room. Message is from USS *Ohio,* Captain. Relaying now to your console in plain text." All done through the fiber-optic LAN.

"Very well, Sonar."

Jeffrey sat and windowed the message in a corner of his main screen.

The message was from Captain Parcelli. It was more than an hour old. Jeffrey waved for Bell to lean over and read it with him. They both got the idea pretty quickly, and gave each other meaningful, worried, annoyed looks. They went back to reading, and finished.

Since Parcelli's ship, as a former boomer, was half again as long as Jeffrey's, this gave the wide-aperture arrays she'd been equipped with—late in her conversion to an SSGN—even more sensitivity than *Challenger*'s. After Parcelli rejoined *Ohio* his sonar people detected the Axis missile launches, much farther inshore than American fast-attack submarines had expected, from what Admiral Hodgkiss had said in his final briefing. Parcelli decided to engage the enemy, as the best available platform within effective striking distance. His nuclear-powered sustained flank speed was almost twenty-five knots, faster by several knots than the enemy class 212s at their very fastest. And the class 212 diesel boats, with only fuel-cell air-independent propulsion and storage-battery power available while running well submerged, could keep to their top speed for only short bursts of time.

Even *Ohio* was noisy at flank speed, especially carrying minisubs with their extra flow noise, and Parcelli intended to use this to charge the launch point of the cruise missiles, then offer battle with the two U-boats. His assessment was that they would have brought a few torpedoes, to fire at targets of opportunity, so they would accept battle, and close the range on *Ohio*. Once within torpedo striking distance of each other, Parcelli intended to suddenly slow, then use his ship's superior quieting, her vastly superior sonars and signal-processing computers, her much larger stock of decoys and countermeasures compared to the little 212s—and other systems advantages—to destroy the U-boats. The message ended by suggesting a revised rendezvous point, well to the north, near where the U-boats would be found. The exact location was specified in the message by an offset to the original classified location, to reduce the already slim chance of an enemy reading the message and arranging an ambush.

Jeffrey fought to keep himself under control. He felt his face turn crimson.

Bell said it for him, by typing on the console so no one would hear. "Looks like we have a real cowboy on our hands, Skipper!" Bell quickly erased the message.

Jeffrey nodded, tight lipped, not trusting himself to speak.

Parcelli had disobeyed orders and was endangering his ship against targets that were not his to attack. *Ohio* was not expendable in this context. Parcelli was even exposing himself to friendly fire—his hunt would surely take him outside today's secret Allied submarine safe corridors.

He's trying to rack up some kills early on, to lord it over me for the rest of the mission.

I cannot allow this. Period.

"You said you smelled something fishy, sir?" Bell prodded.

"Uh, yeah. Thanks, XO."

One thing Jeffrey couldn't do as task-group commander was lose his temper. He would deal with Parcelli in good time.

"The Two-twelves, XO. Never mind how they sneaked so close to Norfolk." *If they had a month or more to cruise along at four or five knots from the coast of occupied France, and drift with undersea currents, or hide under surface storms or neutral merchant ships and so on, I can see that they might have done it stealthily enough.* "The Germans know we put in at Newport News for repairs, that much we couldn't hide. It's even possible they'd originally been dispatched to go after a supercarrier leaving port, or some other high-value target, but then *Challenger* entered the picture, so their orders were changed by ELF."

"Concur, Captain. With you so far."

"And part of the *why* of them sneaking so near is obvious, now that we've got twenty-twenty hindsight from that close shave just now."

"Shorter flight time for their missiles. Less inertial navigation drift, for a better precision assault on our dry dock. And as we saw for ourselves, a lot less margin for our side to man the defenses. . . . We never spotted a hint of the smoke screen we were promised."

Jeffrey nodded. "And leave out how they knew exactly *when* to launch, what day, what hour. It can't be just coincidence. It has to be from signals intercepts, or something they saw on spy satellites, or word they got from informers or moles. We'll hash that through with Mr. Parker and Captain Parcelli later. Another aspect of *why* is much more relevant, here and now."

"Sir?"

"If they come well inside the two-hundred-mile limit, they know we won't use nukes against them. That greatly evens the odds, in a sub-on-sub or sub versus antisubmarine battle."

Bell caught on immediately. "As witnessed by the lack of success of our maritime patrol aircraft and the ASW helos."

"Right. The announced Axis ROEs mean they won't use nuclear weapons within the two-hundred-mile limit of the U.S. homeland either...*assuming* the U-boats obey the ROEs even if facing certain death, or their ROEs haven't been secretly changed." Jeffrey watched Bell grimace. "There's another scary thing, XO."

"Captain?"

"Fuel endurance. By coming this close, and assuming it wasn't a one-way suicide mission, which I seriously doubt, 'cause that's not their culture, they added almost two thousand miles to their round-trip home. The class Two-twelves can't handle that."

"You think they—"

"Yup. They must have had refueling support. Probably a class Two-fourteen long-endurance modified milch-cow sub."

"Oh boy. Undersea replenishment."

"If you were that Two-fourteen, where would you plan your next refueling meet with the Two-twelves?"

"Generically? The last place the Allies would look."

"And where is that place, *specifically,* today?" Jeffrey's role as CO was to teach his subordinates constantly. Making them answer probing questions was an effective way to do that.

The teaching and learning don't stop just because there's a war—they become more indispensable than ever.

"Can I close *Ohio*'s message and bring up a chart?"

"Go ahead." Jeffrey and Bell often worked like this, elbow to elbow, sharing one or the other's console. Such brainstorming had always been vital in the Silent Service, and Jeffrey prided himself on being especially good at it—when the other party played ball.

Bell tapped keys. A nautical chart appeared on the screen.

"I'd have to say, sir, if I were them, rendezvous close to the bottom, to hide in folds in the seafloor terrain."

"That still covers a lot of ground," Jeffrey said. "Now that you have the map, where would you pick the place?"

"If I was some devious admiral in my office in Berlin, I'd tell the Two-twelve attack subs and their Two-fourteen meal ticket back to the fatherland to get it on closer to Norfolk than the point where they launched the cruise missiles."

Jeffrey stared at the chart. "XO, I concur." Then he frowned. "This means we have a problem."

"There's a third Axis sub in the area, and Parcelli doesn't know it. And the Two-fourteen has her own torpedoes, ready to fire."

"Our task group companion allows us no choice, XO. We'll have to run interference for *Ohio,* and take some risks ourselves." Jeffrey cursed to himself all over again. *None of this had been part of the plan. Now* anything *could happen thanks to Parcelli...including Zeno being stranded, and Pandora running wild.* "What do we have in the tubes?"

"Weps?" Bell asked Torelli; Weps was the nickname for weapons officer.

"Six high-explosive ADCAPs, tubes one through six. Two brilliant decoys, sir, tubes seven and eight." Torelli spoke with a thick southern accent; he'd grown up near Memphis.

"Perfect," Jeffrey said. Navy practice demanded that a captain always state his intentions. "We'll use snap shots from tubes one and two if something sudden and bad happens. Be ready on the antitorpedo rockets....Sonar? Nav? Fire Control?" Milgrom and Sessions turned; Bell and Torelli remained attentive.

I've got to think fast with my people, and make up a search-and-attack scheme on the fly.

"*Ohio* is heading northeast at her flank speed to engage the pair of class Two-twelves that launched those missiles. We will proceed in *Ohio*'s support. There might also be a class Two-fourteen in the area, and if so, I need to know it, and I need them to know I know it before they draw a bead on *Ohio*. Sonar, I want to go active on maximum power."

"Sir," Sessions added, "we also need to watch for uncharted wrecks or hummocks on the bottom as we move." As navigator, Sessions always had direct access to Jeffrey; part of his job was keeping the ship from running aground—especially underwater—or colliding with something.

"Concur, Nav. Clearance here is narrower than a shoe box."

"Understood," Bell and Milgrom said together.

"Chief of the Watch, Helmsman, rig for nap-of-seafloor cruising mode. Activate chin-mounted obstacle-avoidance sonar."

COB and Meltzer acknowledged and worked a few switches. A false-color image of the seafloor contours, in an arc ahead of the ship, popped onto their vertical console screens. The high-frequency obstacle-avoidance sonar had sharp resolution, to identify mines, but could see on direct paths only.

The muddy bottom was rolling and rutted, a fact that was emphasized visually by the shadowed areas on the display.

Any one of those shadows could hide a Two-fourteen. I'm damned if I do and damned if I don't. . . . But what else is new?

"Very well. Sonar, one ping."

An undulating siren noise sounded, rising and falling in pitch. It would stop for a second, then resume, interspersed with sharp clicks and deep foghorn tones. It made loose things in the control room vibrate, and the fillings in Jeffrey's teeth hurt. This mix of noises was used to get the most amount of information possible, while making it unlikely that a target could mask the return echo with active out-of-phase emissions of their own. Intentional bounces off the surface and bottom would even probe the places masked from the chin-mounted sonar; data on local water temperature and salinity gradients were used to interpret the complicated paths that sounds at different frequencies took.

The speed of sound in water was five times as fast as in air, but the signal still had to make the whole round-trip to a target and back for *Challenger* to hear any echo. It would take a full minute to search out to twenty-four miles. Longer for the complex returns off terrain and sea life to be sifted through by the signal processors and Milgrom's sonar men, to find traces of an Axis U-boat.

Jeffrey fidgeted. He might have just tipped off the 214, and drawn incoming fire.

"No new submerged contacts, Captain," Milgrom said.

Which means no Axis torpedoes in the water, either. . . . Yet.

"Nothing on *Ohio*?"

"Negative, sir. She must be too far ahead of us. Sound propagation conditions in these shallows are rather poor. My assessment is that she's stern on to *Challenger,* not trailing a towed array because of terrain proximity, and due to her self-noise at flank speed her acoustic intercept might not have heard our ping."

Parcelli doesn't know I'm covering his ass. . . . But he might assume I am, because he forced me to. Cripes, his recklessness makes me be extra cautious, which really isn't my style.

"Very well, Sonar," Jeffrey said, formally acknowledging Milgrom's report. "Fire Control, prepare a laser buoy."

Bell looked surprised.

"We need to protect against a blue-on-blue." "Blue-on-blue" meant a friendly fire accident.

"Wouldn't our coastal hydrophone nets detect us and *Ohio*?"

And, by implication, warn off American antisubmarine platforms.

"They *should*. The captain of *Ohio* seems to be counting on that." *To be fair, Parcelli couldn't launch a laser buoy himself, it would compromise his stealth; no one's supposed to know he's even here. And I can't ask that orders be sent to him to break off his chase, because if our comms are penetrated, I could get him killed.*

"Things malfunction, XO, and people make mistakes, and news might not get where it needs to go soon enough."

"Understood. Buoy-transmission time delay, sir?"

"To the enemy our stealth is gone, so . . . short. Make it one minute."

"Message?"

Jeffrey thought hard. He dared not name *Ohio* in his message, but he needed to work in clues so Hodgkiss could figure out what was happening and issue the proper commands, pronto.

This should do it. Subtle, but Hodgkiss, a submariner, is very smart. . . . I won't identify myself in the message either, just in case some clerk in the loop is an Axis agent, but the admiral will know it's from Challenger *because of this location.*

Gamal Salih had said it well: spies and lies. Jeffrey had never thought he'd need to be so paranoid. He cleared his throat—the dust he'd breathed in still bothered him.

"Flash, personal for ComLanFlt. Am in necessary pursuit U-boats that launched missiles. Base course zero-four-five." *I say* necessary *pursuit, and say base course, not* my *base course, suggesting that someone else's course is involved.* "Prob Two-fourteen in area." *That's the zinger.* "Urge friendly coastal-defense units weapons tight." No launching of torpedoes or depth charges. "Allied submarines stand clear." Friendly fire could work in both directions, and Jeffrey didn't want to sink one of his own kind by mistake. *Coastal defense units excludes* Ohio. *Hodgkiss, knowing what he knows, ought to catch on.* "Surface, airborne platforms limit sonar search above layer. Report contacts via signal sonobuoys." *To* me *for prosecution.* "Fuller sends."

A signal sonobuoy, dropped from an aircraft, emitted a series of loud tones, like Morse code. They could send simple information one way only. But though the U-boats might not be able to read the code, the signal could be heard for miles. It would further telegraph Jeffrey's position to the enemy, but this fit with his need to divert the 214's attention away from *Ohio.*

Bell finished typing Jeffrey's message to Hodgkiss. He arranged for a tight-beam satellite-communications laser buoy to be programmed with the message in code, then launched through a countermeasures tube.

"Sonar, I intend to head for the edge of the continental shelf for better sound-propagation conditions."

"Understood," Milgrom said.

"Helm," Jeffrey ordered, feeling more like a task-group commander every minute. "Make your course zero-four-five." Northeast. "Ahead flank."

CHAPTER 11

Jeffrey gripped his armrests as *Challenger* moved through the water above the continental shelf at her flank speed, fifty-three knots. The ship shook roughly, as she always did when moving so fast, from the immense power being put through her propulsion shaft and into the pump-jet rotors in their cowling behind the stern. Mike cords danced as they dangled from the overhead. Light fixtures and consoles made small squeaking sounds as they jiggled and bounced. Now and then more bits of construction dirt, including that colorful electric insulation, worked their way out of nooks and crannies and fell onto people or onto the deck. Pens, pencils, and computer-screen styluses rattled and rolled.

Everyone was silent now, fixated on their readouts and controls. Tension filled the compartment. Jeffrey could feel it, and *see* it: COB's and Meltzer's neck and shoulder muscles were knotted tight. Meltzer's hands were white knuckled on the wheel as he piloted *Challenger* at a dangerous speed for such shallow water. COB worked switches and knobs on his panel constantly, juggling the ship's buoyancy as she hit one halocline after another—places where salinity, and hence water density, varied because of freshwater outflow from all the rivers and bays along the Virginia and Delaware coasts with their endless series of barrier islands. Everyone else showed concern and traces of fear in the way they sat, in the set of their faces.

Jeffrey too wasn't the least bit pleased. This charge into battle against an unseen enemy, forced because of Parcelli's behavior and now the presence of a class 214 somewhere near, came as a complete surprise. *Challenger*'s people had barely had a chance to catch their breath and slow their pulses from their pounding by the near-miss Axis cruise-missile barrage, and now *this*. Jeffrey, like any CO, hated surprises. And like any proper warrior, he always craved surprise be on *his* side in combat. Worst of all, at flank speed, even *Challenger* with her state-of-the-art sensor suite was half blinded by her own flow noise as she tore through the ocean.

Jeffrey studied the nautical chart and the tactical plot on his console. He did some mental arithmetic. If the pair of class 212s moved toward *Ohio* at high speed, and *Ohio* kept moving toward them as Parcelli had said he intended, then from the moment of those first missile launches as *Challenger* sat in the dry dock, to the moment *Ohio* and the 212s would be in torpedo range of each other, would be about three hours. Half of that interval had already passed. Because of *Ohio*'s head start, the rest of the time might run out before Jeffrey could get very close to Parcelli.

And right now Jeffrey had no choice but to slow down. He needed to find the 214 before the 214 drew a bead on Parcelli. There was a very real possibility that the captain of the 214 already had good firing solutions locked in against both *Challenger* and *Ohio*, and was awaiting his optimum moment to open fire: whenever his torpedoes had short target runs and could come at both ships from angles that gave the German all the advantages.

"Sonar, stand by to check our baffles and do a passive search on the wide-aperture arrays."

"Baffles check on wide arrays, Sonar, aye," Milgrom responded. "Baffles" meant the blind spot behind a submarine's stern.

"Helm," Jeffrey ordered. "Slow to ahead one third, make turns for four knots."

Meltzer acknowledged. *Challenger* gradually slowed.

"Helm, left five degrees rudder."

"Left five degrees rudder, aye, sir," Meltzer said.

Challenger gently began to swing in a circle. Meltzer reported every ten degrees of course change. The ship's wide-aperture arrays, their sweet spots pointing off to either side of the ship, scanned the waters all around as *Challenger* turned, her low speed giving their hydrophones maximum sensitivity.

Milgrom went to work with the senior chief sonar supervisor and the enlisted sonar men. Jeffrey waited for reports.

Meanwhile, he tried to put himself in the faceless class 214 captain's shoes.

Where is he? Which way will he have moved since getting whiffs of Parcelli and me racing along at our very noisiest— and probably also hearing me ping? He'll guess that we're after the pair of Two-twelves. But he won't know I know that he's here.

Where would I lurk if I were him? He has six torpedo tubes. When would he shoot?

Jeffrey stared at the maps and icons displayed on his console. He saw his own ship and the estimated locations and courses and speeds of the class 212s and Parcelli.

Then it all became too obvious.

The 214 would proceed generally north, staying in very shallow water, to support his two friends. He'd try to catch Jeffrey and Parcelli from the inshore flank, from the west, as they were both preoccupied looking down the throat of a dozen other German torpedo tubes aimed at them from the northeast. Inshore, the 214 could hide on the move, where sonar conditions were poorest.

On this part of the Atlantic Coast, the shoreline ran north-northeast, along a line of roughly 030 on the chart. The distance from Jeffrey's ship to the shore was opening only gradually.

"Sir," Meltzer reported, "my heading is zero-four-five."

"Very well, Helm. Rudder amidships." *Challenger* had turned in a complete circle, but Milgrom's people and the ship's supercomputers found nothing.

Jeffrey ordered Milgrom to ping on active, using very-low-frequency noise this time, ideal for finding diesels when ocean surface and bottom lay so close together. The resulting ping was a deeper tone than any foghorn; the entire control room and all in it shivered in resonance. Jeffrey waited for returns from the newest acoustic blast to be received and interpreted. He waited for Milgrom to tell him something useful, something on which he could act. He began to drum his fingers on his armrest, but stopped when Bell noticed and subtly shook his head.

This made the waiting harder. It felt as if a torturer were turning a giant corkscrew through Jeffrey's navel and straight into his abdomen. He wasn't sure which he dreaded more, Milgrom reporting the 214's torpedoes in the water, or her reporting nothing.

Torpedoes at least would mean the fight was joined, and I could fight back.

Again, no hostile contacts. *Ohio* was racing northward, at the extreme range of active sonar detection in slightly deeper water, with no sign at all of stopping to check for local threats like Jeffrey was. This meant that for now Parcelli was drawing ahead of *Challenger.*

For a moment Jeffrey felt reassured that, since the 212s had launched so many cruise missiles in their attack, they couldn't have very many torpedoes left. But then he remembered that for years before the war, the 212s could also carry an external harness that held up to two dozen mines. If this harness had been adapted to hold and launch cruise missiles instead, the U-boats might still have plenty of torpedoes.

Now Jeffrey felt as if the devil had yanked out the corkscrew, and pulled half of Jeffrey's insides with it. He forced himself to stay rational, and analyze all that he knew.

If the 214's captain gets the geometry and ambush timing just right, when the undersea brew up begins it'll be three versus two in submarines, and eighteen to twelve, against, in loaded tubes.

Tubes to the front of us, tubes to the left of us. . . .

Jeffrey's brain changed gears. Now came the really hard part. He knew he needed to make a choice, then stick with it to the bitter end. The fact that Milgrom hadn't detected the 214 with her latest ping suggested that it was farther away than he'd hoped, probably still heading north-northeast along the shore.

To break away from *Ohio* and do an independent pursuit of the 214 would violate that prime war-fighting rule, concentration of forces. Head to head, in isolation, *Challenger* could overwhelm the milch cow, but he'd leave Parcelli against the 212s outnumbered two to one in vessels, and outgunned twelve to four in tubes. No amount of arrogance and fancy tech on Parcelli's part would make up for such long odds.

No, I have to stay on Parcelli's tail, and keep acting as his wingman, like it or not. When we draw closer, I can try to reach him via secure undersea acoustic link. Then he'd better do what I say, and I can properly coordinate the engagement.

"Helm, maintain course zero-four-five. Ahead flank."

Meltzer acknowledged. *Challenger* began to regain speed. Jeffrey pursed his lips.

I can feel each one of these half-blind, nerve-racking sprints take a toll on my cardiovascular system. This can't be good for my health.

But, what the heck? We could all be dead in an hour anyway.

At times like this, Jeffrey knew, an hour was an eternity.

"Fire Control," Jeffrey addressed Bell by his formal role

during an approach and attack. "How many torpedoes could those Two-twelves still have? Assume they used an external harness to carry some of their cruise missiles."

Bell motioned for Torelli to join the discussion. "Figure a cruise missile is about the size of four naval mines?"

Torelli nodded. "So twenty-four mines means the harness could hold six missiles, in protective capsules, say."

"Given the total number of missiles we know were launched," Bell said, "and assuming each Two-twelve came with a full six torpedoes in her torpedo room plus a missile or torpedo in each of her six tubes, they'd have what left?"

"About ten torpedoes apiece," Torelli said.

"A salvo of six, and then a salvo of four," Jeffrey stated. "Maybe. Maximum. We don't know how much space they used up for missiles they fired toward Newport News well after we departed."

"Concur," Bell and Torelli said together.

"But we have to assume the worst, including that the Two-fourteen has a full load."

"Two salvos of six," Bell said. "If those are the tactics they follow."

"It'll be a close call as to who runs out first," Jeffrey said. "Them out of torpedoes, or us and *Ohio* out of antitorpedo rockets."

CHAPTER 12

Twenty minutes and almost twenty miles later, Jeffrey ordered Meltzer to slow the ship and turn in a circle again. Jeffrey dared not go farther without another check for targets and threats. The icons on his computerized tactical plot were mere abstractions, but he knew that what they stood for was totally real. The positions of the pair of 212s was an estimate, but that was far better than nothing. What scared him most was the phantom that didn't even have an estimate icon: the milch-cow 214, whereabouts completely unknown.

Jeffrey dearly wished he could trail his ship's special fiber-optic towed array. This new array, installed before his previous mission, had three parallel lines of sensors instead of just one. The array was ideal in hunting for diesel subs in shallow waters.

But Jeffrey was handcuffed. The array took many minutes to reel out on the special winch and then reel it all back in again. The array didn't work at flank speed, and might even be damaged by flow drag through the ocean at such high velocity. In water so constricted, with many uncharted wrecks on this part of the U.S. Eastern Seaboard, the danger of snagging the array and losing it altogether was serious.

But unless I detect the Two-fourteen soon... Whoever gets in the first accurate salvo in a sub-on-sub engagement usually wins.

Somewhere out there is a strong steel tube, half as long as Challenger *and only one quarter the weight. But she has two dozen officers and men inside, each of them hell-bent on destroying my ship. And they're doing what they're best at— staying invisible, toying with me.*

The pair of smaller 212s and their crews in front of Parcelli's mad dash were bad enough.

Challenger continued making another gradual turn. Once more Jeffrey, torn by frustration, waited for word from Milgrom on any contacts.

"Sir," Meltzer reported, "my course is zero-four-five."

The ship had completed another circle.

"Sonar, anything?"

"Nothing on our passive hull arrays, Captain."

"Very well, Sonar.... Helm, my intention is to resume flank speed on course zero-four-five after doing another active search."

"Understood, sir."

"Sonar, ping on—"

"Torpedoes in the water!" a sonar man screamed. "Multiple Seehecht torpedoes inbound, bearing two-nine-zero, range twelve thousand yards!" West-northwest, six nautical miles. All sonar contacts were listed with true bearings, as if from a compass centered on Jeffrey's own ship; *Challenger*'s course wasn't relevant.

The Two-fourteen has sprung its trap.

Jeffrey needed good information now more than ever.

"Sonar, go active, melee search mode."

Challenger's bow sphere emitted another powerful crescendo chorus of sound.

Data started pouring in.

Milgrom called out each contact.

Bell updated the tactical plot.

Jeffrey hated what he saw. *Ohio* was directly ahead of *Challenger,* by four miles. She'd slowed to do her own target search. The 214, contact designated Master 1, was off to the left, in between them—past *Challenger*'s port bow, and in the broad blind spot of *Ohio*'s baffles. Both class 212s, contacts designated Master 2 and Master 3, were ahead of *Ohio,* as Jeffrey expected, by about another ten thousand yards—one beyond *Ohio*'s port bow and one beyond her starboard bow.

The German subs used updated Seehecht torpedoes, wire-guided from the parent sub. The Seehechts' top speed was almost forty knots; Jeffrey could outrun them easily. But the Seehechts were much faster than *Ohio,* so the last thing Jeffrey could do now was run. *Ohio* badly needed Jeffrey's help, even though all vessels were still well inside the two-hundred-mile limit, so German nukes—hopefully—were precluded.

Challenger moved slowly through the water; the 214's Seehechts were gaining by more than a thousand yards per minute. It made Jeffrey's nerve endings feel like they were on fire.

Patience. Don't rush the ballet or you'll botch it.

"Contacts on acoustic intercept," Milgrom called out. "Masters One through Three have gone active!"

"Sonar on speakers," Jeffrey ordered. The control room was suddenly filled with quadraphonic sound, eerie echoes of enemy pings and the frightening mechanical screams of electric torpedo engine sounds.

"*More* torpedoes in the water," a sonar man yelled. "Fan spread, mean bearing zero-four-five, inbound at eighteen thousand yards."

"They've got superior position and better immediate fire-power," Jeffrey said to Bell. "Masters Two and Three can shoot a dozen torpedoes at *Ohio* compared to her four in any one salvo. After they overwhelm her, they'll all close in on *Challenger.*"

"Concur."

"We fight the fight their way, we've had it. We need to change the rules, make this a battle of maneuver."

"Bearing rate on *Ohio*," Milgrom said. *"Ohio* turning to starboard.... *Ohio* has fired four torpedoes, sir, two each at Master Two and Master Three."

Parcelli needs time to reload. At least those shots might force the 212s to run, and break the guidance wires to their weapons in the water, and give us a chance to outsmart the torpedo software with our human brains.

"Fire Control, signal to *Ohio* on acoustic link: 'Maintain your turn, steer onto course two-two-five.'" Southwest, the opposite of the way they'd just come. "'Put yourself in my baffles, direct all further fire at the class 214 I designate Master One.'"

Bell typed madly and had the message sent.

"Ohio acknowledges!"

"Sonar, speakers off. Go active. Melee ping."

The noise, even with the speakers off, was almost unbearable. Jeffrey told Milgrom to turn the speakers back on—he craved sensory data. Seconds later he could hear each echo come back off the German subs, and the quadraphonic surround sound gave him a three-dimensional feel of the battle.

The tactical plot was refreshed, with new positions and courses and speeds—including icons for over a dozen torpedoes dashing this way and that.

"Fire Control, snap shots, tubes one and two, on bearing to Master One, *shoot.*"

Bell acknowledged and relayed commands. Torelli's team quickly programmed the torpedoes, flooded and equalized the pressure in the tubes, and opened the outer doors. The force of water pent up behind big, stiff elastomer membranes quietly shoved the fish out of the tubes. As they came free of the ship, their closed-cycle liquid-fueled engines started.

Snap shots lacked a proper fire-control solution to lead a

moving target; they were done to save time in a combat emergency. But the homing sonars and software on the fiber-optic wire-guided Mark 48 Improved ADCAPs were very good.

"Tubes one and two fired electrically," Torelli reported, his voice dead flat, as always in combat. By making himself sound almost bored, he kept his people calm and focused.

"Both units operating normally," Milgrom confirmed by using passive sonar.

Jeffrey's opening shots in this battle were well on their way. But to win would demand subtle strategy, not just brute strength.

"Decoy in tube seven, set speed to fifty-three knots, snap shot on bearing to Master One, *shoot.* . . . Helm, ahead two thirds, make turns for twenty-six knots." Twenty-six knots was *Challenger*'s top quiet speed, one knot faster than *Ohio* at her fastest and loudest. The decoy was meant to follow Jeffrey's torpedoes, which moved at almost seventy knots, to make the 214's captain think that *Challenger* was charging at him right behind Jeffrey's own fish.

I've got to shake him up, and force him to make a hard turn, and make him break the wires controlling his weapons.

Jeffrey watched on the tactical plot and listened on the speakers as *Challenger* and *Ohio* passed each other in opposite directions; *Ohio* was rushing down *Challenger*'s starboard side.

"Fire Control, signal *Ohio.* Reverse your course, assume station five hundred yards off my stern. Increase to flank speed, steer your weapons well clear of my decoy at rough bearing two-nine-zero. Support appearance that decoy is *Challenger,* shielding you from the class Two-fourteen. Do not use your active sonar. Rely only on active search by your fish."

The *Ohio*'s active sonar system—as a former boomer whose job was perpetual stealth—was less capable than *Challenger*'s. If *Ohio* pinged, she'd give *Challenger* away via echoes the Germans would hear off of Jeffrey's hull, or she'd reveal a big, quiet hole in the water—*Challenger,* backlit by *Ohio.* Either way would ruin Jeffrey's intended deception.

And if I ping now, I betray that my decoy's a decoy. It's all up to the ADCAPs and my passive sonars now.

Jeffrey was taking a gamble, but out-positioned and out-gunned, he had no choice. There was an awkward moment while he wondered what Parcelli would say in response to his latest orders. Jeffrey was trying to make it look like *Ohio's* captain was confused about what to do, turning and then running and then turning and then seeming to stop.

"*Ohio* acknowledges! . . . *Ohio* turning into our baffles."

This way *Challenger,* silent, might shield *Ohio* from the 212s, who'd be tracking Jeffrey's decoy, which was chasing the 214. Both American ships had the same outside diameter—forty-two feet. And the close spacing brought *Ohio* and *Challenger* under the protective umbrella of each other's antitorpedo underwater rockets, which had an effective range of only a thousand yards before their solid-fuel motors burned out.

Five hundred yards of separation was less than three ship lengths, from *Ohio's* perspective. The two vessels were tucked in tight. Jeffrey now planned to pretend to the Germans that *Challenger* was *Ohio.*

It's time to go on the all-out offensive.

"Fire Control, snap shots, tubes three and four, last known bearing to Master Two. Have both units begin active search after running for two thousand yards. Shoot!"

Bell relayed the commands; Torelli and his weapons-systems technicians were kept very busy.

"Fire Control, snap shots, tubes five and six, last known bearing to Master Three. Have both units begin active search after running for two thousand yards. Shoot!"

The noise of torpedo engines was very loud now. The weapons, both friendly and enemy, began to ping more and more in search of targets. Silvery *tings* filled the air in the control room, musical and sweet, disguising the relentless menace each note stood for.

Jeffrey glanced again at the tactical plot. The 214 was moving northeast from her ambush location at twenty knots, fleeing a clutch of inbound fish. She fired a series of noise-makers, which gave off bubbles and made loud gurgling sounds—but the ADCAPs weren't fooled. One of Torelli's weapons techs controlled the fifty-knot decoy to keep following in their wake. Jeffrey prayed the other U-boats still bought his trick, that the decoy was *Challenger* going after the milch cow.

They did. Grouped together as if to present a united front, the pair of 212s moved boldly toward *Ohio*'s last-known position—toward *Challenger*—at their own flank speed, twenty knots.

There was just one catch. The 214's first set of weapons closed constantly from the side, even as *Challenger* led *Ohio* northeast. The Seehechts might be slow compared to AD-CAPs, but their high-explosive warheads were nearly as large.

I can't ignore them forever.

A new sound came over the speakers. Dull rumbles rose to heavy roars.

"Assess Masters Two and Three have fired antitorpedo rockets!" Bell said.

"Let's see how effective they are."

Jeffrey and Bell waited. *Ohio*'s four weapons ran on, their wires undoubtedly broken now. Torelli had his technicians make *Challenger*'s torpedoes from tubes three through six jink to try to evade the rockets. But the antitorpedo rockets were more nimble.

There were dull *thud*s and tremendous *crack*s as each rocket fired its warhead, a high-explosive shaped charge full of depleted uranium pellets, like a shotgun blast; Parcelli's and Jeffrey's ADCAPs were smashed, and two of their war-heads were set off by the effects of the U-boats' defensive rockets. Echoes finally died away, and the torpedo engine noises were lessened compared to before.

This won't do. . . . We need to use more fish, in quicker succession, from much shorter range.

"Fire Control, reload tubes one through six, high-explosive ADCAPs."

Jeffrey hadn't reloaded before, because doing so would cut the wires to the weapons already in the water. Jeffrey's first two fish, aimed at the 214, were on their own now. Sinking Master One was Parcelli's job, and a salvo of four of his ADCAPs was already on the way.

Both class 212s pinged. Milgrom used active out-of-phase emissions to suppress the echoes off *Challenger*'s bow and the front of her sail. "Assess echoes successfully suppressed."

"Very well, Sonar." The Germans had to be wondering where *Ohio* had gone. *Good. Perfect. Let them wonder.*

The reloading of all empty tubes was done very quickly, thanks to *Challenger*'s torpedo-room hydraulic autoloader gear. Six tubes were soon ready to fire.

Enemy torpedoes began to draw too close for comfort. Jeffrey ordered Bell to have Torelli open fire with *Challenger*'s antitorpedo rockets.

Once more, roars and rumbles began and raced through the sea. The rocket detonations, and the sympathetic explosion of several Axis high-explosive torpedoes, were much louder this time, close enough to rattle *Challenger* bodily.

It was time to try to give the 212s' captains the biggest surprise of their lives.

Hopefully the last *surprise of their lives. They'll think* Ohio *just fired those rockets, while sitting stationary, maybe behind a big fold in the terrain.*

"Helm, ahead flank."

Challenger accelerated.

Jeffrey ordered more snap shots fired, three each at Master Two and Master Three. They closed the range toward the pair of 212s very rapidly, since Master Two and Master Three had been lured before by Jeffrey's sudden disappearing act into charging straight toward his quiet, invisible presence. The net closing rate of 212s and ADCAPs was almost 100 knots.

Jeffrey ordered the six tubes reloaded. As soon as they were ready, he fired another six fish.

They'll know that I'm not Ohio, *and they were fooled before.* Ohio *can't shoot six fish in one salvo.*

The melee was in its end stage now; a stand-up slugfest at barely arm's length. There was nothing subtle about it. Antitorpedo rockets flew back and forth through the water. Torpedo engines screamed, moving away or coming nearer. Homing sonars pinged at different pitches, all of them high and now seeming strident, not sweet. Noisemakers gurgled. The hiss of *Challenger*'s own flow noise made a continuous backdrop over the speakers.

The 212s, in desperation, fired more antitorpedo rockets, and launched more Seehechts, and turned away to attempt evasive maneuvers. But they were running out of ammo, and Jeffrey's gigantic torpedo room was still more than half full. Even in a stern chase, Jeffrey had a speed advantage of over thirty knots. And in these shallow waters, where the sonar layer had never once come into play, the 212s had scant room in which to evade.

This is where I find out if the German captains go nuclear.

Torelli's technicians struggled to follow the action, and control their fish through their joysticks and the guidance wires. Three ADCAPs ran at each 212, homing in independent mode, drawing the fire of German antitorpedo rockets. Three more ADCAPs ran behind each first triplet, a second wave of weapons taking commands through the fiber-optic wires. This was Jeffrey's final offensive fire.

But defense counted too.

One Seehecht through Torelli's screen of rockets and we're doomed.

There was a sharp *crack* and a merciless pummeling.

"Most recent unit from tube one has detonated!" Bell shouted. "Assess direct hit on Master Two!"

Crewmen cheered.

"Quiet in Control," Jeffrey shouted. It seemed an absurd request, given the decibel level, but he needed his people to stay steady, and concentrate.

More roars and blasts resounded outside the hull. Inbound torpedo icons vanished as Torelli's antitorpedo rockets scored hits.

An erupting *vroom* enveloped *Challenger*'s hull, the worst noise and physical punishment yet. Jeffrey was shaken in his seat so hard his vision was blurred.

"Most recent unit from tube seven has detonated!" Bell called out, projecting his voice above the cacophony. "Assess direct hit on Master Three!"

That abruptly, the whole feel of the ocean outside changed. There were no more rockets, and no more torpedoes. Instead there was the terrible sound of the sea slamming into fractured hulls. The 212s had no subdivided internal watertight compartments. The water-cannon noise subsided soon. There was a final gush of escaping bubbles, and both dead U-boats thumped into the bottom mud.

"Sonar," Jeffrey ordered, almost whispering in the sudden quiet, "melee ping."

Another acoustic fist probed everywhere on an arc in front of the ship.

Jeffrey waited.

Milgrom reported no submerged contacts.

"Helm, slow to ahead one third, make turns for four knots." Meltzer acknowledged.

Jeffrey waited for *Challenger* to slow. As her speed came off, the steady vibrations of her own movement diminished, then grew still.

"Helm, right ten degrees rudder, make your course zero-nine-zero." Due east, to bring *Ohio* into the field of view of the starboard wide-aperture arrays, and into the effective coverage of the secure acoustic link. The turn would also avoid a potential collision, until the fast-moving *Ohio* realized that Jeffrey had slowed and was talking to them.

"Fire Control. Signal *Ohio:* 'What is your status, and what is status of prosecuting Master One?'"

Bell typed. It took a few moments for the response from Parcelli to come back and be decoded.

"'Master One destroyed while you were sinking the class 212s.'" Parcelli had sunk the 214. "'Status my ship is outstanding. Why? Were you really concerned about the outcome?'"

Jeffrey forced himself not to curse. He was drenched in sweat, and starting to shake as the overdose of adrenaline wore off. He felt horribly thirsty and drowsy. Looking around in the red-lit control room, his crew seemed in no better shape. They all knew they had barely survived, and only because Jeffrey's split-second decisions had changed all the terms of the battle more than once. They also knew that they'd saved *Ohio*'s backside from a lethal bushwhacking just in the nick of time.

And then I get this message from Parcelli. That snide son of a bitch.

CHAPTER 13

Jeffrey sat in his stateroom, the closest thing he had to a private office on *Challenger.* He listened as people talked to him while he thought about something else—and felt torn in more ways than just that.

Bell and Lieutenant Willey, the engineer, were giving Jeffrey reports on the progress of repairs on the damage sustained in the battle. Jeffrey nodded absentmindedly. Through long practice at this sort of thing, he took in their key points even though mentally preoccupied and emotionally drained. His stateroom, with its fold-down desk to one side and a filing cabinet bolted to the deck in the opposite corner, didn't leave Willey and Bell much space in which to stand and speak; there was only one guest chair—as a courtesy to each other, neither man used it. Both of them looked exhausted.

Willey finished. The shipwide damage was minor, repairs should be easy over the next few hours and days, and he obviously wanted to get back to the work. Jeffrey thanked him, and dismissed him.

Once Willey was gone and the stateroom door was closed

again for privacy, Jeffrey studied Bell, standing there in front of his desk.

"How's morale?"

"Terrific, Skipper. We just scored another two kills. Nothing lifts the crew's mood faster than *that*, sir. And you know how quickly word gets around. Everyone's very impressed by the tactics you ordered. The guys who understood it all explained it to the guys who didn't. How you went with our strengths. Used our superior sonars and quieting to do that disappearing act, then used our sustained hitting power with a flank-speed charge and those multiple salvos."

Jeffrey smiled, and felt some renewed energy. "Good. I want you to do double duty as my chief of staff for the task group, XO."

Bell stood up straight. "Sir?"

"You can start by drafting an after-action report."

"Yes, sir."

"A de facto step upward in authority, so you outrank *Ohio*'s XO." *Which might come in handy soon.* "Good experience for you too, which I'll make sure is appreciated later."

"Thank you, sir."

"And, of course, the ulterior motive."

"Captain?"

"Takes more of the paperwork load off me, and dumps it in *your* lap."

Bell grinned. "All good things come at a price."

Jeffrey grew more sober. He glanced at his navigation console. *Challenger,* with *Ohio* in company, was beyond the Eastern Seaboard continental shelf now, out in much deeper water. "Have me informed when Captain Parcelli's minisub is docked. You and I will meet him at the lock-in trunk."

"Yes, sir."

"I'll need maybe twenty minutes with him alone in here. Then we'll have a classified briefing in the wardroom. Him and me, you, Sonar, Nav, and Weps. Plus our three main guests, Mr. Parker of the CIA, Mr. Salih our Turko-German friend, and Lieutenant Estabo, CO of our embarked SEAL team. . . . Have COB arrange for a couple of off-watch chiefs to stand guard outside the doors to the wardroom. Everything is compartmented, strictly need to know."

———————

Parcelli was sitting in Jeffrey's guest chair. He came alone, except for his minisub's crew; he'd left his XO in charge back on *Ohio.* He wore unwrinkled formal dress blues— compared with Jeffrey's rumpled short-sleeve khakis—suggesting that he expected an argument and meant to win it. His expression was hard and his body language confrontational.

Jeffrey felt reservations about what he needed to do, because this was a first for him. He had to firmly discipline a man who until barely a day ago was his definite senior. And he had to do it in such a way as to not compromise the mission success of Task Group 47.2.

Jeffrey loathed face-to-face hostile confrontations. As commanding officer of USS *Challenger,* discipline within the ship's hierarchy was handled mainly by Bell and COB as a standard part of their roles. *Challenger* had a good crew, so Jeffrey's need for direct involvement was minimal. In his brief stint as XO of the ship himself, in the middle of a war that had galvanized everyone to do their best, he'd encountered few occasions when a junior officer or enlisted man needed any tough talking to.

Commander Parcelli, CO of USS *Ohio,* was something else. Jeffrey had no clear precedent to go by. *Ohio* had almost twice the number of people aboard as *Challenger,* and also weighed twice as much—which by the navy's long-standing culture gave Parcelli major clout, and both men knew it. Crew size and ship's displacement mass defined a standard pecking order, imprinted deep in Jeffrey's instincts throughout his years of being in uniform.

Jeffrey had to keep all this completely to himself while he

dealt with Parcelli. Nothing had ever prepared him for such a trial, and he knew he would have only this single chance to get it right. Despite all the tension and fear involved in combat, Jeffrey found it easier to do battle with enemy submarine captains. *An Axis captain doesn't watch my every physical move, my expression or how I sit in a chair, or how I set my eyes or how I breathe. It's a clear win-lose situation, enemy action, and the end of the battle provides decisive closure. Everything now is so different from that, and brand new to me.*

"Your accusing me of disobeying orders has no basis in fact," Parcelli stated crisply. "Since the rendezvous had not been made, the task group was not yet constituted. I had full freedom of action, and chose to take the initiative while in independent command."

"The task group was constituted when the president ordered it activated, and I was made its commander in a meeting both you and I were at. Your rushing off on your own endangered everything. It endangered your ship, it compromised our stealth, it risked failure of our primary mission. Your orders of where to rendezvous, and when, were very explicit. A pair of class Two-twelves pale, utterly pale, in comparison with our main assignment."

"Nope," Parcelli said, irritatingly nonchalant. "Every U-boat sunk is one step closer to victory. We need to destroy them faster than the Germans can build more, and you know that perfectly well. The very fact of my stealth, which I *chose* to compromise, gave me the element of surprise. And the acoustic modems I left for you assured *Challenger* would come in my support. That's your job while in the Atlantic, Captain Fuller, to provide *me* with support."

"Suppose the modems had malfunctioned? Suppose acoustic conditions had been poorer than they were, and I never heard any modems? What then?"

"I'm perfectly able to take care of myself."

"That entire point of view, that attitude, violates the letter *and* the intent of our orders. You're supposed to provide *my* ship with support in the Med, if we make it that far. And it's not about your ship *or* mine, it's about a task group our ships form *together,* and a mission, something essential we both need to do in the Med. . . . You didn't even realize that a class Two-fourteen was out there."

Parcelli's eyes darted about, as if he'd been caught off guard. *Good. I can play his game too.* But Jeffrey cautioned himself because he had to suppress a smirk. *I must keep this from getting personal, no matter how hard Parcelli tries to reduce it to that level.*

"Undetected opponents are always a risk," Parcelli shot back, as dismissively as he could.

"There's undetected, and then there's *unsuspected.* How clearly do I have to spell this out for you to hear the message?"

"What message?"

"That I was put in charge of this task group for a reason. . . . How many U-boats have you sunk?"

"Counting one off Central Africa a few weeks ago, and giving my ship full credit for the Two-fourteen this time, two. Had you taken on the Two-fourteen, as I expected once contact was made, I'd've sunk the pair of Two-twelves, as I intended all along, and my score would now be three." Parcelli made it sound like an accusation, that Jeffrey had grabbed the best kills for himself. He decided to ignore Parcelli's latest jab.

"You know how many Axis subs I've destroyed?"

"No, frankly I don't."

"Frankly, neither do I. I've lost count, which says something right there. But I can tell you I've been in over a dozen separate engagements, many of which went nuclear, and I'm still here to talk about it. I've got a *lot* more combat experience than you. In this context, in this war, *experience leads.*"

Parcelli stared at Jeffrey hard. "You really don't get it, do you?"

"Get what?"

"You've got all this wonderful experience because you hog the ball. You don't even know what's being said behind your back."

Parcelli sat back triumphantly.

What does he think he just won? And what the hell is he talking about?

"Explain yourself, Commander." Using his rank, rather than Parcelli's title as captain of *Ohio,* was a rebuke that Jeffrey knew Parcelli wouldn't miss.

"Your one-of-a-kind ship cost a fortune, and is an absolute maintenance nightmare. The navy could've had three or four *Virginia*-class fast-attacks for what it cost to build *Challenger.* A lot of influential people think we'd've been better off. You spend so much time in dry dock between your different vaunted missions, you're draining skills and materials that other ships badly need.... You had no idea of the resentment this is causing? Up to and including at flag rank in Undersea Warfare?" Parcelli meant some admirals at the Pentagon.

"None of those decisions was mine to make. *Challenger*'s speed and diving depth, her number of tubes, the size of her torpedo room, all outweigh a *Virginia*'s, as fine as those ships are."

"It doesn't outweigh *four* of 'em, and in this present conflict we need as many subs in service as we can get."

"It's too late, and it's irrelevant. I'm not the type to look over my shoulder. And I sure as *hell* do not intend to have to keep looking over my shoulder now, to make sure you're where you're supposed to be, doing exactly what I tell you to do, no more and no less."

"I'll be full captain long before you, and I'll be rear admiral and you'll never be, from the way you behave."

"All that," Jeffrey said as coldly as he could, "remains to be seen. You'll never wear your fourth stripe if you don't survive this mission. You'll never don that first star if you get killed in the next week or two. So I strongly urge you to concentrate on the here and now, *Captain* Parcelli. As far as *I'm* concerned, *as* task-group commander, you led us both to expend a large amount of offensive and defensive ammunition to sink three lower-value targets that other of our forces could have, should have, and would have sunk on their own. And since unlike other units, you and I will *not* be able to replenish our now half-empty torpedo rooms until after our current mission, your behavior decreased our chances of success."

Parcelli hesitated. Jeffrey decided to throw his hardest punches.

"This isn't some game about whose dick is bigger. This whole mission is for *real,* and its success is by no means guaranteed. If it fails, we might all be dead in two weeks, and the whole world might be dead soon thereafter. *The whole goddamned world might be dead.* Thanks to your impetuous conduct, the Axis might know *Challenger* is in the company of another nuclear submarine, which was supposed to have been top secret.... Lower your sights and tone down your ego, *Commander* Parcelli. Understood?"

"Er, yes."

"Unquestioning obedience or I won't hesitate to relieve you of command."

"But—"

"For the remainder of this mission, I have the authority. You can complain about it later, but I doubt the incident would do very much for your precious chances for further promotion. As for this whole discussion, I now consider the matter settled. If you want to complain about *that,* and you and I are both still alive in two weeks, I cordially invite you to do your worst. *Understood?"*

"Yes."

"Now we have a briefing. There's plenty you still don't know. With my officers and my guests, you and I *must* present a united front.... There's no reason for more animosity. Any *hint* of a schism between you and me could prove catastrophic."

"Concur." Parcelli seemed to be pulling himself together.

The man's nothing if not practical, Jeffrey thought. *If I play things right, he might even feel beholden to me after-*

*ward. Better someone like him as a supporter than an oppo-
nent down the road. . . . I have to plan ahead to the next wave
of peacetime navy politics too, just in case the U.S. Navy and
I both make it that far.*

Jeffrey and Parcelli stood. Parcelli moved to open the door
for Jeffrey—which Jeffrey took as a good sign, of concilia-
tion, at least temporarily.

More to the point, Jeffrey had succeeded after all, in the
first truly no-holds-barred, head-to-head bureaucratic contest
of his career. But he needed to get in one more thing for good
measure. A final, seemingly casual and harmless afterthought—that was really meant to be a very rough stiffener.

Jeffrey had learned this technique from commodores and
admirals who'd used it on him. He leaned toward Parcelli,
while the door was still closed, and whispered in his ear.

"Forget for now about raising that flag with your first star.
Cast your thoughts even higher, up at the sky, and picture
global nuclear winter instead, in a month or less. I think
you'll find the image highly motivating."

CHAPTER 14

Jeffrey's key people were assembled in *Challenger*'s wardroom. Jeffrey, as captain of the ship and commander of the task group, sat in his usual sacrosanct place at the head of the table. To Jeffrey's left sat Gerald Parker. To Jeffrey's right, in what was considered the place of honor, he'd put Captain Parcelli. Jeffrey hoped this gesture wasn't lost on the man.

Farther down the table sat Bell, Gamal Salih, Felix Estabo, and Jeffrey's officers who needed to be present. Lieutenants Kathy Milgrom as Sonar, Bud Torelli as Weps, and Richard Sessions as Navigator all had to know what was coming next.

The foot of the table was empty, because beyond it, on the bulkhead, was a flat wide-screen display. Jeffrey's laptop, already open and on, connected to the display by a fiber-optic cable. Bell got up and checked that chiefs were posted outside the door into the passageway, and also outside the door leading into *Challenger*'s galley, the kitchen and pantry area.

Bell nodded to Jeffrey, and retook his seat.

Jeffrey cleared his throat, and at once had everyone's full attention.

"First, ground rules. For security, all crew are to know as little as possible in advance at each stage of this operation. Just in case we get into trouble, and there are survivors whom the enemy can capture and interrogate."

Jeffrey looked around the room meaningfully. Even though this was hardly the first time his people had had to cope with such a concern, his officers got more serious.

"This map will give you an idea of our general route." Jeffrey tapped some keys. The big display screen showed a chart of the Atlantic Ocean, extending through to the Mediterranean Sea and the start of the Black Sea, and also down to the Red Sea and the Arabian Gulf at the doorstep to the Indian Ocean.

Sessions, Torelli, and Milgrom immediately groaned.

"I see it has not been lost on you that we face some difficult choke points to and from our destination. Steps are being taken by higher command to assist us. Whether or not these diversions work, we have to press on at each stage."

Jeffrey ran through the basics about radio silence, forbidden use of nukes in crucial areas, and other topics covered in briefings he'd attended earlier in Washington or Norfolk. He couldn't tell them about the defector, Klaus Mohr, aka Peapod, aka Zeno, or about Plan Pandora—and this requirement to deny his key subordinates an understanding of what was truly involved weighed heavily on Jeffrey.

"The enemy is meant to believe we're going south, after *von Scheer* in South Africa. You who were present then I'm sure remember our last delightful encounter with that beast." People nodded and murmured uncomfortably.

"The first leg of our course will support the outward appearance of this incorrect conclusion. False signal traffic that the enemy may be able to read will further reinforce the impression that *Challenger* and *Ohio* are heading south. Farther out in the Atlantic, however, we will turn east. In the interests of time, we will then take the shortest route to the Strait of Gibraltar. Nav," Jeffrey said to Sessions, "you can work out the details." Sessions nodded, and Jeffrey could see gears were already turning in his mind. "Our course will take us north of Bermuda, and then north of the Azores. The steaming formation and routine I've chosen is this: *Ohio* will remain below the sonar layer, but otherwise Captain Parcelli and his crew will determine their depth along the way as they see fit. *Ohio* will periodically trail her floating wire antenna to provide updated tactical data for both ships. *Challenger* will stay as close to the seafloor as practicable, for stealth, keeping about ten thousand yards ahead of *Ohio*. *Challenger* will scan passively for threats, using the deep sound channel and various sonar modes as apply. That's your division's main task, Sonar, as usual."

"Understood, sir." Milgrom sounded chipper enough, but there were bags under her eyes and her shoulders drooped more than usual from fatigue. Jeffrey sympathized. He continued.

"*Ohio* as the slower ship will set the pace. Our mean speed of advance will be eighteen knots. Our trip to Gibraltar should therefore take eight days. *Ohio* will, at Captain Parcelli's discretion, trail her towed array, which was recently upgraded to be the same type as *Challenger*'s, i.e., triple-line fiber optic.... The two ships will remain in contact by the secure covert acoustic link. *Challenger* will maneuver so as to remain in direct acoustic line of sight with *Ohio* as much as possible. Given the complex paths that sound rays take between different depths, and *Challenger*'s occasional proximity to bottom terrain, this will call for careful coordination between Sonar and Navigation, on both ships. However, again, since *Ohio* will be setting the pace, and as the shallower unit she's more inherently vulnerable, the onus is on *Challenger* to keep the acoustic path open. If the two ships become separated, with both being so quiet, it may prove very difficult to reestablish contact, even if both try calling by using the link. The result of such separation could be disastrous. . . . I cannot disclose more, but suffice it to say that a sword of Damocles hangs over our heads by one strand of hair, and that strand gets weaker with every day that goes by."

Sessions and Milgrom glanced at each other, both carefully poker faced.

"Although we all did well in our combat with those three U-boats, I have to emphasize that whenever possible, we must avoid further contact with enemy units. Detection of either of our ships by the Axis now risks seriously compromising the mission. Any further combat also risks damage to *Ohio* or *Challenger* or both. This, again, could be disastrous, even if neither of us is actually sunk."

Torelli raised his hand. "Skipper, won't two subs trying to sneak through Gibraltar get noticed? The gap there's so narrow, and the Germans have controlled both sides for most of a year at this point. They'll have all kinds of sensors and weapons aimed our way."

"All true. Hydrophone arrays, undersea smart minefields, the works. That's the next part of the deception process. This much, you all do need to know now, since we've got to start working out our penetration tactics right away."

Milgrom raised her hand.

"Sonar?"

"Captain, why weren't we told any of this before? A week to develop cooperative tactics with *Ohio,* computer models, simulator rehearsals, contingency planning... It's awfully rushed."

"For security. You were to be told this only after we left port." Jeffrey had by now, in private, opened the first sealed pouch from his safe.

"Of course. Understood, sir."

"It won't be quite as difficult as you think," Jeffrey said to the group in the wardroom at large.

He tapped keys and another image appeared on the screen. It showed one submarine towing another, both submerged.

"The way we'll increase our chances of sneaking through safely is to make use of a big-time diversion scheme.... You're aware that some months ago USS *Texas* was damaged in combat and had to ground on top of a seamount near her crush depth." *Texas* was a *Virginia*-class, steel-hulled sub. *Challenger* had helped rescue her surviving crew—just before the Germans could get to them. "The engineering compartment was completely flooded. Some of you may have heard rumors of plans to refloat and salvage the ship, repair her, put her back in action."

People nodded again.

"Well, yes and no. *Texas* has been refloated, basically by robotic minisubs inserting gas bags as floatation bladders inside the flooded spaces. But rather than be salvaged, she'll be sacrificed."

People gave each other doubtful looks.

"It's supposed to work like this," Jeffrey said. "The Royal Navy's HMS *Dreadnought* will tow the submerged but refloated *Texas* to near the Gibraltar Strait. *Dreadnought* is ideal for the job since her ceramic hull gives her a very deep crush depth. If something goes wrong with the tow or buoyancy control, and the *Texas* starts to sink again, the *Dreadnought* at least won't need to worry about being dragged below her own crush depth. And before you ask, yes, a system is in place to cut the towing cables, just in case, and also one to make *Texas* heavy if she threatens to bob to the surface. Of course, implosion of the floatation bags and the unflooded forward hull of *Texas* would be heard for hundreds of miles, and prematurely give *that* game away, so we better hope this part goes smoothly. If it does, *Dreadnought* will release *Texas* near the Strait to free-float at her normal operating depth, and then subtly draw the attention of Axis antisubmarine forces. This should stir up a nice hornet's nest, and the *Challenger-Ohio* task group will sneak through while the enemy's busy attacking a derelict *Texas* and a very capable *Dreadnought*. *Texas,* already stripped of most classified gear, and her reactor compartment filled with special high-strength sealant, will suffer hits and seem to be sunk by Axis fire in water ten thousand feet deep. *Dreadnought* will then withdraw, also in very deep water.... It's rather convenient for our side that the continental shelf by the strait is extremely narrow compared to the eastern U.S.... The Axis will thus be left with the impression that a two-sub task group attempted entry, with one vessel destroyed and the other repulsed. This will strengthen Axis confidence that the Strait is secure, when in fact, God willing, *Challenger* and *Ohio* will have gotten inside and we'll have a good laugh at German expense."

Bell leaned forward. "Making this work will take some precise coordination, sir, between us and *Dreadnought.*"

"That'll be accomplished by a coded ELF radio message. The same message will also be our final go-ahead to proceed with the main part of the mission, inside the Med. And it's one more reason why we *must* keep to a very tight schedule. If *Dreadnought*'s ready and we aren't there yet..."

"Even with this diversion, Skipper, we need more than just acoustic-link contact with *Ohio* to work out the details for passing Gibraltar."

"Yes, thanks, XO. You anticipated my next point. Two more minisub rendezvous are planned between now and when we reach the Straits. *Challenger* will have to come shallow enough to respect the crush-depth limits of *Ohio*'s mini. And for one of these two meetings, I intend for people from *Challenger* to use our mini to visit *Ohio*. This will create greater task-group cohesion. Besides, it's necessary. All of you here on *Challenger* can best appreciate what *Ohio* can and can't do by going aboard her in person.... This wraps up the briefing. You'll each be fed more info when the time comes. Lieutenant Estabo and his men, and Mr. Salih, will be having briefings and rehearsals among themselves. For security, they'll need to use the wardroom. The enlisted mess is too public. XO, you and Mr. Parker and Lieutenant Estabo can work out the schedule needs."

"Right," Bell said.

"Thanks," Felix acknowledged.

"So," Jeffrey said, "everyone, this coming week, pray we don't hear a *Virginia*-class hull imploding prematurely. That happens, we know *Dreadnought*'s diversion effort flopped and put the bad guys on highest alert. We drive on anyway, but our job gets a lot more complicated."

Jeffrey's wry comment left a glum silence in the room. He realized his officers' moods were becoming brittle, a reaction to built-up tiredness and the prospect of yet more overwork.

"Lieutenant Milgrom," Jeffrey said, "I know you served in *Dreadnought*. All goes well, we'll be practically within shouting distance of your shipmates for a little while. Sorry you won't be able to say hello."

"I'm sure all will go as planned, sir," Milgrom answered. She sounded as if she was trying very hard to believe what she said.

"We'll proceed at ultraquiet, but secured from battle stations until absolutely necessary."

"Normal watch-standing routines?" Bell asked, hardly believing the good news—and the departure from Jeffrey's usual workaholic command style.

"Affirmative. I want everyone to make sure to get lots of rest, and plenty of nourishment."

The feeling in the room lightened noticeably.

"Any questions?"

Sessions raised his hand.

"Nav?"

"Sir, if you don't mind my asking."

"You can always *ask*."

"Mr. Salih," Sessions said, "are you at all related to someone else I used to know?"

Sessions, getting into the spirit of this constant need-to-know business, was trying to be cagey. Coming from him, the most laid-back and unflappable of Jeffrey's officers, it seemed slightly funny—and ominous.

Salih glanced at Jeffrey. "They'll figure it out pretty soon on their own. Best I tell them now. You think, Captain?"

Jeffrey shrugged. "Go ahead."

"I'm the same Gamal Salih who had the honor to serve with you before Christmas."

"But—" Sessions started.

"Plastic surgery, and acting lessons."

"I think we better wrap this up," Jeffrey broke in. "Captain Parcelli needs to get back to his ship." Jeffrey turned off his laptop. "Thank you all for attending."

He walked Parcelli aft. An enlisted man stood at the watertight hatch to the lock-out trunk, leading up to the docked minisub from *Ohio*. Jeffrey told him to move out of earshot.

Jeffrey shook Parcelli's hand. "Thanks for coming."

Parcelli's hand was much larger than Jeffrey's, and the palm was warm and not at all sweaty.

A very self-composed person. I could learn from him.

"I have to admit, Captain," Parcelli said, "you surprised me back there."

"Back where?"

"In your stateroom. From things I'd heard, I didn't expect you to assert your authority so, well, so *authoritatively.*" Parcelli rubbed his jaw, pretending that Jeffrey had physically slugged him.

Jeffrey decided that the curtest answer was best. "You gained two important lessons today. One about undersea warfare tactics, and one about me. On both fronts, be impetuous, you get hurt."

CHAPTER 15

Felix Estabo was busy inspecting *Challenger*'s captured German minisub. He had to admit it did have important advantages over the U.S. Navy's Advanced SEAL Delivery System minis. It was faster and had longer range, and the control compartment's instrumentation and sensors were more sophisticated. The equipment and procedures for docking with a parent submarine, or pressurizing the central lock-in/lock-out trunk so divers could come and go through the bottom hatch, were similar to the American design. The adjustable seats in the passenger compartment in back—room for eight commandos plus their gear—were more comfortable than those on the ASDSs Felix had ridden in before, to and from combat.

Felix paid very careful attention as he examined things. This particular minisub was indispensable to the whole mission. The quick trip to and from *Ohio*—for a working group on tactics in a few days—would be a useful dry run. This German mini, actually made and exported by Sweden, was the only way to sneak through the Dardanelles Strait and the

Sea of Marmara to reach Istanbul, which sprawled along both sides of the Bosporus Strait, just before the Black Sea. The Dardanelles was thirty miles long, but parts were barely three miles wide. The exit into the Marmara was shallow—seventy-five feet—and studded with wrecks. *Challenger* or *Ohio* could hardly hope to get through without being detected, and their presence was strictly forbidden by international law. An incursion by the minisub was ticklish enough, from the diplomatic perspective as well as from the navigational one.

"Lieutenant Estabo?" a young voice called from the bottom of the ladder leading into *Challenger* proper.

Felix stuck his head through the wide-open bottom hatch of the mini. "Yo." Felix recognized the kid down there looking up at him. A messenger.

"Sir, Captain Fuller sends his compliments, and requests your presence in his stateroom with the two chiefs from your team."

"Coming." Both chiefs, Porto and Costa, were in the control compartment, so Felix asked them to follow him. He climbed down the ladder, through the functional gray-painted metal air-lock trunk that connected *Challenger*'s in-hull pressure-proof minisub hangar to the rest of the ship. Felix and his chiefs came out near the enlisted mess. Between meals now, some men were watching a movie, others studied for their qualifications to earn their silver Dolphins, and two crewmen played very competitive checkers.

Felix admired the ability of the new guys to concentrate despite the sound track of the movie and the chatter in the mess, as they crammed diagrams of hydraulics or electrical or compressed-air systems. He knew they could have used their sleeping racks as study carrels, where things would be very quiet—but many submariners craved company above privacy, enjoyed the constant crowding and found it, if anything, cozy, and soon learned to tune out irrelevant noise.

It's a unique lifestyle these people lead.

Gamal Salih was standing there, waiting for Felix.

"Feel like a coffee, Gamal?"

"By all means."

Felix glanced at the messenger and raised an eyebrow.

"The captain didn't say not to."

The summoned foursome helped themselves. Brown plastic mugs were stacked by the dozen near two large metal pots of very strong coffee. Carrying the mugs throughout the ship was normal practice—it was sometimes hard to get through a six-hour watch, manning a console or piece of machinery, without a stiff dose of caffeine.

The group arrived together at Captain Fuller's stateroom. The door was closed, so Felix knocked.

The door opened. "Lieutenant," Jeffrey told Felix, "have one of your men stay outside my door here as a guard, for security. Have the other walk through my stateroom and the connecting head to the XO's room, and then stand outside his outer door. The only person you should see along the way is Mr. Parker. The XO and Lieutenant Milgrom are in the control room now."

"You heard the captain," Felix said; the CO and the XO cabins shared a common, private bathroom.

Porto and Costa did what they were told; Felix and Salih went inside and Jeffrey closed the door. Gerald Parker stood up, and everyone made quick hellos.

Jeffrey sat down behind his tiny desk. Parker, a senior person himself, kept the guest chair. Salih perched on the filing cabinet. Felix, faced with the choice of standing in a corner or leaning against the bulkhead next to Jeffrey's dressing mirror, decided to stand.

Parker turned his chair so everyone could see each other better. "Captain Fuller was asking about how we'll make contact with Peapod. This seems as good a time as any to brief all of you."

Felix and Salih nodded.

"There are two parts to it," Parker said. "One is letting him know we're coming, so he can get ready. The other is the actual rescue snatch. For the latter, he also needs instructions in advance. And contact with Peapod has to be made right away."

"So he doesn't chicken out, you mean?" Felix asked.

"Something like that. So he knows what to do and when. And what not to do, like panic or spill his guts to his bosses because he thinks we've abandoned him."

"With you so far," Jeffrey said. "But something's missing. Who, or how, does someone get a message through to Peapod? Since that raid on the brothel where he almost got killed, they'll have extra bodyguards and keep the guy under lock and key."

Parker nodded. "There are times when the most covert approach is to move in plain sight."

"Go on."

"Peapod's cover provided by the Germans is as a trade attaché. Someone we own will meet with Peapod right there in the consulate during his regular office hours."

"What do you mean, 'own'?" Jeffrey asked.

"Remember, we're dealing with very different cultures, not America. Turkey is a secular state, but the majority of the population is Muslim. The person we own is a Pakistani citizen, also Muslim, employed by one of Pakistan's major import-export firms at their Istanbul office. This person, whose code name is Aardvark, happens to be bisexual, with a personal orientation to mostly be a practicing transvestite. Turkey generally tolerates gay behavior in private, but they're self-contradictory. They detest men who dress as women for sex. Aardvark would also be in big trouble with his employers if his lifestyle became known to them, partly because he's been a naughty boy and often does what he does on the company's time and the company's dime. Exposed, he'd lose his job for sure, would be expelled from Turkey, back to Pakistan, and would be unemployable and humiliated in front of his family there. Aardvark likes the city he works in now very much. He likes the cosmopolitan feel of Istanbul, the active nightlife, and he likes to party."

"Party? You mean like alcohol, drugs, orgies?"

"We have very explicit video of him with other men. You don't want to know the details.... That's how we own him. ... We pay him, through a covert intermediary of course, to soften the pain of his servitude."

"And to compromise him even more," Felix said.

"Yes, there is that." Parker didn't even blink.

"But how is Aardvark supposed to get a message to Peapod?" Jeffrey asked. "Just by making an appointment about trade and then walking into his office? Won't the place be totally bugged?"

"Of course."

"And how do we get Peapod to trust Aardvark, and fast?"

Parker smiled. "Aardvark will offer him a gift he can't accept, then give him an invitation he won't refuse."

CHAPTER 16

Klaus Mohr, age thirty-seven, a German fit and hand-some in the classic Aryan way, sat at his desk in his office, in mid-morning. This was the time of day when he acted as a trade attaché for real, to maintain his diplomatic cover—his clandestine work for Plan Pandora took place after lunch and into the evening, in a more secure part of the building, or in safe houses from which field tests of the ruggedized black boxes' stealth and reliability were staged.

He glanced at his appointment book, then at the ornate antique clock on his big cherry-wood desktop. He had a few minutes until his next engagement. Although Germany's trade mission to Turkey was important to the Fatherland, Mohr considered this part of the day as his special quiet time. The routine paperwork and meetings with foreign business-men never taxed his energy or nerves. There were too many other things weighing on his mind already—and the really serious stuff, about bilateral agreements, tariff and customs arrangements, and investment cooperation was taken care of by genuine experts on the embassy and consular staffs.

Mohr got up and paced to one of the windows. An oil painting of the new kaiser, crowned Wilhelm IV less than a year ago, looked down at him from the wall. Knowing that the man was a figurehead, and as used as anyone else in Germany by the ruthless new regime, Mohr felt slightly sorry for him.

Mohr was also feeling sorry for himself. The excitement of surviving the brothel ambush had worn off. But his superiors were still angry with him for taking such serious risks for his own selfish pleasure; Mohr, for all practical purposes, was confined to the consulate grounds until further notice. His two bodyguards had died on Turkish soil, and the Istanbul police and Turkish counterintelligence service were both investigating hotly. Mohr's diplomatic credentials might grant him immunity from any prosecution, but that couldn't prevent him from being declared persona non grata and expelled from the country. He'd really been an innocent victim at the legal brothel, but his involvement in the subsequent foot chase and multiparty shootout exposed him to piercing questions by local law enforcement. This, Germany could not and would not allow. Mohr was still needed for Plan Pandora; to be forced to leave Turkey soon could be a disaster for the Axis war effort. Yet because of his own good work, Mohr was needed less and less each day. This, he knew, made him increasingly vulnerable not only to Turks but to fellow Germans.

If I slow things down, backpedal, try to subtly sabotage the technical work, others will eventually know. My life expectancy then would be very short.

The window of his second-floor office was half open, since it was a very warm and humid day and the air-conditioning in this older part of the building was weak. The noise of street traffic and babbling voices and snatches of exotic music came in through the window, from beyond the high concrete wall that protected the consulate. In one direction, Mohr could see modern skyscrapers. In another, he saw palace towers and mosque minarets. The huge city really had something for everyone.

Everyone but me. Mohr stretched, feeling trapped. He was still very sore from his recent physical exertions in surviving as bullets flew. In one way, being confined to the consulate was a blessing. *At least I got caught up on sleep, with nowhere else to go at night after work.* But in another more important way, the confinement was terrible. *I don't see how the Americans can possibly extract me, or even tell me if they're on the way.*

A commando raid on the consulate, in the middle of downtown Istanbul, was doomed to fail, aside from being an act of outright war. The consulate had its own concealed but heavy defenses, and neutral Turkey would tolerate no attack by American special operations forces, even if the consulate itself technically was sovereign German territory.

Mohr was also feeling down, racked by remorse and depression, because he was actually happily married, and had three lovely kids back at home in Berlin. His sexaholic behavior was all an act, a subterfuge on several levels. It had let him shop around until he found a prostitute who was a plant of the Americans'. He also meant for his frequent nocturnal excursions to make it look like he was callously abandoning his wife—his real aim was to protect her from Axis retribution if he did succeed in defecting, or got caught. He'd been censured repeatedly by his superiors for the marital infidelity, but it always came down to dismissing his penchant for hookers as a character flaw that paled compared to his rare brand of genius.

This whole multitiered gambit was increasingly wearing and draining on Mohr, even before the twin mortal perils of possibly being found out by Imperial German State Security, or being killed by the too-suspicious and ever-vigilant Mossad.

Mohr's secretary knocked on the door.

"Come!"

The young man stuck his head in and told Mohr his eleven o'clock appointment had arrived five minutes early. Mohr said he'd see the man now.

His secretary showed the guest in and closed the door. The slender man wore a fine white linen business suit. He introduced himself.

Awais Iqbal was Pakistani, in his mid-forties, and seemed the nervous and excitable type. Iqbal spoke good English, as did Mohr, so Mohr decided a translator wouldn't be needed.

He showed Iqbal to an opulent, overstuffed guest chair in front of his desk, then sat in his own expensive leather high-backed swivel chair.

A bit much, but we do have to make a good impression on the outside world.

Iqbal tried to move his chair, but it was so heavy he had no luck. He seemed flustered and embarrassed. Mohr offered to have coffee or soft drinks brought in, but Iqbal declined.

After brief pleasantries they got down to details. Iqbal, a long-term resident of Istanbul employed by a Pakistani firm, said his company wanted to do business with Germany.

Mohr asked what his business was, exactly.

The man said it was sensitive, which was why his firm preferred not to deal directly with Berlin. Since Pakistan was neutral, doing so would be legal, but doing so directly might have negative diplomatic, economic, and even military ramifications with certain other countries. Mohr took him to mean Allied countries, or maybe India, also neutral but on a hairpin trigger with Pakistan these days—a serious problem since both were nuclear powers, and psychological restraints against using nuclear weapons had been badly weakened lately by world events.

Mohr saw where Iqbal was going, but let him speak: dummy corporations, as cutouts routing trade from Pakistan by air to Istanbul, from there by ship across the Black Sea to Odessa in Ukraine—part of the pseudo-neutral expanded Russian Federation—and from there sent up the long, navigable part of the Danube River, or by rail, into German turf. All this made sense to Mohr. It wouldn't be the first time such deals were made and devious routes were used.

Mohr asked Iqbal what product he proposed to sell to Germany. Iqbal said missile parts, and other weapons.

"I'll need to refer this to my superiors," Mohr said, which was true. "Do you have any documentation I can show them about your products?"

"Not at this stage."

Mohr wasn't surprised. Usually there'd be a courtship ritual first, establishing rapport, building trust, the usual salesman dance.

"I do have something else for you." Iqbal smiled, and began to reach into his briefcase.

Here it comes.

Iqbal brought out something wrapped in bubble pack, with brown paper under that. He placed it on Mohr's desk. "Open it, please. It's a personal present."

The item was flat, rectangular, and heavy. Mohr carefully undid the tape until there was quite a pile of wrapping material on his desk.

Inside it all was a book. The book was bound in maroon leather. The lettering and cover art looked like gold inlay. The book was obviously very old, the binding certainly handmade. The title was in classic, florid Germanic script.

Mohr read the title. His heart began to pound.

The book was a treatise on ancient Greek history and mythology.

"Go ahead, open it," Iqbal said. "Admire it."

Mohr took a paper napkin out of a desk drawer and carefully wiped the skin oils from his hands. He knew this book was something you didn't want to get greasy fingerprints on. The title page said the book had been printed in Mannheim in 1752.

Iqbal stood up. "May I?" He reached for the book. Mohr nodded.

"Let me show you the quality of the printing, the exquisite etchings. Some are in color, hand painted, you know? Read it to yourself, not aloud, or you'll spoil the whole effect."

There was something strange behind how Iqbal said that.

He opened the book to one page, and held it for Mohr to look. Beneath a rather dramatic and beautifully done illustration was an entry discussing the myth of Pandora's box.

Mohr blinked. It might be just a coincidence.

"Allow me to show you something else." Iqbal turned to a different page. He made eye contact with Mohr and held it, and his gaze seemed to bore into Mohr's soul. "This is for you. For *you.*"

Mohr was almost afraid to look, because of what the page might show—or what it might not show.

He looked. The entry covered the philosopher and mathematician Zeno. He was surprised to learn that Zeno was really Italian, and hadn't moved to Athens until he was forty.

Mohr did everything he could to cover up his emotions. He was sure the room was rigged with listening devices, and feared there might be hidden miniature video cameras too. He noticed that Iqbal was carefully shielding the book against his body as he held it out for Mohr to read.

Klaus Mohr knew he had to think very fast. *The Americans are making contact! How do I respond? What am I supposed to say? What do I do next?*

He decided to try a dangerous gambit.

"I, I can't possibly accept this. It must be worth thousands. This belongs in a museum."

"Yes, it is very valuable, I'm told."

Told by whom?

"We're not permitted to accept personal gifts of more than nominal cost."

"Why not take it on behalf of your government, and if it belongs in a museum, why not one in Germany?"

Again Mohr had to think fast. Then he caught on. He was meant to say no. He *had* to say no.

"The, uh, the paperwork involved, the approvals needed, delays for something like this in time of war . . . Mr. Iqbal, you have no idea how much trouble that would cause. Why don't you, or your company, donate it somewhere yourselves?"

Iqbal sighed, his exhalation a bit overdone, even ragged.

Mohr saw that he was under terrible stress, going through this ritual.

"I suppose I shall have to do something like that." Iqbal began to gather up the wrapping material, and put the rare book back in his briefcase.

"You're permitted to have dinner with people, at least, aren't you? The theater, sporting events, and even . . . parties?"

Iqbal once again made that intense eye contact with Mohr. But this time as he spoke he seemed confident and knowing, suggestive even, experienced, almost . . . leering?

Is he saying what I think he's saying?

Of course! The book was just to prove his covert purpose for being here. He knew I'd have to refuse the gift. Then, when he made a counteroffer of a sales-related get-together, I couldn't turn him down without appearing rude—and risk spoiling the deal.

He knows where I like to go at night. He's obviously been briefed, up to a point. He knows they need to get me out of the consulate, and he's provided a perfect cover plan.

Mohr was pretty certain that Iqbal wasn't a German agent sent to check his loyalty. Axis counterintelligence wouldn't be this indirect, this ambiguous, and leave so much room for Mohr to protest his innocence. But still, Mohr needed to proceed with great caution.

"I'll have to ask my superiors. There are concerns these days, you understand. Kidnappings, shootings on the street . . . As I say, my country is at war."

"Herr Mohr, I assure you, my firm does pay attention to what some would call executive protection. . . . If I come collect you at the consulate front door in an armored town car, would that not be satisfactory? . . . The party will likely go on all night. Don't you live in a safe house or apartment, where you can change clothes and pick up anything else you might need?"

Mohr cringed when he heard the phrase "safe house"—it could be taken more than one way, and he was sure Iqbal intended it so. Mohr thought ahead, and an icy feeling ran through his body. Special hardware and software would need to be grabbed from the hands of the Kampfschwimmer who were training to use the quantum computer field gear under combat conditions soon; they and Mohr were stationed here for final calibration under climate and terrain conditions as similar as possible to the coastline and mountains of Israel.

Mohr knew he had to answer very carefully. Iqbal had just asked him a hidden question—about logistics and resources needed for the extraction by the Americans. "Something like that sounds good. I do share a house with a few other Germans. . . . Will your friends have a pool? Should I bring swim trunks? I'm glad I remembered to mention that. Many people I know here rather enjoy exercising that way." Mohr was trying to convey that German battle swimmers were part of the picture for this all-night party: exercise, as in a military exercise. In a way these back-and-forth veiled hints and signals seemed silly, but Mohr didn't think they had any choice. Iqbal has started it, so he assumed this was the way spies sometimes worked.

"A pool? Yes. Swim trunks? Of course." Iqbal appeared to get the message.

"Where will the party be?"

Iqbal gave the name of a wealthy neighborhood near the Bosporus. Mohr at first was surprised. He'd expected someplace seedy or secluded.

Then he saw that the arrangements would be most plausible this way. He was sure that Iqbal's employer was legitimate, so everything would check out. Missile parts from Pakistan. Mohr didn't think his superiors would say no to this too quickly. . . . They would definitely put a security tail on the town car.

And that quantum computer equipment is vital. The U.S. has no idea how absolutely vital. What I think of as the attack software and operating system for it would be opaque gibberish to any American machine, even a quantum computer of their own. . . . This could all get very messy, but I can't turn back now.

"When do you suggest we have our little outing?"

"Alas, I'll be traveling for several days."

Mohr's heart pounded. Iqbal made a show of removing his calendar book from his briefcase. The briefcase and the calendar book were also bound in a nice maroon leather.

"As you see, I appreciate the finer things, as I'm sure you do, Herr Mohr. Date books one writes in by hand for some people, computer gadgets for others. Perhaps we are opposites, no?"

CHAPTER 17

*G*rand Admiral Doenitz had obeyed the procedures announced by the Allies for neutral submarines to transit the Greenland-Iceland-UK Gap submerged. Egon Schneider's hardest job had been to act like a Russian captain would: cooperative, but impatient.

Schneider smirked. Things had been very suspenseful. There was always the risk that enemy spies had pierced *Doenitz*'s cover story. But Allied inspection platforms bought his ruse. Active and passive sonars, dipping laser line-scan cameras, human divers—Schneider watched and listened to them all through his ship's sensors while they watched and listened to him, the first-ever 868U to venture into the Atlantic.

As he'd expected, *Doenitz* was picked up by an Allied nuclear submarine that, two days later, still followed in trail, using the hull flow noise and propulsor wake turbulence that Schneider intentionally gave him by making a steady twelve knots. He was half-surprised that it wasn't what he considered one of the Allies' first-line fast-attacks. The *Dread-*

nought, Seawolf, and *Connecticut* must have been given other, more pressing duties.

After all, their war opponent is Germany, not Russia.

The trailing sub was one of the refurbished *Los Angeles* class. Though the earliest ones had been broken up for scrap years before, the later models were upgraded repeatedly. Within their speed and depth envelope they were good, very quiet and even retrofitted with sonar wide-aperture arrays. The captain of this particular Los Angeles boat was surely eager to learn about the 868U's own maximum speed and depth capabilities.

And this, of course, as a pretend Russian captain, Schneider was not supposed to allow. *What I am supposed to do, and what fits with my mission orders from Berlin, is lose him, evade the trail—without betraying my true identity.*

At the command console, Schneider thought over how he would do this. All around him his crew were intent on their screens and instruments. The air-circulation ducts gave off a constant rushing sound—though the fresh air couldn't dispel the compartment's aroma of ozone and stale sweat, and brought with it the pungent smell of amine from the carbon-dioxide scrubbers aft. The control-room lighting was bright because it was daytime on the surface.

Schneider felt just enough pressure to make his analysis interesting. He knew he might have committed some error back in the gap, or that the Allies might have picked up something about his ship at point-blank range, and at any moment they could deduce that *Doenitz* was really German, and the Los Angeles would be ordered to open fire. But that hadn't happened yet, and every hour that passed made it seem more unlikely. Meanwhile, he enjoyed toying with the American captain, lulling him before Schneider gave him the shock of his life.

"The most important thing is not to rush."

"Sir?" Knipp asked from the seat to his right.

Schneider sent a duplicate of the large-scale nautical chart he was using to Knipp's console screen. *Doenitz* was off of Ireland, running at 300 meters in water four kilometers deep. "We'll continue our base course southwest, until we get *here*." With his joystick he moved a cursor on Knipp's chart, marking a spot on the endless Mid-Atlantic Ridge where the water for a stretch was barely seven hundred meters deep—a high plateau in the underwater mountains along the volcanic spreading seam that had formed the ridge.

"We need to lose the American without him understanding why he lost us."

"Yes, sir."

"We can't exactly accelerate to sixty knots in plain view, and suddenly vanish on his passive arrays while he listens."

"No, sir."

Schneider used his screen cursor to measure distances, then did a calculation. For something this simple he didn't need help from the navigator. "Pilot, make your speed twenty knots."

"Make my speed twenty knots, jawohl," the junior officer at the helm acknowledged.

"Sir?"

"It's natural for us to move faster now that we're reaching the open Atlantic. . . . I've picked a speed so we'll reach that nice place on the ridge in twenty-four hours. Since it will thus be broad daylight again, the deep scattering layer should be near six hundred meters."

The deep scattering layer was a zone thick with biologics— sea life—that blocked passive sonar at many frequencies and made false echoes on active sonar. The biologics, from large to microscopic, migrated downward each dawn, feeding, as traces of sunlight penetrated to almost two thousand feet; at night they moved back upward to more like 500 feet.

In the bright sun expected by the latest weather forecasts Schneider had, this time tomorrow the deep scattering layer would be deeper than a Los Angeles sub could dive without imploding.

"We go below that, Einzvo, and enter the rugged ridge terrain that's well above our own crush depth, and twist and turn and vary our speed. The American won't be able to keep guessing our position. Suitably masked by terrain, we'll go to flank speed. He'll lose contact and won't regain it and won't even understand why. He'll look really bad to his crew and squadron commander. We can't sink him, but we *can* ruin his career."

An intercom light blinked: the circuit for the radio room. Schneider grabbed the handset. "Captain. Speak."

"Sir," the junior lieutenant in the radio room told him, "an ELF message with our address has come in."

Schneider didn't like this. "A request to come up to floating wire-antenna depth?" That would allow a much faster data receipt rate than the on-hull ELF antenna, but the depth change and the sounds of unreeling the wire would be noticed by the trailing American boat—which might become suspicious.

"Negative, Captain." The junior lieutenant read Schneider the decoded text. Schneider snapped, "Jawohl." He hung up, then cursed under his breath.

"Sir?" Knipp queried him cautiously, seeing his sudden dark mood.

"*Challenger* already put to sea, more than a day ago. Intelligence indicates their destination is Durban. The *von Scheer.*"

"That's what we expected, sir, no? It makes the most sense strategically."

"Sailing so early is something we *didn't* expect." Schneider felt disgusted. "I don't see how they do it. Every time *that ship* goes into dry dock for repairs, Fuller takes her out again weeks ahead of what we predicted."

"Perhaps our other captains' damage estimates were too optimistic, sir. Or our spies have been turned, captured, made to feed us misleading information to catch us unawares?"

"Speculation is useless. What matters is confirmed fact."

Knipp nodded. "Your intentions were—"

"I *know* what my intentions were." Arrive at Durban well before *Challenger* could, and set up an ambush. *But* Challenger *is on the move two weeks too soon, and another American submarine is following me.... I can't imagine a more adverse scenario.*

Despite all the practice and training in Russian waters, and the exhaustive virtual battles in the attack simulator onshore, this was *Doenitz*'s first combat crisis at sea. Schneider met the command dilemma head-on. He made his decision.

"We continue to act like a Russian. If we show any sudden move, the Los Angeles could get excited enough to report it. If the Allies are reading German ELF codes, and make the connection, we'll have given ourselves away."

"Understood, sir. Concur."

"No, we pretend we don't know or care a thing about Fuller and *Challenger.* I'd love to go very deep, quickly, and put a nuclear torpedo up that trailing captain's ass, but he might release a buoy with a warning before he dies."

"Maintain our present course and speed, then, and use the deep scattering layer and the ridge as already planned?"

"For now we proceed sedately, as Ivans who are anything but crazy. Then we embarrass that clown behind us who thinks he's so very smart to have stuck with us this far.... Once we break into ultraquiet at our special flank speed, we'll turn southeast and just keep going at sixty-plus knots. We'll still get to Durban and poor Beck's lair in plenty of time to slow, and reconnoiter and hide, and then blow Fuller's head off."

CHAPTER 18

Before dawn the next morning, Ilse Reebeck settled in at her workstation, in the big and bustling war room of Admiral Hodgkiss's headquarters in Norfolk, Virginia. Just like last night—at the end of her previous very long day—large display screens on the walls showed the status of friendly and enemy forces in the Atlantic Ocean theater of battle. Other screens provided maps and icons of the Mediterranean and the Red Sea, including parts of Allied Central Command whose naval affairs were put under Hodgkiss's control. Information was given as well on the Indian Ocean theater.

But what was happening right now wasn't the troubling issue. It was what *wasn't* happening, and why, and the half-hidden buildup to the next major move that most bothered Ilse. The aftermath of recent events, and the unfathomable near future, riveted her attention—and kept everyone in the war room on pins and needles at their desks, or picking at their food in the cafeteria, or tossing and turning sleeplessly in their racks. Though there was much Ilse hadn't been told, anyone in the war room with eyes and a brain could see that something nasty was heating up in the Mediterranean, and the Axis direction of advance this time would be east.

Her job was to serve as a military oceanographer. She was the liaison between Admiral Hodgkiss and the U.S. Navy's Meteorology and Oceanography Command—METOC— that supported the navy's fighting fleets with tactically important science-driven data interpretations, predictions, and recommendations. METOC had their own separate headquarters, with supporting centers around the globe, but a handful of staffers from METOC sat at the workstations to Ilse's right and left.

Ilse glanced at the two armed marines who stood against the wall, at the end of her aisle of consoles. Hodgkiss's orders for the constant escort hadn't been lifted yet.

Ilse shifted in her seat, tried to loosen up her shoulders and neck, and went back to work. Arrayed before her at the console were computer screens, a sophisticated keyboard, and a bank of secure in-house telephones. Hard-copy procedure and specification manuals, scratch pads full of scribbled notes, empty coffee cups, and well-thumbed reference books covered most of her desk, leaving little free space. Her trash bin, marked CLASSIFIED: SHRED AND BURN like all the others in the war room, was half-overflowing with crumpled papers from late into the evening before. Around her, many voices droned, phones rang, announcements came over the speakers, and couriers and messengers moved about in a constant hubbub. Ilse tuned them out.

Her task involved an ongoing analysis of acoustic conditions in the waters from outside Gibraltar through the whole long Med. It was a gigantic undertaking. Information poured in nonstop from remote sensors in the air or in outer space, and from small underwater robotic probes—called ocean rovers—that could snoop and scoot and then upload their precious data by laser or radio to communication-relay satellites. All of this was vital for modern undersea warfare. The Axis did it too. Whoever did it more and better stood to gain a decisive edge.

The people around Ilse assisted, and the building's super-computers did the numbers crunching. Ilse checked summary reports, and she'd devil's-advocate conclusions. She offered helpful hints as needed, to solve technical problems that constantly came up, or to enhance the customized modeling software used. Hodgkiss, through his aide Johansen, had said Ilse's valuable contributions were being made known to the Free South African legation at their embassy in Washington. She wondered if this amounted to lobbying for the Free South African Navy to promote her to lieutenant commander, or if it had to do with fending off the FBI's mad mole hunt.

Certainly one or the other, and maybe both. Hodgkiss never does things without good reason. Since being awarded the Legion of Merit by her government-in-exile's tiny navy a couple of months ago, Ilse hadn't had direct contact with either her navy or her embassy. Lately, she wondered if maybe she ought to have done more to stay in touch, even shown her face.

Ilse was startled when Captain Johansen appeared, looking over her shoulder.

"Come with me, please," Johansen said.

Ilse made sure the people near her had things well under control, then silently followed the captain. His manner suggested that he didn't want to talk. He waved for the marine bodyguards to accompany them.

Johansen positioned the two marines outside a metal door that was posted with security warnings. He led Ilse inside. The small room had a workstation like her other one.

"We're putting you on something else, Lieutenant."

Ilse was puzzled, then annoyed and angry. "Is this about my security clearance?"

"First of all, that sort of attitude won't help anyone."

"Sorry, sir."

"More to the point, we need you at the moment for something new and different. *Too* new and different, is the problem."

"Sir?" Now Ilse was confused.

"The Russians have deployed the first in a new class of nuclear-powered fast-attack submarines."

"I thought their fleet was mostly defunct."

"When you start out with a few hundred operational subs at the end of the Cold War, and are down to a couple of dozen twenty years later, mostly defunct is *mostly* accurate."

"So..."

"The two dozen SSNs they've got left are among the best in the world. They've had decades now to perfect the lessons they learned from the Walker spy ring, and from other spies we probably still haven't caught."

"You're saying two dozen very good subs is a lot?"

"It's a lot when they're playing at being neutral, while they hold over us the threat of joining the Axis side. It's bad enough they announced after your last trip on *Challenger* that they'd consider any American use of hydrogen bombs on land in the Eastern Hemisphere as a direct attack on Russia herself, and retaliation in kind would be swift and merciless."

Ilse nodded.

"We need to know everything we can about this new sub. The code name we gave it is the *Snow Tiger* class."

"Like with the old NATO names, Golf or Delta or whatever?"

"Correct. The Russians themselves we do know designate it the 868U, and they call the class the Malakhit-B, after the Malakhit Design Bureau, their people who came up with the thing."

"Where do I come in?"

"You're aware that since the war broke out and Russia declared her supposed neutrality, we had to stop sending American spy subs into the Barents Sea?" The Barents lay north and east of Norway, and led to the Russian Northern Fleet ports and supporting maritime-bomber airfields.

"Too provocative if one was detected?"

"Exactly. But a submarine like the Snow Tiger isn't built to rust at a pier, like most ex-Soviet Navy hulls are doing. This one came out, just a little while ago. It went through the G-I-UK Gap according to standard procedures for innocent passage. While verifying that it wasn't actually a German unit, we got to look and listen.... This console has access to everything we have on the Snow Tiger so far, which isn't much. We want you to go through the sound profile, the visuals, tell us everything you can about this ship."

"Don't you have experts who are much better at this sort of thing?"

"Of course. You're not the only person on this."

Ilse winced.

"But the admiral wants your conclusions. You have a unique perspective, from working with the sonar people on *Challenger,* and from your experiences on her in combat against advanced new Axis submarines. You're available, whereas battle-seasoned sonar men are deployed fighting other battles."

"Understood, sir."

"The admiral does not expect miracles. He does want a second opinion."

"About what, exactly?"

The captain pointed at the console desk. "That manila folder has your instructions. Basically, tell us everything you can about the Snow Tiger's hull design and materials, propulsion system, sensors that you see or suspect, and anything else you can think of. It's open season. Give us all you've got."

"How long do I have?"

"I need your initial findings by eighteen hundred." Six P.M. "Food, drink, coffee will be brought to you. There's a rest room through this side door here. You need anything, or see anything important you think I should know before eighteen hundred, call me. The green handset is my direct line; the staff will find me if I'm not in my office. The other phones aren't live, by the way. Your console does have access to a walled-off portion of one of the basement supercomputers."

"When will I go back to helping *Challenger*?"

"Between you and me, Lieutenant, I've no idea if there's even an if, let alone a when."

"But you said—"

"Just stick to the Snow Tiger until you're instructed otherwise. Step one, sign these receipts and security forms."

"But what about my team outside in the war room?"

"They'll be perfectly fine without you. METOC has plenty of bench strength, believe me."

"Why do I have the feeling I'm being locked up and shunted aside?"

The captain stared at Ilse. "You tell me. From what we do know, the Snow Tiger design is very good, and more are being built. We can't afford to have Ivans trailing our fast-attacks in a war zone, putting our boomers under greater threat, snooping outside our submarine bases, gathering intell for Moscow to pass to Germany. To *me* this sounds like a choice assignment for someone with your credentials and rank. If *you* think you're being locked up, maybe you've got a persecution complex. Outward paranoia is often a warning sign of a guilty conscience. Ever since that U-boat cruise-missile attack against Newport News, questions are being asked everywhere about how the Germans could have known *Challenger*'s sailing time so exactly."

"That wasn't a nice thing to say, sir. With all due respect." Actually, Ilse found the comment stinging.

"I'm not nice, this war isn't nice, the Snow Tiger isn't nice, and most of all counterespionage isn't nice. If you like, think of this as a test of your loyalty as well as your skill." Johansen pointed abruptly at the console again. "Come up with some good stuff for Admiral Hodgkiss in your written report by eighteen hundred. Hold back, throw in red herrings, we'll know. Like I said, other people are looking at the same data."

"What if I—"

"Draw a blank? Your value to us will be called into question."

"You *know* I'm not a specialist at this kind of work."

"Commander Fuller's reports say you're adaptable and

smart. I certainly hope he didn't exaggerate for personal reasons." Ilse held her tongue with difficulty. Johansen knew it. "Private acts have public consequences. You're an adult, you should know that without being told. . . ." The captain looked impatiently at his watch.

"This is—"

He waved a hand forcefully to cut Ilse off. "Look, the admiral has many demands on his time. Fighting with the FBI over you could become a distraction. More and more signs do point to there being a mole. The FBI is under tremendous pressure to find the culprit and halt the leak. The sheer weight of personnel numbers versus a suspected junior navy staffer *is* on their side, and the politics and jurisdictional issues remain in flux. If Admiral Hodgkiss starts to get too much heat from above, he'll only stick his neck out so far."

"But he's a four-star admiral!"

"One of several, and not the most senior. Every one of whom wants to be the chief of naval operations before they retire. And each of whom has to please civilian Pentagon and cabinet secretaries, and the U.S. Senate, to ever get that topmost uniformed job. . . . Being familiar with the admiral as I am from two solid years as his right-hand man, if your utility declines, so will his support."

"Then what? I'm thrown to the wolves? To that lynch mob of so-called special agents?"

"Again, Lieutenant, you said it, not me."

CHAPTER 19

A message arrived for *Challenger,* in a code that only Gerald Parker knew. Parker went and decrypted it on his laptop.

"Captain Fuller, contact has been made between Aardvark and Peapod. Your SEALs need to be briefed."

Parker didn't seem at all happy. This made Jeffrey uneasy, but he knew to hold his tongue for now. He decided to conduct the briefing on *Ohio;* it was high time to pay a visit to his task group's other vessel, Parcelli's ship. *And if there's trouble, let everyone hear it at once from our master spook himself.*

The German minisub, still docked inside *Challenger*'s pressure-proof in-hull hangar, was overcrowded. Felix and his team alone made eight, which would be full capacity in the passenger compartment. The mini had an operating crew of two—standard doctrine had one man be a submariner and one be a qualified specialist SEAL. Jeffrey picked David Meltzer, *Challenger*'s battle-stations helmsman, as the submariner pilot. He'd driven the Swedish-built minisub, as well as the American ASDS version, on combat missions several times. Jeffrey wanted him to keep in practice for what was to come. One of Felix's chiefs, Costa, a quiet and serious man, sat next to Meltzer in the tiny control compartment of the minisub as the SEAL copilot. But the mini also held Jeffrey and Gerald Parker, Gamal Salih, Lieutenants Milgrom and Sessions—plus Felix's other chief, Porto, with his jocular temperament and always-lively eyes. Jeffrey squeezed into the control compartment behind Meltzer's seat, and suggested Parker stand—or rather, stoop, with the low overhead—next to him behind Costa. Since there weren't enough seats to go around, two of the enlisted SEALs crouched in the lock-out chamber.

The minisubs had crush depths comparable to a full-size steel-hulled submarine. *Challenger* had to carry hers in her pressure-proof hangar—otherwise, when diving to depths that were comfortable for Jeffrey's ceramic-composite ship, the mini would implode. Not only would the horrible noise ruin the task group's stealth, the German mini's loss would cripple the mission to extract Klaus Mohr. This forced Jeffrey to bring *Challenger* up to near *Ohio*'s depth for the briefing-planning rendezvous. Jeffrey left Bell in charge as command duty officer—acting captain—on *Challenger,* and Lieutenant Willey had the deck and the conn in the sub's control room.

Meltzer and his copilot finished going through their prerelease checklist; an intercom connection let them speak with COB. The control compartment's front and side bulkheads were dominated by four large display screens. Switches, gauges, and indicator lights filled consoles wrapping tightly around the pilot and copilot. Main controls—the throttle and steering joystick—were mounted between their two seats. Behind Jeffrey was the heavy watertight hatch into the lock-out chamber. A similar hatch led aft from there to the passenger compartment.

"Green board, sir," Chief Costa told Meltzer.

"Challenger, Minisub Charlie," Meltzer said into his lip mike, giving his call sign. "Ready for pressure equalization and opening hangar-bay doors."

———

Jeffrey had ordered Parcelli to hold *Ohio* ahead of *Challenger,* a few hundred yards off *Challenger*'s port bow, while *Challenger* pointed northeast and *Ohio* aimed herself southwest, toward Jeffrey's ship. The plan was for each vessel to stay within the arc covered by the other's wide-aperture array on their facing sides, to keep in acoustic-link contact, while not blocking each other's arrays from hearing outward to both flanks. By pointing in opposite directions, each ship's bow sphere covered the other's baffles; with minisubs maneuvering about, Jeffrey wanted neither ship to trail a towed array. He'd ordered Parcelli to hold *Ohio*'s depth at 600 feet, 250 feet shallower than his own ship, to avoid any risk of collision.

To maintain proper formation in the currents that varied at different depths, both ships needed some speed so their rudders could bite. Three knots was fast enough, but this meant that to keep together, one ship had to move backward. Jeffrey had decided *Challenger* would be the one to do so. He'd ordered the task group to steer southwest, *away* from Gibraltar, to disguise their true base course and implied destination.

The mini's bow nosed up as Meltzer worked his controls. He activated the photonic sensors, and images of the ocean outside appeared on some of the screens. Too far east to hide in the confusing sound-propagation eddies of the Gulf Stream, and too far north of the Sargasso Sea to hide under the layer of floating seaweed there, Meltzer had his work cut out for him as he approached *Ohio*. One of Parcelli's minis had vacated its place so the German one could dock, but *Ohio*'s other ASDS still sat firmly attached, just to one side of where Meltzer needed to come in for a landing. For stealth, Meltzer dared not make any noise, and dared not use his floodlights. This meant he had neither active sonar nor good visual cues to guide his final approach.

Meltzer changed the outside displays to image-intensification mode. At first Jeffrey saw nothing new on the screens, then a school of small fish darted by. Then something huge came into view, a gigantic cylinder. As Meltzer worked his joystick and throttle, Jeffrey saw that this cylinder had a sail. Meltzer needed to dock right behind that sail, but instead of bow planes near the cylinder's nose, *Ohio* had fair-water planes that jutted from her sail. Meltzer had to steer well clear, or the edge of a plane could tear a gash through the minisub's hull.

─────────

"Permission granted to open our bottom hatch," Meltzer reported.

Jeffrey, the most senior, climbed down *Ohio*'s air-lock ladder first, and walked out into the SSGN. He was now on the topmost deck of the missile compartment. The first two silos had been turned into lock-in/lock-out chambers; he'd just come through one of these. Altogether, two dozen massive silo tubes marched aft, twelve each along two side-by-side rows. Years ago, Jeffrey knew, all of them had held a Trident long-range ballistic missile, the ultimate strategic deterrent that worked—because it never once had to be used. Now these silos held SEAL equipment, or large-size undersea probe vehicles, or airborne recon drones that could be launched with *Ohio* submerged, or seven Tactical Tomahawk cruise missiles each, or a big clutch of Polyphems. The missile compartment was festooned with fire-fighting gear and protective suits, chemo sensors in case of toxic or flammable leaks—from weapon fuel and warheads, and stored SEAL explosive ordnance—plus radiation detectors.

Jeffrey glanced at the overhead; he could readily see the curve of *Ohio*'s pressure hull, wrapping downward to both sides. Outside the hull, up there, bathed by the ever-squeezing ocean, sat an ASDS and his German minisub.

As a small crowd of his people gathered behind him, he saw Captain Parcelli coming along the narrow passageway from forward, to offer greetings. Jeffrey was glad to see Parcelli smiling, and was pleasantly surprised that Parcelli wore a blue cotton jumpsuit—instead of his previously inevitable dress uniform.

"Welcome aboard, Captain," Parcelli said. His handshake was firm but not bone crushing, and he held it long enough to show that the welcome was sincere.

"Thank you, Captain," Jeffrey responded.

Parcelli nodded to those he already knew among Jeffrey's group. Other introductions were made.

"Feels like a homecoming?" Jeffrey joked to Felix, since he'd served on *Ohio* before.

"I forgot how *spacious* she was," Felix said under his breath.

Parcelli turned back to Jeffrey while they all walked forward. "Let's head to the Special Operations Forces spaces, SEAL country as we *Ohio* Gold people call it. We can use the briefing facilities there."

Jeffrey nodded. He still sensed Parker's concern about something, and wanted to know right away what it was.

Ilse, alone in the small room with the workstation, had already spent several hours going over the available data on the Russian submarine that Hodgkiss's aide had called a Snow Tiger.

She almost jumped out of her skin when Johansen shoved open the door and stalked into the room. He looked very unhappy.

"More data for you." He gruffly handed over some ultra-high-density optical storage disks.

"With respect, sir, your manner. Why is more data bad?"

"Because this batch might be the last we get."

"Captain?"

"Displeasure is being passed down from the top."

"Displeasure with what? Or with *whom*?"

Johansen sighed. "One of our subs was trailing the Snow Tiger rather close in, gathering everything possible, but her captain was somehow outsmarted and the Russian simply vanished in the middle of the North Atlantic. Now it could be anywhere, doing anything, at the worst imaginable point in the war. There are red faces, and purple faces, up to the CNO level and beyond."

Ilse frowned. "Do we need to warn *Challenger*?"

"What have you figured out so far?"

"Look at this." Ilse showed Johansen her work on the Snow Tiger's midships magnetic-field signature, recorded while it was stopped in the G-I-UK Gap. He watched as a 3-D color animation moved and changed shape on her console screen, the fields overlaid on an outline of the Snow Tiger's hull. "I think the Snow Tiger has twin reactors, cooled by liquid metal, and coolant circulation is driven by electromagnetic pumps. The moving shapes are the pulsating fields of the pumps."

"Others have already come to that conclusion. The Snow Tiger could be the fastest, quietest submarine afloat. This new data covers the Snow Tiger accelerating to twenty knots. Tonals, broadband, flow noise, and measurements of wake turbulence when the trailing sub got directly behind her."

"And?"

"Try to figure out the Snow Tiger's maximum speed, and what she'd sound like then."

"Sir, that'd require a team of experienced people to even come close to meaningful answers!"

"From the mood I sense at the Pentagon, you'd better come up with whatever you can, and soon. An embarrassment to an Atlantic Fleet sub, of the magnitude and significance we just had, is ultimately a political embarrassment to

Admiral Hodgkiss, who is, as I already told you, not without his rivals and enemies."

"Don't people have better things to do, like win the war?"

"Sometimes ranking officials get more concerned about their future position if we *do* win than if we lose, especially when they know that failing means we could all be dead anyway. There, I said it out loud. With this other business *Challenger* is involved in going on too, everyone's into backside-protection mode. Scapegoats, witch hunts, you *don't* want the details."

"You're setting me up, aren't you? Giving me a task you know full well is impossible here."

"Hasn't it occurred to you that this workspace is not a prison, but a sanctuary?" Johansen gestured at the four walls. "That hostile FBI interview was obviously meant to get you to panic and make a mistake, or bolt, or send a call-for-help message to your control that special agents could intercept and get enough goods on you to make an arrest. Those odd phone messages and brush-bys suggest that *somebody,* maybe Axis operatives or maybe even a traitor in the FBI, *is* setting you up. The enemy tried to kill you outright a month ago. The next best thing is framing you. In wartime captured spies hang. And the timing isn't an accident either. Your best character witness, Commander Fuller, is incommunicado indefinitely. The FBI director knows it, and Axis intell surely sensed it coming too."

"Does Commander Fuller know about the accusations?"

"He stood up for you forcefully to the director himself. The director took him to pieces in front of the president."

Ilse blanched.

"Do you really think Admiral Hodgkiss would assign you a seemingly endless task without good reason? Your intimate knowledge of Commander Fuller's combat personality and tactical mind-set makes you invaluable, but it also makes you a target. The admiral is keeping you out of sight and out of mind of those who are busy casting about for victims, at any price."

"METOC. A submariner complains that they didn't give adequate support for his boat to maintain contact. I was on that desk, they could pin it on *me*. Add *that* to the FBI file, I'm toast."

"Good, Lieutenant. You're finally catching on."

CHAPTER 20

J effrey was impressed that Parcelli ran a tight and happy
ship. The pride and confidence of *Ohio*'s Gold crew
couldn't be hidden, and couldn't be faked either for
someone with Jeffrey's practiced eye. This was a first for him,
appraising another captain's leadership ability during an inspection of his vessel. *Ohio*'s crew were clearly fond of Parcelli, as Parcelli was of them, which was good. With over two
hundred men aboard, the corridors teemed like a beehive.

After more greetings were made in *Ohio*'s control room,
with her chief of the boat and some of her key officers, the
group, larger now, went down two decks to the wardroom.
This one was much less cramped than *Challenger*'s. Jeffrey
left Milgrom and Sessions here to begin a working meeting
with *Ohio*'s people.

Parcelli led Jeffrey and those with him up ladders and
along passageways. They arrived at the Special Operations
Forces command-and-planning center. This space had once
held the sophisticated navigation equipment *Ohio* needed to
make sure each of the H-bomb warheads on each of her missiles hit its target very precisely—after leaving the earth's at-

mosphere and then reentering thousands of miles away. That equipment had all gone with the SSGN conversion. Now the compartment was filled with communication and SEAL mission-planning consoles and workstations. The consoles were manned; the space was busy.

Parcelli reintroduced Jeffrey to Commander McCollough, in charge of *Ohio*'s sixty-six SEALs. They'd last met on-shore in Norfolk, when Hodgkiss assembled the players and told them their roles.

"Welcome aboard, Captain, and welcome to my domain."

"Thank you, Commander. A pleasure to visit your lair."

"Changed a lot from your day, I bet." McCollough playfully raised an eyebrow. His Boston-Irish accent was as charming as ever; he possessed impressive natural charisma.

"I'll say," Jeffrey told him, looking around and smiling. In the short time Jeffrey had been in the SEALs, in the mid-1990s, before being wounded, ASDS minisubs and SSGN conversions of boomers were projects in the R&D stages—efforts that might easily have both been given the budget ax.

"There's my man!" McCollough exclaimed when he saw Felix. McCollough was clearly not someone to stand on cere-mony—but then SEALs seldom were when among their own kind. "You did us proud. Still wanna go back to master chief?"

There was a familiarity present that wasn't shown in front of Hodgkiss. It was McCollough who'd put Felix in for the commission from master chief to full lieutenant, before Felix left *Ohio* for *Challenger*—and then, under Jeffrey's com-mand, had gotten his bayonet wound from a German Kampf-schwimmer while doing other things that won him the Medal of Honor.

"Well . . ." Felix pretended to be thinking about it. "Nah, I think I'll stay being an officer. My wife would kill me if I had to tell her I took a pay cut."

McCollough made eye contact with Jeffrey; the man had a very clear, no-nonsense gaze. "I suggest we use the large conference room, Captain."

Everyone settled down at their places around the conference table. The furnishings were spartan, with exposed wires, cables, pipes, and air ducts everywhere. The emergency air-breathing masks stored in plain sight, and the fittings in a pipe on the overhead for plugging in the masks, left no doubt that they were riding in a submarine.

The main display screen on the bulkhead glowed to life. Gerald Parker put a disk into a laptop provided by someone on Commander McCollough's staff.

Parker stood at the front of the compartment, next to the screen. His blasé attitude showed that he was used to doing such presentations, and had no trouble addressing groups. Parker's stance was erect and aloof; Felix thought he came across as a tight-ass, and a preppie.

Felix glanced at his men. All eight of them were attentive. This operation was highly compartmented, so they didn't know much of whatever was coming. Like any SEAL about to be clued in on something dangerous but important, these guys were excited.

A map of Turkey popped onto the screen. The map zoomed in on the stretch of water between the Aegean Sea east of Greece, crowded with islands and shoals, through the narrow Dardanelles Strait, and into the wider bathtub-shaped Sea of Marmara.

The map also showed the bottleneck from the far side of the Marmara into the big dead end of the German- and Russian-controlled Black Sea. This bottleneck, less than half a mile wide in many places, was labeled "Bosporus Strait." The city of Istanbul lined both banks. Bridges spanned the Bosporus, giving road access between the parts of the sprawling metropolis.

Right away the difficulties started piling up.

"This is where you're going," Parker stated to Felix, pointing to Istanbul. *"Challenger* will drop you off outside the Dardanelles. Your team with Mr. Salih and me goes the rest of the way, there and back, in the captured German minisub. One hundred fifty nautical miles each way. A long, slow trip. Call it fifteen hours in each direction at a cruising speed of ten knots to save fuel. Go faster for any reason, you get less mileage, we won't make it back. And deep-draft merchant shipping will be a constant menace while the mini navigates. I will remain in the minisub while the rest of you go ashore."

"Contingency plan?" Felix asked.

"Ohio's minis will both be engaged in delivering Commander McCollough's teams to Axis-occupied Greece. Covert recon and overt diversions. This is the first time the U.S. has entered the Med in such force since the start of the war. Every use must be made of the opportunity."

"So no mini is available to come and meet ours and bail us out? If we run out of gas, we have to swim?"

"If you run out of gas, we have to improvise. So kindly don't waste gas. Your passenger and cargo are too important."

"Specifically? My men haven't heard this yet."

"I know. We're going to extract a German defector."

"Right, Peapod. How do we know we can trust the guy?"

"We can't be positive of anything. Our National Command Authorities deem it worth taking the risk. Contact with Peapod has already been made by a third party, Aardvark, who now steps aside after telling his secretary to make some seemingly innocent phone calls that will later assist your efforts. . . . The extraction is set for next week, Friday night."

"That's not much time."

"It's a very tight schedule."

"We'll be violating Turkish neutrality," Felix said.

"Does that bother you?"

"I've done this sort of thing before."

"I know. And *you* know, get caught and you get interned for the duration of the war, if you're lucky. If you're not, you'll be shot as spies. Either way you stick the U.S. with a major diplomatic incident. We want Turkey on *our* side, not neutral and *not* going Axis. Make a mess, Germany will make the most of it."

"Understood."

"A serious complication has arisen."

Something always does. "Meaning . . . what?"

"The extraction won't be as straightforward as we'd hoped. The problem is, we need not just the defector, but some special equipment he uses. Computer gear. That's all Aardvark could confirm, with the Moscow-rules script we provided."

Felix's jaw set. Moscow rules meant the greatest possible spy-tradecraft care taken, when working on a deadly enemy's most closely guarded ground. "And our friend can't just walk out of the consulate with his software on a disk in his briefcase to meet us somewhere, or put a computer in some luggage and saunter out the door. 'Bye, I'm going yachting this weekend.' How heavy, bulky is the equipment? Do we know?"

"It's man packable by a Kampfschwimmer team, we *think,* from what our contact was able to tell us. We do know that German battle swimmers are directly involved."

"I'm liking this less and less."

"The equipment will be at a safe house. The safe house will be used and guarded by the Kampfschwimmer, from what the defector implied. Mr. Salih will pick up the defector at the consulate when the time comes."

"I speak fluent German and Turkish," Salih said. "My job will be to say that Aardvark has been delayed outside the country on his business, and I've come instead to take Peapod partying."

"It's gonna be one hell of a party," Felix said.

"Affirmative," Parker responded. "The defector will undoubtedly be tailed by a security escort, to protect him and keep an eye on him. We don't know if they suspect his loyalty. If they don't now, they might by next Friday."

"Terrific."

"Your team will have to reach shore at Istanbul from the

minisub without detection, and change into civilian clothes. Obtain transportation. Conceal your weapons and ammo as best you can about your persons or in rented or purloined vehicles. And watch out for Turkish police. They're everywhere, they're good, and some patrols go around in armored personnel carriers mounted with heavy machine cannon. Not squad cars."

"Where's the safe house?"

"We don't know. The defector and Aardvark dared not discuss more than that it exists. Peapod will have to give you directions, with Salih as his handler until you all can bring the man back to me in the minisub, where I will immediately begin his debrief while we return to *Challenger*."

Felix took a deep breath. "So we have to attack a safe house full of Kampfschwimmer, without damaging fancy computer gear, without getting killed by the Germans or by the Turkish police, and we don't even know where this safe house is till we get there?"

"Correct. And without getting Peapod or Salih killed. They'll need a rally point to hide in with their heads well down, then you collect them there on your way out."

"And just for starters there's the security tail of Germans whom we need to neutralize quickly and quietly, before they can call a warning or summon help and blow the whole deal?"

"Correct. That part isn't new."

"No. But with more direct action to follow it now, there's a lot more pressure to this phase. And rather severe consequences if there's any screwup." To SEALs, direct action meant combat.

Parker nodded, deadpan.

He's an awfully cold fish when he wants to be, Felix thought. "Do we know the architecture of the safe house building at least? Or the neighborhood it's in?"

Parker shook his head. "Too dangerous to have been broached in any way by Aardvark with Peapod. You'll have to choose your tactics on the spot."

"So we use the time between now and next Friday to plan and rehearse a totally open-ended mission profile?"

"Yes. And while you plan, also take account of Russian and Israeli operatives in the immediate area, who are very interested in our man. Protecting him, or killing him."

In front of Parker, Captain Fuller, Captain Parcelli, and Commander McCollough, Felix couldn't let on how suicidal this whole thing had started to sound.

I'm sure that's one reason they're holding the meeting like this, with all the task-group senior officers present.

Felix sat there steely eyed, and his men implicitly understood that they should follow his example. Though they were naturally competitive, and welcomed very difficult assignments, this particular one seemed over the top. Felix knew them well enough to see it in their faces.

"Okay," Felix summarized. "We sneak ashore, we grab cars to get around a giant city infamous for its traffic jams. We pick up a defector right outside his consulate, and he picks up a tail. We take out the tail without anyone noticing, and then take out a safe house manned by German elite special forces. Except without blowing up computer equipment we don't know how to recognize, and without hurting or killing innocent civilians or cops in a city of twelve million people. We elude armed Russians and Mossad types who won't like us mucking around. Then we all scurry back to the minisub and sail merrily away, obeying a speed limit slower than a guy on a bicycle.... Did I leave anything out?"

"Yes, you did," Parker said.

"What?"

"Think."

Felix saw it. *Oh shit.* "Our cover, our legend, for who we were, after we leave a bunch of dead German bodyguards and Kampfschwimmer behind, and Peapod or his corpse can't be found."

"This has been discussed at the highest levels in the State Department, the CIA, and the Pentagon. We need to befuddle the Germans as long as possible as to what happened and who actually did it, to buy time for us to receive and debrief the defector and harness his help. We also need to assume that the Turks will conduct full investigations of their own, both law enforcement and counterespionage."

"So what do we do?"

"Lead them away from suspecting the U.S. or Israel. Israel is most directly under threat from the impending Axis offensive, and our relations with her are strained. The last thing we can afford to do is have multiple shoot-outs on Turkish soil, and leave Israel holding the bag with the slightest inkling that Americans were responsible."

"The Mossad are too good, and they probably have better relations with Turkey than we do."

"Affirmative. Their outright diplomatic relations, and clandestine human intelligence contacts, far exceed ours."

"So what's the answer? We pretend we're from some other Islamic country?"

"*No.* We need the Muslim nations staying neutral. We can't try to stick them with a crime they'll know they didn't commit. If we want a prayer of getting them to join the Allies, *ever,* we have to leave them out of this."

"Then what do we do?"

"You and your men are all Brazilian-Americans."

Felix and his guys looked at each other and shrugged. "We know that." Brazilians were a varied mix of white and black and native Indian blood; Brazil's official language was Portuguese.

"You and your specific team are hearing this, assigned to this, not simply because you worked successfully with Captain Fuller on *Challenger* before, though that's certainly a big part of why you were picked."

"What's the rest of it?"

"You'll operate there as Portuguese expatriates. Stranded in Turkey by the war when your mother country was occupied.... Few Turks can tell apart Portuguese accents from Brazil versus Portugal, or notice any American tinge to the speech.... That was the plan all along, when the only issue was taking out Mohr's bodyguards. Now you'll be leaving a much bigger footprint, with a safe-house assault involved. So your motivation, your *legend,* has to be amplified. You're a splinter faction of self-appointed partisans, incensed at the Germans for occupying Portugal, and you're getting even. Heckler and Koch MP-5 submachine guns are made under license in Turkey. That's the reason you were issued the particular MP-5 versions you have, with Czech-manufactured shells, and thus appropriate shell-case markings, to add to the confusion."

"Freedom fighters?" Captain Fuller asked. "A scratch resistance group that nobody heard of before?" He seemed to buy into the concept.

Parker nodded. "A savage hit-and-run raid, hurting Germans where they're most exposed, at the edge of territory where they have any real control.... An e-mail will be sent to an Istanbul newspaper after you're gone, taking the credit."

"There's just one problem with all that," Felix said.

Parker hesitated. "I don't follow you."

"Probably because it's so obvious you can't see it.... How do you think this'll look to the Turks?"

"I just told you how it'll look. I'll be providing you all with casual clothes made in Turkey, falsified Portuguese passports, phony Turkish ID cards, internee visas, and the rest."

Felix knew the CIA had warehouses full of foreign goods for use on special ops, and extremely talented document forgers. The SEALs had all been given what Felix now realized—from glancing at Gamal Salih—were Turkish-style haircuts before joining *Challenger.*

"You left out one little detail," Felix said.

"Lieutenant?"

"Mr. Parker, you can glorify the cover story by calling us freedom fighters if you want, but the Turkish authorities will think we're terrorists. Their military is strong. The minute we start stabbing and shooting and blasting down doors in some house in some suburb, they'll send their very best rapid-reaction teams. They'll have helicopters, to look down and shoot down and fast-rope down and leapfrog over gridlock in the streets. They'll do everything they can to wipe us out, and we're not even allowed to shoot to kill to defend ourselves."

Parker opened his mouth to continue just as someone knocked on the door. It was *Ohio*'s communications officer.

"Captain Fuller, Captain Parcelli, we've just gotten an ELF message. We're ordered to use our periscope raft, raise the SHF mast, and copy a high-baud-rate data dump from the satellite." SHF meant super-high-frequency radio.

This took Jeffrey by surprise, and made him uncomfortable. Even the stealthy raft could be noticed by an enemy on or above the surface.

"Who gave the order?"

"ComLantFlt, to Commander, Task Group 47.2, imperative, no recourse, and smartly."

Admiral Hodgkiss had just told Jeffrey to use *Ohio*'s raft, and use it now.

"Very well," Jeffrey said. "We're coming." He and Parcelli hurried into *Ohio*'s control room.

Parcelli was tight-lipped. He didn't like having to break stealth, even by the slimmest margin. He made sure the sonar men and fire-control men held no contact on nearby subs or ships or planes. "You want to take the mini back to *Challenger* before I float the raft?"

Jeffrey almost said yes. But as task group commander he was supposed to be as cool as a cucumber, no matter what. The tactical uncertainties would only get worse as the mission progressed.

"No. Let's both see what the good admiral has to say."

Parcelli told his XO to take the conn and get ready to deploy the antenna raft. Jeffrey asked for a message to be sent to his own ship by the acoustic link, to inform Bell of what was going on; this was quickly done.

"Captain," Parcelli said, "join me in the radio room?"

Ohio's radio room was a compartment off of the control room. Its door was thick, and was equipped with two different mechanical combination locks and one electronic hand-print scanner. A big red sign warned unauthorized personnel to never enter.

Parcelli turned the combinations and held his hand to the scanner. Jeffrey preceded him in, then Parcelli locked the door behind them.

Jeffrey felt it strange to see blue lighting instead of the red he was used to—red or blue were used to make staring for hours at console screens easier on watch-standers' eyes. Otherwise, the radio room wasn't much different from *Challenger*'s. The SSGN's special communications gear for SEAL operations, and for connectivity with surface action groups, carrier battle groups, or amphibious strike groups, were in other spaces, aft.

This radio room was small, crowded with technicians and state-of-the-art equipment, and was warm from the heat that human bodies and racks of black boxes gave off.

The lieutenant (j.g.) who was *Ohio*'s communications officer oversaw things as his people did final checks on the receivers and the decryption gear. They also tested the connections to the raft antenna, threading inside the winch cable on its drum in *Ohio*'s sail. All was in order. Every transmitter was cold, long switched off, and would stay switched off, to avoid the slightest chance of an accidental signal being sent out that would ruin the undersea task-group's stealth.

"Raft on the surface," a technician announced a few minutes later. "SHF mast deploying.... Good contact on the satellite." Equipment in the small space came alive. Recorders began to run, digital signal-strength meters fluctuated, and red and green indicator lights flickered rapidly.

Parcelli addressed the radio-room phone talker as the download came in. "Chief of the watch is to prepare to retract the raft on my order."

The phone talker spoke into his mike, then listened. "Chief of the watch acknowledges, retract raft on your order, aye."

"Download complete!" the communications officer called out, sounding jumpy.

"Phone talker," Parcelli snapped. "Retract the raft."

"Chief o' the watch acknowledges raft retracting, sir."

"Very well . . . Radio, decrypt the download."

"Header decoded, sir. Message is to Commander, Task Group 47.2, personal, copy to CO, *Ohio,* personal."

"Sir," the phone talker said, "XO reports no threats detected yet."

"Very well," Jeffrey said. *Maybe we got away with it. Nobody noticed the raft.* "Give me the disk when the decrypt is completed. Captain Parcelli, may we use your stateroom?"

Jeffrey waited while the decoding computers continued to run. The time they were taking suggested that either an extremely long text message had come in, or the message included a heavy amount of supporting numerical data. *Or both.*

"Decrypt complete, sir," a senior chief said.

"Give the disk to Captain Fuller," the lieutenant (j.g.) ordered.

Jeffrey took the disk in his hand, holding it by the edges so he wouldn't get fingerprints on its surface. They left the radio room and went into Parcelli's cabin. They used Parcelli's laptop to read the disk.

The message began with a cover memo that referenced a number of attachments. Several were raw acoustic recordings from a Los Angeles submarine's sonars. *Those would be very data intensive, for sure.*

There were also several reports and analyses attached, including—this caught Jeffrey's attention—one that mentioned work performed by Ilse Reebeck.

But the cover memo itself was enough.

Jeffrey and Parcelli looked at each other.

"So the Russians have a new, extremely quiet fast-attack sub loose somewhere in the Atlantic." Parcelli's usually unflappable expression seemed worried. "Our paths might cross. This isn't good. We know too little about her. She might detect us and we wouldn't even be aware of it."

"Concur," Jeffrey said. "At least she won't fire on us.... But she may pass a contact report to her base, and from there to Moscow, and from there to Berlin. If she sees us in the North Atlantic, steering east, our cover of heading south to Durban is ruined, totally blown. The Germans could deduce real easy from our latitude that we're aimed for the Med. And the *Texas* sacrifice by *Dreadnought* right outside Gibraltar? Instead of a diversion, it becomes the circumstantial proof that we're definitely there."

"What are your orders?"

"Like Hodgkiss says, press on. Be doubly on our guard."

"And pray."

"Yeah," Jeffrey said. "It's a very big ocean around us. We might not come within a thousand miles of the 868U."

"But what if the Axis or their Kremlin friends suspect our side will be doing something aggressive, given the German buildup on the eastern North Africa front? What if this Snow Tiger is abusing her neutrality to establish a barrier patrol outside Gibraltar? What if instead of a very big ocean, she's been deployed specifically to hunt for something like our task group at the most obvious, the *only* choke point? She doesn't *need* to fire at us. She just needs to warn the Axis defenses by radio or a laser buoy. The Germans in the Med can take care of themselves if they know what to look for. Once we're caught inside there, it'd be like them shooting fish in a barrel."

"Get me two copies of this disk to take back to *Challenger.* Your sonar people and mine can each go over the sound profile of the Snow Tiger, and I want to examine what's on here myself alone in my stateroom." Jeffrey exhaled, displeased by the ever-mounting complications. "I'll leave Estabo and his SEALs with you and McCollough until our next rendezvous. They need the special-warfare planning and rehearsal facilities now more than ever. The simple existence of this Snow Tiger requires more caution, but caution would cost us time in the Atlantic and then in the Med, which could give the extraction team too little slack when they get to Istanbul."

Parcelli nodded soberly. "The master schedule's locked in. The *Texas* business and then the defector snatch, hopefully soon enough for Peapod to help us before Pandora is launched. Hodgkiss sees what we see. He knows that if there's any delay, our entire effort might collapse on itself."

"I'll grab my officers and Parker and Salih and head back to *Challenger* at once. Recall your ASDS from visiting *my* ship."

"And then?"

"We resume our tactical formation for steaming east. You high, me low, and I range ahead as the scout. You trail your towed array, I use terrain for concealment. The key to eluding this Snow Tiger lies in who detects whom first."

CHAPTER 21

Late that same afternoon, alone at her private console, Ilse was deeply immersed in seemingly self-contradictory data about the new Snow Tiger. Studying on-line references about known and historical Russian submarine design approaches made her even more confused.

Johansen burst into the room. Ilse stood up and mentally pulled herself together. "Sir?"

"METOC won't admit it, but it appears that they need you after all."

"You want me back in the war room?"

"No. Continue here. Take this."

Ilse reached out and palmed a disk. "What is it?"

"That's what METOC wants to know. You tell me, and I'll tell Admiral Hodgkiss."

"But, I mean, what is it?"

"It's a sound. Something strange. They're not even sure it's real. It might be an artifact of the signal-processing algorithms having a flaw, or electronic noise internal to the system and they just can't pinpoint the defect."

"Such things happen."

"Don't let what I say bias you. The admiral thinks it would be opportune if you could identify the sound for sure, and soon. Think outside the box. He said you're supposed to be good at that.... I have a meeting. Good luck."

Johansen left.

Ilse shrugged to herself. She inserted the disk from METOC into a reader on her console and went to work.

The disk had a text explanation. The data included a noise recording made a few hours ago, by a navy ocean rover patrolling over the Mid-Atlantic Ridge close to the equator. Ilse put on the headphones that came with the console. She tapped keys to replay the sound, then closed her eyes and listened.

A rushing, whooshing noise rose in strength and then fell. Ilse displayed its power spectrum over time—a jagged, wriggling graph of intensity versus frequency from moment to moment. There were no signs at all of pure tonals that a submarine would give off, no mechanical transients, or anything else man-made.

Played at normal speed, from start to finish, the entire recording of the detection by the ocean rover lasted thirty seconds. There were a couple of breaks, where the sound disappeared and then began again two or three seconds later. Ilse guessed these were caused by jagged terrain in this relatively shallow stretch of the Mid-Atlantic Ridge, blocking the sound source from the ocean rover intermittently.

Ilse called up specifications on the ocean rover and its sonars. Unfortunately, the unit was too small and its hydrophones weren't sophisticated enough to give her much with which to estimate the range between the rover and the sound—the whole rover was barely larger than a fat torpedo, and traveled at a mere four knots for long endurance.

The unidentified sound source was moving roughly north to south. She knew this because of how the bearing to the center of the sound changed with time, according to the ocean rover's positional data. Knowing its range from the rover would help to indicate its speed. Its speed might help her figure out what it was.

She did more analyses. Eventually, from a variety of technical factors about how the power spectrum behaved, she narrowed down the source's velocity to maybe thirty knots, minimum, and maybe a hundred knots, tops.

This was very fast, even too fast, for a sub or a decoy or a torpedo. The tonals would've been glaring.... And the signature was all wrong for a supercavitating rocket weapon. There was no sign at all of a missile engine firing, or exhaust bubble collapse, and anyway, those things went more like two hundred or three hundred knots.

Progress of a sort.

This sound is definitely a natural phenomenon of some kind.

Its intensity was stronger at lower frequencies—what acoustic engineers called gray noise. As an oceanographer Ilse knew the gray-noise quality was a sign suggesting that whatever had happened involved the displacement of rock or mud or lava. What was odd was that the fragmentary data she had did seem to imply—unless the navigational instruments on the rover were badly out of calibration—that the motion she was hearing was nearly horizontal, and its true velocity was almost constant. This didn't make much sense among steep peaks atop an undersea mountain range, which was probably what had most puzzled METOC; other readouts Ilse examined and cross-compared said the ocean rover's orientation and navigating were good.

Ilse struggled for hours, skimming research reports on tectonic behavior.

A slant-wise avalanche, she finally concluded. Ancient volcanic rubble, unstable from washing by eons of particle-laden current fronts, suddenly gave way, confined to a ravine so it slid sideways instead of falling straight down. It was known that the leading edge of such landslides could hydroplane, skating on a thin trapped layer of water, reaching at least fifty knots. Water resistance against the front face would keep it from accelerating much more than that.... After thirty seconds, the whole mess had rolled and bounced out of sound-path contact with the ocean rover.

It was obvious once you saw it. It had been right under the METOC peoples' noses the whole time.

———

Felix Estabo was not a happy camper.

He and his men were running the same scenario for the fourth time. The first three times, he'd been killed.

The SEAL mission-rehearsal equipment aboard *Ohio* was superb. The virtual-reality capabilities of the helmets everyone wore far surpassed any video game the public could buy. Much of the software was so good it was rated top secret, and the system ran on *Ohio*'s supercomputer. The imagery looked completely real, and the detail of the scenario was astonishing. The compartment in which the rehearsal was played was temperature controlled, and fans created wind that affected trajectories of notional bullets fired inside the game. There were even sprinklers on the overhead to make real rain—which would show up on the pictures inside the game helmets too.

Each man stood on a treadmill, mounted on its own turntable, which sensed the speed and direction in which a player ran, and stopped if he stopped. The slope of the treadmill could vary constantly, depending on the terrain defined in the game and the player's coordinates. It was able to imitate the physical effect of climbing stairs. The treadmill surface was wide enough for a man to lie prone, as if taking cover. Mechanical actuators underneath could also inflict the teeth-jarring, gut-pounding shock of a nearby artillery round or grenade.

The only thing lacking, Felix thought, were environmental odors.

A genuine battlefield stinks, even through a gas mask.

Since the CIA lacked much information on the safe house in which Peapod's crucial equipment would be held—other than that it was *some* kind of house—Felix and Commander

McCollough's planning staff considered everything, and then did their best to prepare. Gerald Parker had brought data disks with building codes and architectural data for Istanbul. But as in any infiltration or forced-entry exercise, some types of structures and landscapes were easier or harder than others to penetrate.

The mission profile they were rehearsing now was intentionally made as difficult as possible. It involved a big mansion surrounded by a high wall, with a front and back gate protected by armed guards. The mansion's exterior was stone, mostly granite or marble. This was based on an actual piece of real estate in Istanbul, something specific meant to represent one generic type.

The personality and voices of the mansion's guards were played by SEALs from McCollough's staff, all of whom had been in combat before. They pretended they didn't know at first that Felix's men were hostile, they just behaved in a careful, vigilant way.

And after dark on a Friday night, Felix thought, at a very wealthy person's home, it can be hard to convince the guards we're delivery boys or plumbers.

The SEALs communicated with the guards just as they would in actuality in Istanbul, using Portuguese-accented fractured English, improvised sign language—even notes, written in advance for the SEALs by someone who spoke good German, that Felix handed to the guards.

From previous run-throughs of this simulation, Felix had already decided that his team would have to kill all the guards, quickly and silently, before they could sound an alarm. The biggest risk was that real guards might be wearing life-sign monitors, which would transmit a warning if their respiration or heart rate fell outside the normal range. Jamming the transmissions would be guaranteed to alert every enemy in sight—or out of sight, inside the mansion, or elsewhere in a property holding backup troops. So transmissions had to be sniffed for in the ether, to know if monitors were worn by the adversaries on the perimeter. Then, if so, signals of fake live people—on the proper frequency—had to replace the real vital signs of the guards, seamlessly, as they died. Felix's men came aboard *Challenger* with the portable equipment needed to do this. They were also trained in working down in utility manholes, to cut power and sever fiber optics on cue, to surprise and isolate their objective.

But past the guards was a wide lawn with no trees. It made a perfect killing field against intruders. Automatic weapons from the stone mansion had unobstructed arcs of fire . . . and the high stone wall and solid metal gates would stop the bullets from hitting elsewhere in the neighborhood. Such a lawn might have motion detectors, including pressure-sensitive strips hidden under the earth. These detectors would call the Kampfschwimmer to arms instantly, and might even set off booby traps to kill or wound the SEALs, or stun them for capture.

The team was prepared for this too. Probes could detect buried objects. Big rolled-up sheets of lightweight composites that flattened and became rigid under battery power would let the SEALs crawl through a field of buried mines if need be—but only assuming that the German traps weren't set to be too sensitive, so as to avoid false alarms from stray cats or free-roaming guard dogs.

Then there was the safe house itself. Infrared visors helped penetrate walls to some extent, to identify body heat.

The technology list went on.

The gadgets and the tactics interrelate. They have to. Need dictates form and function.

Felix's heart was pounding as the scenario played on. To him and his men, this was no game. The pretend assault was a matter of life and death, because soon the bullets and knives would not be make-believe.

Felix cursed to himself.

The defenses were too deep and strong. His team couldn't push past the wall, and across the lawn, and inside the mansion without being seen and shot at while their only cover was hopelessly inadequate. Felix led from in front, it was his duty, and that was why he kept getting killed. . . . But unlike in real life, he got to see how the battle continued without him. Every time, they failed in their critical goals: Enter without too much disturbance for a neighbor to call the police, and exit with Peapod's gear intact and not too many friendly losses.

Felix took a deep breath. His team was about to try once more to get inside the mansion without getting slaughtered.

Suddenly, Commander McCollough's giant face stared at him as if through a fish-eye lens, replacing the scene from the simulator.

This must be the man's idea of a practical joke.

Most SEALs liked practical jokes, unless the joke was played on *them.*

"Time's up," McCollough's voice sounded in the earphones of Felix's virtual-reality helmet. "The minisubs to *Challenger* will be ready for us soon."

Felix pulled off the helmet. Underneath, his hair and forehead were drenched in sweat.

He glanced around at what *Ohio*'s SEALs called, with dry irony, the dance floor: the set of treadmills on turntables. His men stood there, panting, their weapons in one hand and their simulator helmets in the other. The team all looked at Felix. He could see that his chiefs felt discouraged.

"Well," Felix said, "maybe this time we would've made it."

Costa and Porto were skeptical. His men stared at the deck, their morale visibly low, which wasn't like them.

"Look sharp!" Felix snapped, showing his displeasure forcefully. "We learned a lot the past few days. Mistakes were corrected and weak habits fixed, so they won't cost us bad when we go with live ammo."

But Felix asked himself a tough question: Did they need more men? Should he convince Commander McCollough to lend him another team for reinforcements?

No. Too many operators on something like this gets too complex and conspicuous. Integrating new guys, doubling the number for whom we need to steal local transport, coordinating a bigger group, and then everybody escape-and-evading to a badly overloaded mini. . . . That's not the answer.

Felix saw the truth, which he knew Captain Fuller and Gerald Parker would like even less than he did.

They needed a human Trojan horse to have the slightest chance of pulling this off. Gamal Salih would have to do much more than just make contact at the consulate and pick up Peapod for a night of partying. Salih, an ethnic Turk who spoke fluent Turkish and German, would have to be the SEALs' shill, right there when they assaulted the German safe house. Even then, from these simulations, the outcome stacked up as iffy.

Felix led his men toward the showers built into a lower part of the first two missile tubes, under the pressure-proof lock-out chambers. They'd tidy up before returning to *Challenger* for the duration of the mission; after days of this practicing with little sleep and even less hygiene, the team smelled like a pack of billy goats.

CHAPTER 22

Jeffrey and Bell sat in Jeffrey's stateroom. It was late afternoon on a Sunday—the Sunday before the Friday that Felix's team, with Gamal Salih, would arrive in the German minisub at Istanbul. The final task-group planning and coordination meetings, held on *Challenger,* were done with, a final rendezvous with *Ohio* in the eastern Atlantic completed. Jeffrey and Parcelli had wrapped it up with a firm handshake, determined expressions on their faces, and wishes of good luck.

But we also knew it might be the last time we saw each other alive.... It's as if we made a contest of it, which of us would outwardly betray less tension or doubt. We were very closely matched. I'd have to call it a draw—we both won.... Not that that changed how we really felt inside.

Among many other items, a set of simplified code words had been agreed on, to supplement the standard list, for the fastest and most unambiguous use of the secure acoustic link, in the special war-fighting conditions the task group might encounter.

Challenger and *Ohio* would stay in a flexible tactical for-

mation, varied on Jeffrey's orders as the situation evolved—
until that fateful moment when Lieutenant Estabo either did
or didn't return with Klaus Mohr and his special equipment,
most likely early on Sunday, a week from now. If things went
well, *Challenger* and *Ohio* wouldn't again conduct a rendezvous to exchange any people before then. The task
group's egress orders for after that remained unopened in
Jeffrey's and Parcelli's safes. Jeffrey had no idea what the orders might say.

At least Gamal Salih welcomed the chance to be more involved in the excursion into Istanbul. Jeffrey knew well from
his previous mission involving Salih, where submarine captain and freedom fighter had bumped into each other under
fire in northern Germany, that the man was very handy with a
pistol or a knife. He had good reasons of his own for craving
vengeance, and the killing of German combatants ran in
Salih's blood as a natural talent.

Right now, a nautical chart showed on Jeffrey's laptop
screen. The place, inside the Med but farthest from land,
which he'd have to try to reach to self-destruct his ship in a
worst-case outcome, was marked on the digital chart by a
red dot.

The dot was an abstraction. The dangers and uncertainties
summarized by its being there were real.

Bell, sitting patiently, followed his gaze.

Jeffrey noticed this, and said, "We'll find out soon what
the Axis ROEs truly are in this theater. If they identify
Dreadnought while she creates a diversion for us using
Texas, and the Germans go nuclear less than two hundred
miles from land, things might turn ugly fast and spread far
and wide from there."

Bell nodded. He was usually much more talkative in private, especially when under stress, when he seemed to like to
verbalize his anxieties. His taciturn conduct emphasized too
clearly that the strategic issues hanging in the balance put this
mission way beyond any situation they'd dealt with before.

Jeffrey thought of Plan Pandora, whatever exactly it was—he still didn't know for sure, and only Klaus Mohr could tell him. He thought of those modern ekranoplans that Russia sold to Germany—the ultimate amphibious-warfare assault craft—and of the land offensive, thrust at Israel, that the Afrika Korps seemed on the verge of launching.

He thought of the Israeli atom bombs planted in Germany, and of Israel's remaining nuclear arsenal, over a hundred warheads at least. Some were deployed on her diesel subs for deterrence. Some were suspected of even being hydrogen bombs.

Jeffrey's intercom light blinked. He grabbed the handset. "Captain."

It was the lieutenant (j.g.) in charge of the radio room. Jeffrey listened. "Very well, Radio."

Jeffrey looked at Bell. "ELF code came through. The *Texas* and *Dreadnought* action starts right after sunset. Our extraction mission for Peapod is on, definitely confirmed."

Bell nodded soberly, but again said nothing.

"You go into Control. *Ohio* should've copied the message themselves, but use the acoustic link to make sure."

Bell stood. "Man battle stations, sir?"

"Not yet. I'll be with you in a minute."

Bell left. Jeffrey sat alone in his stateroom, staring at the chart on the computer screen. The shores of Spain and North Africa converged like the mouth of a funnel. The neck of the funnel, the Strait of Gibraltar itself, was seven nautical miles across at its tightest, and twenty long. The Bay of Gibraltar, now a German naval base, was at the far end of the Strait.

Texas and *Dreadnought* *are approaching from the north-west. They'll be somewhere off Cape Trafalgar soon.*

Jeffrey thought of that great battle fought near Trafalgar, by the UK's Vice Admiral Nelson against a merged French and Spanish fleet, over two hundred years before. Nelson won, but was killed in the battle.

Challenger, with *Ohio* in company, was approaching the

Strait of Gibraltar from the southwest, as prearranged, much closer to Casablanca than Trafalgar.

Jeffrey turned off his laptop. He glanced one last time at the picture of his parents, taped to a bulkhead. He touched the photo gently, and traced the two figures on it longingly with his index finger. He knew how badly it would tear them up if they outlived him, their youngest child, their only son.

He paused to listen to the gentle hushing from the air-circulation vents—soon they'd be turned off for added stealth, to prepare for battle. Jeffrey's senses were heightened, colors appeared more vivid, and he thought he could hear his heart as it beat.

He looked at his hands while he held them out in front of his body. They were perfectly steady, but his fingers felt ice cold. He rubbed them on his pants legs so the friction would warm his palms.

He opened the door to the corridor, and strode into his control room. He stopped near the command console, where an officer from Torelli's weapons department had the conn. Bell already sat at the console, next to the lieutenant (j.g.).

"This is the Captain," Jeffrey announced to everyone in the compartment. "I have the conn."

"Aye aye," the watch standers said. The junior officer got up and Jeffrey took his place. The seat was still warm, and Jeffrey adjusted it to be more comfortable for himself. Satisfied, he projected his voice clearly and evenly.

"Chief of the Watch, sound silent battle stations antisubmarine."

"Silent battle stations, ASW, aye."

COB had found some excuse to kibitz in the control room, inspecting and checking the readings and settings on different equipment, something usually done by a junior crewman. COB immediately took the seat at the ship's control console, as battle-stations chief of the watch.

Jeffrey couldn't help smiling.

"Fire Control, pass the order to *Ohio,* man silent battle stations antisubmarine." Bell was now fire-control coordinator.

Bell repeated the message back to avoid misunderstanding or error, then saw to having it sent.

"*Ohio* acknowledges, sir, manning battle stations ASW."

"Very well, Fire Control." *Parcelli was obviously expecting the word any minute. He'll know what to do from here for a while.* Jeffrey refocused on *Challenger* business.

"Chief of the Watch, rig for ultraquiet."

"Ultraquiet, aye."

COB spoke to the phone talker, who repeated the message, then held down the switch of his sound-powered mike and passed the order around the ship.

"Chief of the Watch, rig for depth charge."

"Rig for depth charge, aye."

As COB and the phone talker ran through their litany again, Lieutenant (j.g.) Meltzer hurried into the control room to relieve the man at the helm.

"*Ohio* has signaled us, Captain," Bell reported. "All stations manned and ready."

Jeffrey glanced at a chronometer. "Acknowledge and tell *Ohio* I say, 'Quick work, well done.'"

Jeffrey windowed the nautical chart, the gravimeter display, and the tactical plot on his console screen. The gravimeter would be most useful as they approached the coasts and the water got shallower.

From a depth now of five thousand feet, the seafloor would quickly slope upward toward the continental shelves of Europe and Africa as they converged. Currents and countercurrents, and tectonic collision and folding, had gouged a notch 2,000 feet deep or more through most of the Strait. But along the western approaches, the water went down only six hundred feet. The deep path through the strait itself was studded with seamounts—extinct undersea volcanoes—rising almost a thousand feet from the bottom.

On the tactical plot, amber icons showed neutral shipping moving in and out of the Strait. Red icons that crossed the plot at greater speed were small Axis surface warships patrolling the waters outside. Aircraft were sometimes detected in the distance, streaking across the sonar waterfall displays like comets or meteors.

Lieutenant Milgrom's technicians identified any new contacts, and Lieutenant Torelli's fire-control technicians tracked them all for the plot. The minefields outside the Strait showed on the tactical plot and the nautical chart. Their positions had to be announced by international law; neutral ocean rovers verified the data.

Jeffrey's greater concern was antisubmarine minefields inside the Strait, ones the Germans might not have announced. *Challenger* and *Ohio* carried remote-controlled probes designed to scout ahead for such hazards, but his intended tactics precluding using them. He was also concerned about bottom sensors, and hydrophone arrays, sprinkled around and stretching across the whole floor of the Strait. Then there was the biggest unknown: the whereabouts and intentions of Russia's *Snow Tiger*.

For all this, and more, Jeffrey's and Parcelli's officers and chiefs had developed careful plans in intensive working sessions each time they'd rendezvoused.

Jeffrey knew from bitter experience how rapidly plans could come undone. He'd seen that the most crucial tactics usually had to be dreamed up on the spot. . . . But doing so, repeatedly, for more than six months with too little leave to rest had begun to deplete him.

Something's missing. I see what it is.

I don't have my usual relish for combat this time—I feel stale and weary.

I'll just have to gut it out. Performing while exhausted is a constant aspect of war, and almost four hundred lives on two vessels depend on me.

Jeffrey spoke again to Bell, but knew everyone in the control room could hear him.

"Now we wait for the sun to go down, then the tide to begin running out. Then the shooting starts, hopefully well northwest of us, near Cape Trafalgar."

CHAPTER 23

Ilse Reebeck sat at the console in her private workroom. It was starting to feel like solitary confinement.

To take a break, she called onto her screen a situation map for the Med, a duplicate of what would loom large now on a wall in the war room, and would also be closely watched by top brass at the Pentagon.

The display showed four Allied nuclear submarines in the eastern North Atlantic, coming in two pairs toward the Strait of Gibraltar. The types of icons used showed that the positions were only estimates, based on prearranged operational plans. The plot didn't name the individual subs, and Ilse hadn't been told what their intentions were. But she assumed that soon at least some of them would try to force their way past Gibraltar and into the Med. She also knew that one of them was *Challenger.*

Part of the map displayed different identified enemy units, all around the Med, belonging to the various branches of the German armed forces. Enemy lines of communications—routes of logistics support—were also shown on the maps, along with known depots and data on their contents. The map showed the array of military units in Egypt and Israel too, dependent for resupply on air transport and the shipping route up through the Red Sea. The map was so large scale that it even reached down to Ethiopia, where the Great Rift Valley formed the northeast flank of the beleaguered Allied pocket in Central Africa—cut off from Egypt by German forces and local auxiliary fighters holding Sudan.

Ilse figured that this picture was assembled from many forms of intelligence, including visual and infrared surveillance, radar, signals intercepts, message decryptions, human-agent reports, plus expert conjecture and surmise at the CIA, the NSA, and the Pentagon's own various intelligence offices. She knew that hundreds of sensor platforms, and thousands of clerks and analysts, were needed to keep the big picture reasonably complete and up to date.

She called up another display that she found even more interesting, though disturbing, an ever-changing collage of visuals from spy satellites and unmanned aerial vehicles. These would zoom in on a crowded harbor in occupied Italy, or a group of German tanks on the move in the Libyan desert, or a rail yard in Greece choked with rolling stock. These pictures made the icons on the tactical plots seem much more concrete. Ilse reminded herself that many millions of people lived in these places, would be involved directly in fighting the war, or would be enveloped by the German surprise onslaught when it started.

The green phone on Ilse's console rang. "Lieutenant Reebeck."

Johansen's yeoman said he was putting through a call from outside the base. The person who got on the line was a lieutenant commander in the Naval Oceanographic Office, a major component of METOC, headquartered at the John C. Stennis Space Center in Mississippi.

"I have something you'll be interested to know," the lieutenant commander told Ilse.

"Yes, ma'am?" The woman was a superior officer; she

spoke with a nasal twang, as if from the upper Midwest, maybe Minnesota.

"Remember that datum you called a slant-wise avalanche?"

"Yes."

"We heard something like it again."

"In the same place?"

"No, not in the same place." The woman sounded like she was smiling, and this put Ilse on her guard.

"Where? Using what platform?"

"In the South Atlantic. In waters we keep a careful eye on these days."

"Ma'am?"

"The Cape Plain." Off the South Africa coast. The woman gave the coordinates.

"Do you want me to study the data?"

"That won't be necessary." Now she sounded vindictive. Ilse didn't like this at all.

"For your information, the datum was detected at a depth of about two thousand feet, with the seafloor there at sixteen thousand feet."

"So it couldn't have been an avalanche."

"Nope. Your analysis was incorrect. As a matter of fact, misleading."

"So what do your people think they were, ma'am? Turbulence between conflicting underwater storm fronts?" The ocean could have major storms down deep, where strong currents formed temporarily, much like high winds blowing over the surface. The currents were just a few knots, but the moving water—much denser than air—carried tremendous energy.

"Either that," the woman said, "or gas seeps spreading sideways at a density discontinuity, or some other natural phenomenon. We're making new discoveries all the time, as you well know."

"Were there tonals?"

"No. There were no tonals. The rest isn't your concern."

"Then why did you phone me?"

"To say we don't appreciate your meddling and ineptitude." The lieutenant commander hung up on Ilse.

Ilse was livid.

She put down the phone, then picked it up again. She wanted to call someone to complain, but realized that that would be childish. Captain Johansen had already told her that politically motivated blame games were intensifying.

A moment later he knocked, then walked into the room.

"You aren't doing too well."

Ilse knew what was coming.

"It seems your technical analysis of that odd flow noise, discredited now, gave the FBI more ammo to use against you in this spy witch-hunt."

"Can't my own embassy do something to get them off my back? It's getting hard for me to work with all these distractions."

"The FBI beat us in getting there. The director talked to the Free South African ambassador in person. The embassy says that when push comes to shove, they're unable to vouch for you. Your being in the U.S. at the time the coups and the war broke out looks bad given everything else. It's too much as if you were put in this country as a sleeper agent."

"But I was here at a conference! I had no idea what would happen back home! If I hadn't gone to the conference, I'd've been teaching at the University of Cape Town and would have been executed right next to my family!"

"That's what the FBI director said you would say."

CHAPTER 24

It was the dead of night in Istanbul that same Sunday. Klaus Mohr struggled to keep his brain divided into three totally separate compartments: scientist, traitor, family man. The first two had to stay active at once, while the third he was forced to hold deeply repressed. This was hard enough, but worse yet, the two active parts of his thoughts contradicted each other. The strain of the constant balancing act was terrible in itself, but also posed the problem that all his scheming might fall apart in front of armed witnesses.

"I don't understand the problem this time," the Kampf-schwimmer lieutenant said. "We did everything the exact same way we always do. We checked the connections over and over." His team of seven men nodded. Their eyes looked tired, but their bodies held coiled energy, like panthers. Their leader, the lieutenant, like the others was tall and trim and very fit. He had a hooked, pointy nose, and very thin lips, which made his already gaunt face seem more pinched. "We know we drew a good load for the power supply. I thought the ammeter was faulty, but the cables we tapped were live, they sparked."

Mohr took a deep breath. The Kampfschwimmer all smelled of sweat and sewage, though they'd washed well enough for sanitary purposes. The room held a permanent, stale cooking odor, like rancid grease and strange spices, left over from the previous tenant. Mohr pretended to feel frustrated, as he should have been under these circumstances in his role as a scientist. This part of his act was effective, because his frustration as hopeful defector was vivid enough.

Klaus Mohr was meeting with the Kampfschwimmer field team in a Plan Pandora safe house. Blackout curtains were drawn, and the lighting in the small room was dim. Istanbul, an open, neutral city, had no wartime blackout, but the curtains were essential for security. The furnishings that came with the rented building were sparse, so some of the commandos squatted or sat on the floor, with their submachine guns worn on shoulder straps or cradled on their thighs. Other Kampfschwimmer were elsewhere, inside or outdoors Mohr didn't know, standing guard. Mohr himself slumped in an easy chair whose stuffing poked through tears in its back. The lieutenant sat on a metal kitchen stool that creaked as he moved. Between them, as the center of attention on the rugless worn wooden floor, was the portable quantum-computer equipment. The commandos had just returned from a test. Their test had failed, as Mohr intended. He'd set the equipment out of calibration intentionally.

Klaus Mohr had to act like he was surprised by the problem and badly wanted to fix it. Otherwise, his cover would be blown. From his meeting with that Pakistani last week, Awais Iqbal, Mohr knew he needed to stall until Friday, then hold another meeting like this or his entire plan would come unglued.

Mohr had no illusions now: The device he'd created was a new type of weapon of mass destruction.

He'd received permission from his bosses to attend the party on Friday. He needed to tread very carefully so the permission didn't get yanked when he announced the need for another field test, back-to-back with Iqbal's affair. The waiting was taking a toll on Mohr's nerves. *Five more days.* Each day heightened the chances that Mohr's arrangements for defecting would be found out.

"Everything worked fine last time," the lieutenant said, trying to be helpful, sounding puzzled both at the equipment trouble and also at Mohr's blank stare; Mohr snapped out of his introspection. "The systems crashed just like they should have." The lieutenant laughed. "Total chaos at the Izmir airport for a few hours, till we let them come back up. But this time, at Zonguldak? Cell phones, bank machines, nothing." Izmir lay on Turkey's southwest coast; Zonguldak faced the Black Sea.

Mohr nodded, distracted. His feelings of remorse at having to turn against his own country grew stronger constantly. His sense of grief and regret at abandoning his family, and his worry that they'd be punished despite his best efforts to distance himself from them, weighed on him every morning like a boulder squashing his chest. This was the part of his mind he needed desperately to wall off.

He also had another difficult task because of Iqbal. He'd need to describe the layout and defenses of this safe house to his rescuers, in the greatest detail possible. This made him view his surroundings in a whole new way.

Mohr tried to memorize the floor plan and physical arrangements. He tried to gauge the thicknesses of the walls, interior and exterior. He wondered if the floors were thick enough to stop soft-nosed bullets. He wondered if there was an easy way down and inside from the roof.

"Herr Doctor Mohr?" The lieutenant had caught his mind wandering again.

"I was thinking," Mohr responded, which was true. He pretended to be annoyed with the Kampfschwimmer. "I'll need to check through everything carefully. Break each module down, go through systems integration step by step, troubleshoot."

"How long will it take to fix the gear?"

"I can't even guess till I figure out what's wrong."

"What should we do, then?"

"I'll have to stay here awhile, to work."

"Thank you. Should I have one of my men inform the consulate?"

Mohr's driver and bodyguard, who'd dropped him off near the safe house, would be staying on the move through the streets—parking might attract the wrong attention.

Mohr nodded to the lieutenant, and the lieutenant passed an order to one of the enlisted men, who left.

"Maybe we should get some sleep, sir," the lieutenant said. "It's very late. I can use the couch. I've slept on much more uncomfortable things. You can borrow my bed. It has the best mattress and pillows."

"First help me bring the equipment to the clean room. I want to examine a couple of items. Then sleeping sounds like a good idea."

"Jawohl, Herr Doctor."

Mohr and the commandos stood. Some hefted the equipment modules. They climbed a flight of stairs and came to one room whose ceiling and walls were completely covered with transparent plastic sheets held on with brown duct tape. More of the plastic sheets, like curtains, hung across the only way in, to keep out dust. This was the improvised clean room. Through the plastic, Mohr could see the table with tools and instruments where he'd tinkered with the equipment before.

"Leave these outside. You're all too dirty."

The lieutenant apologized. "We had to get to some rather inaccessible places."

"I'll take them from here. I don't need you or your men now." Mohr tried to sound imperious, arrogant. Then it occurred to him that if the Americans did assault this building and won, he was talking to a dead man. *Is he close to his parents? Married? Does he miss his wife and kids? . . . Will they miss him?*

Mohr cleaned off the module cases in the hallway. The

commandos went into other parts of the house. He assumed that, as usual, they'd rotate through security watches while the remainder of the team slept.

Klaus Mohr lifted the first module with both hands, and slipped through the curtains into the clean room.

The high-capacity photon quantum-entanglement unit. How I wish to God I'd never invented the thing.

———

Jeffrey fretted, pacing in the aisle in *Challenger*'s control room. With the fans turned off for greater stealth, and twenty-plus people squeezed into the compartment, the air tasted increasingly stuffy. It was also getting uncomfortably warm from all the electronics running, even with the water outside the hull at a cold fifty-five degrees Fahrenheit. The lighting was nighttime red, and Jeffrey's eyes were well adapted by now.

COB and Meltzer sat at their ship control stations with little to do. Jeffrey had his task group in a holding position, drifting silently with the tidal currents, being pulled slowly away from the mouth of the Strait.

He glanced at a chronometer on a bulkhead. "Two hours late. We should've heard something." He was talking mostly to himself.

"They may have a problem on *Dreadnought,* Captain," Bell said, "like releasing *Texas* from the tow."

Jeffrey grunted. "If it's bad enough, it could take them all night. That's even assuming *Dreadnought* got to her proper place on time."

"No change in pattern of enemy antisubmarine patrols, sir."

Jeffrey almost snapped at Bell. He could see for himself exactly what was or wasn't happening, just by looking at the tactical plot. But Bell, as fire-control coordinator, was doing his job, giving Jeffrey regular updates.

"Very well, Fire Control."

Much more of a delay and they'd lose the wrong-way tide

Jeffrey wanted, and they'd also be forced to cross the deep Alboran Basin just inside the Strait in broad daylight.

On the sonar speakers, Jeffrey heard the churning, swishing noises of surface craft, enemy and neutral, all tracked on the tactical plot. He paced some more, and kept peering at the chronometer as it ticked away each second, on and on.

He heard a sound like distant, rolling thunder.

"Loud explosion bearing three-two-five," Milgrom shouted. "Underwater explosion, nonnuclear, range one hundred thousand yards!"

Northwest, fifty miles. Exactly where it should be. Jeffrey rushed to his seat and buckled in. "Fire Control, signal *Ohio:* Get under way, formation for passage through Strait."

CHAPTER 25

*C*hallenger and *Ohio* began to approach the Strait of Gibraltar. For now they made ten knots, the fastest they dared go here if they hoped to retain their stealth, to try to beat the clock on the all-important changing tides. Challenger's eight torpedo tubes held six high-explosive ADCAPs and two brilliant decoys. *Ohio*'s four tubes held three ADCAPs and one decoy.

Ohio's twenty-four eight-foot-diameter missile tubes bristled like an underwater battleship's big guns. Her dozens of SEALs were geared up for action, with both of her ASDS minisubs already loaded and ready to deploy on a moment's notice to harass the nearby African coast if needed; more SEALs could lock directly out of the ship in scuba very quickly. *Ohio*'s hundred-plus Tomahawks would already be programmed for targets on land or at sea that might threaten Jeffrey's task group. The silo containing *Ohio*'s forty-two Polyphem missiles had its top hatch open, to ripple-fire immediately at anything in the air that could drop torpedoes, depth charges, or sonobuoys within dangerous range of herself and *Challenger*.

Ohio's crew and SEAL company were set on a hairpin trigger. All Parcelli and McCollough needed were acoustic-link orders from Jeffrey. The mouth of the Strait loomed closer by the minute.

But if we do have to open fire, our goose is cooked. At this of all places we must *stay invisible. The prearranged diversion by* Dreadnought *and* Texas *simply* has *to work.*

Jeffrey kept his focus roving between the displays on his console and the crew sitting or standing all around him in the control room. High tension and anxiety were visible on faces and in body language. COB's and Meltzer's necks and shoulders seemed unnaturally stiff as they sat with their backs to Jeffrey, steering the ship and controlling her buoyancy. Some crewmen had growing crescents of sweat around their underarms. Others used pieces of toilet paper, kept handy for cleaning their touch screens, to dab at their foreheads instead. A few of the newer people endlessly squirmed in their seats, or gripped their armrests much too hard. One youngster started to wipe his console screen repeatedly, compulsively, causing a pile of wadded tissue to accumulate on the deck—until a senior chief squeezed his elbow and whispered reassuring words.

The inner effects of fear and worry, or excitement and battle lust, that people around him were feeling, Jeffrey was unable to see. Thoughts of home and family, prayers, grim determination, or daydreams of valor and glory? He could only guess. Tightened chests, churning stomachs, cramping intestines, these he imagined all too well from how his own body protested.

Jeffrey knew he had to say something, do something, for himself and for everyone else.

"Chief of the Watch," Jeffrey ordered in as calm and routine a tone as he could muster, "put gravimeter display and tactical plot on all periscope-imagery monitors."

COB acknowledged. The unused, darkened screens around the control room came alive.

Now at least they all saw what Jeffrey saw. He couldn't make the risks and the burdens any less than they truly were, but he could make this gesture of sharing. Sharing the one thing that, as warriors with no turning back now, they'd crave the most: information, situational awareness, the big picture of what was going on outside the hull and beyond the narrow horizons of their individual consoles.

The gravimeter showed the shorelines of occupied Morocco and Spain. It showed the hills and mountains beyond, and the folds and humps and pillars in the seafloor under the water. It showed Morocco and Spain getting closer and closer together, and the water ahead getting shallower.

Another distant rumble sounded over the sonar speakers.

"Loud explosion bearing three-two-five," Milgrom reported, "non-nuclear, range ninety thousand yards." Closer than the previous blast; Milgrom's voice was controlled, but subdued.

"Captain," Bell said, "enemy platforms converging on site of explosions."

Jeffrey watched the tactical plot on his screen. Crewmen without the same data on their consoles glanced at the monitors very briefly, when they dared shift their gazes from fixating on their own displays.

German airplanes and helos were dashing to join the escalating fight between their brethren on the one hand, and *Dreadnought* and *Texas* on the other. Enemy surface warships went to flank speed, and headed northwest like the aircraft. Merchant shipping altered course to stay well clear.

"Sonar, status of any submerged contacts to northwest?"

"No submerged contacts held, sir."

It was too far, and *Dreadnought* and the sacrificial hulk of the semi-salvaged *Texas* were too quiet. Jeffrey knew he'd asked a dumb, impatient question: New contacts were always reported immediately, without prompting from him.

"Nature of detonations?"

"No torpedo engines detected yet. Conjecture weapons expended were Axis mines or depth bombs."

"Very well, Sonar." *Did Dreadnought use an off-board probe to set off a mine on purpose? A faked blunder to draw attention, as was her job?*

Jeffrey hated not knowing what was happening with the two Allied submarines forty-five miles away. "Fire Control, status of communications with *Ohio?*"

"Acoustic-link carrier waves still open in both directions, sir."

Jeffrey's task group was keeping in formation with each other, and maintaining a sonar signature with as few changes as possible, by sending a steady stream of random numbers through the low-probability-of-intercept acoustic link. The transmissions served as navigation beacons or running lights that—hopefully—only the task group units could hear, and that neither unit would lose.

"Sir," Milgrom called out, "aspect change on Master Fourtwo." Master 42 was a passive sonar contact held on the bow sphere and the port wide-aperture array. She was a German antisubmarine frigate, of the modern *Brandenburg* class. "Master Four-two relative bearing now constant, signal strength increasing."

"Master Four-two is approaching us, sir," Bell reported.

"Blade-rate increase on Master Four-two," Milgrom said. "Flank-speed blade rate, sir!"

The tactical plot showed the Brandenburg accelerating toward thirty knots—faster than *Challenger* dared go because she'd be too noisy, and faster than *Ohio* could possibly go. The frigate, a formidable type of warship somewhat smaller than a destroyer, was coming from west-northwest, pinning Jeffrey's task group against the African shore. She was only twenty nautical miles away, closing fast, and she carried four torpedo tubes and a pair of Super Lynx sub-hunting helos.

Jeffrey regretted having put the tactical plot on the unused periscope monitors: A shock wave of consternation ran through the control-room crew, more than would have been the case without all those reminders of the peril that was increasing for *Challenger* and *Ohio* every moment.

Barely at the portal to the Strait, and already we're detected and trapped.

As if to foreshadow their doom, another loud explosion sounded in the distance, and Milgrom reported Axis torpedo engine noises near where *Texas* and *Dreadnought* would be.

"Captain," Bell said, interrupting Jeffrey's thoughts, "*Ohio* signals, 'What are your intentions regarding Brandenburg?' "

"Signal *Ohio,* 'Steady as you go.' "

Bell looked surprised, but repeated the message aloud and then had it sent. Parcelli acknowledged.

Milgrom reported more explosions in the distance, and Allied as well as Axis torpedo-engine sounds.

The Brandenburg was still closing.

As the reverb from the distant torpedo warheads died away, Milgrom reported two airborne contacts approaching at over a hundred knots.

The Brandenburg's sub-hunter helos, working as a team, just like in our own standard doctrine.

"Contact on acoustic intercept," Milgrom almost shouted. She steadied herself. "Axis air-dropped active sonobuoys."

"Close enough to detect us?" Jeffrey demanded. He couldn't hear them on the speakers.

"Not yet, sir. But helo search pattern developing suggests high risk of detection at their closest point of approach."

"Sir," Bell said, "*Ohio* signaling, 'Repeat, Flagship, what are your intentions?' "

"Fire Control, reply to *Ohio,* 'Repeat, steady as you go.' "

"Sir," Bell objected, "you heard what Sonar said, they'll be on top of us any minute."

"Send the message to *Ohio* as I dictated."

Bell acknowledged, and then Parcelli acknowledged receipt.

"Listen up, people," Jeffrey said. "We don't know for sure that the Brandenburg knows we're here. The Axis might just be checking this area in case the two Allied subs they're fighting off Trafalgar are a diversion."

"But, sir, that means the diversion failed."

"No, XO, it means the Axis aren't stupid. We'll have to make a mini-diversion of our own and hope our stealth holds up."

"Captain?" Bell was obviously confused.

"They're working hard to make a contact on any Allied sub or subs near Morocco, correct? Let's satisfy their appetite. Give them something to detect."

"Sir?"

"Fire Control," Jeffrey snapped, "program brilliant decoy in tube seven to sound like HMS *Dreadnought*." Jeffrey studied the tactical plot, and weighed the range and speed of the Brandenburg and her two helos. The picture was kinetic, dynamic, making it very hard to project ahead.

"Captain," Bell said, *"Dreadnought* is presumed detected well northwest. Enemy will know our decoy is a decoy."

"Exactly. Have decoy run at stealthy speed due north for five minutes." For Jeffrey's trick to work, he couldn't rush it, but five minutes was cutting things close. "Then have decoy go to *Dreadnought*'s flank speed on course zero-eight-zero." Toward the mouth of the Straits; the real *Dreadnought* was as fast as *Challenger.*

Lieutenant Torelli's weapons-system specialists went to work. He downloaded the full acoustic profile of *Dreadnought* from Milgrom's people, from their huge database of different vessels' signatures. The brilliant decoy was programmed.

"Fire Control, Weps," Torelli reported. "Decoy ready."

"Decoy ready, aye," Bell said. "Captain, decoy ready."

"Decoy ready, aye. Firing-point procedures, decoy in tube seven."

Bell and Torelli began reciting orders and acknowledgments and status reports.

"New contacts on acoustic intercept," Milgrom said. Her voice was an octave lower than the first time they'd been pinged, but now she was gritting her teeth. "Air-dropped active sonobuoys, much nearer to *Challenger* task group."

This is going to be tight.

"Fire Control, make tube seven ready in all respects, including opening outer door."

Bell acknowledged and passed orders down the line. Torelli announced when tube seven was flooded and equalized and the outer door was open.

"Tube seven, *shoot.*"

"Tube seven fired electrically," Torelli said.

"Unit is running normally," Milgrom said

"Five minutes till that decoy starts making a racket," Jeffrey thought out loud. *Five minutes in which either helo's sonobuoys, or their dipping sonars, might find us.*

"Signal from *Ohio,*" Bell said. " 'Decoy will reveal task group's presence.' "

"Signal *Ohio,* 'Message received. Steady as you go.' "

"But—"

"Send it, XO."

Bell did as he was told.

Jeffrey glanced at a chronometer. *Still four minutes before the decoy starts to get rambunctious, as its built-in active sound emitters give off conspicuous noise.*

Enemy sonobuoy pings began to be audible over the sonar speakers.

"Attempting to suppress hull echoes," Milgrom stated. Using active out-of-phase emissions.

"Don't attempt," Jeffrey told her. "Do it."

"Sonar, aye."

Now Jeffrey could hear, fading in and out, the roar of helo engine turbines and the clatter of their rotor blades.

We're dead ducks if they find us.

He looked again at the tactical plot and the chronometer. It was a race against time, and a test of each side's technology and tactics, whether the sonobuoys would see through *Challenger*'s and *Ohio*'s acoustic masking before the brilliant decoy kicked in.

Jeffrey's people were all on the edge of their seats. The

control-room air was stifling from so many overstressed bodies packed so close. For now, there was nothing they could do but wait. A few of them were so sweat soaked that Jeffrey was concerned they'd become dehydrated. There were nervous coughs from dry throats, stifled desperately to maintain ultraquiet.

Suddenly, pings came very close—some of the crew were jolted in their seats. There were also distant explosions, as other German forces battled with *Dreadnought*. Milgrom made her usual announcements, and gave assessments. Underneath her impressive self-control, Jeffrey knew she had to be very worried for the safety of her Royal Navy friends.

Inside his own control room, Jeffrey saw that a few men's hands were trembling. The phone talker and some others with not enough to keep themselves busy stared at the overhead in abject fear, as if waiting for a depth charge or a torpedo from a helo to be dropped right down their throat—inside the arming radius of *Challenger*'s antitorpedo rockets, and coming at a very unfavorable angle for using noisemakers. Jeffrey sympathized with how they felt. He had to force himself to not rock back and forth in his seat with his fists clenched, as if to physically urge his decoy to do its thing soon and do it well. The Brandenburg was still charging in their direction.

And I'm sure she has torpedoes in each of her tubes, to add to the punch of her helos.

There was a series of *booms* due north, close in. People who didn't realize what they were looked terrified. A roaring, throbbing, whining noise rose in strength very quickly. The roaring got deeper, the throbbing got faster, and the whining rose in pitch.

"That's our decoy," Jeffrey announced before Milgrom could report it. "Faked reactor-coolant check valves slamming open, boom boom boom. Then phantom *Dreadnought* going to flank speed."

The sound of the decoy competed with ever-closer and louder enemy sonobuoys.

Then the helo engines and rotor blades also changed in strength and pitch.

"They're going after the decoy," Jeffrey said, with self-satisfaction that he hammed up intentionally for his crew. "They know it's not *Dreadnought* herself. They think it's a decoy she launched a while ago to create a diversion at extreme range."

Bell finally understood. He grinned. "Since she wouldn't create a diversion right next to other Allied submarines, they think there aren't any Allied subs in this local area."

There were splashes over the sonar speakers, then shattering concussions came through the water. This time, as the reverb and vibrations diminished, Jeffrey could only hear the enemy helos, receding.

"Assess our decoy destroyed by depth charges," Bell announced.

"Aspect change on Master Four-two," Milgrom called out. Now it sounded like she was trying to suppress a smile. "Bearing drift is left. Assess Master Four-two in tight turn, maintaining flank speed."

"She doesn't want to miss the tail end of the fun with *Dreadnought* and *Texas*," Jeffrey said. Soon Bell confirmed that Master Four-two had steadied on a course for Cape Trafalgar.

Jeffrey listened to the echoes and rumbles outside. Some were from the nearby depth charges the helos had dropped out of spite, to kill the decoy. Some came from the much more serious battle in which *Texas* was supposed to die, but from which the real *Dreadnought* was meant to escape, back into the Atlantic—repulsed from trying to enter the Strait of Gibraltar.

"Signal from *Ohio,* sir: 'That was hairy, but I'm impressed.'"

"Fire Control, make signal to *Ohio:* 'Maintain formation, increase speed to thirteen knots.'"

CHAPTER 26

With the fans switched off, the air shipwide was getting very dank. In *Challenger*'s hushed control room, Jeffrey and Bell gripped their armrests. Their knuckles were clenched almost bloodless, not so much from fear—though there were plenty of reasons for fear—as from the need to brace themselves in their seats. *Challenger* shimmied, plunged and rose and fishtailed. The ride was never this rough at such a modest speed when the ship was out in the open ocean and nicely submerged. But *Challenger* wasn't in the open ocean. Jeffrey's displays told him so, and his crew's intensely careful work reemphasized the point. They were inside the Strait of Gibraltar.

At the digital-navigation plotting table, Lieutenant Sessions and his team were standing, bent over their main horizontal display. They swayed clumsily as the deck pitched and rolled, with no predictable rhythm they could use to anticipate which way the ship would act next.

As *Challenger* made an especially violent sudden drop, and then rose like an elevator, Jeffrey gave thanks for this turbulence. His task group was following their entry plan for the

Med; its keystone was to do the last thing the Axis expected. This was why Jeffrey was fighting the outgoing tide.

Most of the Mediterranean Sea had very little tidal range; from low to high was only a foot—almost nothing. But the Strait of Gibraltar was different. The tides through the narrow gap ran very strong.

The wind-driven prevailing surface current flowed into the Med from the Atlantic. The surface current was offset by another one underneath. This balancing countercurrent flowed steadily outward, from the Med toward the Atlantic.

When the tide flowed into the Med, it intensified the inward prevailing surface current's speed. *This is what any sailor would expect; it's common sense.*

But when the tide flowed out of the Med, peculiar things happened. At shallower depth, the outflow would be strong along both shorelines of the Strait. Yet in the middle of the Strait, contradicting the outgoing tide, the water down to about 150 feet still flowed inward. All these different currents and tides could run as powerfully as four knots.

When water at one temperature and with one salinity level flowed one way, and adjacent water at a different temperature and salinity flowed the opposite way, extremely chaotic eddies and gyres resulted. This badly garbled local sound propagation. And the outward tide ran at a different speed from the deep, outgoing current; where they touched, one sliding over the other, fluid shear and friction made acoustic conditions even worse.

The sonar speakers confirmed what Jeffrey knew. The gurgling, swishing sounds picked up from all around were uneven, jagged, unsettling. They were much louder than *Challenger*'s or *Ohio*'s flow noise would ever be at this speed.

Jeffrey's task group was using this. Instead of riding an incoming tide—with the ship's propulsion very slow for total quieting, an old submariner trick—*Challenger* and *Ohio* followed a route through the maximum turbulence ever available here. They hugged the southern boundary between the outgoing tide and the incoming shallow current, at the depth where the outgoing deep countercurrent began. Water to port ran westward. Water to starboard ran east. Colder, saltier water beneath the keel ran westward too, but not as fast.

Jeffrey was depending on this turbulence for acoustic concealment. It gave him and Parcelli a fighting chance to be missed by Axis hydrophones of many different varieties, on guard for movement through the Strait by Allied subs.

And staying relatively shallow, but not too shallow, provides several other benefits—though the effect on our odds of survival is rather mixed.

Both subs were below the keels of all but the deepest-draft surface ships; laden supertankers could reach down over 100 feet. Supertankers inbound here should be empty except for ballast, and riding high. It was the outbound ones full of oil, heading from the Middle East to neutral countries like Sweden or Finland, that were accidental submarine killers. By keeping to the south in the Strait, Jeffrey intentionally stayed at the edge of the inbound lane of the shipping traffic-separation scheme. But merchant mariners were notorious for sloppy navigation and for ignoring the rules of the road. Anything could happen.

Then there was the problem of mines. There weren't supposed to be any in the Strait itself, and the surface traffic in front of the task group served willy-nilly as minesweepers. But a moored mine somewhere in the Med—or protecting the Axis fortress at Gibraltar—might have broken loose and drifted into their path, without being set off for them by some unfortunate merchie. *Challenger* and *Ohio* had off-board probes designed to hunt for mines, but these couldn't be deployed. They were too slow to keep up with their parent subs at thirteen knots, and their active sonars wouldn't work well in such acoustic turbulence—while any pings from them could betray the task group's presence.

It occurred to Jeffrey that the Axis had probes and military ocean rovers too. *Ohio* or *Challenger* might crash into one and suffer serious damage. The noise of the crash could be loud enough to get noticed. The loss of signals from their probe would surely alert the enemy to investigate more closely—that was the whole point of using rovers for ASW patrols, and of cultivating an ASW commander's mind-set of vigilant paranoia.

And while cruising at only 150 feet with their sonars underperforming, an enemy helo with dipping LIDAR might see *Challenger*'s or *Ohio*'s hull before they had any chance to react and defend themselves.

Milgrom announced another surface contact on the bow sphere. Since this new contact was ahead of them, it was slow: *Challenger* was overtaking.

Jeffrey watched the contact icon pop onto the tactical plot. The icon indicated an unknown vessel type and nationality. Jeffrey didn't like this.

Milgrom's people identified the vessel as a merchant ship.

The icon was updated. Jeffrey began to hear the ship on the speakers. Her screws swished and churned in a manner different from the current-boundary turbulence. She hissed and pounded as her hull cut through the water and met each swell. Then Jeffrey could hear mechanical growling and throbbing from the big diesel engines that modern merchants used instead of steam, and he listened to the humming of her auxiliary machinery. The sounds died abruptly in *Challenger*'s baffles.

The way that ship's noise stopped so suddenly reminded Jeffrey of one of his other tactical problems. Because of the close proximity of Jeffrey's and Parcelli's subs, plus the bad sonar conditions and the vicious eddies and gyres, only *Ohio,* aft of *Challenger,* trailed a towed array. To avoid leaving the area of highest water disturbance—and thus become more exposed—neither sub would circle to do a baffles check in the Strait.

Challenger was blind to her stern, with *Ohio* acting as Jeffrey's seeing-eye dog. They would learn soon the hard way if he'd made a wrong decision on this. *Ohio*'s towed array wouldn't work well in such troubled waters, and might

even snap or be cut at its root by her screw as *Ohio* dipped
and bucked. Plus, when she did make a detection, she needed
to send Jeffrey a report via the acoustic link—which could go
out at any time.

Long minutes passed. A German destroyer went by from
behind, heading inward, then another, presumably returning
from the engagement with *Dreadnought* and *Texas*. Their
hull-mounted active sonars pinged, setting Jeffrey's every
nerve on fire. The Germans acted as if they didn't notice him,
but that might be a trick, to lure his task group farther in to be
bottled up and clobbered. Military aircraft overflights were
detected faintly; no incoming weapons materialized, at least
not yet.

"Enemy's Gibraltar base off our port bow," Sessions announced. "Closest point of approach in ten minutes."

Jeffrey and his crew hunkered down. Gibraltar sat on the
north side at the inner end of the Strait, its famous Rock on a
long peninsula enclosing the massively defended harbor
within a bay. Parcelli's weapons officer would have his giant
battery of Tomahawks pretargeted at Gibraltar now. In an
emergency, the task group might wreak enough havoc to battle their way back to the Atlantic—or go down in a blaze of
useless glory. The air in the control room kept getting stuffier
and stuffier.

CHAPTER 27

Fresh from a full meal and a catnap, Egon Schneider exercised his privilege as captain of *Grand Admiral Doenitz* and took a long, hot shower. So far, he was satisfied with the performance of his new ship and his crew.

He dressed in a black jumpsuit and seaboots, and strode into his control room. A junior officer had the conn. Schneider's einzvo, Manfred Knipp, kept an eye on things. Schneider read different displays, to update himself on the overall situation.

"I have the conn," he announced. Acknowledgments were duly made, the junior officer vacated his seat, and Schneider sat down at the command console. The control-room lighting was red; it was nighttime on the surface.

Schneider's trip through the whole South Atlantic Ocean at sixty knots had gone well. *Doenitz*'s sonar men performed repeated self-noise checks using the arrays mounted along the hull. The special superquiet cladding materials layered around the propulsion system's various components suppressed the flank-speed tonals beautifully. To slow once he reached his station outside Durban, Schneider ordered all machinery to suddenly be turned off. He kept the temperature in both reactors just high enough to prevent the liquid-metal coolant from solidifying.

Nice to not have to worry about any signature from the coolant pumps. With no moving parts, the electromagnetic pumps emitted no decibels at all. Schneider drew electricity temporarily from *Doenitz*'s massive battery banks. The ship glided to a halt making nothing but flow noise. Then he ordered a patrol speed of three knots, with the turbogenerators back on line. This was enough to let his crew maintain control on the planes and the rudder, and was also enough to let him trail a towed array and recharge his batteries.

Schneider glanced again at his gravimeter display. He liked this setup a lot. The continental shelf by Durban, facing the Indian Ocean on South Africa's east coast, was very narrow. Only fifty sea miles offshore, the bottom dropped to two thousand meters and then kept going deeper. Before reaching the rises of the Agulhas Plateau to the south, or the Mozambique Plateau to the east, the depth reached three thousand meters—ten thousand feet—and then four thousand plus.

Genuine blue water. Ideal for antisubmarine work.

Manfred Knipp came over. "Respectfully, Captain. Your intentions?"

"No change, Einzvo." Schneider had taken the conn merely to keep his hand in. He felt no need to justify himself. "Jawohl."

Schneider eyed the tactical plot. "I see those two *Los Angeles*–class boats are still keeping their close blockade on the port."

Ernst Beck's damaged *von Scheer* was being repaired in the hardened underground sub pens dug into the bluff that formed one side of Durban Bay. The whole top of the bluff was crammed with internment camps for American and British businesspeople and tourist families—including hundreds of children—to discourage attack before the *von Scheer* put to sea. The human shields had all been corralled from South Africa and the countries to her north when the war broke out.

"No indication either Los Angeles unit detected us, sir."

"Not surprising," Schneider said dryly.

He had ordered *Doenitz* into a racetrack search pattern, a long oval, moving back and forth along the coast farther out than the two old American subs. He expected that the high-value targets the Allies would use in this blockade, *Seawolf* or her sister ship *Connecticut,* and *Challenger* or even *Dreadnought,* would also establish a more distant blockade. The Seawolfs had very strong and thick steel hulls, which let them dive much deeper than a *Los Angeles* or a *Virginia* class. They also had more torpedo tubes, and a substantially higher flank speed.

My advantage is, I can move slowly, since I'm already in position where the American vessels will want to be. To get here with reasonable promptness, they need to move much faster than three knots. . . . I'll be quieter and my hydrophones will have better sensitivity. Sonar superiority, *that's the key to victory in any sub-on-sub battle.*

Now it was just a question of continuing to patrol, and waiting—and pretending to be a snooping Russian submarine if a low-value Allied unit somehow came within its own detection range of *Doenitz* before Schneider's sonar men heard it, so he could evade. The Boers had been warned that a Russian nuclear sub was in the area, doing espionage on the U.S./UK blockade of *von Scheer.* This prevented a friendly fire accident, and maintained the subterfuge that Schneider's ship was a Russian 868U, not a German one.

At the moment, *Doenitz* was heading southwest, paralleling the coastline on the inshore leg of the racetrack search pattern. The Agulhas Current ran at this depth, one thousand meters, at about three knots. Combined with Schneider's speed, this let him cover more ground over the seafloor every hour. He'd chosen to make the offshore leg of the oval be the one that went back northeast, because well away from the coast the current was weaker, and worked against his progress less.

Schneider's intercom light blinked. It was the communications officer, a junior lieutenant in charge in the radio room: *Doenitz* received a code block through her on-hull ELF antenna, saying Schneider had to prepare to receive a message through the secure undersea acoustic transmitter the Boers had installed in the deep Transkei Basin with help from Imperial Germany.

"Navigator, give me a course to aim our starboard wide-aperture array at the Transkei Basin."

"One-one-five, Captain."

"Pilot, rudder starboard five degrees, steer one-one-five."

The pilot acknowledged. *Doenitz* turned.

This is irregular. Why are the Boers sending me a message?

The bottom-emplaced transmitter system had much greater range than the sub-to-sub covert acoustic link that Schneider was more familiar with using. He waited for the message to be received.

Eventually, the communications officer decoded the header. It said the rest of the text was in Schneider's personal captain-only code.

So the Boers relayed it, without being able to read it.
Good.

"Pass the message to my cabin."

Schneider next addressed the junior officer who'd had the conn before. He'd remained in the control room, standing in the aisle, because he still was officer of the deck for this watch. Schneider told the young man to take the conn, and get back on course for the racetrack patrol.

Schneider went into his cabin and locked the door. He used his private passwords and top-secret software to decode the message. After he read it, he used the intercom to summon Knipp.

The einzvo knocked on his door in a moment—both men's cabins were only a few paces aft of the control room.

"Sit."

Knipp did what he was told.

"It seems the high command's priorities are changing."

"Sir?"

"They plan a new offensive soon, eastward, by the Afrika Korps. That's all the message indicates, nothing about its objectives, but I assume it's been planned for a while."

"After the battle for the Central Africa pocket?"

This struck a raw nerve in Schneider. That battle was the one where Beck had commanded *von Scheer* and had not done well.

"The relevant thing for us is that Berlin suspects the Allies have seen the logistic movements preparatory to this offensive, and they might intend a spoiling attack."

"To break up the offensive before it builds any momentum? Does the message say how?"

"Allied carrier groups, with their escorting submarines, are expected to stop protecting the shipping lanes from the Persian Gulf to the Pacific, and make a sudden lunge toward the Arabian Sea instead. This would get their aircraft and cruise missiles within striking range of our army's line of advance through Egypt and Israel. We're ordered to break off our patrol here and proceed at once to the Arabian Sea, and be ready to engage those submarines and carriers. At our discretion, we can enter the Red Sea as well. Further information on enemy naval movements, and permission for us to open fire, will be sent by ELF."

"Understood, sir."

"Since time is of the essence, we'll need to head north at flank speed. This means we need to find terrain that's shallow enough to mask us as we accelerate."

"Jawohl."

Schneider grabbed his laptop angrily. He called up a nautical chart. "We'll head through the Mozambique Channel." Between the huge island of Madagascar, and Africa. "Plenty of seamounts and shoals there to hide us while we're noisy."

"Understood, sir."

"Tell the navigator to work out a course."

"Speed, sir?"

"Twenty knots. We'll be stealthy enough, and that should put us at the start of the Mozambique Channel in one day."

"Understood."

"Dismissed."

Knipp left Schneider's cabin.

Schneider called up a larger-scale nautical chart. This one showed the whole east coast of Africa, and the western part of the Indian Ocean, as far north as the Arabian Sea.

Once we achieve flank speed, it's a few thousand miles to my new destination. Another three or four days. Enough time to think up good tactics. But not enough time to get back here before Challenger *arrives and* von Scheer *sails. Whichever way that rematch goes, I'll never gain command of* von Scheer *now.*

Schneider stared at the nautical chart and cursed.

CHAPTER 28

Late Tuesday morning, toward the end of his regular office hours as a trade attaché, Klaus Mohr hung up from a puzzling phone call. He sat at his desk and brooded. Traffic noise coming through the open window broke in on his thoughts. A muezzin called the faithful to noon prayer from loudspeakers on the minaret of a nearby mosque. As if in counterpoint, radios and disk players outside blared as each passed by, in cars or held by pedestrians, an ever-changing mix of Western and Turkish and Arabic music that ebbed and flowed in exotic dissonance.

The musical dissonance, and the tug-of-war between theological and secular, seemed to Mohr to reflect his own mental state.

The phone call had left him concerned and confused. The voice was pleasant, female, young, and spoke German with a Pakistani accent. She'd told Mohr she was a secretary at Awais Iqbal's company. Mr. Iqbal sent apologies that he wouldn't be able to make the party Friday night; an export-import deal abroad had hit some snags. Instead, one of his local friends would pick Mohr up, with the same arrangements as before. The new person would be Turkish, and unlike Iqbal, he spoke fluent German. Mr. Iqbal hoped Herr Mohr would have a better time than ever.

Mohr didn't like this. *What if Iqbal was captured by German security, and interrogated? What if the substitution of someone else on Friday night is a trap?*

I need to be very careful.

The strain of it all was becoming too much. Just yesterday, he'd received a message from his wife in Berlin. She'd said she'd heard too much of his shameful philandering with prostitutes. She demanded a divorce, with full custody of their children. Legal papers were being prepared in case he resisted, and to show him she hadn't the least desire to try to reconcile. The tone of her message was bitter.

Mohr would curtly agree to all her terms, of course. It meshed with his broader scheme perfectly. This was the ideal way to protect his family from Axis retribution—if he defected successfully, and also if he was caught.

But the reality of her message pierced Mohr's soul. He dearly loved his wife and children. If only he could explain. But there was no way he could ever explain.

Other things troubled Mohr too. Activity in the classified part of the consular facilities was suddenly heating up. He feared the Axis knew there was a leak somewhere. The pressure to finalize everything for Plan Pandora had skyrocketed. He saw that this forced his hand.

I must be sure the equipment is working smoothly, very soon. No further delaying tactics or I'll be faced with a guaranteed no-win: Lingering equipment trouble will mean I can't go out Friday night with the Turk, a trivial matter compared to Pandora from my superiors' point of view. . . . I might be put under scrutiny for sabotage, or arrested, if the technical work develops further glitches now. . . . And I won't be able to assure that one Kampfschwimmer team with their crucial gear are in the safe house Friday after midnight.

That last thing screamed to be Mohr's top priority. Without the gear, and with the Pandora schedule moved up, his knowledge by itself became quite worthless to the Allies—the same way his special gear, without him alive and present to explain it, would do the Allied cause no good.

Mohr pondered in near despair . . . *Got it!*

I'll pretend one attack team's gear set is a lemon. Plagued by gremlins, as the old American expression went. . . . Yes. The set I started fiddling with on Sunday, which I'll fix but then miscalibrate in a different way before it's field-tested again in the daytime on Friday.

Mohr knew he needed to have the other gear sets functioning flawlessly, to save his skin and keep viable his last-ditch hope of defecting—which meant he had no choice but to leave behind for German use ten copies of a working, terrible weapon.

Mohr's stomach turned as he had another realization. If he told his bosses about the call he'd just received, they could, for entirely different reasons, refuse to let him go: A last-minute change might make his bodyguards suspicious. Iqbal had been inside the consulate before, and after meeting with Mohr he'd been covertly photographed, then given a discreet background check. Who was this other person? Mohr hadn't even been given a name. He only knew that Iqbal's secretary had said Iqbal told her he vouched for the man. Assuming that some clever explanation by the Turk when he showed up, or maybe a note signed by Iqbal—whose signature the lobby log had on file—kept that part from becoming a problem later, the altered invitation gave Mohr's bosses an easy opening to order him to decline it now, and simply stay on duty and stick to Pandora. . . . Yet if Mohr's phone calls were monitored by consular security, for him to not tell his bosses early would definitely raise a red flag.

He'd never dreamed that espionage could be this complicated.

Mohr had to report the change immediately. He prayed he'd still be allowed to attend the party. Smooth-talking his superiors got harder every time—he was running out of ideas and excuses, and they were getting visibly annoyed.

The answer stared at Mohr from on top of his desk. His callousness surprised him. He would use the letter from his soon-to-be ex-wife as a tool, as his ticket to go with the Turk on Friday night: Now of all moments, divorcing, he needed thoroughly decadent release to clear his head. But the people he reported to might answer in just the opposite way: Now of all moments, he needed to reserve his head for essential business only.

If he couldn't attend the party, but was instead taken directly to the safe house with strengthened bodyguards, he'd never make contact with the Turk, never brief his rescuers on the safe house's inner layout, or even be able to tell them where it was. Even if his rescuers managed to tail him anyway, he'd never evade his own bodyguards and the Kampfschwimmer—if shooting started he'd probably die in the cross fire.... And that assumed his bodyguards and the Kampfschwimmer didn't have secret instructions to make sure Mohr was never captured alive.

———

Wednesday morning, Captain Johansen, with Admiral Hodgkiss himself, came into Ilse's workroom. Ilse stood to attention, surprised to see the admiral there in person.

"At ease, Lieutenant," Hodgkiss said, "though nothing about this will be easy."

"Yes, sir." Ilse was crestfallen. She had an idea of what was coming. She was also frightened—to land in the clutches of America's overstretched, imperfect criminal-justice system as an accused foreign spy in a war could be the end of her.

"The director of the FBI has gone over my head to try to convince the CNO to pull your security clearance and sever your relationship with the United States Navy."

"What now?"

"I placed my reputation on the line to back you up. This bought us time, but not a lot. The FBI is having an indictment drawn up against you for espionage. They say they had enough to go to a classified-level grand jury. The CNO told JAG to use some Byzantine jurisdictional issues to delay the indictment as long as they can. The Naval Criminal Investigative Service has also formally complained that they weren't involved in the FBI's work up to now, and the CNO is using that but it'll only give us another few days. Overall, things don't look good. The FBI director can bypass the Department of the Navy, bypass the whole Department of Defense, and cut straight to the cabinet level on matters of homeland security. He's started to already, using something against you for which you aren't cleared, which is circumstantial but he presents as damning, more persuasively each time he recites it. There's also the issue of how the Axis knew when *Challenger* would sail. It might have been by HumInt, and your name remains on the dwindling shortlist of suspects."

"Don't my prior contributions count for *anything*?"

"That's one of the problems. Your most valuable services of all, things you did several months ago, are top secret and highly compartmented. Candidly, Naval Intelligence and the CIA both feel maintaining that secrecy is crucial to the outcome of the war. So crucial, in fact, that it outweighs anything else you might do for the Allies going forward. I'm sorry."

"You mean they're willing to cut me loose? Leave me out in the cold after everything I did for them?"

"From the perspective of military necessity, it does make sense to keep an ironclad lid on your old contributions. Especially since it's obvious that enemy agents are working *somewhere* close to the rest of this, given the incriminating evidence against you that's being manufactured lately. Perhaps not just to negate your effectiveness now, but also force open files that any mole would love to get his hands on."

"Yeah."

"Your two recent technical errors, or let me call them apparent or alleged errors, with METOC, don't help your case."

"I know. So what should I do?"

"Lieutenant, I trust you implicitly, partly because I do know all you've done to aid the Allied cause, and partly because I know Captain Fuller trusts you implicitly and I trust him."

"Yes, sir. But what does that mean I should do?"

"Give me and JAG and the NCIS and the CNO more ammunition. Do something else, something more, of unquestionable significance to prove which side you're loyal to."

Ilse perked up. "Like go on another commando raid?"

"No. You're limited to this workroom, your quarters, and the direct route in between. Adequate food will be brought to you. You're not even to visit other parts of the base without prior written permission from Captain Johansen."

"From now on," Johansen said, "the marine bodyguards will continue to escort you everywhere, but their tasking is changed."

"You mean they're jailers."

"The FBI insisted, as a precaution," Hodgkiss said. "Be glad I won the fight to even still give you a work console. And we're not sure how much longer that will last."

"You may not communicate on any substantive issues with persons other than myself," Johansen said. "All phone calls or e-mails from this room or your quarters to anyone on or off the base will be blocked. Electronic equipment in your quarters has been confiscated, including your cell phone and personal laptop. Data access from this console has been narrowed."

"Solitary confinement, or nearly so. Do I get a lawyer?"

"Only after the indictment is unsealed. Then an attorney will be provided. When things get that far, in a week at the outside, your solitary confinement will be genuine, and total. The gears of the legal process will then begin to grind dispassionately, and as I say at the moment the weight of admissible evidence hangs rather heavily against you."

"So in effect that's my deadline to somehow clear myself."

Hodgkiss nodded. "No more than a week, maybe less. After that you'll be incarcerated, awaiting trial as a spy. Cap-

tain Fuller isn't here to testify in your defense; he won't be
for some time, assuming he comes back at all. The FBI
knows this and is clearly railroading procedures through in
his absence." Hodgkiss pointed at the console. "Apply your
technical skills with dispatch to the projects I previously assigned you. Be the first on anyone's staff to come up with
something really good, to exonerate yourself and forestall
that indictment."

CHAPTER 29

Two and a half days after *Challenger* and *Ohio* passed
through the Strait of Gibraltar, there was still no sign
they'd been detected. For much of that period, Jeffrey
had the task group secure from battle stations, so captains
and crews wouldn't be worn ragged. Both ships returned to
their regular watch-keeping schedules, with good meals and
adequate sleep and recreation, for the one-thousand-nautical-
mile trip paralleling North Africa. In water mostly ten thousand feet deep, they resumed the cruising formation they had
used in the Atlantic, at a speed of eighteen knots.

To pass the time, a checkers tournament was held in the enlisted mess; an electrician's mate, the odds-on favorite, won,
as expected. His reward was to pick the toppings for the piz-
zas baked for midrats, an extra meal served every day at midnight. The chiefs, in their separate quarters, played bridge or
cribbage; some were wickedly good at both. The wardroom,
with Jeffrey joining in now and then, went on a binge of
watching old cowboy movies on the wide-screen video monitor on the bulkhead there, as each officer's workload allowed.

Despite the more relaxed atmosphere, and the lack of sounds of battle from outside, reminders of the impending Afrika Korps offensive never ceased. The on-watch control-room crew tracked noise from a large number of merchant ships, some of them neutral and some of them enemy owned. Many cargo vessels plied the routes between the underside of Europe and ports in Africa. Sonar men reported that most of these rode deep, heavily laden, if going to Africa, but rode shallower, in ballast, heading back north. Jeffrey sometimes wondered what the Allies intended to do to interfere. This logistics buildup made the Afrika Korps stronger every day. As tempting as it was, Jeffrey's orders were explicit: Hold your fire unless first fired on by the enemy and evasion gives no recourse. Avoid at all cost *any* event that might compromise the Zeno extraction.

Over the deep Alboran and then Algerian Basins, the prevailing currents had been in the task group's favor, and they used this to make better time. Then they passed through the strait between westernmost Sicily and Tunisia's jutting Cape Bon—at almost 100 miles wide, spacious compared to Gibraltar. They steamed on toward Malta, the little island now coming up fast. Malta lay between southeastern Sicily and western Libya. All three places were firmly in German hands. Jeffrey ordered his task group to go to battle stations.

Because of the timing forced on him by his mission, it was broad daylight. Visual observations by the enemy would be much easier, Axis personnel would be more lively and alert, and worst of all there was LASH. It turned the sun itself into a mortal threat for submarines while shallow. The acronym seemed apt. The mere thought of it made Jeffrey feel as if he was getting flogged, the skin and flesh on his bared back being flayed by an unseen adversary. LASH really might be the end of them all.

Jeffrey hoped to God that he was doing the right thing. He could no longer put it off; he warily eyed his displays.

North of Malta was a broad bank that extended to the Sicilian coast, barely fifty miles away. The bank rose like a hump from the bottom to less than 300 feet. The water over this hump was the Malta Channel.

South of Malta lay a short stretch of deep water, studded with seamounts in close proximity behind which anything might be hiding—moored hydrophones, antisubmarine mines, or German class 212s. Then came the vast Tunisian Plateau, where all the water was even shallower than in the Malta Channel.

It's time, again, to do the unexpected—according to plan.

"Nav, recommend a course through the Malta Channel. Down the middle."

"Zero-nine-seven, sir." Just south of due east. Sessions obviously had the answer ready before Jeffrey asked.

"V'r'well, Nav," Jeffrey said briskly. "Helm, on my mark, left five degrees rudder, make your course zero-nine-seven."

Meltzer acknowledged.

"Fire Control, signal *Ohio*." Jeffrey gave the information for the course change, on his mark.

Bell acknowledged, then said that *Ohio* acknowledged receipt of warning of the turn.

"Mark."

Challenger turned and *Ohio* followed. The formation turn was executed smoothly, no easy maneuver since *Ohio* handled differently from *Challenger.*

I have to give Parcelli his due. His people learn well from even the slightest practice.

The Malta Channel area teemed with fish, and with fishing boats and their nets. The shoals and banks of the channel also teemed with offshore natural-gas drilling platforms, which made all sorts of machinery noise—and undersea pipes, which gave off flow noise.

Challenger and *Ohio* continued on course for the channel. They adjusted their depth for the rising local topography.

As the water became more and more shallow, the background-noise level rose. The highlight, in Jeffrey's mind, was Mount Etna, a live volcano on Sicily 11,000 feet tall. Magma shifted constantly in widespread underground chambers, and vibrations too subtle for people on land to notice threw valuable extra decibels into the sea. The channel's current made even more noise, as its lower portions flowed over jagged protrusions from what the chart indicated as "Numerous Wrecks," or it gushed past platform pylons. The magma displacements created magnetic anomalies.

Merchant shipping continued to churn the waters overhead.

Jeffrey went through the whole series of orders and responses with Bell and Meltzer, to command the task group to slow to five knots. The reduced speed was necessary for several reasons. In shallower water, as the outside pressure lessened, to go much faster would make *Ohio*'s screw begin to cavitate. This was the submarine equivalent of a car burning rubber from too much torque to the tires and not enough road traction. Cavitation threw off a characteristic hissing, a dead giveaway to the vessel's presence; *Challenger*'s cowled pump jet was much less prone to this than *Ohio*'s huge bronze screw. And too shallow, if they didn't slow, both subs would create a moving hump on the surface above their hulls, with a subtle propulsor wake that trailed behind. Even in choppy water in a busy shipping channel, enemy forces processing special radar bounced off the surface could eke out the truth that something submerged was there.

The blend of these factors robbed Jeffrey of an important option for the next several hours: They dared not put on a burst of speed to avoid a potential problem. To do so would tell the Axis exactly where to zero in.

Everyone in the control room knew it too. People hunched tensely over their consoles. Whenever a fresh, unidentified sonar contact was listed, some of the newer men cringed.

Challenger and *Ohio* entered the thirty-mile-long channel. The clearance between the surface and the bottom became even narrower. This impaired sonar performance, because sound paths bouncing repeatedly between the waves and the seafloor muck lost signal strength before they could spread very far. *A double-edged sword.* The same bad propagation that muffled the task group's signature also made both vessels partly blind.

We won't have much advance notice of ships on a possible collision course. A supertanker's keel is still as dangerous to us as the unseen part of an iceberg would be to that tanker.

Jeffrey's primary worry remained optical detection—including LIDAR and LASH. LIDAR, at least, was active, and photonic sensors on *Challenger*'s and *Ohio*'s hulls could warn if a laser emitter was near. The water in the channel was turbid—cloudy—from biologic waste, erosion silt, particles from undersea volcanoes, dust blown from the deserts of North Africa, and human pollution. So a laser would scatter light in all directions, tipping off the task group to move to one side before the hostile emitter could get a measurable return.

LASH, on the other hand, was completely passive. The sunlight of Sicily this time of year was infamously strong. No storm had brewed up to give fortuitous cover. The weather, confirmed acoustically and photonically by *Challenger,* was fine.

About LASH, Jeffrey could do nothing but sweat and continue to pray. He did both, in deadly earnest. He patted his forehead with his handkerchief unashamedly; when it became too soggy, he used the cloth to squeegee further perspiration down the sides of his temples, away from his eyes.

"Sir," Bell reported as evenly as he could, *"Ohio* signals, deploying three off-board Seahorse Mod Five probes."

It was time to implement the next part of the plan.

"Very well, Fire Control," Jeffrey said very formally. "Signal *Ohio,* 'Commander Task Group acknowledges. *Challenger* now deploying two LMRS probes.' "

"Ohio acknowledges, sir."

The LMRS probes were launched through torpedo tubes, and controlled by fiber-optic wire or via acoustic digital link. The Seahorses were larger, because they could be carried in triplets in one of *Ohio*'s big old missile tubes. They were fully autonomous, had much longer range and endurance, and their sensors were much more capable than the smaller ones on an LMRS; with a minisub in its in-hull hangar, *Challenger* couldn't accommodate even one Seahorse probe—another reason *Ohio* was so vital as an escort.

By using acoustic links, both ships could see the data from all five probes. The off-board unmanned vehicles moved on ahead, searching stealthily for obstructions or hazards, like five fingers feeling their way for items lost under a dresser. The probes' low-probability-of-intercept super-high-frequency active sonars, and passive image-intensification cameras, did most of their work. Transiting the Malta Channel, these feeds were indispensable.

Fishing nets could extend for miles from a trawler, Jeffrey knew. An uncharted wreck could lie on the bottom, with the top of its mast or superstructure rising many feet up from the floor. Loose or misplaced mines, or even unexploded ones left from World War II, could also be anywhere.

In conditions like these, an Axis U-boat might be anywhere.

Jeffrey watched his console as all the data kept pouring in. Murky black-and-white pictures showed him trash strewn on the channel floor—liquor and beer bottles, big tin cans with their opened lids bent back, and empty oil drums were common.

Then some probes found the edges of debris fields leading to wrecks. The control-room mood became grim, fatalistic. A shiver went up Jeffrey's spine as his task group passed each drowned graveyard. He got an all-too-explicit tour of a World War II cargo ship, lying on its side with a huge hole punched below the waterline. The styling of the ship looked Italian or German, not British.

Probably hit by a Royal Navy sub, in the era of the battles for Tobruk and El Alamein.

Now and then Jeffrey needed to change course, coordinating with *Ohio,* to avoid one danger or another in their path. He asked Milgrom to turn on the sonar speakers.

The racket he could hear was reassuring. These waters were noisy indeed.

Milgrom reported aircraft overflights. These included military helos—identified by their engine power and transmission-gear ratio—and fixed-wing maritime patrol planes—also identified by their engine and prop sounds.

Jeffrey did what he could to steer away from the projected path of each aircraft. The formation's own plotted path on his chart became a confusing zigzag, headed vaguely east. It was nearing local noon; the sunshine would aim straight down at them.

Milgrom announced another patrol plane.

Too close. "Hard left rudder! Due north!"

Bell typed frantically and Meltzer yanked his wheel. The task group made a panic turn to clear the zone beneath the aircraft.

"Natural-gas platform dead ahead," Sessions stated between clenched teeth.

Jeffrey ordered another sharp turn, back on course, just as the aircraft flew by.

Two dozen people collectively held their breaths and waited forever.

"No depth charges dropped or torpedo-engine sounds," Milgrom whispered hoarsely once her chief and his men were positive.

Everyone, including Jeffrey, tried to breathe normally.

We sure are doing the unexpected. No nuclear submarine captain in his right mind would go through the Malta Channel if he had any choice. The deep water with its seamount maze was a much more logical tactic.

Not for the first time, Jeffrey asked himself if he'd done the right thing choosing to steer this way, or if he'd let down everyone whose survival depended on his leadership judgment.

And then, before his eyes, the bottom suddenly dropped off to 600 feet, then 1,500, then 6,000, and then 10,000. Jeffrey had been so preoccupied that he was startled to see that they were through the Malta Channel, safe. The Ionian Basin beckoned, the deepest part of the Med.

"Yee-haw," the exhausted assistant navigator, a senior chief from Galveston, murmured under his breath. He typed and called up a different chart on the digital-plotting table, repeated on Jeffrey's console screen; the Malta Channel vanished.

"Yee-haw is right," Jeffrey answered out loud. *Challenger*'s course remained steady, east. The African coastline veered away south, while the heel and toe of Italy lay far north. Well ahead stood occupied Greece.

"Chief of the Watch, secure from battle stations." Officers, chiefs, and other enlisted crewmen began to unwind, waiting for their regular watch-standing reliefs to arrive.

Two minutes later, Gerald Parker strolled in. "May I observe, Captain? Sheer curiosity. I've barely seen your control room since we set sail."

Jeffrey wished Parker would just go away. The chemistry between the two was bad and not getting better. Their personal styles, their outlooks on life, the professional worlds in which they moved were too different. Dinner chitchat in the wardroom kept making this painfully clear. Jeffrey tried every human-relationship management tool he'd been taught over the years as part of his navy training, but Parker saw through them at once. He always bobbed and weaved, as if he were subtly taunting Jeffrey. His attitude stayed adversarial, and he never let down his guard. His goal appeared to be to show Jeffrey that the CIA man was vastly sharper at reading personalities, spotting needs and motivations, and exploiting weaknesses to manipulate people. He never gave an inch, never offered a single gesture of trust, and never tired of verbal jousting—he actually seemed to enjoy it.

But Jeffrey couldn't exactly lock Parker in a stateroom between meals and head visits, and the man had an important role to play soon as Peapod's handler. Jeffrey felt an obligation to respect him, but he didn't have to like the guy. He showed Parker where to sit without getting in anyone's way—at the unused photonics mast-control console, aft of the navigation table.

More crewmen arrived to take the places of those who'd been manning battle stations. Sonar men pulled off their headphones and handed them to fresh people when the new arrivals stated they were ready to relieve them. Lieutenant Milgrom waited until last, as a senior chief stood there to take over from her. She suddenly reacted, as if she'd been hit with a baseball bat.

"Aircraft overflight!" she shouted. "Multiple inbound aircraft! Helos and patrol planes converging from west and north! Sonobuoys! Active sonobuoys at very close range!"

CHAPTER 30

Jeffrey cursed, guessing instantly what had happened: That previous near-miss overflight carried LASH, and saw at least one of the submarines. It radioed in a report, a German commander somewhere made a decision and issued orders, and now armed aircraft were swarming in coordinated, overwhelming force.

"Battle stations," Jeffrey snapped. "Sonar, suppress the hull echoes."

"Echoes suppressed! Port wide-aperture array detecting sonobuoy echoes off *Ohio* rudder and screw!"

If Milgrom can hear them, the Germans might too.

There was pandemonium in Jeffrey's control room, caught transitioning from battle stations to regular watch keeping and suddenly going to battle stations again. *Challenger* crewmen who'd just left ran back. Everyone tried to trade places at once. The compartment became much too crowded. A lieutenant (j.g.) tripped and fell as he passed the helm to Meltzer. Meltzer stepped on the other man's kneecap to get buckled in at the wheel. Bell dashed from aft and practically tore a junior officer out of the fire-control-coordinator seat.

"More air-dropped active sonobuoys," Milgrom called out.

"Rig for deep submergence!" Jeffrey shouted. "Rig for depth charge!" COB acknowledged. "Helm, emergency deep! Down-bubble forty degrees! Increase speed to twenty-six knots."

Meltzer acknowledged, his Bronx accent thick, always a sign that he felt stressed. He pushed in on his control wheel until it was almost flush with his instrument panel.

Challenger's bow nosed steeply down—uncomfortably, desperately so. Jeffery hated doing this, but the ship came first, not the people aboard her. Crewmen still playing musical chairs lost their balance or their grips on fittings. They grabbed for each other, for anything, or slid forward on the treacherous ramp that the flame-proof linoleum deck had become. The unlucky or clumsy ones lay piled in a heap at the front of the space. Two essential fire-control-men stations ended up empty. A stocky chief, dancing to try to stay upright as his shoes couldn't hold against gravity, crashed into the tactical plot on the bulkhead—now tilted wildly off vertical—next to COB's position. The display screen went blank. Jeffrey's seat belt bit into his abdomen, and he was almost folded double while his console top sloped away from him at an outrageous angle.

Challenger gained speed and kept plunging deeper.

"Fire Control," Jeffrey shouted, "to *Ohio,* break formation. Commence full evasive measures. Weapons free at your discretion." Jeffrey had his orders from Hodgkiss; so did Captain Parcelli.

Bell typed madly on his keyboard. *"Ohio* acknowledges! ... We can't just abandon them, sir!"

"We need to, we can, and we will."

"Surface impacts!" Milgrom yelled. "Depth-charge pattern!" The range and bearing she gave were almost identical to *Ohio*'s.

Rumbling detonations sounded at shallower depth. *Challenger* shook but kept diving. She passed through five thousand feet.

"Helm, take her to the bottom, make your course due east!"

"You're *running*?" Gerald Parker yelled as the depth-charge reverb died down. "You can't just *leave* them there defenseless!"

"They're not defenseless," Jeffrey snapped.

"Sir," Bell said, "we need to *do* something. They have *Ohio* localized! . . . Acoustic link to *Ohio* broken!"

"We're doing what we're supposed to do, XO."

More depth charges went off. *Challenger*'s disarrayed crew was buffeted violently. Men tried to claw their way up-hill against the tilt of the deck to reach their stations.

"*Torpedoes in the water,*" Milgrom screamed. "Air-dropped, export-model Mark Forty-sixes." Used by the Germans. "Ranges and bearings indicate the aircraft have *Ohio* surrounded."

Jeffrey heard the torpedo engines scream. Then he heard gurgling, bubbling sounds. *Parcelli launched noisemakers.*

Above the other racket he heard dull *boom*s.

"Reactor check valves," Milgrom stated.

"*Ohio*'s going to flank speed," Bell said, in disbelief that this whole thing was happening.

"Negative!" Milgrom said. "More check valves, different bearing!" Jeffrey couldn't hear them this time. He still had a tactical plot on his console but the data was unreliable.

Where the hell is Lieutenant Torelli? I need his first-squad tracking team. Two fire-control men who should have been to Jeffrey's right at battle stations instead lay badly hurt down by the forward bulkhead. Jeffrey saw the jagged white bones of compound fractures to arms and legs. He saw the bright red blood as shipmates tried to use tourniquets on the wounded.

"Decoys," Bell said. "I think they're both decoys. *Ohio*'s trying to throw the Germans off."

Jeffrey nodded. "He's probably gone as deep as he can and stopped to drift so he can play possum."

The control-room deck began to warp from the outside pressure as *Challenger* dove deeper and deeper at her top quiet speed. Near nine thousand feet, Milgrom called out,

"Hull popping." *Challenger*'s ceramic-composite hull was protesting the punishment. There was no way to avoid this. Jeffrey worried that the crunching sounds would give his ship away—he hoped they'd be drowned out by the wild action raging almost two miles above. He feared a sudden cannon-like influx of the sea. This was the deepest *Challenger* had gone since departing Norfolk; a flaw undiscovered till now in the latest repairs would have horrible consequences. Unforgiving blasts shattered the ocean again.

"Torpedoes have detonated," Milgrom yelled, projecting her voice above the ever-rising noise.

Jeffrey waited to hear the thing he dreaded most aside from a flooding alarm—the sounds of a sinking submarine.

"Assess both decoys destroyed!" Bell called out.

Ohio had only two decoys. The Germans would know they hadn't hit her yet—decoys gave off no floating wreckage, no bodies, no telltale oil slick. Because she'd been quiet, she couldn't have moved fast, couldn't have gotten far. More sonobuoys pinged high above. *Challenger* kept racing east. The melee behind them was at such shallower depth that the angles involved let the wide-aperture arrays pick up what was happening.

Sonobuoys continued pinging. Jeffrey eyed the gravimeter. He was heading into the Ionian Basin, south of Italy and Greece. *Ohio* was cornered against the steep rise leading up to the Malta Channel. Parcelli had contingency orders from Jeffrey that if the two ships needed to separate under attack, *Challenger* would head east and *Ohio* should avoid heading east. If Parcelli went west, back toward Malta, he was dead. His choices were to stay still or make a move either north or south. Jeffrey thought that south would be better: The water was much more open there.

Parker slammed hard against the back of Jeffrey's seat, then leaned on it for support.

Jeffrey was livid. "Get back to your position."

"I need to know what's happening."

"The task group is coming unglued, is what's happening."

Meltzer pulled back on his wheel. *Challenger* began to level off at almost twelve thousand feet.

More depth charges detonated. Milgrom reported more torpedo-engine sounds. Then she reported more pings, coming from the type of sonar on ASDS minisubs. *Ohio* had released them, so they could lure the inbound torpedoes away from their parent. Parcelli was using his minisubs as last-ditch improvised decoys; Jeffrey pitied the crewmen aboard them. But jettisoning the minis let *Ohio* go faster—less flow resistance and noise.

"You can't just leave two hundred people to die," Parker yelled in Jeffrey's ear.

"My orders are explicit! If detected and attacked in the Med, *Ohio* is expendable and *Challenger* must get away."

"You can't play God like this! We still need all those SEALs and probes and weapons on *Ohio*."

"For now they're on their own. We need *Challenger* in one piece so we have the German mini with the range to get Peapod."

"You'd sacrifice *Ohio* for a *minisub?*"

"You're out of line, Mr. Parker! Get back to your post!" Jeffrey pointed at the photonics-mast console. The constant pings and blast reverb and screaming of torpedo engines made their conversation surreal.

"You're the famous Captain Jeffrey Fuller! You're supposed to be the man who never gives up, who does the impossible! Pull another trick out of your ass before it's too late!"

"Get back to your post." Jeffrey resisted shoving Parker.

The ocean was rent by a giant thunderclap, then another.

"Assess both ASDSs destroyed," Bell shouted, horrified.

"More torpedoes in the water," Milgrom said. "Mark Forty-sixes."

"Sir," Bell pleaded, "we all have friends on that ship. You can't just let them die. You saved *Ohio* twice before, near Norfolk and then with a *Dreadnought* decoy."

"I have my orders," Jeffrey said coldly, torn up inside.

"I've seen you disobey orders, Captain." Tears were coming to Bell's eyes. *"Please."*

There was a new screeching roar on the sonar speakers. It was overlaid by other, similar ones. They would stop, and then more would occur, repeatedly.

"Ohio is launching Polyphems," Milgrom said.

Many crewmen turned to Jeffrey, their faces asking him to achieve a miracle. They knew those Polyphems would point right back at *Ohio.* The German aircraft that weren't shot down would known exactly where to aim. Parcelli was making his last stand.

Deeper, ripping roars drowned out the higher-pitched screeching ones.

"Tomahawk launches, Captain," Bell whispered, all choked up.

"Loud surface impacts," Milgrom reported. "Chaotic flow noise, increasing in depth. Assess as aircraft shot down."

There were more blasts from depth charges. Noisemakers gurgled in vast profusion, some old and some fresh, trying to confuse torpedoes. More Polyphems screeched, more Tomahawks roared. Parcelli might still fight his way out to safety.

"New surface contact! Brandenburg tonals identified!" A frigate had joined the battle. Much louder pings sounded now above everything else. "Brandenburg has gone active!" The frigate had a sonar mounted under her bow. It was much more capable than any battery-operated sonobuoys. "More torpedoes in the water! ADCAP Mark Forty-eights!" *Ohio* was engaging the Brandenburg.

"More torpedoes in the water! Mark Forty-sixes!" The Brandenburg was shooting back. Both vessels had four torpedo tubes. *Ohio*'s weapons were faster and smarter.

There were different roars that ended in sharp detonations—*Ohio*'s antitorpedo rockets.

Parcelli still has a chance.

Jeffrey heard an extremely powerful ping, on the opposite side of *Ohio* from the Brandenburg frigate's bearing.

"New surface contact! Contact is ex-Italian *de la Penne*–class destroyer!" Taken over by the Imperial German Navy.

"Six tubes on a de la Penne, Captain," Bell said flatly.

"Help them!" Parker shouted from the rear of the control room. "For the love of heaven, use your Mark Eighty-eights!"

"They'd be a dead giveaway, you fool!" Jeffrey looked at the best-guess plot. The frigate and destroyer had *Ohio* in a pincers, one from the north and one from the south, each making over thirty knots. Parcelli was badly outgunned, ten tubes to four, and must be running out of ADCAPs. If he went west to shallow water now, he was surely doomed. His only escape was east.

Jeffrey had ordered him not to flee east. Would Parcelli obey, to protect *Challenger* from detection and possible crippling or destruction? Would Parcelli and his crew maintain their discipline to the last, and knowingly sacrifice themselves? Or, caught in a squeeze, fighting for life, with layer after layer of defenses peeled away and every tactic failing, would Parcelli come toward Jeffrey and bring enemy fire down on *Challenger*?

Roar after roar meant more Tomahawk launches. These were probably programmed in antiship mode. They moved ten times as fast through the air as a torpedo moved through the water.

Heavy concussions pounded *Challenger* and echoed off the side of the towering escarpment between her and the Malta Channel.

"Loud explosions! Cannot identify!"

The acoustic madhouse made it impossible to follow the battle via hydrophones. The tactical plot was useless without updated data from sonar. All Jeffrey could do was wait.

Eerie moans, and *crack*s, and sounds like breaking glass came over the speakers, garbled by dull thuds and sharper eruptions.

"Assess destroyer and frigate sinking!" Bell said with renewed hope. "Assess explosions were Tomahawk hits!" The breaking-glass noise came when the red-hot piping of gas-turbine engines and diesels was hit by cold seawater; the moans and cracks were tormented steel bending and fracturing as the enemy warships broke apart on the outside and from within; the thuds and eruptions were ready-use ammo and entire magazines blowing up.

Torpedo engines continued to scream. Jeffrey heard another *boom-boom-boom,* then a rising whine as *Ohio* herself tried flank speed. He listened to another long series of anti-torpedo rocket engines light off. *I think Parcelli just fired the last of his rockets.* There were sounds like shotgun blasts, and these began to mingle with torpedo warheads exploding singly or in groups. Echoes and reverb were more intense than ever.

They subsided in a way that felt all wrong, replaced by a two-toned roar—compressed air from an emergency blow, and inward-jetting seawater; the air grew more feeble, the jetting much stronger. It ended with a deafening rumble, louder and distinct from any other sound so far. Crewmen glanced at each other, puzzled or appalled. Jeffrey and Bell grasped at once the special quality of that rumble, like a deep-throated *crump* that tailed off into a rebounding *pshew.* The new noise echoed hollowly, and hopelessly—it was the unmistakable signature of a steel-hulled submarine imploding. A terrible silence ruled in *Challenger*'s control room, broken only by injured crewmen gasping or grunting, and by other crewmen's sobs.

"Maybe a few got away in escape gear," Jeffrey said to no one in particular.

"Don't you think the Germans will know that?" Parker snapped accusingly. "Don't you think they'll be hunting them down?"

Jeffrey didn't answer. His heart told him that, near crush depth, no one could make an ascent from *Ohio* without fatal bends.

The corpsman and his assistants arrived with stretchers and first-aid kits. The uninjured people around Jeffrey seemed like they'd just aged ten years. He felt as if he'd aged twenty.

"What are your orders, sir?" Bell asked quietly.

"Continue east and go on with the mission. Secure from battle stations in three hours if we aren't attacked."

CHAPTER 31

Eighteen hours later, after tending to the wounded and holding a memorial for *Ohio, Challenger* had crossed the Ionian Sea. Jeffrey's next job, the final leg before releasing the ex-German minisub bound for Istanbul, was to penetrate the Aegean Sea between occupied Greece and neutral Turkey. To do this, while Parcelli had still been alive, they'd decided to take the closest way in—the wide but shallow Antikýthēra Strait, one gap in a ribbon of islands that stretched from southern Greece to Turkey; the largest of these islands were Crete and then Rhodes.

Lord, I miss Parcelli. Jeffrey bit down his grief. But he kept seeing Parcelli's face in his mind, and the SEAL commander McCollough, with their egos and strong personalities, both so proud of and caring about their men, brimming with sincerity and confidence, now all gone forever. Jeffrey remembered Parcelli's cowboy behavior off Norfolk, how the two had argued afterward, taken each other's measure, and then—on the accelerated time frame common in war—started becoming almost friends. Jeffrey gazed at his right palm, which had shaken Parcelli's big, warm, reassuring hand. He could still feel that touch, summon up all the sensations of it. Jeffrey's palm seemed so empty.

He ordered battle stations for the passage through the latest strait. Jeffrey was honest with himself that he was nervous—events in the Malta Channel might portend more bad things to come. His crew, still subdued or depressed, went to their positions as if some of them were sleepwalking.

"Pull yourselves together," Jeffrey ordered. "XO, put on report anyone who shows the slightest sign of inattention."

"Yes, sir," Bell answered, sounding drained himself.

This was harsh, Jeffrey knew, but it was appropriate and necessary. *Ohio*'s heroic crew had set an example of superb dedication and discipline to the end. Her loss, with so many lives, was tragic, but Jeffrey couldn't permit his people to mope. For him the hardest part was that most of his subordinates, because of security, had no idea why whatever *Challenger* was doing was so important. Thus they couldn't understand the reason for leaving fellow submariners to die, while they themselves sneaked away to preserve their own lives. Morale had hit rock bottom.

Jeffrey needed to take action on this, but he wasn't sure how. He hoped that as the rest of the mission unfolded—or maybe afterward, if they survived—his people not yet in the know might get some inkling of the immense value to the war effort, and to eventual peace, of what had happened to *Ohio*.

In the meantime *Challenger* had to continue alone. Jeffrey was experiencing an unease he couldn't shake off. It was partly because of Gerald Parker's most recent behavior. The man had a persona for every occasion, and put each on like a mask. Now he was suggesting that the loss of *Ohio* showed that Mohr's extraction might be a trap after all. It could be that Parker was rattled under his always-poised exterior, or it could be that he was setting things up to distance himself from the mission in case it failed, to preserve his career at Jeffrey's expense. The latter fit with his outrageous behavior in the control room during the battle. Jeffrey had chewed him out in his stateroom afterward, but he could tell that Parker was unrepentant. He pleaded ignorance of the ways of the sea and the customs of the navy, and claimed that his job on this mission gave him certain authority anyway. He came as close as he dared to insinuating that *Ohio*'s destruction was somehow Jeffrey's fault.

Observing Parker's conduct, listening to what he said, caused Jeffrey to have his own serious doubts about Klaus Mohr. Jeffrey hated to depend on people he didn't *know* he could trust. Was Mohr, as a supposed defector, for real, or was he a phony? Did he even actually exist, or was the identity artificial, only manufactured bait?

Jeffrey did know better than to second-guess himself on his decisions in and around the Malta Channel. The choice to proceed through there was made in a participative group context, including Parcelli's wise counsel, and input from seasoned officers and chiefs on both *Ohio* and *Challenger*. The final decision had been Jeffrey's, yes, but he was the task-group commander, and task groups weren't run by committee. He was sure there would be an inquiry if and when *Challenger* returned to the States. He'd worry about that later. He had far more compelling issues to occupy—or pre-occupy—his attention for a while. It occurred to him that the U.S. might already be aware that *Ohio* was sunk, if one of her emergency buoys had been released, then worked properly, and its signal hadn't been jammed by the Axis. Remote sea-surveillance data alone would probably be too ambiguous: A frantic engagement in which *Ohio* launched so many missiles, with many tremendous explosions under the water, might have served to disguise her escaping. Jeffrey sighed. He knew better.

Challenger made it through the Antikýthēra Strait unmolested. Jeffrey ordered a turn onto course zero-seven-six, a bit north of east. Using deeper water, this would start to take them through the labyrinth of other Greek islands that sprinkled the entire Aegean all the way to mainland Turkey.

Jeffrey wondered how things really stood now between Turkey and Germany. He wondered what effect his mission

might have. He realized that a safe house full of dead Kampfschwimmer would raise many questions, beyond those already covered in his briefings with Gerald Parker and Felix.
Kampfschwimmer operations on Turkish soil were an act of
war. How would Turkey react? Was there another, clandestine level to Jeffrey's orders, one that had only gelled in
Washington after Aardvark made his final report on his meeting with Mohr? Was there a chance to let sovereign Turkey
discover for herself egregious German duplicity that the U.S.
couldn't simply put in a diplomatic note?

———

Jeffrey got more sleep while he could as *Challenger* tra-
versed the Aegean. Then he took the conn and sounded battle
stations. The loading of equipment and weapons into the
minisub was finished. Meltzer would be the mini's pilot; he'd
boarded already and powered up the vessel and its controls.
At a depth of two hundred feet, inside Turkish territorial waters, Jeffrey bade good luck to Parker, Gamal Salih, and Felix
and his SEAL team. Jeffrey avoided melodrama. No one felt
like giving a speech. Everybody understood what hung in the
balance. It made people tight-lipped, their conversation terse
and clipped, their eyes hooded and hard. Jeffrey watched as
they climbed the ladder inside the lock-out trunk. Hatches
swung shut and were dogged. Crews ran through final checklists. The minisub was released.

CHAPTER 32

In the dim, red, postmidnight lighting of the minisub's control compartment, Felix looked over David Meltzer's shoulder at the navigation display. The upcoming strait was only the first part of the fifteen-hour trip to their destination, and in many ways it was the scariest. The unforgiving Dardanelles ran forty relentless miles, never more than two miles wide, with nasty twists and turns, and wrecks in the most inconvenient places. Two hundred and fifty feet deep at best, it shoaled to barely seventy-five just before opening onto the Sea of Marmara.

The minisub was too small to have a gravimeter. It held no off-board probes for scouting ahead. It wasn't even armed.

Turkey was neutral, and merchant shipping used the Dardanelles constantly. *Challenger* had already done the work of penetrating hostile defenses. But the minisub wasn't neutral, and its unannounced submerged presence was an outright violation of recognized international treaty law. If detected, Turkish patrols had every right to shoot to kill.

"I'm activating sonar speakers," the copilot SEAL chief

Costa said, even more dour than usual; the mouth of the strait was upon them. The now-familiar sounds of churning and swishing, hissing and pounding, growling and humming of surface ships passing back and forth on the moonlit surface filled the tiny compartment.

"Turning into outbound shipping lane," Meltzer stated. The digital gyrocompass readout became a blur, then steadied, but didn't stay steady for long. The mini, only 8 feet high on the outside and 60 feet long, began to pitch and roll. Even down at 150 feet, the endless movement of big ships made the restricted channel not just noisy, but rough. There was almost no current or tide here, but hulls and screws caused wakes that reflected strongly and chaotically off the steep shorelines on both sides of the strait; this shoved kinetic energy deep down into the water trapped between.

The effect of the noise and the turbulence made Felix think of being caught in a giant Jacuzzi.

Felix watched as Meltzer and Costa fought their controls. The inertial navigation system marked their gradual progress. Felix, standing crammed in behind Meltzer, grabbed the back of the pilot's seat for support. Chief Porto, who would relieve Chief Costa later, stood behind him, shoulder to shoulder with Felix.

Now and then the mini's acoustic-intercept array would pick up active sonars coming toward them. The frequency band and other technical aspects of these pings showed that they came from commercial obstacle-and-mine avoidance sonars used by modernized merchant ships. Felix hoped that if the mini couldn't steer aside in time, out of detection range of one of these ships, the crewman watching the sonar readout would think they were only waterlogged debris, or an ocean rover, or just wouldn't care.

Felix decided to go into the passenger compartment and grab some sleep. While a master chief, he'd qualified in ASDS piloting, then on this mission had learned to handle the German mini too, giving better skills redundancy to his team's mix of personnel. He planned to relieve Meltzer for a while, later on. *Who knows when I'll be able to rest again after that.* He was grateful for the corpsman's antiseasickness pills.

"Copilot," Felix said, "mind your trim. I'm going aft."

"Aye aye, sir," Costa acknowledged. The mini had variable ballast tanks, just like a full-size submarine.

Felix inched his way past Porto standing next to him—no easy task in such cramped quarters. Porto, typically upbeat, seemed overflowing with energy, and Felix hoped he didn't peak too soon emotionally. Felix undogged the pressure-proof hatch into the central hyperbaric lock-in/lock-out chamber. He stepped over the hatch coaming, then gently pulled the hatch closed and dogged it. He moved slowly and smoothly through the lock-out chamber; the ride was choppy enough without his shifting weight making things worse. At the aft end of the chamber, he opened the hatch into the passenger compartment. He held tight as the mini was jostled and tossed.

Seven seats were taken: Gamal Salih and Gerald Parker had the front row. Felix's five enlisted men sat farther aft. Salih and Parker were going through briefing files as best they could, for last-minute brushups on mission details. The enlisted men—who viewed the turbulence as a challenge that made things more interesting—were cleaning their MP-5s for the umpteenth time, or sharpening fighting knives that were already as sharp as a surgical scalpel. The combined tone of this activity was notable tension, barely subdued.

Fifteen hours is a long time to sit. It's like flying nonstop from New York to Tokyo.

The chairs, meant for lengthy transits, were plush, and reclined like airline seats. Everyone looked up from what they were doing when Felix came in. "Don't mind me," he said. He took the empty seat, then spoke to the enlisted SEAL across the aisle. "Make sure I'm up in four hours. Wake me if anything happens before then." A supply clerk somewhere had failed to provide enough pillows. Salih, always so considerate of those around him, was first to hand Felix his own.

The mini shimmied and dipped in the swirling confines of the strait, but Felix had learned to sleep through worse in C-17s or smaller aircraft.

By the time they'd enter the more open Sea of Marmara, the windowless minisub compartment would feel claustrophobic, the novelty of leaving *Challenger* would've worn off, and the ride should become much smoother. At that point, Felix would make sure everyone rotated taking good naps. For now his people had too much adrenaline.

Felix tilted his seat back, and put his left arm across his eyes to help him fall asleep.

He wondered if he would dream. The past couple of days he'd been having nightmares, about submarine hulls imploding: the inside air temperature rising like an oven as the atmosphere compressed, Commander McCollough and sixty-five other SEALs bursting into flames before the seawater quenched the crematorium *Ohio* had become in her death throes.

Then Felix recalled that this minisub had been captured from a Kampfschwimmer team by a SEAL team staging from *Challenger*. The Kampfschwimmer were all killed in that action. Rumors back in Norfolk said the SEAL lieutenant and chief from that team were killed on a later op. *Men now dead sat in these seats once, and men now dead once trod this deck.*

The idea caused Felix unease. The metallic scraping and clicking of weapons being cleaned and sharpened didn't make it any better. Felix went to sleep surrounded by ghosts of SEALs and Kampfschwimmer. His last conscious thought was of the families, widows and orphans, forever mourning and missing men lost in this godforsaken war.

"Contact lost with Minisub Charlie," Lieutenant Milgrom reported.

"Very well, Sonar." Jeffrey studied his tactical plot; there were no threats. "Chief of the Watch, secure from battle stations."

"Secure from battle stations, aye." COB passed the order through the phone talker.

It was in the wee hours of Friday morning, local time. Allowing an adequate interval for Felix to reach Istanbul, do his thing there, and then—God willing—make the long trip back with Peapod and his gear, Jeffrey expected them sometime between dusk and midnight on Saturday.

As per the plan, for ultimate stealth, *Challenger* was observing total radio and laser-buoy silence. No summons came through on ELF to trail their floating wire, to listen to any updated intell or orders—the U.S. had had nothing for Jeffrey since *Ohio* went down with all hands, at least not yet. He knew from Gerald Parker that spy satellites would make passes over the Dardanelles and Istanbul to watch for unusual happenings from Friday dawn into Saturday evening.

"XO," he said to Bell, "the best thing we can hope for now is nothing. That we hear nothing for the next day and a half."

CHAPTER 33

Hours later, submerged beneath the daylight of midafternoon, Felix expectantly watched a blank monitor screen. The tactical plot was crowded and uncertain. The water was not very deep, and the busy inlet was less than one mile wide. There was little room for the minisub to maneuver, to avoid being run down while at periscope depth. For Felix and the others in the control compartment, the pucker factor was high. Sonar propagation was bad and signal to noise was high, and the inertial navigation system by now had drifted into too much error for their purposes—pinpoint positioning would be crucial for what came next.

Lieutenant Meltzer began to raise the minisub's periscope mast above the surface. As the navigation plot indicated, they were through the Sea of Marmara now and had turned left into the Golden Horn, a long and tapering body of water off of the start of the Bosporus Strait. The Golden Horn split the western part of Istanbul in half. The Old City sat along its southern bank, on a hilly peninsula that ended at Seraglio Point, on the Bosporus. The New City sprawled beyond the

Golden Horn's north bank. The remainder of Istanbul, on the eastern—Asian—side of the Bosporus, had a few Byzantine- or Ottoman-era monuments and decrepit castles, but was mostly a series of bedroom communities.

Bridges spanned the Golden Horn, and also spanned the Bosporus farther north, toward the Black Sea. Ferries shuttled along different routes, threading between sightseeing boats and larger merchant ships. Some of the merchies moved in and out of the Bosporus, aiming for the Black Sea or going the opposite way, toward the Med. Others of these big ships came into the Golden Horn—part of which formed Istanbul's major industrial port.

The one thing Meltzer didn't need to worry much about— every submariner's dread—was an undetected sailboat on an imminent collision course, gliding silently on the surface by using the wind. Briefing papers said there would be very few pleasure craft in the Golden Horn. Felix soon saw why.

The periscope photonics head gingerly broke the surface. It took a while for the oil and scum to drain off enough for a clear full-color image to show on the monitor. The sun was bright, the sky overhead was clear, but the Golden Horn was anything but golden. It was terribly polluted. Chief Porto took over and panned the periscope head rapidly in a circle: Nothing big was coming at the mini.

Felix got his first, dizzying, live view of Istanbul through that video feed. *"Dizzying" is a good word for it: Centuries of architecture all jumbled together. Crenelated battlements on dark old fortress walls, mosque minarets that frame the main buildings' colorful domes, church spires in gleaming gold or weathered copper, and cement, steel, and glass skyscrapers.*

"Wind northwest, eight knots," Meltzer read off a panel. "Air temperature sixty-six Fahrenheit."

"Pilot, proceed to the drop-off point," Felix ordered.

Meltzer acknowledged. The waters roiled by passing ships would help disguise the raised periscope. Based on the amount of flotsam and jetsam Felix saw floating around, the photonics sensor head shouldn't stand out as the mini slowly moved. But this was a double-edged sword, since all that crap up there could foul or break the sensor head. They needed real-time visual cues to see something coming too close—Meltzer and Porto would have to dip the head underwater and turn the mini out of the way. One added hazard, transiting a semi-enclosed working harbor, was a bobbing steel cargo container that had broken loose somewhere and fallen overboard—Felix knew that around the world this happened thousands of times every year. They'd be as silent as sailboats, perhaps with nothing showing on the surface, and the sharp corner of a heavy container might pierce the minisub's hull.

"Time to get geared up," Felix said. "I'm going aft."

Felix went into the passenger compartment. On the way he passed Chief Costa, doing tests and eyeing a checklist to get ready to use the lock-out chamber.

The entire SEAL team had boarded the mini already wearing black wetsuits. These were made of a breathable, quick-drying layered material, so they were comfortable to wear for lengthy periods out of the water. The team's equipment was all stowed now in waterproof bags that included adjustable floatation bladders; they wouldn't pop to the surface prematurely, or get lost on the murky, muddy bottom either.

The men finished taking turns using the head, one last time, at the stern of the passenger compartment. Soon they all did dive-buddy checks. Felix made extra sure Salih's dive gear was in good order and that he wasn't getting panicky. But Salih seemed to be enjoying himself.

The Turko-German tested his Draeger re-breather scuba mouthpiece with confidence, then manfully slapped the titanium dive knife in a scabbard fastened to one of his thighs. "The CIA trained me in all sorts of useful things," he said to Felix. "I didn't even know how to swim when I first ran into Captain Fuller. Isn't that right, Mr. Parker?"

Parker nodded, very reserved. Salih gave Felix a wink. Felix got the impression that all further details were classified.

Parker and Meltzer shook hands with the team and wished

everybody good luck. The mini would stay still for now in the Golden Horn and hide, submerged in hotel mode—running only its environmental control systems, to preserve the precious fuel supply. Late tonight it was to begin moving back and forth between the north and south banks, at predetermined places, and listen for a high-frequency homing beacon the SEALs would deploy.

Everyone squashed into the lock-out chamber, trying not to step on each others' big combat swim fins. They made sure all hatches were fully dogged. By intercom, Felix told Meltzer they were ready. The air pressure started to rise; Felix felt his ears crackle. He and the others held their noses with one gloved hand, kept their mouths closed, and shoved air up from their lungs. Their cheeks swelled. They did this until the air pressure steadied; their sinuses and ear canals stayed clear this way. Meltzer confirmed that the hyperbaric chamber was equalized to the outside water pressure at the level of the bottom hatch, twenty feet of seawater. Costa knelt and undogged the hatch. It dropped down on its hydraulically damped hinges. Through the hatch coaming was a pool of dark and smelly water. A feeling of expectation, a thrill, passed through the grouped men almost physically. This got Felix over his last-minute nerves.

The team pulled on their dive masks, put their regulators into their mouths, and performed a final buddy check. Their closed-circuit re-breathers gave off no bubbles, for stealth, but also had longer endurance than older compressed-air scuba— and had become popular even with recreational divers, so being seen in them on the surface would not raise suspicion. One by one they sat on the edge of the hatch coaming, rolled forward into the water, and disappeared. Felix went last.

Deciding where to leave the water had needed careful thought. The rushed nature of the mission forced the minisub to arrive at Istanbul in broad daylight. The size of Istanbul's developed waterfront precluded sneaking onto land in a wilderness area—too much distance to cover to the German consulate.

Felix popped his head above the tepid saltwater, not being the least bit subtle or furtive about it. Meltzer had done an excellent navigation and piloting job; Felix saw what he expected—and needed—to see. On the Golden Horn's northern, New City edge, only a few feet in front of him, were an acre's worth of big concrete water-aerating tanks, several gas burn-off towers that flared periodically, an office and a garage building in the mid-distance, and a convenient ladder for getting ashore. The alien setting and the danger gave Felix a wonderful rush.

He smiled, and tugged twice on the lanyard connecting him to Chief Porto, his dive buddy. Porto looked around, tugged on his other lanyard, and Gamal Salih appeared. They unclipped the lanyards and climbed the ladder. Nearby stood outdoor, screened-off showers meant for maintenance divers.

Soon Felix's team were all ashore, stripped naked behind the screens, showering thoroughly and rinsing off their dive gear. Aside from the filth of the water, they needed to remove the last little trace of forensic signs—U.S.–made cloth fibers, dust particles from inside a submarine, whatever—that clung to their hair and in the nooks and crannies of their bodies. They dried themselves with towels made in Turkey, and dressed in casual clothes also made in Turkey. In the week leading up to departing from Norfolk, even their dental work had been redone to Portuguese or Turkish standards.

Salih put a small but heavy velvet sack into his shirt pocket. In deference to local cultural sensitivities—and so to better blend in—none of the men wore hats. They donned cheap watches and synchronized with Felix—3:42 P.M. They checked their forged ID papers and counted their real local money one last time, and slipped out their Turkish-made weapons.

The MP-5s were model A-3s, with collapsible buttstocks and no protruding silencers on their barrels. Slung downward by the adjustable strap in one armpit, and held along the side of their bodies, the firearms became invisible when the men pulled on thin windbreakers—especially with no protruding magazines loaded into the weapons yet; these they slid into pants pockets. They strapped fighting knives near one ankle, under a pants leg.

They picked up their equipment bags, with dive gear plus flak vests, helmets, pistols, and more ammo inside—and a disassembled sniper rifle for long-range work—and sauntered out of the sewage-treatment plant. It was one of the least guarded or hardened targets in Istanbul—raw sewage went into the Golden Horn from other sites anyway. Nobody challenged them.

Away from the plant, the men split up into smaller groups. In their heads were maps and routes and schedules, plan phases and fall-back arrangements, thoroughly memorized. The whole team knew what to do. Some would hail taxis. Others would ride on city buses. Felix and Salih, and Chief Costa and an enlisted man, would walk and then hop aboard a municipal electric trolley.

CHAPTER 34

Felix and those with him survived their half-mile walk to the trolley—something never guaranteed. Istanbul traffic drove on the same side of the road as in the U.S., but beyond that the vehicular rights-of-way were fought for driver to driver, in a perpetual game of chicken whose outcome was left to the will of Allah—literally. Pedestrians had no rights at all other than to be run over. The sidewalks were safe enough, most of the time, but the streets and intersections were maiming zones for people on foot. Red lights were seen as suggestions, often ignored if no policeman was near. Spillback, gridlock, blaring horns, squealing brakes, and frustrated cursing went on nonstop. One car rear-ended another with a loud *smack* and the sound of scattering headlight glass, barely ten feet from where Felix warily paced. The drivers argued, but not violently. Fender benders seemed a matter of course, frequent accidents a normal part of the daily routine here.

And exactly as the briefing papers said, Felix thought, *taxi drivers are so conscious of crashes that they have their blood types painted on the outsides of their cabs. Terrific.*

They threaded their way through milling crowds. Felix and his group passed tea sellers with big silver samovars strapped to their backs, and vendor stands offering fresh-caught seafood, pastries, stews, or mouthwatering lamb. Ever concerned about detection and surveillance by a number of potentially hostile non-American operatives, for security and countersurveillance the SEALs and Salih pretended to not know each other. Their gym bags were different shapes and sizes and colors for this reason. They used the reflections in windows of shops and the windows and mirrors of parked cars to make sure they hadn't already picked up a tail.

At last on the jam-packed trolley, they stood near enough to watch each other's backs and guard against pickpockets. At one stop they shuffled off, covertly taking careful looks at everyone else who left the trolley there. They waited for the next tram to come down the line, and made sure no one else from the previous one had loitered and got back on when they did.

Along the way, in odd snatches when he wasn't preoccupied with remaining clandestine or simply staying alive amid the traffic mayhem, Felix got more of an up-close view of Istanbul's New City. The architecture varied from shiny office buildings to millennia-old monuments whose stone was now blackened by air pollution. The odors of exotic spices wafting from shops and restaurants blended with the bite of vehicle exhaust fumes. Lute and zither music clashed with Arab-style quarter tones and homegrown Turkish evolutions of rock and jazz. Men and women, dressed in Western casual or business attire, mixed freely with others who observed Islamic public-apparel guidelines with different levels of strictness that seemed completely a matter of personal choice. The Turkish tongue that most of them spoke sounded vaguely like Hungarian, but Felix knew there was no linguistic connection.

And modern Turkish was written with English-style letters, as Felix could see on trolley and bus destination boards, street signs, storefronts, and product advertisements everywhere.

Felix kept noticing the large number of Japanese tourists.

As on his last mission, on a different continent, they seemed to take an almost voyeuristic glee in getting as close as they could to a tactical nuclear war in which, so far, they were neutral; Tokyo's recent announcement that they had their own atom bombs, proved by an underwater test, was just one more destabilizing factor in the present increasingly unstable world.

These particular Japanese may be a lot closer to tactical nuclear combat than they realize.

Felix, Salih, and the two SEALs got off the trolley again, this time at their stop. After more death-defying sprints through traffic at what were supposed to be crosswalks where they had the light, the foursome walked on briskly, blending into the crowd and the hubbub. They arrived at their first destination, the storefront of a two-story yellowed limestone building. They did another check for any surveillance tail. *None.* Together, they went inside the upmarket executive-protection rental company.

———

Felix acted as their leader at the rental company. On the trip from Norfolk, with help from Salih, he'd mastered some phrases of the Turkish language, and learned about local conversational gestures.

"*Merhaba,*" he spoke in Turkish to the man at the counter. Hello. The man wore an off-the-rack business suit that didn't fit very well, and had a black mustache and a receding hairline. He chain-smoked, as witnessed by an overflowing ashtray on the desk behind the counter; the air had the strong but not unpleasant odor of tangy Turkish tobacco. A stereo played, of all things, classical music—Vivaldi's *Four Seasons,* a lively, fast-paced section of the piece. Two leather couches with a newspaper tossed on one formed a waiting area.

"*Iyi aksamlar,*" the attendant responded. Good evening.

"*Ismim...*" My name is. Felix pulled out his Portuguese

passport and gave his false name. In Portuguese, he mentioned Awais Iqbal and his firm, and said they had a reservation.

The man shook his head from side to side.

Felix knew he wasn't saying no. He meant he didn't understand. He didn't speak any Portuguese. *"Almanya?"* Did Felix speak German?

"How about English?"

"Yes, English is good." Most Turks who did business in Istanbul spoke at least one foreign language pretty well.

"You should have two cars for us." Felix explained that Mr. Iqbal had been delayed outside the country, and they were standing in for him. Felix gave the reservation number Iqbal had passed on to his handler, which eventually reached Gerald Parker on *Challenger* by radio. This was to confirm Felix's identity as a genuine associate of the absent Iqbal.

The man bowed his head once. This meant yes. "Still not wanting bodyguards?" His English had hints of a British accent, not American, a common thing in this part of the world.

Felix lifted his head back and raised his eyebrows. This was how Turks conveyed no. "We have our own." Felix made sure to speak with a Portuguese accent as best he could; this was another part of his cover that he'd been practicing for days. He gestured at Chief Costa and his enlisted man, who stayed quiet. They were supposed to be bodyguards. They looked the part.

"This your principal?" The attendant glanced at Salih.

"Evet." Turkish for yes. Felix went back to English. "We're taking someone to a party."

The man reached under the counter and gave Felix a pile of forms to fill out, and a pen. "Please show me your documents. All." He cast his eyes over the group.

The SEALs and Salih placed their passports, visas, international driving permits, and other papers on the counter. Salih was pretending he was a Turkish citizen, although both he and his parents had been born and raised in Germany. Salih translated each box on the form for Felix, and showed him where to sign.

While Felix filled out the forms, the man turned to his computer and entered the passport numbers. He seemed satisfied that none of Felix's group had a criminal record, or was a wanted terrorist, or whatever. If anything came back saying the passport numbers were invalid, he didn't react.

He typed on his keyboard again. A printer spat out an invoice.

Felix made a tsking sound, a sign of disapproval. "Too high."

The man leaned across the counter. "This basic rate for the cars. Overnight is two days. Not negotiable. This for insurance, also two days." All insurance rates were steep, with the war. "This for full petrol tanks." Gasoline prices were also astronomical. "This is surcharge because you not taking our bodyguards to go with cars."

"Why a surcharge? You do less work."

"Because, my friend, when customers use own bodyguards, cars come back with more damage."

Felix didn't argue. He pushed the filled-out forms across the counter.

"How payment?"

The team did not bring credit or debit cards, since Parker had said providing valid ones in-country, with false names, was too difficult and would leave a trail. Large amounts of cash were problematic too, because Turkey suffered hyperinflation even before the war, and international currency rates were fluctuating wildly. Precious goods had become a reliable form of exchange amid so much financial instability.

Salih reached into his pocket, and opened the velvet sack. He offered two high-quality emerald rings. The stones were large, and more valuable than diamonds.

The attendant called someone from an office, then took another puff on his cigarette. This second man, younger and thinner than the first, also wore a business suit, except with the obvious bulge of a pistol holster under his left armpit. He used an eye loupe to assess the stones. *"Iyi."* Good. *"Guzel."* Beautiful. He went in back and put the rings in a safe.

"Will you need weapons?" the attendant asked.

"No. We have."

The front-desk man eyed the team's windbreakers and gym bags.

"I must see weapon licenses. The law."

More forged documents proffered, and accepted; more paperwork.

"There now must be collateral for cars."

The team expected this. Salih handed Felix two wristwatches. Both were Harry Winston models, a very prestigious brand, for the extremely wealthy only. Felix gave them to the attendant. Each, in the U.S., would cost about a quarter of a million dollars new. They were sold worldwide, and Felix expected that the CIA had bought these in some neutral country, in an untraceable transaction.

The appraiser came out again, inspected the watches, and nodded.

The front-desk man took digital photos of both, printed the photos, recorded the Harry Winston serial numbers on their photos, filled out and signed a form, and gave Felix the receipt for the deposit. The watches went into the safe. They'd be returned when the cars were returned. He finished his cigarette, stubbed the butt in the ashtray, and lit a new one with a gold lighter. He exhaled another cloud of smoke.

"One more thing. Need pictures, each of you. Here please." One by one, Felix and his guys stood where the attendant showed them to, and he took photos. He checked that these came out okay on his computer screen, printed hard copies and added them to his paper files, saved the data to a backup disk, labeled it by hand, and put the disk into the safe.

He called out into the rear office area, louder. Another Turk—rather unfriendly and with a knife scar on his cheek to rival Felix's—appeared soon and took over at the counter. Like the appraiser, he had a big pistol bulging from under his suit jacket.

The attendant made a downward scooping gesture with one hand, which signified that they follow him. He led Felix's group through a door, down a dusty cinder-block corridor, then, after punching keys in an electronic lock, through another door.

They came out into a large, enclosed space in the backmost part of the building. It smelled of fuel and exhaust fumes—both gasoline and diesel—and lubricants. The ceiling lights were harsh, bare, functional fluorescents. The floor, spotted with stains from oil and transmission fluid, was poured concrete. To one side, Felix saw a well-equipped maintenance area, with a hydraulic vehicle lift not now in use. A late-model Audi sat near there, with its front windshield and hood removed.

Must've taken incoming fire, Felix thought. *Wonder who the client was.*

And who shot at them.

Farther on, half a dozen cars were parked as if at an indoor garage, except with more room between them.

"I suggest this one for your guest." The car was a 2012-model, sparkling-clean, black Mercedes-Benz sedan. He opened the driver's door, and showed Felix the window. It was armored, and double glazed. "Other windows all like this." Felix knew that the double glazing prevented eavesdropping by someone bouncing an infrared laser beam off the glass to catch vibrations from people talking inside the car. *Good.* "Between glass is vacuum, not air. Protect more for RPGs." Rocket-propelled grenades. The vacuum would help break up a shaped charge's supersonic jet of hot gas and molten metal. *Very good.* "Doors have armor panels, also front, back, top, two layers, stop RPGs. Special plate under chassis absorb even land mines. See? Look."

Felix peered under the Mercedes. He saw a plate protecting most of the underside of the vehicle. *Ceramic composite.* The plate was backed by a sheet of metal formed like bubble pack, designed to crumple and take the force of a blast.

Felix stood. "No dark window tinting?" This was common on stretch limos used by celebrities, for privacy.

"I can stick on sheets of tinting quick, but not recommend. Draws attention, and harder for you to see out at night."

"Agree, no tinting. . . . What's this?" Felix pointed to small nozzles in the roof of the passenger compartment.

"Fire-suppression system. Automatic. Engine space have same. New gas, like halon, but not toxic. . . . This one, good chase car." The Turk pointed to a dirty, dented jalopy, a brown Hyundai four-door at least ten years old.

"It looks like it's been in an accident," Felix said skeptically.

The attendant smiled, for the first time. "You blend in. That just sheet metal. Chassis, suspension strengthened, engine new, two hundred fifty horsepower, whole drive train new. Passenger place, engine compartment, boot, all armored." The "boot" meant the trunk.

"Petrol tank?" Felix used the British word for gasoline.

"Main and reserve, total one hundred fifty liters." About forty gallons. A large supply, even for something so heavy because of all the hidden armoring. "Tanks hard steel with self-sealing rubber bladder inside. Mercedes same. Tires, both cars, bullet resistant."

Felix waited while his chief and enlisted man opened the hoods, checked in the trunks, sat in the driver seats. Both cars had manual transmissions, which the men expected and knew how to use. They took electronic instruments from their gym bags, and carefully did a visual inspection and swept for bugs or tracking devices.

The attendant smiled again. "Professional. Trust no one."

Salih got in back in the Mercedes. Felix would drive. Costa was tasked to drive the chase car, with the enlisted man in the front passenger seat. The attendant punched a button and the garage doors at the back of the building opened onto a side street. Traffic was heavier now, because it was getting late in the day and the weekend was starting.

With the driver's door ajar, sitting, Felix reached out and

offered to shake the attendant's hand. He switched back to Turkish to close the deal politely.

"*Cok tessekur ederim. Allaha ismarladik.*" Thanks very much. Good-bye.

"*Gule gule,*" the attendant said. So long. "*Hosca kalin.*" Stay safe.

CHAPTER 35

Felix could feel his heart pumping almost as hard as it would in combat. In a way, he *was* in combat. He was trying to negotiate downtown Istanbul traffic in the middle of evening rush hour. The clock on the armored Mercedes's dashboard, which he'd synchronized to his digital watch, said 5:57 P.M. They still had a lot to do before picking up Klaus Mohr at eight.

An auto coming the other way, ignoring the lane-dividing line, almost sideswiped Felix as it used a momentary opening on his side of the street. Horns behind Felix blared—at *him,* for not driving aggressively enough. An accident would cause delays and draw unwanted attention, and make Felix and Salih very vulnerable. Felix wasn't concerned so much about personal injury. With the vehicle's hidden armor, on top of its regular air bags, he and Salih were protected. The danger was hurting someone else in a crash, or hitting a reckless pedestrian.

"The ride's surprisingly smooth," Salih said.

Felix glanced at him in the rearview mirror for an instant.

"Good engine mount. You'd never know the power under the hood. And good shocks. Not too stiff, not too mushy." Both men used English—but accented either Portuguese or Turkish—as the language they had in common according to their cover stories.

They drove on, following a long-preplanned route. Felix tried to keep an eye on the banged-up Hyundai a few cars behind him, but it wasn't easy. And Salih couldn't keep looking out the rear windshield to give him status reports. Though the car was soundproof, a trained observer could still read their lips and watch their movements inside the car; Salih staring backward a lot would be a sure tip-off that he was doing spy tradecraft.

The odds of a tail at this point were much higher. They'd had to sacrifice their anonymity when they rented the cars, and associated themselves with Awais Iqbal and thus with Klaus Mohr—this step was essential, so that they would appear genuine to German consular security and could pick up Mohr, and Salih could take him to the party that Iqbal had promised. *If Mohr has been compromised,* Felix thought, *hostile action could break out at any moment.*

Besides the Germans and their Russian friends, there were also the Mossad, and Turkish counterespionage forces, to worry about. The chase car did its best to watch for a tail and protect the Mercedes's rear. But the chase car itself might have a tail. A few sudden turns would help to check. Felix and his chief had talked this all through in rehearsals.

At a street Felix was waiting for, he made a sharp right as the cars in front of him ran the red. He circled the block of stores and apartment buildings slowly. His eyes refocused constantly between the steel-and-flesh obstacle course ahead of the car and his mirrors that let him look behind. Sometimes he had to jam on the brakes, or floor the accelerator. He worked the gear shift constantly, mostly moving more slowly than a man could run; a heavy, armored auto had a lot of momentum needing precise control. He and Salih were thrown forward against their seat belts, or shoved back against their headrests, over and over. Felix made another right turn, this time driving with traffic that had the green.

He slowed for a wayward pedestrian. *Shit.* In the rearview mirror, he saw that a delivery van behind him wasn't stopping. That driver hit his brakes and skidded half sideways, blocking oncoming traffic, and more brakes squealed. Angry drivers everywhere made rude gestures at Felix.

"You have to stop being so nice to people in the road," Salih said. "No one expects it, least of all that person you were afraid of hitting."

"Yeah," Felix said. "I need to drive more like the locals."

Salih threw his head back, raised his eyebrows, and made a loud tsking sound to show sharp disapproval and also remind Felix—by using proper Turkish body language—whom they were *not* supposed to be: new arrivals. Salih put a hand over his mouth and murmured, "You *are* a local. Been living in Istanbul a year, remember?"

Felix caught himself almost nodding American style, but stopped the give-away gesture. He and Salih had to stay fully in character, living their parts every moment. Felix was supposed to be a war refugee, long acclimatized to the ways of Istanbul. *My defensive driving habits might ruin everything.* He made a sudden, unsignaled right as the light went red in his face. He gunned the engine, scattering natives in the crosswalk.

"Better," Salih said under his breath.

Felix didn't answer. He was too busy watching other cars. The Hyundai was up ahead. Felix had gone in a circle not just to watch for anyone following his vehicle, but to get behind the chase car for a while, and become the chase car himself.

With his right hand he patted the MP-5 laid on the seat next to him, covered now by his windbreaker. The feel of its hard metal contours under the thin nylon cloth reassured him; he'd inserted a thirty-round magazine and now there was one in the chamber. The Mercedes, like the Hyundai, had firing ports concealed in the doors. They were covered by a synthetic-fiber cloth akin to Kevlar, which stopped bullets from one side but allowed a weapon muzzle to be shoved through from the other side—this feature of executive-security customized autos went back twenty years.

They arrived at their next destination. Felix double-parked. He cracked the driver's door and slid out before he could be sideswiped and squashed. He jogged into a tobacconist's. Using some of his Turkish paper money, he bought a prepaid calling card, then jogged back to the Mercedes. Traffic now was such a mess that he had to squeeze in on the passenger side, then slide awkwardly over the MP-5 and the transmission hump and gearshift grip to get into his seat.

This time, gamely, he returned the rude gestures of other drivers. Some shouted insults. Felix was glad he didn't understand much Turkish. He saw Salih stifling a guffaw.

"You don't want to know what some of them called you."

Felix nodded his head down once, to agree.

A couple of blocks later, Felix and the other driver ground to a halt: The chief in the Hyundai had stopped, also double-parked, and was buying himself a calling card at a newsstand kiosk on the sidewalk.

Two lights farther on, the Hyundai made a hard left. Felix didn't follow. Instead he watched for trouble, then continued straight ahead. He wanted to become the lead car again. He came to a traffic circle, as expected. He went around twice, again to check for a tail, and to let the Hyundai get in a good position a few cars behind him. A panel truck worked its way in between them. He and the chief lost sight of each other.

Unless commandos burst out of the back of that truck and start firing antitank launchers at us, we're fine. Again Felix patted the MP-5; Salih wore his under his jacket, also loaded now. *But then Salih doesn't have to drive.* Felix switched on the air-conditioning. He was working up a sweat, just dressed in shirtsleeves.

He came to another cross street he knew to expect. He turned and drove into a municipal parking garage, while the

Hyundai circled the block. Salih stayed in the car with the doors locked, to make sure no one tampered with it.

Felix, relying solely on the knife concealed on his right calf for self-defense, stretched his legs and walked as casually as he could out of the garage and into a crowded local Internet cafe. He knew the World Wide Web had been badly fragmented by the war. But Turkey was a forward-looking, technology-loving country, and everyone here was wired or wireless. Despite international firewalls and broken cross-border server connections, the Internet within Turkey was heavily used.

Felix found an unoccupied pay terminal, and inserted his calling card. He went to an e-mail account whose ISP code, account name, and password he'd memorized. The account had been created by an in-country, CIA-connected agent whom Parker told Felix he had no need to know more about. He didn't check for e-mails, but went directly to the drafts folder. It was empty. None of his two other teams, the men who'd hailed a taxi or the men who'd taken a bus, had checked in yet. Felix changed the account password to something only the SEAL team knew, to prevent unwanted intrusion if the in-country agent was compromised. Felix walked back to his car.

Different people accessing the same e-mail account and leaving messages for each other as unsent drafts was the latest version of an age-old spycraft tool: the dead drop, a place no snooping third party would think to look. Because the drafts were never sent, they were never scrutinized by the government's software that monitored e-mail content—and they couldn't be intercepted in transit by covert adversaries either. *The messages are never in transit.*

Near his Mercedes, Felix glanced around, pretending to check for possible muggers—like all big cities, Istanbul had its share of crime. He was really looking for security cameras, or any people in a direct line of sight. Satisfied, he got into the car, put the MP-5 strap over his left shoulder, and donned the windbreaker. Driving now was uncomfortable, but Felix had been through far worse discomfort in training and in battle.

Felix and Salih left the garage, paying in cash for their short stay. Felix, saw the Hyundai as it circled the block. He wanted, and so allowed, Chief Costa to notice him. By maintaining a neutral expression, instead of giving some other prearranged sign, Felix informed the chief: no word from the other SEALs yet.

Felix drove to a high-rise luxury hotel, and stopped the Mercedes at the underground valet parking. He told the attendant his passenger was just checking in for now, and they'd need the car again soon. Felix opened the door for Salih, then unlocked the trunk. He took out both gym bags.

Inside the busy lobby, at ground level, they declined the offer from a bellhop to take their bags. They stood in line at the check-in desk and waited their turn. They again provided the clerk with the name Awais Iqbal, gave the reservation confirmation code that Iqbal had obtained more than a week earlier, and explained the last-minute substitution of Salih for Iqbal. They presented their documents, and the clerk did a quick verification of everything on his computer. Salih paid in advance for the room and for the party buffet with gold South African Krugerrand one-ounce coins. These were readily accepted—the price of gold had skyrocketed since the war, and the coins had long been sold worldwide to investors and collectors. The clerk gave Salih his change in cash, and handed him a plastic key card for the electronic lock to their room. They took the elevator to the twenty-second floor, the highest level. Their room was actually an elaborate corner suite at the end of the corridor, laid out for business entertaining. On one side out in the hall were emergency stairs. The chief quickly checked them—no surprises.

The suite immediately next door was already occupied. Through the walls, Felix and Salih could hear music playing, laughter, and loud conversation in Japanese. Felix put his ear to the wall.

Only men. . . . Their call girls haven't arrived yet.

He glanced at his watch. After 7 P.M.

Felix allowed himself a quick look at the magnificent view, and then pulled the curtains closed. He took a device from his gym bag and did a sweep of the suite for listening devices. *Clean.*

The phone rang. Salih answered, then said something in Turkish and hung up. "On his way," Salih told Felix. In a minute, the enlisted SEAL from the chase car came in, without his gym bag, but with his windbreaker on. Felix knew Chief Costa had dropped the man off nearby and that he'd walked to the hotel. Part of the plan was that he would now change cars to ride with Felix and Salih. All of them went downstairs and out of the hotel, onto the crowded and noisy street. They found another Internet pay terminal. Felix checked again for messages. This time both other teams said they were ready. No acknowledgment was needed; from now on everyone knew what to do. Felix deleted the drafts, then emptied the trash folder.

They walked to the hotel's parking garage, picked up the Mercedes, and drove back into Istanbul traffic. They saw the Hyundai with the chief at the place they'd agreed upon; he'd been maneuvering around the area, still watching for hostile agents watching *him.* Felix let the Hyundai get a few car lengths behind him. Then he set off for his next stop, the German consulate. It was close to Taksim Square, in the heart of the New City, very Westernized and with a very active nightlife.

———

Klaus Mohr waited in the lobby of the consulate. After playing every trick card he could—reinforced by brown-nosing and pleading—he'd been given permission to go out with the Turk who was standing in for Awais Iqbal. He'd been ordered not to get the least bit drunk, to take the usual measures against sexual disease, and to save more than adequate en-

ergy for his work with the Kampfschwimmer later. He was
told in no uncertain terms that he needed to leave the party at
midnight, and would be picked up by a consulate car, with
security—some of which he'd see, and some of which he
wouldn't. Before he left the consulate, the guard at the desk
was to know the exact location of the party . . . and Mohr and
this Turk would be tailed there as a further precaution.

Mohr worked to behave naturally now. The lobby guards
weren't paying him any special attention. They had no reason
to. On the contrary, they'd been warned to act naturally
themselves, alert but nonchalant, despite unmistakable
changes in the work rhythms and moods of the senior staff.
Though they didn't know the reason for their instructions on
how to behave, Mohr did: No clues could be allowed to leak
about Pandora and the stepped-up timing of the Afrika Korps
offensive.

*If these guards only knew . . . But there are also surveil-
lance cameras in the lobby, monitored by hard men who do
know.* Mohr forced himself to not keep looking at his watch
or the clock on the wall, or right at a camera. The Turk who
was supposed to meet him was late. He'd received no last-
minute confirmation that the stag party, the whole extraction
plan, was still on. He could think of a dozen things that might
have gone wrong, things he wouldn't have heard about or
been told about.

There was still the danger that his loyalty was suspect, and
that he was being entrapped.

The worst of it was that only Mohr himself understood
what would really have to be done to halt Pandora. His rescuers, if they even arrived, had no idea of what was truly
called for, and no conception of how narrow the margin of
time had suddenly become.

Mohr tried to redirect his concern and doubt into a difficult
masquerade: He was supposed to be bound for a lecherous night
on the town, to lustfully celebrate his legal separation from a
now thoroughly estranged wife. He was supposed to also be on

the verge of the final fruition of his astounding technical genius, putting into practical effect breakthroughs he'd spent his entire career on. *Hurrah for the Fatherland! Long live the kaiser!* Mohr felt bitter about how he'd been used for years by the coup conspirators, and about how he'd let himself be used.

Someone came into the lobby from outside. Mohr looked up hopefully, his chest tight—but it was only a minor consulate employee.

A few minutes later one of the guards at the outer gate came inside. Again Mohr held his breath. The man popped into the rest room near the lobby, then went back to his post.

Mohr couldn't help but glance at the clock. It was 8:25.

The desk guard read his mind.

"Probably just traffic."

Mohr nodded. He hoped so. He didn't trust himself to speak.

The gate guard came inside again. Mohr's heart skipped a beat. But the guard murmured to the desk guard about something Mohr couldn't hear. Neither of them even looked in his direction. They murmured together further. Mohr shifted his attention to the doors. He reminded himself that to act impatient at this point would be normal. *Not* being annoyed by the delay could give him away. He heard the desk guard typing on his computer.

The gate guard went to the armored glass doors leading back outside. Mohr felt utterly crestfallen. He swallowed so hard his Adam's apple hurt, making a noise he was sure both guards could hear. The gate guard stopped abruptly. He turned to Mohr, with the door propped half open against his back. Now Mohr could barely breathe.

"Herr Mohr, your ride is here."

Mohr almost wobbled, weak kneed, as he got up. He realized with a mix of exhilaration and fear that the gate guard was standing there to politely hold the door for him.

A Mercedes-Benz with a driver and another man in front idled by the curb, in the restricted parking zone outside the consulate compound's security wall. A third man, with dark skin and a thick black mustache, was standing on the sidewalk. He was shorter than Mohr by at least twenty centimeters—about eight inches—and had a heavier, stockier build.

He saw Mohr, smiled, approached, and greeted Mohr in fluent German. They got into the back of the Mercedes, and fastened their seat belts. The driver barged his way into traffic.

"Herr Iqbal again sends his apologies. I think you'll get everything you expected without him, though. I intend to take good care of you."

"You speak German very well."

The Turk sighed. "I used to live in Frankfurt. I was a building engineer."

Mohr wasn't sure what to say next. Was this supposed to be some sort of code he hadn't been told about? Who knew what messages hadn't gotten through to him the past few days?

"The consulate guards know where I'm going, but I don't myself. Where *are* we going?"

"Hotel Mercure."

Mohr was impressed—one of the finest in Istanbul.

The driver narrowly beat a red light, and a pedestrian made a rude gesture. The driver mumbled something that sounded vaguely like Italian but wasn't. The other person in front grunted in response.

"These men work for you?"

"Rent-a-guards, like the car. Refugees from Portugal."

"You speak Portuguese?"

"I talk to them in English. They understand it enough."

Mohr nodded. The motion was jerky; his muscles were tight from nerves.

The Turk took a calendar book out of a jacket pocket, and made some notes in the back with a felt-tip pen. He held the book open in his lap, well below the level of the car windows, and aimed it at Mohr. Darkness had fallen, and the New City streets near Taksim Square were well lit. Enough light came into the car for Mohr to see.

Mohr saw, for some reason written in English, "Quiet until hotel." Then he understood. The Turk had used English to make it look like an improvised phrase book meant for the bodyguards.

Tradecraft every step of the way. God knows who's following us besides my own security backup . . .

No. They're not my own anymore. From here on, other Germans are the enemy.

━━━━━

Once back in the hotel suite, Felix turned on the stereo. He tuned the radio to a Turkish talk show, and turned the volume up until it was very loud. The enlisted SEAL did another sweep for bugs: clean. A buffet of food had been laid out at the bar area during their absence, along with a big urn of coffee.

Klaus Mohr sat on a couch, next to Salih. No one spoke. Costa arrived; he'd left the Hyundai in a public garage nearby. He whispered gently in Felix's ear, "Two cars were tailing you. Both had two occupants. Looked like German toughs. One car parked in the hotel garage; I expect that's the one that'll pick up Mohr later. The driver's sitting, I guess to be on call in case this party ends early or Mohr doesn't like it. The other car's circling, as if to keep up roving surveillance around the hotel." He quickly told Felix the make of the cars, their colors, and their license-plate numbers. Felix memorized the information and shot Costa a thumbs-up.

Costa had a remarkable knack for vehicle surveillance and countersurveillance—one reason he was on the team. Costa had also had an unfair advantage over the Germans. Felix drove Mohr and Salih from the consulate to the hotel using a preplanned route with features that would force any tailing vehicles to exhibit tradecraft—which would show to someone with Costa's trained eye. And since both SEAL cars knew the route to the hotel, they could sometimes split up and then get back together, giving Costa relative mobility even in traffic. But the Germans needed to stay glued to the auto with Klaus Mohr, if they were to provide Mohr with constant protection while in the streets.

Soon Chief Porto and four more enlisted SEALs came in, singly or in pairs. The whole team was assembled.

The house phone rang. Salih answered, spoke, hung up.

He grinned.

There was another knock. Salih went to the peephole, then opened the door to the suite. Three very attractive, well-dressed young women came in. Salih talked to them rapidly in Turkish, and offered each a large amount of cash. The women seemed surprised, but not for long. They took the money, giggled, piled plates with food from the buffet, and went into one of the bedrooms and closed the door. Soon Felix heard male voices and music coming from there, in between the Turkish men speaking on the radio, and the muffled noise of the Japanese next door—both sexes now, sounding very intoxicated.

Our own call girls are watching a movie or TV show. One of Felix's teams had been tasked to arrange for the high-class hookers, by asking around among local taxi drivers for a recommendation, suitable for entertaining a diplomat, and then making a pay-phone call. Felix went into the other two bedrooms, and turned on music on the radios, different stations. He turned on more music in the kitchenette next to the bar and buffet.

Porto took small tools from his bag, opened the hallway door halfway, and worked for a minute on the electronic lock. He let the door slam shut. An enlisted SEAL went through the door to the bedroom area and closed it behind him; Porto put his ear to that door. Satisfied, he stepped back, glanced at Felix, and nodded. The internal door was sound-proof, as advertised.

"It's okay to talk now," Felix said in English. "Don't raise your voice above the radios. I made them loud in case we missed any bugs. Just let the Turkish chatter and the music flow, and talk under it."

"What did you do to the door?" Mohr asked.

Felix hadn't expected the question. Then he remembered that Mohr was supposed to be a techie. "The lock has an electromagnet, right? And all room locks are wired to a central processor, so hotel people can change key-card combinations from downstairs when someone checks out."

"Yes."

"The door acts like a sounding board. When vibrating, trace currents from that lock could be used to eavesdrop on this room."

Mohr smiled weakly, interested in the shoptalk but taken aback by the need for such heavy precautions. "I had not considered that."

"We did. Part of our job."

"And those women?"

"Iqbal promised you an orgy. They're the orgy. Just in case someone unfriendly is keeping tabs from in the lobby, or bribed one of the reception clerks. Everything has to look legit, so we don't raise any alarms too soon."

"You seem to have thought of everything."

"Now is where we start to get more free form."

"What do you mean? Who are you?"

Felix sensed that Mohr was becoming depressed. *Here he is at last in American hands, and instead of bugle calls and parades it's all so furtive and matter-of-fact. Parker and Salih told me to watch for this.*

Felix wasn't sympathetic. He had to stay suspicious of the guy. This meet could still be a setup. Felix needed to act a part, and he psyched himself up. Parker had told him bluntly to *use* the drama of the moment—the initial contact—to establish rapport in case Mohr was genuine.

"Allow me to introduce myself. Lieutenant Felix Estabo, U.S. Navy SEALs." Felix shook hands with Mohr as warmly as he could, and gave him his most sincere, endearing smile. "You have no idea how much we and our government appreciate everything you're doing, Klaus." He used Mohr's given name to speed their bonding. "Call me Felix, please."

"Yes, all right, Felix."

Felix introduced the members of his team, and Mohr shook hands all around.

"Let's dig in. We need the sustenance. Klaus, why don't you go first."

Everyone loaded plates and grabbed hot coffee and started eating. The SEALs made sure to behave with quiet confidence; they'd been briefed to let Mohr feel he held center stage, while reassuring him that they'd come well prepared and could handle every aspect of the high-risk defector rescue. Mohr saw this, and after a few bites quickly perked up.

"What time are your keepers supposed to collect you?" Felix asked.

"Midnight. How did you know they'd do it that way?"

"Professional surmise. That's how we'd handle it if we were them. Then they take you to the safe house?"

"Yes. More surmise?"

"That, plus the info Iqbal could get to us."

Mohr thought for a moment. "Now I understand better. He asked me certain specifics, indirectly."

Felix nodded, then told him things that had stopped being secret anyway. Again, Mohr needed to know that the Americans were competent...plus, it wouldn't hurt to pointedly remind him of who his friends were. "When your brothel acquaintance fled town after that attempted Mossad hit, it really put our side on the spot. Your last message to us got through, but the lady's comm plan with you went out the window when she did. Let's just say other assets were called into play, and it was rough when we found out the consulate had you under close confinement. We did what we could in a hurry. The main thing is, it worked."

Mohr nodded. Everyone finished eating and put the dirty dishes aside. They huddled around a glass coffee table. Costa took writing tablets and pens out of his gym bag. Porto produced a cigarette case and a lighter, lit several cigarettes, and let them smolder in a couple of handy ashtrays.

"Use single sheets of paper," Felix told Mohr, "placed directly on the glass, to leave no impressions on the underneath sheets of a pad. . . . This is flash paper. Touch it with a burning cigarette, it's useless ash in a split second."

"I understand."

"Now, we have very little time for you to tell us everything you know about this safe house, the people who'll be in it, and this unusual equipment of yours."

CHAPTER 36

At first Felix had trouble believing the things Mohr said his equipment at the safe house could do. This set off red flags immediately. Felix's orders were to insist on a summary of what Mohr offered the Allies. He was to judge how forthcoming Mohr behaved now that a gesture of good faith had been made to him—by the U.S. sending the SEALs—and abort the extraction at once if anything at all seemed fishy. Force protection came first. Felix and his team were not to unnecessarily endanger themselves, Salih or Parker, the captured German minisub, or USS *Challenger* without at least some up-front testing of Mohr's credibility.

But sitting on the couch in the suite, Mohr rattled off unclassified research going back decades. He referred repeatedly to Albert Einstein's own expression from the 1930s, "spooky action at a distance." To check this all out, Felix sent Porto to use an Internet pay terminal with its choice of search engines, to verify that these published theories and lab experiments were real. The suite itself had good computer equipment, but Felix had no intention of even touching it.

Porto came back, and reported that everything Mohr had said was true.

Meanwhile, Costa went downstairs, retrieved the Mercedes by using the claim check Felix had given him, made sure to elude any tail, and then drove to the quiet top level of a different garage. He exchanged the license plates on the Mercedes for a different set from his gear bag, then used special aerosol cans to put a lot of dust on the car, and road dirt around the fenders and wheel wells. This step was necessary since the Germans surely knew the Mercedes from when it had picked up Mohr; when Costa was finished it looked very different. He put on a disguise, drove the car into the underground garage at the Hotel Mercure, and went back upstairs.

————————

It was getting late, and the briefing had to end. In an unused bedroom with a private bath, Klaus Mohr stripped and took a shower. He dressed again, and combed his hair, but left his hair slightly damp on purpose. Back by the bar, he took a few puffs of a cigarette, then swirled some Turkish liqueur in his mouth and spat it out in the kitchenette sink.

This is all what my bodyguards will expect.

During the briefing, the SEAL leader Felix had sent men off to run errands now and then; some of them returned and some didn't. The briefing involved a lot of sketching of the safe house, answering piercing questions from Felix's chiefs about the Kampfschwimmer and their weapons, and thinking through each step of a hasty assault. Mohr gave a detailed description of what his field-equipment modules and special tool kit looked like. Salih discussed with him, at length, the personalities and attitudes of the individual Kampfschwimmer in the team they'd be going up against.

Extensive map work followed, choosing routes of approach and escape, picking places to meet if the team got split up, and deciding where Mohr should wait—somewhere well outside the line of fire.

Now, Felix looked Mohr up and down.

"Remember, Klaus, you're a warrior, and you aren't alone. We'll be right behind you. Just make sure you don't lose that knockout pen, and for the love of God don't use it on yourself by mistake."

"Yes."

The chief named Costa and one of his men departed, to get a head start. Then Felix put on a false beard and eyeglasses, so the guards wouldn't recognize him from before, and told Mohr to give him five minutes. Felix and the other SEALs walked out.

In the suite, the radios still played and the call girls still watched TV. It was just before midnight. Mohr left and took an elevator to the lobby. One of the bodyguards from the consulate came into the lobby by a different elevator from the underground parking garage. Without a word Mohr followed him, and got in the back of a dark blue BMW luxury sedan. As Felix had told him to, he sat behind the guard who was in the front passenger seat, and he didn't buckle his seat belt.

———

Felix drove the dirtied-up Mercedes while Porto used the front passenger seat and Salih sat in back. Costa and his enlisted man were in the Hyundai. Mohr had said the safe house was in a run-down neighborhood on the far side of the Old City. The Kampfschwimmer team and their gear were due to be back from their latest field test by eight P.M., to allow for possible delays in their getting there to meet Mohr. Felix was unhappy because this precluded his team from arriving at the safe house first, to ambush the Germans unawares while still outside, or to even just send a point-man observer to do a head count and size things up.

Felix worried that the schedule had been set by the Germans for exactly this reason. Maybe they'd been tipped off to expect an attack tonight—perhaps tipped off by Klaus Mohr himself, or perhaps because Awais Iqbal was a double agent really owned by the Germans, not the CIA. Felix knew nothing of Iqbal but hearsay. Mohr's unclassified technical references, since they were public information, by their nature didn't conclusively prove yet that he deserved Felix's trust; they just suggested that he might be of very high value if he was honest about his achievements and actually meant to defect.

I'll have to find out the hard way.

To reach the Old City, the German driver with Mohr and the German chase car—a black Mercedes—were on the Ataturk Bridge. Mohr had predicted this, saying he'd realized from previous trips that the driver's supposedly random choice of which bridge to take across the Golden Horn fit a pattern. Four vehicles now made an odd motorcade amid the traffic on the bridge: Mohr's car was first, followed by the German chase car. Felix's Mercedes followed the other Mercedes, and the beat-up Hyundai followed Felix. The Germans, while still in the New City, had already used standard techniques to locate and evade a tail. Felix was prepared for this: As long as Felix and Porto, or Costa in the Hyundai, held contact on the Germans' black Mercedes chase car, they could rely on it to keep them within range of Mohr's BMW. As long as Felix trailed the chase car, not Mohr, and worked with the Hyundai for mutual support, the American cars could avoid being spotted by the Germans, and could also better check that they weren't themselves being tailed.

On the bridge, with no cross traffic, their positions were locked in and Felix could take stock for a minute. He knew his reinforcements were already in place across the bridge. A highway, Kennedy Cadesi, ran like a giant U along the whole shoreline of the Old City peninsula. It could take the Germans close to the safe house by a long route, but one where traffic moved very fast—making it too easy for assassins with armor-piercing rounds to do a rolling drive-by hit. Felix thus expected that Mohr's car and its trailing escort would use local streets that cut straight inland across the peninsula, since in the Old City maze, skirting the tangled warrens of

Istanbul's grand bazaar, they'd be better able to make sure no one was following Mohr. Felix was plagued by a similar concern, that he'd picked up an undetected tail, or series of tails.

The Mossad is a main factor. Their tradecraft is superb and they'd have access to a large supply of vehicles if they wanted. They might be on us right now and we wouldn't know. I'm praying they won't interfere with us trailing the Germans, since from their angle we're possibly about to do their work for them by getting rid of Mohr one way or another.

Felix's heartbeat started to rise. They were almost over the bridge. Soon he'd know if the Germans took the Kennedy Cadesi or local streets after all—this was essential to his plan to separate Mohr from his bodyguards soon without alerting the Kampfschwimmer. If he'd misread German intentions, and they did go onto the highway, the whole extraction plan would almost certainly collapse.

———

When it happened, it happened fast, because Felix and all his men knew that once they sprang their trap, every second counted. They had to do it early, soon after the Germans came off the bridge, before their choice of paths became too varied, and coordinating the SEALs' redeployments would become a mad and iffy scramble.

For the first time, Felix and his men used their radios. The radios were digitally encrypted, and broadcast their spread-spectrum signals in a radar frequency band—the transmissions bounced around intervening buildings better, and were also much less likely to be overheard.

Felix got right behind the German chase car, but then lagged back, allowing space to open up. He pressed his radio's talk button, said a single word in Portuguese, and released the button. He heard two one-word responses quickly: The reinforcements were in position, and no Turkish policemen were visible. Felix pressed to talk again, and gave the go-ahead signal.

A taxi came out of a side street and T-boned the German chase car. The impact was loud enough that Felix heard a *bang* even through his own car's soundproofing. The momentum of the impact swung the German vehicle at an angle and carried the taxi into the middle of the intersection. A gypsy cab came from the opposite direction, and swerved and screeched to a halt in front of the German car, barely missing it. Felix floored the accelerator. The armored Mercedes rear-ended the German, hard enough to deploy air bags in Felix's and Porto's faces. Felix coughed from the dust kicked up.

The drivers of the Istanbul taxi and the gypsy cab—both SEALs—got out and started shouting at each other, and at the Germans in the chase car. Felix and Porto also got out. Broken glass from smashed headlights and taillights littered the street.

To passersby, yet another Istanbul fender-bender pileup had just occurred. Auto horns blared.

The SEAL chase car, the Hyundai, added to the ruckus by driving onto the sidewalk to bypass the wrecks.

———

The noise and chaos behind Mohr were impossible to miss. His driver halted in traffic, cursing, the moment he realized the chase car had been involved in a bad accident. The bodyguard in the front passenger seat reached for his radio, and Mohr reached for the special pen. Felix had said to just touch it to the skin at the back of the neck. He leaned forward, as if to speak to the bodyguard, and applied the pen. He belched to cover the slight hissing sound it made when pressure on the point activated the injection spray.

The driver finished putting the gearshift in park. He looked backward as Mohr leaned toward him.

"Wass?" What?

Mohr pointed in the other direction, ahead of the car. The

driver, confused, turned to look, and in that instant Mohr got him with the pen. Seconds later, both men were slumped forward against their shoulder belts, heavily sedated, with no needle marks on their necks. The compressed-air-powered, high-pressure spray drove the sleep drug through their epidermis, and capillary absorption did the rest. Mohr palmed the hip flask Felix had given him, and while pretending to see what was wrong with his driver and bodyguard, got high-proof schnapps on their chins and down their clothes. With a handkerchief he wiped his fingerprints from the empty flask, leaned farther forward, wrapped the bodyguard's right hand around it, and rested the sleeping man's hand in his lap. Still using his handkerchief, he unlocked the right front door.

An old brown Hyundai pulled up on the sidewalk next to Mohr's BMW. Mohr recognized Chief Costa; he'd been expecting him. With help from an enlisted SEAL riding with Costa, they moved the pair of Germans to the BMW's backseat without taking them out of the car. Mohr switched to the Hyundai while the enlisted SEAL took the BMW driver's seat.

Salih, speaking rapid-fire Turkish, reassured pedestrians that no one was badly hurt. More SEALs, passengers in the gypsy cab and the taxi, joined the accusations and wild gesticulating that raged back and forth in German, Turkish, and Portuguese. Two of the SEALs, hamming up concern, reached out to calm the German driver and bodyguard. Felix knew both SEALs held knockout pens. The Germans staggered, increasingly woozy.

Salih shouted in Turkish. Felix knew he was supposed to be saying. "They're going into shock! Concussion! You, you, help me!" Salih pointed at Felix and Porto. Salih said something else to the gathering crowd; he was telling people that he and his friends would take the men to a hospital.

They carried the nearly unconscious Germans and put them in the back of Felix's Mercedes. The gypsy-cab driver and his passenger got back into the undamaged cab and moved it out of the way, into the street facing the halted German BMW and Costa's Hyundai up ahead. The taxi driver, with help from other SEALs, pushed his ruined taxi to the corner of the intersection, blocking the crosswalk, but at least not blocking traffic, and left it there. He ran to the gypsy cab and crowded in.

Salih got into the damaged German Mercedes, pretending that the drive train had been bashed out of commission—so no one would suspect it was armored and thus get too nosy or have the car stick in their mind. Salih worked the steering wheel while Felix prepared to push from behind with the SEALs' own armored Mercedes, damaged superficially but totally driveable.

Ahead of them, the BMW and Hyundai were both moving now, down the street. Felix used his knife to cut away his spent air bag, and tossed it onto the sleeping Germans' legs. The SEAL in back arranged it like a blanket. Horns died down as traffic started crawling again. But Felix heard sirens in the distance, getting closer. Someone had phoned 155 or 112 or both, the Turkish equivalents of 911 for police or for an ambulance.

A hundred yards farther on, Salih and Felix came to an alley. They both knew it would be there. As Salih steered the Germans' Mercedes, Felix used his car to shove the other into the alley, to get it out of the way and more or less out of sight. Salih joined him, again in the front passenger seat. Now Felix's Mercedes was chock-full, with two unconscious Germans and a very pumped-up SEAL in back.

Felix took the first right turn he could. He knew the stolen gypsy cab, the rented Hyundai, and the commandeered German BMW would split up and take shortcuts to a nearby deserted industrial area. They'd avoid entanglement in a Turkish police investigation of the accident—they'd rendezvous again at a prechosen isolated point. Temporarily abandoned autos were a common sight in Istanbul after accidents, and drivers not lingering to be questioned by the cops was normal. What wasn't normal was that the damaged taxi was stolen, and the damaged and dumped Mercedes had a license plate that might be traced to German consular ownership.

"Did they use their radio?" Felix demanded of Salih. "Or a cell phone?" He hadn't noticed himself, and was afraid the Germans he'd rear-ended had called the consulate for help before they'd gotten out of their car.

At least their air bags didn't deploy, so I don't think the crash set off an emergency signal.

"I couldn't tell either," Salih said.

Felix squeezed the steering wheel harder. "Time is of the essence now." In minutes the consulate might figure out what was happening, talk to someone senior enough to make a decision, and then send a warning to the Kampfschwimmer in the safe house. Felix and his team had to beat that deadline or they'd lose the vital element of surprise.

But first, they had to dispose of these two drugged Germans.

The hardest part of murder is disposing of the bodies.

Bloody corpses dumped somewhere would attract immediate attention.

Felix came to a pair of old, dark warehouses; he shut off his headlights and turned in between them. He, Salih, and Porto got out and hurried to remove the two Germans.

They arranged them side by side, slumped against one of the buildings. Porto splashed cheap whiskey in their mouths and on their clothes—he didn't need to get any into their stomachs or their bloodstreams, since by the time they revived, the SEALs hoped to be long gone. He opened a canteen, which he and Felix had filled earlier to have ready. The chief poured stale human urine into the crotches of both unconscious bodyguards. Felix knew, per the plan, that the two drugged Germans from the other car would be dumped elsewhere the same way. The original Turkish civilian drivers of the taxi and the gypsy cab had been relieved of their vehicles in a similar manner by some of Felix's men much earlier:

The SEALs had hailed taxis repeatedly, chatting up drivers in fractured English during short rides, and picked ones who were self-employed and just starting the evening work shift—so the thefts wouldn't be reported prematurely.

Public drunkenness in Istanbul is an increasing problem, despite the many Muslims who don't drink. One thing that doesn't draw much notice is a wino or two conked out, especially when they've pissed themselves. Even a local cop is very unlikely to haul them in. They're messy and they really stink.

CHAPTER 37

U nder a railroad trestle, Mohr dashed from Costa's
      Hyundai to the armored Mercedes that Felix and
      Salih had rented. The BMW and gypsy cab stood
guard from farther off. Then, with four vehicles to work with
now, they did a much more extensive check for tails—there
were no signs of any.

The autos drove on as a group, making no attempt at
stealth now, running badly behind schedule. Felix parked the
Mercedes in the shadows between the rare streetlamps in the
seedy neighborhood near the safe house. Inside the car with
the doors locked, Mohr ought to be fully protected from any
hooligans who might bother him. Mohr was visibly nervous.
Felix gave him a spare pistol just in case, and to make him
feel more a part of the team.

"We'll be back. Sit tight."

"You have to kill them all before they can damage the
computer modules."

Felix had a horrible thought for the first time. *It comes
from being so rushed.* "Do the gadgets have self-destructs or
booby traps built in?"

"No. Too risky. But they aren't bulletproof either."

"We have to go. Slouch like you're taking a nap, but keep your eyes open."

"If I see Kampfschwimmer, not you, I'll shoot myself."

Felix knew Mohr meant it. *That's probably the best thing for him, if this safe-house attack does come unglued. . . .*

Felix jumped into the back of the gypsy cab, and the little assault convoy roared off. They halted at their preselected staging area. Everyone piled out of the cars and opened the trunks.

———

The Kampfschwimmer safe house was well chosen, in the middle of a dark street of old two- and three-story buildings. The entire block seemed to Felix to reek of neglect and poverty and crime. *I wouldn't want to walk down this street alone, even armed.* Felix and his team were now geared up for battle. They wore black flak vests and ceramic-composite helmets, with equipment harnesses and lightweight night-vision goggles. Under the helmets and goggles they wore gas masks. The fighting would be at short range—no sniper rifle, no fragmentation or lethal-concussion grenades.

They knew from Mohr that the safe house appeared to not have any external security cameras, and he'd never seen displays for them inside, but one of Felix's chiefs made as sure as he could with image-intensified binoculars. Then Salih walked down the street, still in casual civilian clothes, and tried to see if there were miniaturized surveillance lenses after all. Past the safe house, he gestured that he didn't spot any up close. Felix thought it would be hard to tell with the little moonlight to go by. *But, lenses in a slum?* Everyone *knows how to spot them these days. Here, with nosy and paranoid neighbors, they might make a safe house less safe. . . . In sixty seconds we'll find out.*

Felix's team moved up both sides of the street, hugging the shadows, in a tactical formation. Most of their magazines were loaded with flat-nosed bullets, to avoid any chance of overpenetrating two structural walls and going into the occupied buildings on either side. On the back of their flak vests they had stenciled "EMNIYET," Turkish for police, in white.

When they were near the targeted building's front, Felix used an infrared scanner to locate people inside by their body heat. No image. He turned it off and on again. Nothing.

The damn thing's broken.... Mohr said to expect ten men.

A chief with a directional mike also had it aimed at the building. He tried different windows, then made hand signals.

No conversations overheard. Not even radios playing.

Salih knocked on the door of the safe house. Somebody on the other side said something, and Salih answered, disguising his voice. His tone was sniveling, pathetic, but persistent—as if he refused to go away. He got louder, on the verge of hysteria.

Expecting Klaus Mohr momentarily, and wanting to be rid of this nuisance before Salih might make a scene, a Kampfschwimmer unlocked the heavy, rusty, metal-slab front door.

Felix knew Salih would start in Turkish, then switch to fractured German if the Kampfschwimmer didn't speak Turkish. He was pretending to want to make a heroin buy, and a friend had said this was the place. The German would assume he had the wrong address, causing a moment's hesitation.

Felix gave the signal. His men dashed forward, their MP-5 shoulder stocks unfolded, rounds in the chambers, safeties off.

On the run, shoving Salih aside, Felix authoritatively yelled *"Polis!"*—another Turkish word for police.

"Lutfen," Salih begged as he fell to the ground and rolled out of the way. *Please.* Then in his normal voice he yelled up and down the block in Turkish. Felix knew he was announcing a police raid, and telling everyone to stay inside and stay down.

On this block, a drug-house raid is believable. Most of the residents are probably glad it's not them being raided.

For another crucial moment, the Kampfschwimmer would be confused. They knew one thing—their safe house was not a heroin connection. They'd assume a Turkish SWAT team had followed Salih, and thus also had the wrong address.

Felix's team poured through the door, shouting *"Polis!"* over and over, fanning out and climbing the staircase as the metal door slammed shut behind them. Felix picked a human target and his weapon barked, the recoil pounding against his shoulder as spent brass flew. On that cue his team opened fire.

Kampfschwimmer darted for their weapons. Felix's chiefs both threw flash-bang gas grenades. They detonated, and Felix saw spots even though he'd known to close his eyes. Military tear gas filled the air.

Felix was panting and his gas-mask lenses were fogging already. He pumped round after round into every Kampfschwimmer's face or abdomen he saw, with his weapon set on two-round bursts. He wasn't sparing of ammo, and quickly had to change magazines.

A bullet struck his flak vest, knocking him backward. SEALs on either side fired past him; another German screamed and fell, dead.

"First floor clear!" Porto shouted in Portuguese. His voice was muffled by his gas mask.

"Go! Go! Go!" Felix bellowed, also in Portuguese.

"Cellar clear!" came from below.

Felix's ears were ringing painfully now, from the grenades and loud reports of weapons indoors. But the noise was part of the plan. Through the mental tunnel vision of combat, Felix caught glimpses of his men moving from room to room, covering each other, looking down the sights of their weapons. They swept their gazes and MP-5s in unison from side to side. Their muzzles spit fire as they shot at Kampfschwimmer, and more muzzles flamed as the Germans shot back. Chipped plaster fell from the walls where stray bullets hit, and upholstery stuffing flew around like windblown snow. Felix heard breaking glass and smashing porcelain.

He advanced and almost slipped in a dead German's

blood. Tear gas mixing with more and more gun smoke further obscured the view outside his mask. There was a sizzling blue-white flash and all the lights went out.

The fuse box must've been hit.

Muzzle flashes punctuated the dark.

Felix flipped down his night-vision goggles.

"Second floor clear," Porto shouted.

The surviving Germans had retreated to the top floor.

The top floor, Mohr said, held his clean room and tools.

"Go! Go! Go!" Felix yelled. Four SEALs dashed up the rickety stairs, Costa and Porto tossing two more flash-bang tear-gas grenades. Felix heard the Kampfschwimmer coughing.

They got a strong dose already, even if they've pulled on gas masks by now.

Felix and his three other men rushed to a spot on the second floor and reloaded with custom armor-piercing ammo. Felix gestured upward to exactly where they should shoot. They began to fire straight through the ceiling. They were creating a wall of enfilading fire, to keep the Kampfschwimmer from moving into Mohr's equipment clean room—if they hadn't reached it yet.

But I can't stop the Germans from firing into there, and my men must be very careful. Mohr's modules aren't bulletproof.

A body tumbled heavily down the stairs to the third floor. Felix kept pumping rounds along a perimeter in the ceiling. His magazine ran empty. Again he had to reload.

A stream of bullets came back through the ceiling. The man next to Felix was struck on the top of his bulletproof helmet, so hard he was knocked out. He fell, reflexively squeezing his trigger; his MP-5 fired as Felix ducked. Another burst from upstairs stitched the unconscious man's chest. Rounds were stopped by his flak vest, but one leg jerked when it took a hit.

Felix had to keep firing through the ceiling at all costs. He was running low on ammo. He was afraid his armor-piercing rounds would punch through the roof, despite their reduced propellant charge, and come back down through the air and hurt or kill an innocent person somewhere. A main cross beam, too splintered, snapped, and part of the ceiling sagged.

"Cease fire! *Cease fire!* Third floor clear! Roof clear!" That was Chief Costa, still using Portuguese.

"Man down, second floor!" Felix shouted.

Da Rosa, the SEALs' first-aid specialist, hurried from above and went to work on the wounded man's leg.

"Sir," he reported, "we lost a man."

Oh, Jesus. Even through the gas mask, Felix could hear da Rosa's distress. "Who? Where?"

"Fernando, sir." Fernando Gabrielli, one of Felix's enlisted SEALs. Da Rosa said he'd been shot twice in the head as they'd assaulted the top floor.

That was him tumbling down the stairs.

Felix had no time for grief or regrets. His breathing inside his own mask was very ragged now.

"Find Mohr's modules! Find his tools!" Without them, all this carnage would have been for nothing.

"We're in the clean room!" Chief Costa's voice came from upstairs. "Tool kit looks okay! No modules up here!"

"Check again!"

"We did, sir! Negative modules on roof or third floor!"

Felix felt a stab to his heart. *What if they'd left the field gear somewhere else, as a security measure?*

Felix's men from upstairs clambered down. Chief Porto was clutching a bullet wound through his forearm. Da Rosa helped him bandage it. Another SEAL held a box by the handle: Mohr's tool case. One man just stood there in the dark. Even through his night-vision goggles, Felix could tell he was in a daze.

That's one dead and two wounded. At least I didn't see arterial blood spurt from either wound. But I think the chief's got a broken bone in that arm.

He saw that da Rosa was putting a splint around Porto's wound.

And where in hell are the modules?

"Switch to flashlights!" Felix pulled one out of his equipment vest and checked that it still worked. He raised his night-vision goggles on their bracket attached to his helmet front. Felix started to look around on the second floor.

He found the modules.

All four stood together on the debris-littered floor, on the far side of bullet-riddled couches. A German corpse lay draped across the computer boxes, as if the Kampfschwimmer died shielding them with his body.

Felix pulled the corpse off the modules. They were covered in blood.

"Sir," Costa called. "There's too much smoke...Something's burning."

"Find it," Felix snapped. "And find a fire extinguisher."

Felix left the drying blood where it was on the computer modules, so as to tamper with them as little as possible. He hefted each of the modules into a separate waterproof sack, to protect them and camouflage what they were.

"Chief! Did you find what was burning?"

"The fuse box, sir! I turned off the main. That stopped it sparking and smoking. I dug around with my knife, no sign of hot embers."

"Get a body bag." SEALs never left a man behind, dead or alive.

Gabrielli was placed in the body bag, one of a pair the team had brought just in case. As the shifting flashlight beams from Felix's men weirdly lit the smoke and floating dust and lingering tear gas, he went into the kitchen. The plumbing was shattered, and water was spraying under the sink, forming a widening puddle on the floor. He looked around for a bucket or big pot that didn't have a hole in it. He found one and managed to fill it with water.

He walked back to the body bag. His boots crunched on broken glass and splinters of wood. Spent shell casings clinked as he kicked them aside; they lay everywhere, the brass glinting brightly in his flashlight beam.

He used the water to wash the outside of the body bag of

Gabrielli's blood and brains. He and the others used more water to wash the blood and gore they'd stepped in off of their boots.

The SEAL with the leg wound, de Mello Vidal, had revived from the blow to his head. He complained of seeing double and feeling nauseous.

Concussion.

Between two wounded men, a full body bag, four heavy computer modules, and one tool-kit case—and all their weapons—Felix's team had a lot to carry. They helped de Mello Vidal to stand up. His concussion didn't seem too serious, but he needed to lean on da Rosa to be able to walk.

They went down to the first floor and left the building.

Felix was sure they were being watched from some of the darkened windows around them.

With luck it will take someone a while to call the police. After all, so far as they know we are *the police.*

Salih came up from the steps down to a basement apartment in the building next door. That little stairwell, which Mohr had told him about, had served as an effective foxhole during the raid.

Felix saw him do a head count and look at the body bag. Salih said nothing.

"Could you hear us shouting in Portuguese out here?" Felix whispered in English. The real police were meant to think the attackers were splinter-group partisans.

"Plenty. Especially when your men were on the roof."

"Hear any wounded civilians?" Felix noticed broken window glass on the sidewalk in front of the building.

"No signs of human activity at all, actually. I heard some ricochets, but I don't think they hit anyone."

"Okay, good."

"They knew to keep their heads down. This sort of area, stray bullets are not unique to tonight, believe me. . . . Sorry about your man."

Felix grunted. He was starting to get choked up. He *hated*

the after-action adrenaline crash, especially when his team took losses.

Salih and Costa trotted down the block and around the corner, returning in the gypsy cab and the Hyundai.

Everyone quickly squashed into one vehicle or the other, equipment and computer gear and body bag and all. Salih drove over to the parked German BMW. Costa in the Hyundai, with Felix and two men in back and the dead Gabrielli across their laps, sped to Mohr in the Mercedes.

They distributed their loads more evenly. Gabrielli was placed in the trunk of the Mercedes. The cars roared off in four different directions—just as the sounds of sirens began in the distance.

———

By splitting up and blending in, the cars were able to evade police and regroup at their final meeting point. To make better time, they used different roads than before, choosing routes that were more open, less congested—hostile surveillance was less of a problem now than direct interdiction by Turkish authorities.

Some of the cars went straight north through a belt of university campuses. Others, including Felix in the Mercedes with Salih and Mohr, looped northeast and then northwest, past a big synagogue and a massive cathedral—then came mosques, palaces, harems, and an ancient Roman arena, made into museums, all closed this time of the night.

The team got back together in a dark and deserted park, on the south shore of the Golden Horn, between the Ataturk Bridge and the Galata Bridge. They unloaded all their equipment, the wounded men—Porto and de Mello Vidal—and the body bag with Gabrielli inside. Then the four vehicles were driven off to be concealed behind bushes close to each bridge. The SEALs left two damaged Turkish MP-5s, magazines of Czech ammo, and phony "EMNIYET" flak vests in some of the cars; the uncleaned submachine guns had very obviously been recently fired, and some of the flak vests had bullet hits in them or blood on them. By morning the real police would find them, maintaining the SEALs' cover story of being rogue Portuguese anti-German extremists. The cars dumped by the two bridges would make it look like the guerrillas had changed mounts after the attack and driven into the New City.

Felix and three unwounded SEALs all ran back to the meeting point after disposing of the cars. The distance they'd each had to cover was half a mile, but they put every ounce of remaining endurance into it, and they were worn out.

Felix lowered the sonar transducer into the putrid water of the Golden Horn, and activated it. While they waited for Meltzer to hear them and approach in the minisub, Salih and the unwounded SEALs changed from battle dress into their dive gear.

With binoculars Felix scanned the water for Meltzer's periscope. The meeting point was in a little cove on the shore of the park, giving a bit of added privacy. *There.* Felix saw the periscope, looking straight back at him, not moving. He knew the photonics head had an image-intensification mode just like his binocs did, so Meltzer surely saw him. Meltzer had come as close in as he could, without the top of the mini showing or the bottom lock-in chamber hatch becoming mired in the mud.

"Chief, you and me." Felix and Costa clipped themselves together with a six-foot lanyard and quietly entered the water. Soon they returned, carrying what looked like a streamlined coffin.

"Klaus," Felix said, "you first. Then your equipment. Then we take the wounded, one by one."

Mohr had already been briefed. Felix undid the watertight clamps and opened this pressure-proof personnel transfer capsule. Mohr lay down inside and Felix strapped him in and turned on the air supply. He resealed the capsule. Mohr gave him a thumb's-up through the little window where a passenger's face would be, riding inside with no need to wear scuba gear or even be able to swim.

Felix adjusted the buoyancy tanks of the capsule. He and Costa went underwater with the grand prize of their extraction mission safely cocooned—Herr Doctor Klaus Mohr, alias Peapod to the CIA, code name Zeno to the Axis.

CHAPTER 38

At noon on Saturday, Jeffrey tapped his foot impatiently outside the air-lock trunk that led up into *Challenger*'s minisub hangar. The mini had docked and the hangar doors were closed; the ship was secured from battle stations. The minisub had returned seven hours earlier than seemed possible, and Jeffrey *really* wanted to know why.

He'd verified that Felix was in the mini and not under duress by using the acoustic link to ask questions only Felix himself could properly answer. And he knew there were casualties.

Felix half-stumbled out of the air lock, exhausted and elated all at once. "Woo, was that one hell of a ride!"

Challenger's chief medical corpsman and his assistants moved in and climbed up to assist the wounded SEALs. They would work on them inside the minisub first, then lower them strapped into Stokes litters, stretchers covered with protective wire cages.

Gerald Parker came down the ladder from the mini, also visibly frazzled—and frustrated, irritated, even incensed.

An unfamiliar figure appeared behind Parker. He was tall

and slim and handsome, blond with blue eyes. Jeffrey thought he looked as thoroughly German as a German ever could; he had to resist his natural impulse to hate the man on sight as the enemy. His hair and clothes were a mess. His face was gaunt; he needed a shave and his eyes were bloodshot.

The stranger glanced around at his new environment, bewildered at first. He quickly got his bearings, and recognized Jeffrey. *From my picture somewhere?*

Parker and Felix opened their mouths to say something, but the German beat them to it.

"Captain Fuller, it is a great honor to meet you at last. My name is Klaus Mohr. We must speak in private immediately."

Parker butted in. "Captain, I would not recommend it. Mohr has been uncooperative since he stepped into the minisub. He repeatedly refused to give me a debrief of any kind. He's holding something back when he should be spilling his guts out to me."

Mohr gave Parker a look of contempt. Perfect Aryan specimen and haughty Ivy League WASP glared at each other.

Jeffrey, feeling bombarded, turned to Felix. "Lieutenant?"

"Well, yeah. He said he needed to rest, and wanted to have to go through the details only once, with the man in charge. You, Captain. Then he told us that every hour counted, and that the minisub couldn't waste fuel. He suggested a way to solve the latter problem."

"And?"

"I assessed it to be feasible, and also advantageous since our fuel margin was already slim. It worked—I have to give him that much. In the big picture, I don't know. My job was to deliver the guy. He's here." Felix shrugged.

Jeffrey decided to slow this conflict down to get control over it. He'd take things step-by-step. He sized Mohr up. He wasn't surprised that there was antagonism between Mohr and Parker, considering how badly Jeffrey and Parker got along. Parker was overbearing, a bully, a snob. That might work in other contexts, with agents Parker thought he owned because of extortion or whatever, but it was clear at once that

Klaus Mohr knew nobody owned him. He had a very intelligent face, a dignified bearing, evident self-pride, and, if half the CIA's guesswork was right, he'd also have heavyweight academic credentials. From Mohr's point of view, if sincere, he was doing the Allies a favor, not the other way around.

Parker is the wrong man for this job. . . . But I've learned a few things from him. I can manipulate too.

Jeffrey intended to put Mohr through the wringer. And he'd do it subtly, only after first breaking the ice.

"What was your time-saver, Herr Mohr? May I call you Klaus?"

"In my role as trade attaché, I know . . ." He frowned to himself. "Excuse me, I *knew* the sailing times of shipping bound for Axis-occupied ports. Several were leaving Istanbul before dawn. I said we should hitch ourselves to one."

"A routine dive task when you think about it, sir," Felix said, sounding much more tired now. "We used the mini's tow cable to attach it to the bottom of the rudder pin of a big merchie that mostly did twenty-two knots once she got under way. At twelve thousand tons displacement, we figured she wouldn't notice the drag of a sixty-ton mini. Hair-raising trip, submerged right under her wake, but it did get us to you faster."

"How'd you unhitch at twenty-two knots?"

"Near this end of the Dardanelles we used the switches that jettison the mini's tow cleats from inside. . . . The merchie gets tangled in that loose cable, well, score one for us. It'll look like some kind of accident, right? Remember, sir, everything's German."

Jeffrey watched in silence as the two wounded SEALs were brought down and under the corpsman's supervision their litters went into the wardroom. Gamal Salih helped, not his usual irrepressibly chipper self now, but still glad to have had a chance to hurt Germany as a front-line freedom fighter again.

The body bag with the dead SEAL came down, carried by four of Felix's men.

Jeffrey pointed aft. "The freezer. The mess-management people will show you." Bodies were stored there when space permitted. "My condolences on your loss."

The SEALs left with their burden, not saying anything.

We paid a high price to get you, Klaus Mohr, including the sacrifice of Ohio, *and there's still a long way to go to arrive home safe.*

"Mr. Parker, Lieutenant Estabo, Herr Mohr, follow me *now.*"

———

Jeffrey had the three of them—Gerald Parker of the CIA, Felix Estabo the SEAL, and Klaus Mohr, German defector—wait in Bell's stateroom while Jeffrey went and fetched Bell.

"Time to open my egress orders," Jeffrey said when he and Bell were alone in Jeffrey's stateroom. He unlocked his safe and pulled out the bulky envelope, then carefully entered the code to bypass the anti-tamper incendiary mechanism.

He read the hard-copy orders silently. "No surprises to us. Let's hope they'll be a big surprise to the enemy." He handed the orders to Bell.

Bell looked them over, his expression becoming haunted for a moment. "It's awful seeing the references to *Ohio.* I keep feeling we should have done *something* to help them."

"That subject is closed," Jeffrey said curtly. *Ohio* was to have separated from *Challenger,* to lurk in the Med, so her vast weaponry could be used to help repulse the Afrika Korps offensive. Then she was supposed to sneak out past Gibraltar, the same way she'd sneaked in.

Turned out to be a one-way trip for Parcelli. Jeffrey pushed the thought from his mind. It was too poignant, and he had other difficulties—two of which were that *Ohio*'s arsenal was gone from the playing field at a critical time, and her loss left lingering, unanswered questions about an Axis mole or trap.

Jeffrey took the orders back from Bell, entered the code to

rearm the incendiary, and gingerly put the pouch in his safe. "XO, have a messenger get our guests in here. They're right next door but I want to stand on ceremony. . . . For now, you're command duty officer. Stay in the control room and keep an eye on things. We're by no means out of the woods."

"Understood."

"This could take me a while. Our defector seems in a mad rush about something not yet specified, and he hasn't exactly hit it off with our CIA friend."

"Trouble, Skipper?"

"When have we had a mission that wasn't trouble?"

———

Felix, Parker, and Mohr stood around Jeffrey's tiny fold-down desk. They all tried talking at once.

"Quiet," Jeffrey snapped. "One at a time. Klaus, you put yourself in harm's way to help us. We did the same for you. So we're even. Calm down, prioritize, tell me what I need to know."

"Plan Pandora's purpose is to collapse the Israeli command, control, and communications net."

"We suspected that already," Parker said.

"Don't interrupt. Continue, Zeno."

"The method of attack is based on a new type of quantum computer. . . . Let me brief you the way I briefed officials in Berlin."

"Finally," Parker said under his breath.

Mohr ignored him. "What I do uses quantum entanglement to achieve something called quantum teleportation, to infiltrate enemy firewalls and virus filters."

"What's quantum entanglement?" Jeffrey asked.

"Two entangled photons act as if they're directly connected regardless of how far apart they become. That was one of Einstein's discoveries, a basic property of nature, part of the way the universe works."

"I don't see where this is leading."

"You will, Captain, soon, and getting this from me is necessary. In quantum computing in general, information is carried by the photons' spin, their polarization, instead of the zeros and ones in conventional electronic binary computers."

"How does this help you attack anybody?"

"I control swarms of entangled photons moving in a sequence that makes them look like random strays, the ultimate in seemingly harmless noise. I send one photon from each entangled pair into the targeted networks. That's step one. Then, at my end, I slow their partners to a walking pace for a microsecond, long enough to be able to alter their spins to become specific bits in a computer worm's program-code string. That's step two."

"I still don't see what this has to do with cyberwar."

"The distant photons automatically acquire the same new spin because they're entangled with the ones at my end. So they too suddenly form into the worm, already past every firewall. It's as if I reach across into someone else's systems through another dimension. That's why scientists call it teleportation."

"It happens instantly, this spin change at the far end?"

"As I said, that's what quantum entanglement means. There's much more to it, to be able to harness that instant action-at-a-distance without violating the light-speed restriction on any transfer of measurable information. Solving that was one of my most significant insights. Unlike all the other countries working on practical teleportation, I looked for and found a way to accomplish it where I didn't need someone cooperating with me at the far end, performing the things required to keep Einstein's speed limit satisfied. The lack of that need for friendly assistance is what starts to make the quantum computer a weapon instead of a calculator.... There's the lesser issue of decoherence, which is the term for the entanglement gradually falling apart as the photons interact more and more with their environment. I invented a method to hold back decoherence for much longer than anyone else has been able to do."

"And then what?"

"The other crucial thing was that I realized the Israelis and everyone else were viewing quantum computing in a very different way. They wanted it to replace much slower classical computers. I worked toward *hacking* normal computers, servers, and routers using quantum computer entanglement teleportation. That's my second breakthrough. It completes the weaponization concept. And I and my team, in secret, we got there first."

Parker snorted. "It sounds like a bunch of science fiction gobbledygook to me."

"How much do you know about nuclear physics?" Jeffrey asked.

"Nothing, frankly."

"Well, I know a little something. Proceed, please, Herr Mohr, but try to wrap it up."

"To summarize, a flood of seemingly random photons are made to collate themselves into countless copies of the worm, too late to be stopped. The quantum worm then propagates further once inside each infected processor. There's no need to dupe any users into opening attachments. The worm paralyzes operating systems and launches a massive denial-of-service attack at everything from military headquarters to fighter-jet avionics to cell-phone switching centers to battle-tank fire-control computers, and power plants and even digitized data-link radios carried by infantry. The multiplier effect, the negative synergy, of so many nodes and facilities crashing at once is catastrophic." Mohr was breathless by the time he was done.

Jeffrey glanced at Felix. "Lieutenant? How much on-scene vetting could you do before the final extraction?"

"Klaus gave references to unclassified work on the theory, and some lab experiments that showed the principles did work. Tunable laser diodes, narrow band-pass wavelength filters, beam-splitter crystals, semireflecting mirrors, and a bunch of other, weirder stuff. We checked them on-line at a pay terminal. Some of the papers were even written in Israel. Tel Aviv University, and the Technion in Haifa."

"Well," Jeffrey told Mohr, "there's plenty of time to sort this all out when we get you to America."

"You don't understand. Plan Pandora has been moved up. Berlin must have suspected something, either a leak or a spoiling attack by the Allies against the Afrika Korps. Their worst fears will be confirmed when they find the dead Kampfschwimmer and no sign of my corpse."

"What's their launch date for the offensive?"

"Six A.M. Tuesday, Berlin time."

Jeffrey was shocked. "That's way earlier than we thought. Way, *way* earlier."

"We have to stop the computer attack *soon,* or all is lost."

"You want us to go after the attack team?"

"There are too many of them."

"Explain."

"There are eleven separate teams, to make sure that at least one succeeds. Every gear set in existence has been thrown into this. Different approach routes and methods of attack. Some are going by U-boat, after covert pickup on the Turkish coast. Others will ride on merchant ships. At least one will go with help from local anti-Israel extremists into southern Lebanon."

"Details? Routes? Specific targets?"

"I was insulated from that part, for security. But there are two methods of inserting the entangled photons for the worm. One is by directly tapping a fiber-optic land line."

"So the teams need to get into Israel?"

"And survive long enough to hook up the equipment to the lines, which takes less effort than you might think."

"What's the other method?"

"It's heavier, less mobile, but it can work from outside Israel's borders."

Jeffrey didn't like the sound of this at all.

"It involves more hardware to protect against quantum decoherence through the open air, and a special transmitter."

"Transmitter?"

"Some military radars work at frequencies ideal for my purposes. Radar, like all radios, and in fact all electromagnetic radiation, uses photons too, just as light does."

"Yup."

"The transmitter is what's called a maser, the equivalent of a laser for the proper sort of radar beam.... There's a big radar installation on Mount Hermon in northern-most Israel. Their antennas are one portal for picking up a maser beam of entangled radar-frequency photons. Others are any patrolling radar-surveillance planes. Even a fighter aircraft can have its radars infiltrated, and a maintenance or intell avionics download would then inject the photons into the wider networks. Entangled photons imprint on photons of different energy, and even on electrons, so they pass right through all the modems, amplifiers, and connectors involved."

"How perfect, pervasive, would this assault really be?"

"There'll be isolated pockets that escape contamination, but most such people won't be able to find each other amid the chaos. Nothing wireless will work because the central-station software won't be functioning. Remember, Israelis for years have been heavily dependent on cell phones instead of land lines. Cell phones can only talk through central stations via towers, they can't talk one to one, on their own. The same applies to modern data-link army radio sets. They aren't walkie-talkies."

"So what are you suggesting?"

"We have to get to Israel before *any* of the attack teams. I have a patch that counteracts the worm, but only if it's injected before the first worm arrives."

"It's like a vaccine, not a cure?"

"Exactly. I can get it into Israel's networks, the same way the German teams plan to attack."

"So you want me to take *Challenger* toward Israel, raise an antenna mast, and beam in this patch?"

"If only it were that simple, Captain. To be absolutely sure of success, it has to go in through a fiber-optic line. That version of my equipment is the only type I could possibly bring out with me. The other type is nowhere near man packable."

"Say that again. Slowly, in simpler words."

"You need to sneak me into Israel, *now,* so I can tap into a fiber-optic trunk somewhere."

CHAPTER 39

Mohr's statement hung in the air pregnantly.

Parker exploded. "This is absurd! This man is asking us to do his dirty work for him! He's using *us* to deliver the virus!"

Mohr was deeply offended. "I am not a saboteur. I gave up everything to help you."

"Quiet," Jeffrey said, "everybody.... I have one big question for you, Klaus. Why didn't you warn Israel directly?"

"Warning alone would do no good. You can't stop the worm simply by knowing it's coming. No normal computer-security methods have any effect against quantum teleportation. If Israel shuts down all their radars and signals-intercept equipment to avoid penetration that way, they'll leave themselves blind before an imminent Axis blitzkreig, and they'd *still* be wide open to the worm via fiber optic."

"Couldn't you slip them the patch conventionally, on a disk, like with regular virus protection?"

"The patch's being distributed by regular means to all the users in Israel who need it would be spotted at once by German agents. I'd have been dangling from a noose within hours, and Berlin would work to replicate the unique expertise I intentionally hoarded. It might take them a year, but eventually they'd be able to recalibrate each of the handmade gear sets with a different worm, while also making more gear sets."

Jeffrey nodded. "And you wouldn't be there to help Israel the next time, because you'd be dead."

"The only reason I'm valuable to *you*, Captain, now that the consulate knows I disappeared, is that the Axis is under such immense strategic pressure to keep up their war momentum after their recent setbacks. The Afrika Korps juggernaut is primed to jump off from their starting positions *soon*. To cancel things and wait a year to try again would be militarily unacceptable. They need to use the worm I already programmed for them, the one for which I have a patch. That's why we must hurry. Berlin's best choice is to push their quantum-attack teams forward urgently. Think of what that means, Captain.... Israel is in tremendous danger."

"Or at least, so you say. Don't try to stampede me. I want to understand why you didn't offer your full assistance to Israel weeks ago, quantum-computer equipment and everything."

"I did. I contacted them, indirectly, before I reached you more elaborately. The Israelis traced me back to my group. That's when my staff at the consulate started dying, and then they took a shot at *me*. The Mossad must have thought the simplest way to stop Pandora would be to kill me right away, in Istanbul. And they're viciously untrusting people, Captain. With the atom bombs they planted in Germany several years ago, sometimes I think they're outright fanatics."

"Mr. Parker?"

"That last part in and of itself makes sense. It's consistent with things we know independently, including the report of the hit attempt by our agent in the brothel. But as you and I discussed with others at the Pentagon, Israel wanting to murder Mohr doesn't somehow make him more reliable for us."

"You seem to have done a flip-flop since that meeting."

"That meeting was before I had to sit in your control room and hear *Ohio* being destroyed, *Captain.*"

Jeffrey winced. Mohr looked dismayed at hearing this news.

Jeffrey grew angry that Parker carped on the subject of *Ohio,* undermining Jeffrey in front of other people. He pointedly changed the subject, and became more distant and formal.

"Lieutenant Estabo, report your assessment of what the first contact with Herr Mohr and your assault on the safe house indicate. Mr. Parker here did not *sit in* on any of that."

Felix took a deep breath. Reading Jeffrey, his manner became more crisp. "Our on-site validation was based on unclassified reference sources only. It looked good enough to continue with the extraction, but, objectively speaking, proves nothing about Herr Mohr's claims.... And while from the German perspective the outcome of the safe-house battle would have been uncertain, it *is* conceivable that the supposed need to assault the Kampfschwimmer was in actuality a design to drag us into a double bluff."

"Lieutenant?" Jeffrey didn't follow Felix.

"Sir, the requirement for a firefight with casualties on our side might have had an undercurrent of psychological warfare. People value most those things that are scarce and hard to get. It's human nature."

"Granted. How does that apply here? I still don't see it."

"The need to prepare and execute combat against a fortified place, suffering potential KIAs and WIAs, as indeed we did, could be mental sleight of hand to get us to believe that the thing we fought for and won was a valuable treasure... when in fact the thing we obtained was, is, an infernal device we've carried into our own fortress, *Challenger,* I mean, and maybe Israel."

"So the computer modules are like a Trojan horse? The Germans let you win at the safe house *on purpose?*"

"That scenario can't be eliminated, sir. It's possible the Kampfschwimmer were sacrificed intentionally by the Axis

High Command. It's even possible they were volunteer suicide troops."

"They *let* you kill them?" Jeffrey asked in disbelief.

"They might not have *let* us, sir, knowingly, themselves, but Herr Mohr did provide us with tactical information and the element of surprise, which German planners ought to have been aware made it likely that our attack on the Kampf-schwimmer team would succeed."

Mohr began to back into a corner, literally. "How can you all be so *paranoid*? There is no time for such bickering!"

Jeffrey didn't respond. He considered everything Felix had said.

"Lieutenant, sweat the details of your hypothesis. Was there anything during the safe-house assault that raises doubts about what really went on?"

"I hadn't considered it that way, Captain."

"Do so."

"Well...Our initial entry might have been a little too easy. The way they opened the door to Gamal Salih without him having to make more of a scene."

"Anything else?"

"Hmmm...The way one German lay over the quantum equipment, as if protecting it with his body."

"He wore a flak vest?"

"Yes. And not all of them did as we went in."

"So one Kampfschwimmer shielded the gear instead of helping repulse your team?"

"Maybe," Felix said. "And you'd think that when it was evident they were being overrun, he'd have destroyed the computer stuff to keep it out of our hands, not sacrificed his life to keep the gadgets intact."

"Where was Herr Mohr while all this went on?"

"Well out of the line of fire, in an armored limo."

"And what did you mean when you said that they might've been suicide troops? Suicide fighters kill themselves to *kill* other people, not help them."

"Not necessarily, sir, if you think about it. They could try to be fall guys without us realizing it, as part of the psychological gambit. That's what I meant about it all being mental sleight of hand. Plus, they *didn't* help us. They *pretended* to help us. That's how they got the Trojan horse through the gates."

"Oh boy," Jeffrey said. "Talk about wheels within wheels."

"But the quantum gear *works*," Mohr insisted. "I saw the results of the field tests in Turkey. We shut whole areas down until the worm's built-in time limit expired."

"That's consistent with things we do know," Parker said. "Turkey has suffered some inexplicable system outages lately."

"Why wasn't I told that before?" Jeffrey demanded.

"It didn't come up. And you didn't need to know. And it only strengthens the case against Mohr. If it's cause and effect between his equipment and those outages, which I remind you all is unproven, that would merely indicate that the malevolent hardware Mohr has with him does work. It demonstrates nothing whatsoever about him having a patch that would save Israel from some bizarre teleportation virus."

"Herr Mohr," Jeffrey said, looking directly at the man, hard. "You're asking us, in effect, to invade an ally, Israel, with which American relations are already strained. You're asking us to not tell them we're coming, go in covertly ourselves, and jigger with their command and control, supposedly for their own good."

Mohr stared right back at Jeffrey. "If you tell Israel you're coming, they'll never agree. Never! With the way you all keep showing so much skepticism, how can you possibly expect them to take seriously whatever arrangements *you* present before Tuesday that have anything to do with quantum patches? That's totally obvious already, isn't it?"

"Granted."

"And you can't ask them for permission to do the patch even if you believe me, because if they hear one word about this, they'd refuse and you forfeit the option to go in secretly!

If they learn that I and my device are getting anywhere near them, they'd do everything possible to stop us!"

"What's this *us*?" Parker snapped.

"Ease up," Jeffrey cautioned him sharply. "Don't distract me." He turned back to Mohr. "You're telling me that if I take you in there at all, the whole operation has to stay invisible."

"Yes. Do you at least accept that part, Captain Fuller, in isolation from everything else?"

"Yeah.... What do you have to say for yourself about Lieutenant Estabo's comments? His views on the safe-house raid?"

"I knew those men from training and working with them. They all had wives and children. They had every reason to live, to fight for their lives for the sake of their families."

"*You* abandoned your family," Parker stated. "Supposedly for some higher cause. Why couldn't the Kampfschwimmer too?"

"I did it to *protect* my family! The Kampfschwimmer would have gained *nothing* for their dependents by allowing themselves to be killed! They'd have left widows and orphans! No German ideology or military tradition has *ever* glorified such conduct!"

"All right," Jeffrey said. "Let's leave that particular point aside and cut to the chase. Is there a way to demonstrate your device for us?"

Mohr sighed. "Not convincingly, Captain. The patch and then the worm? Nothing would happen. The worm alone? Your ship would be crippled. A single laptop? Without close verification by scientists in your country, you'd just see a dead computer. You wouldn't know absolutely that quantum hacking was what I did to kill it."

Jeffrey nodded, making a sour face. He knew Mohr was correct on this bit, which only made the broader issue harder to resolve. "Just out of curiosity, what keeps this worm from taking over the world?"

"The worm is programmed to know where it is by detecting characteristics of the host systems it attacks. It's also set to expire, six days postattack. Damage outside of Israel and Egypt should be minimal. Affected computer networks there will come back up, after the Axis has occupied both countries through the land-and-cyberspace envelopment."

"Is the U.S. homeland under threat from the worm?"

"Not over intercontinental ranges. Quantum decoherence makes the entanglement deteriorate from too many collisions with external matter and energy. The error-correction packet needed gets impractically large. . . . Decoherence with range is why a fiber-optic tap is preferable to beaming at a radar dish, and why you can attack a nearby plane but not a satellite directly."

"Are Axis systems protected?"

"Yes, as one of many standard periodic security updates. Remember, the worm manifests itself, it runs, like a normal program. The difference is how quantum teleportation gets it past firewalls and antivirus screening. . . . In fact, I recommend that you let me inject the patch into *Challenger*'s systems, since I'm not sure how safe you'd be under Israeli airspace otherwise."

Parker sputtered, "You can't possibly trust this guy. This is *way* over the top."

"I'll be the final judge of that. I'm in command of this ship."

"I've already seen what happens when you're in command."

"How *dare* you?"

Parker backed down, and put a more conciliatory tone in his voice. "I dare because I need to get something across that you don't seem to be willing to hear, Captain. What Mohr says is too pat. This talk about teleportation is beyond me. Even if it's true, *especially* if it's true, we definitely haven't precluded that the Germans could be using us as their messenger boys. Also, it's outside the plan and it violates orders."

"You mean bringing him back to the U.S. for a long debrief?"

"Precisely. Let the National Security Agency get hold of his equipment and pick his brains and see what the hell he's talking about. If what he claims holds up under studied scrutiny, and from the Allied perspective his intentions are benign, there's plenty of time to warn Israel convincingly and *then* give them his gear with the patch."

"But Mohr says the offensive opens Tuesday morning."

"That's another part that's too pat. How do we know, except for his say-so? A standard part of any con is pressure to make the victim decide before common sense can kick in. To me, his talk of a moved-up timeline is a warning in itself."

"Lieutenant, your opinion?"

"From the parts of the technical stuff that I can follow, sir, the hacker attack *is* plausible enough to be scary. If Herr Mohr is telling the truth, and we don't help him, Israel will lose, big time, and the Allies will lose big too."

Jeffrey turned to Mohr again. The German seemed annoyed by the fact that everyone had been talking about him as if he wasn't there.

"Herr Mohr, lay out for me *explicitly* how Pandora is supposed to help Berlin with the atom bombs that Israel planted in Germany."

"The worm will prevent Israel from getting the go codes to their agents within Germany to detonate the bombs. Also, the worm does not destroy data files. The Afrika Korps and German intelligence experts, with pretasked special-forces strike teams, expect to capture people, documents, and disk drives they can use to quickly identify the agents who control the bombs and also learn the location of each bomb. That's how they preempt any potential dead-man switch in the Israeli ROEs."

"Makes sense," Jeffrey said. "It also neatly explains why they'd dare an offensive against Israel when Israel already holds a prepositioned deterrent in Germany."

"No," Parker insisted. "Mohr himself implied that the success of the quantum attack isn't fully guaranteed. This scheme to find the bombs and catch their Mossad trigger agents before Germans see mushroom clouds on their soil is also much too iffy. No commander in his right mind would trust to luck like that.... Which only makes me more sure Mohr's whole story is ridiculous."

"Knowing the high command in Berlin the way I've come to know them," Jeffrey said, "I think they'd take the risk of having some bombs go off on their soil if the odds are low enough and the rewards are high enough. From what Herr Mohr here says, this attack greatly lowers the odds of high cost inside Germany. And the Afrika Korps offensive, by succeeding, offers great rewards in terms of influencing Turkey and the Persian Gulf nations to turn Axis, with all their strategic geography, and their oil.... Besides which, if one or two bombs do go off, the Germans can blame it on Israel and gain sympathy from the Muslim states."

"We both already covered that in Washington."

"Yes. And the president decided it was worth the risk to send a task group to fetch Herr Mohr."

"There was no talk then about *us* invading Israel."

"We were not aware then that there was a need for us to invade Israel."

"Then get in touch with Washington. Ask what we should do."

"I can't."

"Why not?"

"My orders insist on radio and laser-buoy silence until we're far outside the Med. To maintain total stealth we can't transmit."

"You're contradicting yourself."

"How?"

"You're happy to obey one part of your orders, yet ignore another part of the same orders, and go entirely outside your orders in certain other very material respects."

"As in...?"

"Radio silence, but entering Israeli waters. And not only entering them, but *invading* them, taking a German with German equipment onto friendly turf without permission."

"True."

"You can't do that."

"It's my job to know when to bend or disregard or even re-formulate my orders."

"I—"

"Look. If we did break stealth to transmit and thus gave away our existence and our position to the enemy while in hostile waters, *and* we didn't then end up getting sunk like *Ohio* already did when she was detected, messaging the Pentagon or Norfolk wouldn't accomplish much aside from me covering my ass, and maybe you covering *your* ass."

"What are you insinuating?"

"Come on, use your head. The situation is so complex, nuanced, and ambiguous that we'd be going back and forth with senior people in the States till kingdom come, just to convey what the issues and uncertainties are. Think about how this whole conversation has already gone, just between the few of us face-to-face in this compartment. Anyone above us in Norfolk or Langley or Washington probably won't have any more information than we do with which to decide. If they did have something relevant, they'd know we needed to know and we'd've heard something by passive ELF, and we haven't. If anything, the higher-ups will have much less feel for the real-time dynamics of what's happening now with Pandora. I'm the commander on the spot. I'm supposed to show initiative. Maintaining stealth is a matter of common sense, of self-preservation. Breaking stealth just to protect my backside could get us all killed—it's absurd. The status of *your* backside is not pertinent to my decision."

Parker turned beet red. "Then don't break stealth. Just stick to the original plan. We have Mohr. Let's go home."

"I'm beginning to think that I need to change the original plan."

"Christ."

"Listen. We've gotten a lot of new information since we made contact with Herr Mohr, staggering information, because we did what the president himself decided we should do. The idea that Germany needs us to sneak this quantum worm into Israel seems unlikely. Herr Mohr himself says

they have eleven attack teams on the way. I know for a fact
that Kampfschwimmer are extremely good at their jobs.
Lieutenant Estabo and I have personally seen, at bayonet
range in recent months, that their training and equipment,
their courage, and their battle skills are superb. *You've* never
smelled a Kampfschwimmer's breath while you grappled
hand to hand, both sure that one of you would certainly die in
that encounter. They *don't* need *Challenger* to run their errands. But I think the Allies do need *Challenger* to do a different job, finish the job for which the president sent us into
this theater, by using the most up-to-date information we
possess."

"We're going in circles. I simply cannot concur with your
willingly violating Israeli sovereignty at the behest of a German agent we barely know. Mohr could just be using you to
clinch the effectiveness of his overall virus attack by us becoming *another* team, *Challenger,* with Mohr himself as their
first team, to *reinforce the Kampfschwimmer.* You believe
him, and deliver him, but he still works for Berlin. He inserts
the virus instead of immunizing against it. Nothing you've
said, *nothing,* precludes that from being the true scenario. . . .
And while he's at it, he could compromise *Challenger* while
you violate Israel's sovereignty. Mohr plans to ruin your
stealth, maybe by something with this so-called *patch* he
wants to give you, and Israel gets rather irate at America. You
aid the Axis cause. You might even get sunk *that* way, by accident or on purpose. Remember, Israel shot USS *Liberty* to
pieces for snooping during the 1967 war."

Jeffrey couldn't refute that logic. The whole business could
be a different sort of trap, with Istanbul merely a way point,
and the bristling coast of jumpy Israel as *Challenger*'s grave.

"Lieutenant, find Mr. Salih. I want his read on Herr Mohr."

"Yes, sir." Felix left.

"Captain, I must warn you, I think you're making a terrible
error in judgment."

"I understand, Mr. Parker. I've listened carefully to everything you've said."

"Then why are you ignoring it?"

"I'm not. I'm weighing all the factors I have in front of me. We do know that the Afrika Korps plans an offensive. We do know that the offensive only makes sense if they have some way of crippling Israel's command and control. We knew that before we left Norfolk. In his last message, the one he got out through that brothel contact, Peapod said he held the key to Pandora. Now that we're here, and Klaus Mohr's here, he's offered us that key in specific detail."

"That's what I mean. I'll say it again. It's too pat. You can't trust Mohr by going solely on what you now know. To invade Israel based on the word of an untested defector goes beyond irresponsible. It's criminal negligence. Letting him co-opt your ship for his own purposes is entirely outrageous!"

Before Jeffrey could answer, someone knocked. "Come in!"

It was Felix. "Salih said he thinks Mohr is sincere, and unless he's somehow been misled by Berlin, or brainwashed, we should trust him."

"There," Parker said. "Misled or brainwashed. Even Salih is hedging. How can we know Mohr isn't a Trojan horse and doesn't realize it himself?"

"Because it's *his* equipment the Germans are working with!"

"But—"

"No more buts. Mohr is the smartest man in the German computer-espionage shop. Nobody there understands his hardware and software better than he does. No one misled him on anything. Gamal Salih says to trust him, and I trust Salih. My own instinct at this point says to make the choice to trust him. No known fact tells me *not* to trust him."

"I—"

"Lieutenant, please take Herr Mohr and wait in the XO's stateroom."

Felix and Mohr went next door.

"Mr. Parker, you're welcome to put your official disagreement on record. My XO will show you how to have an entry

made in the ship's formal log. I have no problem with you
disagreeing with me. However, this ship is not a democracy. I
am the ship's commanding officer. I have used you and
everyone else as sounding boards and sources of information. And I've made my decision. *Challenger* is the ideal
platform for sneaking up to Israel and dropping off operatives with no one noticing. And for God's sake, I'm not a
fool. I intend to put Mohr through his paces very rigorously
between now and then. He won't have a single moment to
himself. No one can keep up an act under the pressure and
scrutiny I intend to apply.... And you'll note that I'm not
breaking laser-buoy silence to get out a warning that the
Afrika Korps will move on Tuesday, important as such news
is, precisely because it might be some sort of a trick. Our National Command Authorities have other ways to monitor that
and warn Egypt and Israel if they don't see it themselves."

Jeffrey reached for his phone handset and called the control room. "Give me the navigator." Sessions answered.

"At top quiet speed, by the most direct route, how long to
the coast of Israel?"

Sessions was taken aback. "Which point on the coast, sir?"

"Oh, the middle somewhere. For now, use Tel Aviv."

"Wait one, please.... Twenty-seven hours, sir."

"Thank you. That's all." Jeffrey hung up. "Twenty-seven
hours." *That would be midafternoon tomorrow, Sunday. I
think it's a working day, with Israel's overstrained economy
on a war footing.*

Jeffrey got up and went through the connecting head and
brought Mohr and Felix back. Jeffrey's stateroom was
crowded again.

"Herr Mohr, I gather from what you said about there being
so many attack teams that the portable equipment can be operated without you."

"Yes."

"Can the particular gear set you brought with you with
your patch be worked by a properly trained commando team,
without you actually being there?"

"If nothing goes wrong with the hardware, and the team is properly competent. To train them will be grueling, with a significant chance of failure. Why can't I go with them? I strongly advise it. I have practice at such things now from the extraction process in Istanbul."

"Because anywhere in Israel, especially with no proper papers, you'd stick out like a sore thumb. You're much too valuable to take such risks. The SEALs, at least, with their builds and complexions, can try to pass as Mediterranean Jews. It's also a precaution just in case you are a double agent. I'm sure you understand that."

Mohr nodded. "If I'm not there, I can't do something to draw attention to the SEALs and reveal the presence of *Challenger.*"

Someone knocked on the door.

"Come in!"

The SEAL chief Costa squeezed into the compartment. "Excuse me for interrupting, Captain." His face was etched with concern. He nodded at Felix to acknowledge his superior officer, but then met Jeffrey's eyes.

"What is it, Chief?"

"We've got big trouble, sir."

"Go on."

"We've been cleaning off the computer-module cases. There was a lot of dirt and dried blood caked together on the outsides."

"And . . ."

"One of the cases took a bullet through a corner."

Mohr went white.

Parker smirked. "I guess that settles it. No trip to Israel."

"Quiet," Jeffrey said. "Chief, which module?"

Costa described it.

"That one is the power unit," Mohr said.

"Chief, I need to ask you a very important question."

"Sir?"

"Can you tell from the damage whose bullet it was?"

Mohr and Felix looked at each other meaningfully. Both

knew what Jeffrey was getting at, and how significant the answer would be: Both sides' MP-5s and pistols all used the same ammo, 9-millimeter rounds. Which side in the firefight hit the module?

"Captain, powder burns show the round was fired at point-blank range."

Parker's jaw set. Mohr and Felix didn't say anything; instead they peered expectantly at Jeffrey.

"That dead German was trying to destroy your modules, Herr Mohr."

"Yes."

"Lieutenant, he was stopped from going further by you and your team."

"Concur, sir."

"That's all I need to know. Chief, where's the module now?"

"Azavedo should have it here in a minute." Paulo Azavedo was one of Felix's enlisted SEALs.

Someone knocked. "Let him in," Jeffrey said. Everybody scrunched together to make room. Parker showed distaste at having Felix and Costa press against him, defiling what he considered to be his innermost personal space. Jeffrey had no sympathy whatsoever for Parker's discomfort.

Azavedo came in with the module. He held the heavy box high for Mohr to examine, causing his ample muscles to bulge. Azavedo had a broad, open face. He peeked through the exit hole while Mohr sighted through the bullet entry point. Jeffrey watched them make eye contact this way; neither man was smiling.

"Herr Mohr," Jeffrey asked, "can the damage be fixed in twenty-four hours?"

"Perhaps. Perhaps not. It depends on what spare parts and materials you have, and on how much help you can give me."

"We've got quite a lot of things in inventory, and some of the finest engineering and electronics people in the world. . . . Can you also dovetail the repairs with training Lieutenant Estabo's team in how to use your gear?"

"In the next *twenty-four hours*?" Mohr was aghast.

"Well, twenty-seven, actually. That's all the time our mandatory egress schedule allows, before the German offensive begins and we're badly stuck. The rest of that is classified."

"Twenty-seven hours for what you ask is impossible."

"You're positive? Even by staying awake the whole time, throwing as many of my crew into the job as you might need?"

"Captain, I understand what it means to make heroic efforts under time pressures. I know the American expressions about achieving the impossible, about the word 'impossible' not being in your dictionary. But when I say impossible, I am not using an expression. To accomplish what you ask is impossible."

"Then what do you suggest?"

"Concentrate on repairing the module. Instead of trying to train your SEALs, I then go with them."

Parker gave a harrumph of total disgust. But squashed against the bulkhead, with two other men's bodies in very close contact, he'd lost his fragile dignity. Now, to Jeffrey, his latest objection came across as almost comical.

"Herr Mohr," Jeffrey asked, "if you don't train and you go with the team, is the module repairable in twenty-seven hours?"

"We can only know by trying. Is there any choice?"

"No. Okay, Lieutenant, stay, but your men can leave now."

Once the door was closed, Jeffrey was again with Felix, Mohr, and Parker. "I want to ask you another question, Herr Mohr. Could your equipment, in Allied hands, be used to do to the Axis what they're trying to do to Israel?"

"Eventually, potentially. There would have to be much research on reducing quantum decoherence with range. Israel from north to south, and Jerusalem to Cairo, are each two hundred and fifty miles. German-occupied Europe alone measures five times that in any direction, which means twenty-five times the total target area. Decoherence worsens exponentially. That makes the problem much more than twenty-five times as hard to solve."

"And we'd need a whole new worm, wouldn't we, one the Axis won't have a patch for? Plus, from your work and then your disappearance, the Axis will be forewarned."

Jeffrey called the control room and told Bell to join him; Bell arrived in seconds. Jeffrey filled him in. Bell's eyebrows rose higher and higher. He kept glancing between Felix and Parker and Mohr, and Jeffrey could sense him straining to catch up and digest everything. "We have our hands full, Captain," Bell said when Jeffrey was finished.

"And then some. XO, take Herr Mohr and use your state-room and ask Lieutenant Willey and COB to join you. Start getting everything and everyone you need freed up to focus on repairing that damaged quantum module."

"Yes, sir."

"And have a messenger find out when the wardroom will be clean after surgery's finished. We're tight for working and planning spaces as it is."

Mohr paused in mid-stride as he and Bell began to leave, and Mohr's head jerked to one side. He frowned darkly, not just with his mouth but with his entire face. "Captain, I've thought of something. No, *two* problems I must mention. They interrelate."

"You better tell us, fast."

"The worm is designed to not become active immediately when inserted, but at a specific future moment, to coordinate with the Afrika Korps attack."

Jeffrey pondered this. "So Israel isn't warned of the worm too soon? When it reveals itself in action as regular program code? To keep Israel from writing their own patch, and re-covering before the real shooting starts?"

"Setting the activation clock in the quantum worm is one thing Berlin insisted that I automate in the module sets. A Kampfschwimmer can enter the start time easily. I showed them all how."

Shit. "So their high command isn't locked into Tuesday. They could move up the whole offensive."

"After Friday night's events, it seems likely they will."

"There's more time pressure than we thought."

"Yes. There will also be no way for us to be sure the patch got into their systems ahead of the worm, until the scheduled start time arrives."

"You mean, even if our intrusion goes off without a hitch, tactically and technically, *we can't tell if we beat every Kampfschwimmer team till the main battle starts?*"

"I'm afraid so."

Jeffrey was deeply disturbed. "We do all this work and take all these risks, and we won't know if it *paid off* until it's too late for us to do anything but watch for unfolding disaster?"

"That is an accurate way to put it, Captain. I'm sorry if I caused you to think the result would be more definite sooner."

"XO, you and Herr Mohr better get to work." They left.

Jeffrey focused on Felix. "Lieutenant, you have five fit men including yourself?"

"Correct, sir."

"We need to start planning where and how to make a covert landing on the coast of Israel tomorrow afternoon. You'll have a maximum of six hours to depart *Challenger,* get to the beach, do your thing from there, and return to the ship. That's not negotiable. Six hours. *Challenger* has a fixed appointment elsewhere, later. Beyond that you don't want to know, because you don't need to know and you'll be on hostile turf. Yes, we have to view Israel as hostile. For security, they were never told we're in this theater. If they detect us they won't know who we are, and they might attack. If they detect us and their naval command was infiltrated by Germans, then German antisubmarine forces from Greece or Crete will attack. Mohr's disappearance cancels any advantage we gained from the loss of *Ohio.* The Axis will have seen through the cover story for your Istanbul raid by now, even if Turkey hasn't. They'll know an extraction could have been done via water. That's the score. If you're not back by 2000 Sunday evening, I leave without you."

"Understood, sir." Felix sounded grim.

"Talk to Bell and COB. See if we've got anybody who speaks some Hebrew. Try Meltzer on that, he's a qualified ship's diver. Have Bell pick two of my crew to pilot and co-pilot the minisub. You arrange scuba lessons for Mohr in a partly flooded lock-out trunk. Compressed-air diving in shallow water isn't all that hard. And keep a careful eye on Mohr during this mission. At the least sign he's pro-Axis, kill him. That's an order."

"How will I know if Mohr is really pro-Axis?"

"Learn as much as you can about him and his equipment. Then, on the ground, as unit commander use your discretion."

"What if I misinterpret something? He's about to save the world, but I goof? If I kill him he can't save the world."

"Every op has its downside. Cope. Mohr is not to know about this. I don't want him being on guard. We act as if we accept him completely. Dismissed." Felix left; only Parker remained.

"I repeat that I must protest, Captain. The basis for your decision is sketchy, and the arrangements become more tenuous at every turn. Mohr's latest utterances are the most ridiculous double-talk I've ever heard from a supposed defector's lips. *We won't know if the patch worked until the offensive starts.* He snookered you! Bought himself an out! The cyberattack succeeds and Israel goes under. Mohr says, Oops, I guess my patch didn't get there in time, or, the repairs to the module were flawed. We'll be long gone, too late to undo the damage he did!"

"I haven't decided to trust Mohr. I've decided to implement his recommendations. Those are two quite different statements. If you don't want to help, go to your quarters. When the XO has a spare moment, he'll make sure your protest is recorded nice and legal. Don't make me have to say that again! Your repeated disrespect of my authority has put you on thin ice."

Parker waved, as if that didn't matter in the least to him. "You'll be court-martialed, you realize. You're committing an act of war, invading Israel on your own."

"The court-martial won't be till later. If this new plan succeeds, I exonerate myself by producing results."

"It'll all be on your head. You'll make powerful enemies."

"Mr. Parker, it's all been on my head from the minute we got under way in Norfolk."

CHAPTER 40

During the trip from outside the Dardanelles Strait to the coastline of Israel, there was a frenzy of activity inside *Challenger*. Jeffrey made another round of visits to the racks where lay the crewmen badly injured from his steep dive to escape as *Ohio* came under fire and sank—glum duty, both for Jeffrey and the men he tried to cheer up. It reminded them all of something they'd rather forget, and emphasized how their broken limbs, wrenched backs, severe concussions left them feeling useless while a mood of crisis filled the ship. Then Jeffrey spent most of his time making sure the preparations for his invasion of Israel went as well as possible. The stress and sleep deprivation everyone felt were starting to lead to flaring tempers; Mohr, Felix, and Salih argued often over little things. Bell, Willey, and COB were being worn ragged.

Gerald Parker had accepted the change in plans as a fait accompli. He made himself useful by helping to devil's-advocate Felix's sketchy plan for the clandestine operation in Israel.

He figured out that his life depends on us succeeding. As

for consequences later, at the CIA and the Pentagon, or the cabinet and the White House, I'm too busy to think about that now.

Once *Challenger* passed the island of Rhodes, on the way out of the Aegean, Jeffrey took the conn and stayed just beyond the edge of Turkey's twelve-mile territorial limit. This helped him sidestep German threats as he worked south toward Israel. But Turkey's navy, though neutral, was relatively strong, and she protected her home waters proudly and aggressively. Complicating matters was the fact that Turkey owned over a dozen diesel subs, all of them made in Germany, variants of the type 209, with eight torpedo tubes. It would be tricky to know a submerged contact's true nationality—even if they started shooting.

They gave Cyprus a wide berth as their destination neared.

Bell provided an updated threat assessment. A handful of modern Israeli diesel subs were based in Haifa. Very quiet when cruising slowly on batteries or their air-independent propulsion, *Challenger* might bump into one, with dire effects.

Different Israeli diesels would also be deployed, though their captains would want to evade other submarines at all cost. These were the boats that served as boomers, with nuclear-armed cruise missiles launched through torpedo tubes. Now they most likely hid well west of Jeffrey, to bring German-controlled North Africa in range. Whether they'd serve as a deterrent or an initiator of tactical nuclear war on land remained to be seen. *At least we know they won't target the Aswan Dam if desperate enough, sacrificing their Egyptian allies to create an impassable tank trap.* When Germany nuked Warsaw and Tripoli at the very start of the fighting, mid-2011, Egypt drained the gigantic artificial Lake Nasser behind the dam; experts cautioned that if the dam were smashed, a radioactive tsunami would sweep down the Nile and wash away most human life along the banks—including Cairo, population twenty million.

Bell said Israel also had oceangoing corvettes, 1,000 tons and 250 feet long, such as the Improved Sa'ar V+ class, built for Israel in Mississippi. Though smaller than Turkey's frigates, these each had six antisubmarine torpedo tubes and an ASW helo.

The final approach would be no picnic even for *Challenger.*

Jeffrey was increasingly plagued by a disturbing thought. The Germans might have an entire underground of science wizards. What proof did Jeffrey have that Mohr was truly their head guy on quantum hacking? What if there *was* someone smarter, and—as Parker had tried to warn before—Mohr had, unawares, indeed been misled about what his gear set with the patch would do? *What if he's a Trojan horse of a different sort, an unconscious one?* In that case Mohr could feel all the sincerity in the world, but it would count for nothing.

Later, taking a break for food in the wardroom before he grabbed a catnap, something else bad played on Jeffrey's mind.

He kept thinking about the two dozen ekranoplans Russia had sold to Germany. These would have been the top-priority target for *Ohio,* with her egress orders—as he now knew—to linger and hurt the German offensive. Using more than a hundred Tomahawks programmed in antiship mode, four or five cruise missiles would have ambushed each hybrid seaskimmer aircraft, with the missiles moving at twice the aircraft's speed. *But that was not to be.*

Each ekranoplan could lift eight of Germany's Leopard III main battle tanks, with tank-rider support infantry. When the time came for the Axis assault to open, the ekranoplans might head straight down from Italy to occupied Libya to unload, or they might turn east and threaten the coast of Egypt and Israel.

Both of these Allied countries knew about the ekranoplans, but couldn't know where they'd come ashore to disgorge their cargoes. They'd land wherever Israel's tanks weren't, preferably in their rear—this was elementary strategy. It created multiple quandaries for Israel's generals, since their own tanks couldn't be in two places at once. Israel's tank brigades had been mostly poised in the Sinai Desert—Jeffrey knew this from things he'd heard before leaving Norfolk. They formed a defensive bulwark behind the twin water barriers formed by the Nile and the Suez Canal. This was to try to halt the Afrika Korps formations thrusting east on land.

But the ekranoplans moved much faster than any tank. The exposed parts of Egypt's and Israel's coastlines ran 150 miles. *Where would almost two hundred Leopard IIIs do the most for the Axis?* Then Jeffrey saw it.

If the Israeli brigades stayed in place, or advanced via bridges and pontoon ferries to forward positions in Egypt's western desert, the ekranoplans would just continue coming east at sea. They'd keep Israel's generals guessing, and ultimately deploy the modern panzers in two groups north and south of Tel Aviv. The city was right on the coast, in good tank country. Even with no immediate logistical support—ammo resupply and more fuel—those tanks would surround and cut off Israel's biggest city, a horrendous outcome and perhaps decisive combined with the worm attack if Mohr's patch attempt failed. If Israel kept their own tanks back by Tel Aviv, they left African Egypt and the Sinai Peninsula weaker. The ekranoplans could off-load on the Sinai coast instead, concentrate to spearhead the main body of the Afrika Korps, and the Israeli homeland would become a battleground in a different way.

The ekranoplans would be heavily escorted by Luftwaffe fighters flying from Libya and Greece—also basic strategy. The Israeli Air Force would have no choice but to come out and fight, reducing their ability to support the Israeli Army. They'd suffer disproportionate losses, torn between defense over land and at sea, torn further between conflicting roles of air superiority and antiship or ground attack. With the Luftwaffe so powerful, and the ekranoplans giving them all the initiative theater wide, the Israelis had almost no chance to win.

And none of it would be necessary if Ohio *hadn't been sunk.*

———————

The final run to Israel took *Challenger* southeast. The slope up onto the continental shelf was gradual but relentless. Before, in deep water, if fired on, *Challenger* could outdive conventional torpedoes, which had crush depths of 3,000 feet or less. Now, with the shallower bottom, that option was forfeited when Jeffrey and his ship might need it most.

The SEALs, with Salih, Meltzer, and Klaus Mohr, got ready to depart in the minisub. Jeffrey went to battle stations; Bell sat next to him. *Challenger* used the established shipping lane that led toward Haifa harbor, which presented many perils but helped avoid naval mines. He ordered two off-board probes to be deployed, to scout ahead for uncharted mines or wrecks, bottom sensors, and prowling ocean rovers. When the bottom reached 600 feet—miles into Israel-owned waters—he and his probes turned south, on the inner edge of the corridor for coastal traffic. He wasn't surprised there were so few cargo vessels in the area. Rumors, of a German offensive that would be soon, must have spread far and wide. Merchant mariners would've noticed changed military behavior, and civilian anxiety and dread, in any port of call—including Haifa.

A probe's feed suddenly went dead. Lieutenant Torelli said the fiber-optic line was good, but the probe had broken down. Without its motor working, there was no way to retrieve the 3,000 pound unit, and no time to improvise a retrieval. Jeffrey ordered the line cut. He had no more probes as replacements. *Challenger* needed to go on, half blind, leaving dead-certain proof that an American submarine had been through here. The probe's malfunction might indicate Israeli interference; the loss of its feed could be the prelude to an assault on the mother ship. Everyone braced for the worst, staying quiet, barely moving.

Nothing happened. Then Jeffrey remembered that *Challenger* might have gotten this far because of unwanted aid: Some of the Kampfschwimmer attack teams, with sets of Klaus Mohr's gear, would be doing the same sort of infiltration, in U-boats. They might be diverting Israeli forces that otherwise would be denser in *Challenger*'s area—but their presence could also alert Israel to search with the greatest care for more subs sneaking toward the coast. *And nothing says we won't bump into one of those U-boats. Then there are the Kampfschwimmer, whose movements might warn Israel to watch out on land ... and who might even cross paths with my SEALs.* Things could get ugly.

Challenger opened her hangar doors to release the minisub. Jeffrey timed it between passes of Israeli aircraft and patrol boats. He held his breath; there was no incoming fire, yet. The minisub moved inshore; *Challenger* withdrew to deeper water. The patrol boats had no sonars or antisubmarine weapons. They bristled with .50-caliber heavy machine guns and larger automatic cannon. Their crews' job was to spot intruders using small craft, rubber boats, or scuba. From years of fighting terrorists, they tended to shoot first and ask questions later. They could chew Felix and his men to pieces, in the water or on the beach. Jeffrey hoped Felix's audacious plan would prevent this.

CHAPTER 41

Egon Schneider and Manfred Knipp sat at the command console in *Doenitz*'s control room. Schneider was still displeased by being relegated to a side show: Lurking for *Los Angeles*- or *Virginia*-class American submarines around the Arabian Gulf, plus maybe an aircraft carrier or two.

His flank-speed dash northward through water five thousand meters deep—so fast yet so invisible—had been exciting. Then he waited, but nothing interesting occurred.

"It seems we've beaten the Americans by too wide a margin. We're simply too fast."

"Sir?" Knipp asked.

"Nothing but merchant shipping passing above us. No enemy cargo ship is a target worth revealing our presence and true nationality for."

"Jawohl."

Schneider sulked and studied the large-scale nautical chart. *Doenitz* was in the Gulf of Aden, where the bottom in many places was 900 to 12,000 meters deep. Twelve hundred meters was his crush depth. Now he hugged ooze-covered terrain at almost one thousand meters, moving at only four knots—for quieting, and to assure the best sensitivity for his on-hull passive sonars searching upward.

The Gulf of Aden was an inlet off of the Arabian Sea that pointed toward Africa. At the gulf's western end, the water suddenly narrowed to the Strait of Bab el Mandeb. Through this strait lay the Red Sea. All shipping for Israel and Egypt, to or from the Indian Ocean and the Pacific, had to pass through this one strait, less than sixteen sea miles wide, much of that blocked by islands and shoals, jagged coral reefs, and wrecks.

"Verdammt," Schneider cursed. "This is getting us nowhere. The Gulf of Aden is too wide for us to be sure of catching good targets, and the Bab el Mandeb is too narrow to lurk there. I don't like this setup." One side of the Bab el Mandeb Strait was controlled by neutral Yemen, and the other by the Allies' Central African pocket.

"Your intentions, sir?"

Schneider leaned toward Knipp's main console screen, until his large belly pressed against the edge of the console. "We penetrate the Bab el Mandeb, move to the northern end of the Red Sea, and work *here,* at the tip of the Sinai Peninsula. Once inside the Red Sea we get water that's nice and deep again. Off the Sinai, by Sharm al-Sheik, we'll be astride the Jubal Strait, the start of the Gulf of Suez leading to Egypt and the canal to the north-northwest, and also right outside the Tiran Strait, at the start of the Gulf of Aqaba, leading north-northeast to the harbor and naval base at Eilat in southernmost Israel, *here.*"

"Understood," Knipp said, as obsequious and yet martinetlike as ever.

"That puts us at the center of the Y intersection. The Red Sea is the Y's base, the Gulf of Suez is its left upper arm, and the Gulf of Aqaba is its right upper arm. This gives us several advantages compared to where we're positioned now. Do you see them?"

Schneider knew he didn't have to especially like Knipp to harness him as a good einzvo. *My career advancement depends on bringing up key subordinates, grooming them for eventual independent command, regardless of what I think of their personalities. . . . As far as I'm concerned, proper military leadership is altruistic only superficially. The true political goal is always selfish—to build good-looking paper credentials, thus earning, no,* demanding *my own next promotion.*

Knipp continued studying his screens and thinking.

"I see one thing, sir. The deep water there is up to eighty miles wide. That gives us more options than staying close to the Bab el Mandeb."

"That's tactical. Think big picture."

"Oh. By blocking the central intersection of that Y, we dominate any naval cooperation between Israel and Egypt along their southern flanks, before and during the Afrika Korps' offensive."

"Good. What else?"

"There's more, Captain?"

"Yes. Much more."

Knipp thought about the chart again. "I believe I see another factor now."

"Speak."

"We know Allied fast-attacks need to enter the Red Sea for their cruise missiles to reach useful targets in North Africa."

"Go on." *This much is obvious from the chart.*

"If we run stealthily to the north end of the Red Sea, we can then sweep southward again, and sink the Allied SSNs one by one as they move up to take their designated patrol boxes. Enemies we don't hear first by our superior sonars, we'll certainly locate exactly from great range when they start to launch missiles."

"How do you suggest we get to the north end of the Red Sea stealthily?"

"We'll need to move slowly through the Bab el Mandeb, so our wake hump doesn't show because it's so shallow. We can then continue northward at perhaps fifteen knots, in case any enemy SSNs are in the Red Sea already."

"Navigator," Schneider called out, without bothering to turn his head to look at the man.

"Navigator, aye aye, sir."

"Steaming distance from Bab el Mandeb to Sharm al-Sheik?"

"Eleven hundred and ten sea miles, Captain."

"Very well, Navigator." Schneider leaned back in his seat, and gave Knipp a sidelong glance. "Fifteen knots puts us where we want to be in three days. We don't have three days to dawdle."

"Because the offensive might start soon?"

"And because enemy SSNs going faster than fifteen knots could overtake us from behind. . . . Copilot, activate anti-LIDAR and anti-LASH active hull coatings. It's broad daylight up there."

The copilot acknowledged.

"Attention in Control. I intend to penetrate the Bab el Mandeb at five knots. Soon thereafter we'll reach rugged seafloor terrain off several large islands. This terrain will block our noise as we accelerate. I will then go to flank speed and make the entire transit north at sixty knots along the bottom. We will therefore arrive on station in early afternoon, local time, on Monday."

"Understood," the watch standers said.

The Red Sea's floor, right down the middle as it ran north, was conveniently at or close to *Doenitz*'s crush depth. This route was lined with black-smoker hot vents, petroleum seeps, and volcanic sinkholes filled with extra-salty scorching brine, all of which would aid concealment.

Schneider's intercom blinked. *Verdammt, what is it* now? He palmed the handset: the radio room. An ELF code ordered *Doenitz* to trail her floating wire antenna.

Schneider did this while still on the bottom, to help mask the antenna winch's mechanical transients. Then he ordered the pilot to reduce depth until the floating wire could reach up toward the surface. A message started coming through. The message was in Schneider's private captain-only code.

Another change of orders? Are those nincompoops on shore in Berlin ordering me back to Durban after all this time and labor wasted to get where I am? . . . It's worth it, though, to have a crack at Challenger *before* von Scheer *is ready to break out.*

Schneider gave Knipp the conn and went to his cabin. He opened his laptop, entered his passwords, and read the decoded message. At the beginning he cursed again, but then he was positively delighted.

CHAPTER 42

Klaus Mohr reminded himself, with savage and poignant irony, that he had wanted, *demanded,* to be here. He fought down the urge to panic, and forced himself to keep breathing in and out through his scuba regulator. This was the culmination of a quest that had been eating Mohr alive for many weeks. The interval for possible success was exceedingly narrow, measured in a handful of hours, with no margin at all for mistakes.

Vertigo, claustrophobia, and fear of drowning made his heart race, and his respiration was faster than the effort to kick with his legs should have required. The shallow water was so murky through his dive mask, even on a sunny afternoon, that his only guides on where to go were the tug of the lanyard between his waist and his dive buddy, Gamal Salih, plus the dive computer strapped to his left wrist. Mohr needed the direction the bubbles of his open-circuit scuba took just to show him which way was up. The computer's glow-in-the-dark readouts said it was 4:08 P.M. local time, an hour behind schedule already, and he had only twenty minutes left of air. He could never reach the Israeli shore, a quarter mile away, in twenty minutes at the rate he was going. Worse, the hostile shore was on his right, due east, and his compass said he and Salih were swimming north.

That was the point. The team sent to infiltrate Israel—at Mohr's own vehement urging, and on Captain Fuller's finely debated orders—walked a delicate high-wire act that, with this swim, had barely begun.

Steady mechanical buzzing and growling filled Mohr's ears. Underwater, it was hard for even a seasoned diver to tell where sounds were coming from. This was Klaus Mohr's first-ever dive, aside from the hurried training inside one of *Challenger*'s lock-out trunks. He was keenly aware of the reasons for why it might also be his last. The surrounding murk that made it hard for Salih to aid him in an emergency was the least of his worries.

The murk diminished as Mohr swam farther north, maintaining ten feet over the bottom that was only twenty feet deep. Now he could see Salih, and then to each side the whole team. But this cut both ways, since others could see them too, just as easily.

Felix Estabo and Chief Costa and the three enlisted SEALs put Mohr to shame. Each of them dragged a waterproof bag holding one of Mohr's computer modules or his tool kit, with adjustable buoyancy bladders to keep the bags from rising or sinking. Lieutenant Estabo really had his hands full, since his dive buddy was Lieutenant (j.g.) David Meltzer—one of *Challenger*'s qualified safety-and-inspection divers, but never schooled in undersea special warfare tactics.

Yet Meltzer's help was essential. He'd spent a summer in Israel in high school, and had been top of the class in his Hebrew school before that. Along with the SEALs and Salih, Meltzer—like Mohr—used conventional scuba that gave off bubbles. Stealth was not part of the plan; when properly equipped, and so heavily burdened, traveling submerged was much more efficient than raising constant splashes along the surface, as long as their air supply held out.

The notion of hiding in plain sight, in the water and then

on the land, made Mohr feel naked. He kept going on willpower alone.

A new buzzing noise began, at a higher pitch, growing loud and then diminishing. Mohr watched as a black rubber raft with an outboard engine bounced through the gentle swells above, busy on some errand. It passed the team a bit farther out to sea, carefully avoiding their telltale bubbles, meanwhile casting a moving shadow on the bottom. Mohr looked at the seafloor, and amid the rocks and sand and mud, and starfish and colorful coral, he could see the shadows of eight men, including himself, with their gear bags.

Ahead, almost a soccer-field length away, a large boat sat at anchor, its hull below the waterline looming dark and menacing. That dive-support boat was the main source of the steadier, throaty buzzing and growl, but the boat didn't move. The support boat was the team's first destination.

Between Mohr and the boat—a fifty- or sixty-footer—there was much human activity on the bottom. Felix changed course slightly, and the invasion team followed. They swam close enough to the other group to be spotted but not interfere, and not have their swim fins kick up silt to disturb these divers intently at work. Some noticed Mohr and his companions, glanced up, and waved. He waved back. The strangers took his presence for granted. But Mohr knew that to them, it was *he* who was a stranger, and a mortal enemy.

This was the easiest part. With dive masks over their eyes and nose, and scuba regulators in their mouths, it was hard to tell people apart.

Mohr's heart beat even faster. He calmed down by observing the work as the team swam on, his scientist's curiosity aroused. These mental notes would be vital soon. They might make all the difference to whether or not his cover story could bear scrutiny. He was the team's most indispensable member, but also its weakest link.

The edges of the working site were marked by orange nylon cables, rising from concrete blocks on the bottom to orange balls on the surface that served as buoys. Another black rubber raft, its outboard engine idling, was moored nearby. Mohr expected that this one held the diver lifeguards and a radioman, in case anybody below got into trouble. That raft would also be flying a larger version of the flags attached to each buoy: a blue-and-white swallowtail pennant, the international warning signal to passing ships that divers were present.

The site itself was laid out in a coordinate grid of one-meter squares, formed by stretches of white plastic pipe. Two black hoses, each about as wide across as one of Mohr's slim thighs, extended along the bottom and up to the anchored boat, whose heavy pumps Mohr realized caused most of the growling he heard. A pair of divers used one of the hoses like a vacuum cleaner; Mohr could see it sucking things in—sand, silt, pebbles, and any small artifacts. Around them, in an indentation in the seafloor, were the fragmentary ribs of an ancient shipwreck. Nearby, other divers operated cameras in clear plastic cases, where intact and broken pottery jars lay jumbled in a heap atop round stones that had once been the ship's ballast. They made notes on white plastic clipboards that held no paper, with what looked like regular pencils. Different divers were using the other hose to gently spray water, not suck. They shifted the hose back and forth systematically, raising a cloud of bottom material that was thrown against a mesh backstop so no valuable finds would be lost. They were clearing an additional area of its overburden of sand and silt, to expose more of the wreck and the debris field strewn around it centuries or even millennia ago.

Mohr closed his eyes for a few seconds while he made his legs continue to kick. He burned the images he'd seen into his brain. The whole team would be doing this. Felix had told them sternly, before they left the minisub, that their lives and their mission depended on a long series of such small details, to support big lies.

———

Felix and the others broke the surface near the support boat. He let Meltzer do the talking. *"Shalom!"* Meltzer shouted above the boat's pump engines. He waved to get the attention of someone, anyone, on deck. A teenage boy leaned over the rail behind the wheelhouse. After some Hebrew they changed to English, which most Israelis spoke well from studying it in school—if they weren't English-speaking immigrants themselves.

"Can you get us a ride to the beach?" Meltzer yelled.

The teenager looked at the group in the water. As rehearsed, all of them had their dive masks up on their foreheads, and breathed the open air as they trod water, to seem less furtive. The northerly current that paralleled the shore brought them slowly, relentlessly, down the length of the boat.

"Who are you? I don't know you."

Felix assumed the kid was helping on the underwater dig because he was too young for the army. But he wasn't too young to be suspicious of intruders.

Meltzer gave a false name, then pointed toward another dive-support boat nearly a mile to the south, whose noises the minisub had homed in on by sonar. Someone was dumping buckets of waste silt, already sifted through screens that would catch any artifacts, over the up-current side of that boat.

"We're from NYU!" New York University, whose archaeology department sponsored digs in the Middle East. Meltzer had been to their Manhattan campus often enough to fake it if grilled.

"I said I don't know you!"

"We're supposed to be working the other site. Got mixed up in the silt from the river, went the wrong way, couldn't find the boat, and got caught by the current. Before we knew it, we were carried too far to swim back easily. So we drifted toward you, to stay clear of the minefield."

A stretch of beach between the two underwater dig locations was cordoned off by barbed wire, and seeded with mines and posted with conspicuous warnings. Just south of the other boat was one of Israel's few rivers that hadn't run dry for the summer by May, the Crocodile. The river was muddy and also polluted. To become disoriented in the outflow near its mouth, underwater, was plausible—barely.

"Don't you have compasses?" the kid shouted back. He seemed argumentative, skeptical by nature.

Meltzer shrugged while he kicked with his fins. "I screwed up. The other guy tried to tell me, but I wouldn't listen." Meltzer gestured at Salih.

"Who are *you*?"

"Professional divers hired by the dig. We're from Ashqelon." A port far down the coast, dozens of miles past distant Tel Aviv.

"Turkish?"

"Me, yes. The others are Portuguese, guest workers, stuck." By the war. "The bald guy is also from NYU." Klaus Mohr had shaved his head, and dyed his eyelashes black with waterproof face camouflage Felix had given him, to appear less Germanic. Meltzer and Salih did the talking to divert initial attention from Mohr.

"Look," Meltzer said, "we're exhausted, we need fresh tanks, and we might need to make another dive before nightfall. *Can we please cut the crap so you can call us a ride to the beach?*"

Meltzer was mirroring the kid's argumentative attitude. He'd told Felix that Israelis often spoke this way as a matter of course. Seeming defensive could ruin everything.

As if to punctuate Felix's worries, an Israeli Navy fast-patrol boat roared by, a thousand yards farther out in the Med.

The kid disappeared without answering Meltzer. The boat's pump and vacuum engines, mounted amidships on deck, suddenly stopped. Felix heard snatches of Hebrew, and static from a radio. Two men in their early twenties took the teenager's place at the rail. They wore green combat fatigues, and aimed assault rifles at the eight men clustered in the water. "You," one of the soldiers shouted to Meltzer. "We called both beach camps. They say they never heard of you, or anybody from NYU." His accent was more noticeable than the kid's, with a singsong quality that would have been lyrical if it hadn't been so venomous.

Felix's team had come unarmed except for their dive knives: Archaeologists and hired-hand diving assistants would not carry guns. To flee would surely draw fire from these soldiers, and a quick call to the patrol boat would put an end to the matter. The soldier who wasn't talking seemed too trigger happy to Felix as it was. Meltzer would have to bluff it out, as he'd been scripted to in advance.

"Come on!" Meltzer shouted back in his best Bronx accent and rough New York City style. "There's a goof on the roster, all the admin's like chaos here. This whole thing's a mad rush, you know that better than I do! Why do you think we had to use Turks and Portuguese?"

Meltzer meant the site work was all a mad rush, to telescope most of a summer's worth of excavating into just a few weeks, between the recent end of northern Israel's rainy season and the start of a German offensive whose precise timing wouldn't be known to civilian researchers. Extra volunteers and workers made the site areas hectic. The professors running the project needed good data to publish or perish and get tenure—or not—and the grad students needed to finish their dissertations, to earn their doctorates—or not. Meltzer was pretending to be such a grad student, flown in from the U.S.

"Why weren't you drafted?" the soldier questioned Meltzer. The draft had been reinstated in America because of the war.

Felix tried not to cringe. They hadn't thought of this in the hurried role-playing rehearsals. Meltzer, in his mid-twenties, physically fit and in reality on active duty, needed an excuse.

"I have Crohn's disease."

"Mah?" What?

Felix was impressed. The soldiers might just fall for this.

"A chronic inflammation of the small intestine! Bad news! . . . Relax! It's genes! You won't catch it!"

"So how can you dive?"

This soldier just wouldn't quit. Felix saw for himself that

Klaus Mohr wasn't exaggerating when he said wartime Israelis were totally paranoid.

"I wear a diaper."

Felix laughed, almost giddy with relief. Meltzer had come up with the perfect answer—with an assault rifle aimed at his face. The soldier thought Felix was snickering.

"We all do on long or deep dives," Salih threw in, which was true for both recreational and professional divers.

"One at a time," the soldier said. He gestured with his muzzle toward the ladder from the water at the stern of the boat. He pulled back the charging handle of his rifle and let it snap forward, chambering a round. "First hand up your sacks."

The team swam to the stern. Their bags with Mohr's cases were passed to one of the boat's other crewmen, someone tanned bronze, in his mid-fifties, potbellied but surprisingly strong. He moved with a sailor's ease. Felix assumed from his proprietary air that he was the vessel's owner. Meltzer climbed the ladder, followed by Salih, then Mohr, then Felix.

"Maspik!" the soldier shouted. Enough! He'd shrewdly divided Felix's team in half, with four SEALs still in the water. He'd also separated the team from their equipment bags. The teenager and the older man had opened them without asking permission, and started searching the contents. They pulled out clipboards resembling the ones used at the wreck site, improvised from what had been available on *Challenger;* the ship's vast on-line e-book library of tour guides for crewmen on leave had told Felix this much, the same way it let him and Gerald Parker identify this site and assess its probable present active status.

Like many items in the bags—including pencils, an underwater camera with blank film, and Mohr's quantum computer and tool case—the clipboards were damp with saltwater. Everything had been soaked while still on *Challenger,* to appear more authentic when examined. Were they authentic enough?

Felix and those with him stood on the deck, dripping. Their compressed-air tanks and weight belts were heavy out of the sea. Standing upright in the head-to-toe loose-fitting wet suits was serious labor. They had to squint in the bright sun reflecting off the Med, because their hats and sunglasses were in side pouches of the gear bags. Even with a light on-shore breeze, and the temperature in the seventies, Felix felt much too warm as he waited to see what happened next.

"What's in these cases?" the boat owner demanded.

Felix's tension worsened. Explaining the cases couldn't be avoided. Neither could Mohr keep mute forever, and Meltzer was too junior to lead a major university archaeological expedition, even a last-minute add-on by a school not a principal dig sponsor.

"May I show them to you?" Mohr asked politely.

The soldier pointed his rifle angrily at Mohr, stepping back to keep the foursome covered. His partner held his own weapon pointed at the men still in the water. Felix had seen that the rifles were Galil ARs, with their safeties off. Long, curved magazines projected down and forward from their receivers; each held fifty rounds of the same ammo as an M-16. Felix did *not* want to take a bullet—or a burst of bullets. None of his team wore body armor.

"You have a German accent," the soldier said to Mohr, his voice thick, bloodcurdling, hate-filled.

"So?" Mohr answered back aggressively. "And I suppose that no Israelis speak with German accents? *Hmm?*"

"You are not Israeli."

"Did I say I was?"

"What are you?" The soldier had his Galil's unfolded stock on his shoulder now, and peered down its sights at Mohr's head.

Uh-oh, Felix told himself, sweating, *here's the punch line.*

"I'm German. And an adjunct professor at New York University. And *not* a supporter of Imperial Germany or I wouldn't be here, would I?" Mohr advanced on the soldier, loaded Galil and all, in a rage that he summoned from deep inside himself. "Don't you know there are *good* Germans? Do you know how many of my friends were shot for resisting tyrants last year *in* Germany?" Spittle began to fly from Mohr's mouth. "Do you think I *like* having to explain myself wherever I go, as if I'm some kind of vile insect? *Do you think I like it?*" His nose almost touched the flash suppressor at the Galil's muzzle now.

Felix thought that if they survived this, Mohr deserved an Oscar for his performance.

"Where are your papers?"

"At the hostel. We don't take them with us *on dives.*"

"What are these boxes?"

"Magnetometers, gravimeters. For finding and mapping out underwater wrecks. I'm testing them on working sites to calibrate them. You understand the word *'calibrate'?*" Mohr folded his arms across his chest defiantly, over the straps of his scuba and his uninflated buoyancy vest.

For an uncomfortable minute the soldier kept his rifle trained on Mohr. Then his eyes drifted to the equipment cases sitting on the deck. His eyes darted back to Mohr, testing for a reaction, any excuse to open fire. The tactic was as transparent to Mohr as to Felix. Mohr gave the soldier a dirty look, then spoke quietly and evenly. "Get us a ride to the beach, or shoot me. Make up your mind."

The soldier lowered his rifle, snapped the selector onto safe, and shouted to the wheelhouse, then to his partner. The other soldier safed his weapon. The boat owner talked on the radio; a response crackled in Hebrew. Soon a young woman on the beach, at the primary camp north of the minefield, pushed a rubber raft into the water and started its little engine, heading for the boat.

The soldier glanced at Meltzer. "Eight people and those bags, you need two trips." The deck's pump and vacuum engines came back to life, making noises and giving off smelly exhaust.

CHAPTER 43

Chief Costa and the enlisted SEALs had already gone to the beach with some of Mohr's gear. Now Felix, Meltzer, Salih, and Mohr rode the raft steered by the young woman. She'd spoken to Meltzer briefly in Hebrew, but ignored her other passengers. To her, Felix could tell, he and Salih were underlings. Klaus Mohr kept his mouth shut, not pressing his luck. The woman, her expression serious, purposeful, handled the raft with skill.

They approached the shore quickly. To the left of the beach the land rose to gray cliffs, with an indentation forming a cove. There were structures and activity on the cliffs. Felix knew this was Tel Dor, one of the most extensive ongoing land-based archaeological digs in Israel. Farther north was a promontory, topped by a Crusader fortress crumbling from neglect. South by a few miles, also directly on the shore, lay another Crusader ruin, with the base of what had once been a tall, massive tower.

Large rocks stuck out of the water near the beach. The rubber raft wove between them, kicking up cool spray that sprinkled Felix's body and face. The sea altered from deep blue to turquoise green, the surf was barely three feet high, and white water lapped against yellowish sand. The raft ran up on the beach. The woman turned off the outboard to save scarce gas.

"Todah," Meltzer said. Thank you. The woman nodded, then went about checking the raft. The narrow tide line here was mostly free of detritus from naval battles a hundred-plus miles to the west; Felix saw bits of charred driftwood, and small blobs of oily gunk, easily sidestepped.

He scanned the setup on the beach. Open-sided canvas tents gave shade, where people at long tables rinsed artifacts, then immersed them again in buckets for preservation; records were kept on laptops. A close-sided tent had a sign that said "East Carolina University Underwater Archaeology Group." Another such tent had a sign in Hebrew and English; the English part said "University of Haifa." Farther off, a generator purred. Cables were strung over tall planks driven into the sand, providing power to different parts of the encampment. A tank trailer with diesel fuel sat near the generator. A bigger trailer had "Fresh Water Do Not Drink" marked on its tank. One open-sided tent held coolers, coffee urns, and food; workers wolfed down snacks there.

Closer to the multilane coastal highway stood a row of chemical toilets, and a few parked vans and cars—Haifa was twelve miles straight north. Felix also noticed a big stack of white PVC pipe, a pile of empty compressed-air scuba tanks near the highway, and rows of filled tanks standing upright on wooden pallets close to the water. The sand in many places was wet; it was crisscrossed by countless footprints and sets of tire tracks.

Rolls of barbed wire stretched along the whole south edge of the area, from the surf to the highway. Portable floodlights on poles, switched off now, pointed both at the encampment and toward the deserted beach beyond the wire. Hundreds of yards off, on a twisting corridor through the minefield, Felix saw a sandbagged heavy machine-gun emplacement.

He went to the co-ed shower area. Burlap screens on stakes

gave minimal privacy. Chief Costa and his men had by now washed off, cleaned their gear, and changed into casual civilian clothing from dry side pouches in their bags. Felix and those with him did the same, then strapped dive knives near their ankles, under their slacks.

They carried their dive gear to an open-air spot with wooden tables and clotheslines equipped with plastic hooks. All sorts of gear was piled on the tables; wet suits hung from the hooks; an attendant kept an eye on everything. Felix and his men tied numbered tags to their gear, and the woman gave them claim checks. She spoke good English. Meltzer said they'd be back in two hours, to put in another short dive before dark. He asked how they could get a lift into Zichron Yaakov, a town a few miles away where he said they were staying. She pointed to a van.

As the team trudged up the beach to the van, hefting their equipment bags, Felix noticed more barbed wire, and other young women guarding the inland perimeter exits. They wore army uniforms and carried Uzi submachine guns—an old design, used mostly by rear-area troops, but deadly if well maintained. Felix's group was challenged at gunpoint by two of these women.

They spoke little English. While Felix's heart was in his throat again, they questioned Meltzer and he responded as best he could. He gestured out at the boat, and the raft they'd ridden in on. These soldiers insisted the team open their equipment bags and unlock Mohr's module cases and his tool kit. They looked them over carefully. They waved electronic wands around each case: detectors for explosives, poisons, radiation, and germs. Finally one of the women nodded and pointed the team toward the shuttle van. Felix knew that the hardest part by far was yet to come.

As they clambered into the van, he realized that none of the soldiers had names or rank insignia on their uniforms, for security. Meltzer told the driver, another woman, their supposed destination. The driver wore civilian clothes, but had a loaded Uzi on the seat beside her. The van's windows were all rolled down. With a jerk it picked up speed and cut onto the highway, heading south. A nice breeze came in the windows. Traffic was conspicuously light, except for crowded buses and long military convoys.

Soon swamps and lagoons mixed with eucalyptus groves, date trees, and tilled fields. Ahead was a coastal kibbutz—a socialist collective farm—and a road sign said it was called "Nakhsholim." The van turned inland instead at the first intersection. They crossed a rail line, then another north-south road. Their side road began to gain altitude. They were climbing the foothills of the Carmel Range, only 1,500 feet tall at its peak, but compared to the flat coastal plain running south, these green hills before them seemed high. They passed large vineyards along the road, then soaring, narrow, fragrant cypress trees. Behind the van, the view to the Med with the late-afternoon sun above the sea was stunning.

The van made a sharp right turn. Soon they were on a street of Zichron Yaakov: population six thousand, employment mostly in agriculture or light industry, plus tourism—the latter was sluggish because of the war, except for the ubiquitous Japanese. The street was lined by stucco one-story buildings with red-tile roofs. It was paved in places with cobblestones, and the streetlamps were decorative old-fashioned gas lights; the first Zionist settlement at Zichron Yaakov had been founded in the 1880s.

The van stopped at the hostel. The driver gave Meltzer a card, then touched the cell phone on her dash: Call if they wanted transport later. Everyone waited on the sidewalk until her vehicle was well gone. Their jaws set. It was time to assume new identities, and do the thing they'd come here for.

CHAPTER 44

It wasn't easy finding the type of manhole Mohr said they needed. He'd deduced that one of the buried fiber-optic trunk cables from Tel Aviv to Haifa had to pass under Zichron Yaakov *somewhere*. It was by far the largest town on a straight line from the Mediterranean shore to the West Bank Territory's border, barely sixteen miles eastward from the sea. Such placement of the cable was forced in part by the need to protect it, and in part by the need to give good connection service in the town. The size and shape of the maintenance-access manholes—rectangular, one by two meters or so—were set by the need to sometimes move big parts and equipment in and out.

Felix knew this was at best a series of hopeful assumptions. *Challenger* lacked maps of Israel's fiber-optic grid, because in Norfolk no one thought they would ever use them. The idea of stealing the information in Israel was dismissed right away, with Gerald Parker's wholehearted agreement. He'd warned that any physical or computer-hacking break-in or search for such data could be spotted instantly by the Shin Bet, Israel's ruthless internal state-security apparatus. The

SEALs' raid would end in catastrophe, the team either captured or killed.

The group began walking the streets, lugging Mohr's gear, looking for the manhole that would let him hook up his quantum computer. Meltzer preempted suspicion by people they passed as best he could, acting friendly and making quick greetings to Israelis they met on the spotless sidewalks.

Felix often glanced at his watch. He was in a race with almost a dozen Kampfschwimmer teams to get into the Israeli systems first. He also kept thinking of the hard deadline Captain Fuller had set for minisub pickup. Even if they found the cable, even if Mohr's gizmo functioned correctly—and Mohr didn't show any signs that he was in fact a double agent for the Germans—Felix realized they might not make it back before *Challenger* sailed. They'd be stuck in Israel lacking a good explanation of how they'd arrived, with an all-out Axis offensive charging toward them very soon. The American embassy would surely be watched, might be penetrated, and going there could betray *Challenger* and Mohr.

Face it, this effort was launched on a swim fin and a prayer. The fatalistic mood of the Israeli pedestrians Felix saw didn't help. They all knew that the war—which up to now had spared their homeland, though it nearly bankrupted their economy—would soon become a vicious fight for survival, a fight to the death. Memories of previous wars and terrorism fueled the communal concerns. Knowing what a different generation of Germans had done to a different generation of Jews added an edge of fury that Felix could tell was seething all around him. The scenic views between the leafy trees reminded him of how much could still be lost. Few of the locals he went by were males between sixteen and fifty—they'd been mobilized, massing nearer the front where the Afrika Korps would be.

Mohr pointed into the road. Meltzer walked to the manhole cover, consisting of four smaller pieces placed side by side flush with the pavement, and read the words on the heavy metal castings. After reading them he said, "Right type of manhole, but welded shut." Security.

Felix's mind raced, trying to think of where they could steal an acetylene cutting torch.

"No," Mohr whispered. "This is good. It means we're in the proper area. We need to trace the cable's route and find one kept open for quick repairs and testing. You see?"

Felix nodded. He considered splitting up his team to search in opposite directions. But this would probably waste as much time as it saved, since he needed everybody when the work began. His instinct told him to go north.

After snaking for blocks through the streets of Zichron Yaakov, they found another manhole for the fiber-optic line, also welded shut. Felix's frustration level was almost unbearable.

Then it dawned on him. Technology-dependent firms would want to be close to the fiber-optic main, to have the shortest, least expensive, reliable high-baud-rate connections. To find the main he had to find such companies. A commercial area would be busier too, so a manhole there might not be sealed against tampering like these unguarded ones in quieter residential districts. Felix led the way southwest, to an office park near the modern town center. Following curving streets that ran steeply uphill and down, they located what they needed.

In plain sight of people on the street, and of others who might glance out the windows of their offices, the team put down their equipment bags. Chief Costa and his three enlisted SEALs—da Rosa, Azavedo, and Magro—opened the bags, chatting as casually as they could in Portuguese to keep up their cover as hired guest workers. Meltzer began to fuss about, pretending to be their foreman, waving his arms, pointing, and issuing commands in English and monosyllabic Hebrew. He understood conventional fiber optics from qualifying on *Challenger*'s systems. The supposed cable-maintenance crew removed eight uninflated orange life jackets, which everybody put on as if they were traffic-safety vests. The team donned hard hats brought from the ship.

Costa pulled out a crowbar. Rosa, Azavedo, and Magro stepped into the street, and began directing vehicles around and away from the manhole. Costa used the crowbar to lever the sectional covers off; Felix and Salih helped him slide each awkward piece to one side in a pile facing on-coming cars. Below these was a sheet-metal pan for chan-neling rainwater into drains. Costa lifted it, exposing an opening into cool, musty blackness. Mohr climbed down the ladder with a flashlight, and the SEALs passed him his modules one by one, then his tool kit. As his team manhan-dled the cases, Felix saw the silicone that plugged the holes in the power unit where the German bullet had gone through. He thought to himself that the repairs made on *Challenger* had better work—or they, Israel, and the world were in trouble.

Felix and Salih climbed down to help Mohr, then Meltzer went down partway. Like this, Felix could see his alleged foreman standing above, in a rectangle of tree-shaded day-light, with torso exposed, watching for any problems at street level. Meltzer tried to appear as matter-of-fact as he could, not furtive. He'd be the team's liaison with any locals, and while underground Felix needed someone on the ladder to be surveillance and verbal communications relay for the surface element of the group.

The maintenance space itself, beneath the manhole, was maybe four times the size of the three-foot-by-six-foot entry hole. Felix found a light switch, flicked it, and weak bulbs came on, leaving the crowded and dank space in semi-shadow. Thick cables emerged from the concrete wall in a side of the prefabricated chamber, entered a floor-mounted unit that Mohr said was a fiber-optic signal amplifier, and then the cables disappeared into the wall on the opposite side. Thinner cables ran from junction boxes to the amplifier and through the other sides of the chamber. There were old spiderwebs in the corners by the low ceiling that supported the street. Mohr, tallest, brushed the top of his hard hat against the roof when he stood up straight.

Mohr crouched and opened the modules with help from Salih. He removed neat wire coils and furiously started to hook together his gear, then plugged a cord from the power unit into a 220-volt utility socket in the chamber wall. Lips pursed, very tense, Mohr pressed buttons on the modules, starting the first complete, all-up test allowed by a protective Captain Fuller since the damage in Istanbul. The modules began to hum and whine. Indicators glowed, green and amber. "All self-check correctly."

Felix thought he might feel something being so close to the quantum-entanglement process. *A tingling, a numbness, distorted vision? . . . Weird stuff is going on inside those cases.* But the only sensation he noticed was one of relief.

The next step would be to tap into the Israeli trunk cable.

"Mah zeh?" a man snapped from somewhere above.

Meltzer glanced down the ladder and said that meant "What is this?" He left the hole. Felix heard him speak in Hebrew, to a person who answered sternly, unsatisfied.

Felix feared that the inevitable confrontation with authorities had struck much sooner than he'd hoped. "Keep working," he said to Mohr. Felix climbed the narrow ladder. He smiled, which was the only thing he could do under the circumstances. Right there was an Israeli policeman, on foot patrol. He was thirtyish, muscular, and had a swarthy complexion with unreadable predator's eyes. His body posture told Felix enough. The man kept his fingers poised by the butt of a hefty pistol in his belt holster. His radio crackled, a staticky voice, then was silent, pregnantly.

"He's asked to see our work papers and IDs," Meltzer stated to Felix in English, deadpan. "I've explained that I'm an American engineer helping on cable-system upkeep since everybody else is in the army, and you lead the work gang assisting me."

"What are you wearing?" The cop fingered Meltzer's orange life vest.

He speaks some English. He's establishing more control.

"For emergencies. Flash floods, in sewers..."

"I want to see your passport."

Something had to be done, and Meltzer waited for a SEAL to do it. Chief Costa was standing behind the cop. Costa sneaked in a hand sign asking Felix if he should knock the guy out.

The policeman's free hand began to reach for his radio mike. Felix envisioned the entire scheme falling to pieces, with them all arrested for sabotage. Costa couldn't attack the cop in broad daylight, in the middle of the street. Pedestrians were glancing too attentively as it was.

Felix counted on the cop not wanting to swamp his headquarters with yet another false alarm about what could be perfectly legitimate newcomers to the area. Felix faked a noisy sneeze, then begged pardon in Portuguese—a prearranged signal. The enlisted SEALs continued directing the sparse road traffic, but they moved subtly to block the manhole from the view of the nearest civilians on the sidewalks beyond parked cars. Felix gestured for the cop to approach him. Costa backed off. The policeman walked nearer, touching his pistol. His expression was opaque, hard. He unsnapped the nylon strip holding the weapon snug in its holster; he was preparing to draw.

Felix held up a hand to the policeman as if to mean, Please wait a moment. "I bring you all the documents. They're with our things in the hole. Okay?" He hammed up hesitant English, in his thickest Portuguese accent, displaying his sweetest smile.

Felix climbed down before the cop could object. Inside the maintenance space he whispered urgently to Salih. "Your turn. Take my place. Charm the guy and lure him in real close."

"Plan B?"

Felix nodded curtly. The next few seconds were critical. "Keep working," he hissed to Mohr.

Salih stood on the ladder and spoke in gabby Turkish, trying to convey to the cop that he was a foreign guest-worker technician; he said "Turk Telecom" repeatedly, but that was all Felix could understand. The idea in this contingency—at least as briefed in the hectic mission rehearsals—was to try to puzzle a cop just enough, by a seemingly innocent barrage of different languages and people going in and out of the manhole. This mental sleight of hand, a jack-in-the-box show, was a long shot, and improvising under pressure would be key. From the shadows, peering up, Felix saw the cop look into the manhole, past Meltzer and Salih to where Mohr fiddled with his modules.

Felix smoothly reached and grabbed the policeman's ankles and yanked him past Salih and into the opening. The cop yelped and tumbled through feet first; Felix grunted with effort as he and Salih caught him. Felix chopped him in the side of the neck with the edge of his palm, and lowered the stunned policeman to the floor. He barely fit, taking up most of the free floor space.

"You all right?" Meltzer yelled into the manhole. He pretended to wait for the policeman to answer. "Yes?" Meltzer said. "Good . . . Here's your hat." He held the hat below the lip of the manhole, then let it go; it dropped. This pantomime was supposed to make locals think the policeman had been clumsy following Felix into the manhole, and was safely inside examining documents. Meanwhile, Felix had grabbed a roll of duct tape from Mohr's tool kit. He swiftly bound and gagged the cop before the man could regain his senses. He tugged the pistol from its holster and placed it on top of the waist-high amplifier: a newly acquired firearm, a possible asset for his team, kept in reserve. Felix would use it only as a last resort. He held his breath, listening for hints of alarm from above. Salih went up to check.

Felix rubbed a painfully bruised shoulder.

Mohr looked at him. "Wonderful. Now what?"

"Keep working. How much more time do you need?"

"I'm not sure yet."

The cop, wedged beside the amplifier cabinet, fought against the tape. "Relax," Felix mumbled. "Be quiet and we won't hurt you." The Israeli glared and fought harder. Felix raised a hand, threatening another karate chop. The policeman levered his bound legs, fast, and almost clobbered Felix on the chin. He ducked under the man's flailing heels and dealt him another, much sharper blow to the side of the neck as he tried to bodily smash Mohr's equipment. The Israeli slumped, in a stupor. Felix removed his gear belt, tossing it out of reach.

"What are you going to do with him?" Mohr asked as he applied his tools to one of the fiber-optic cables.

"Leave him here," Felix said, securing the cop's feet to one drainpipe and his upper arms to another with lots more duct tape.

"And no one will notice that he went in, but didn't come out even after we finish?"

"Passersby who saw him go down won't be around to not see him climb back up. They'll have passed by."

"And people in offices? They won't have passed by."

Crap. "Keep working."

Mohr peered at whatever he was doing, frowning. "You already said three times to keep working."

The policeman's radio crackled again. Something about the tone of the voice made Felix wary. He stuck his head out to where the others were making sure no one drove into the manhole. He caught Meltzer's eye; Meltzer came inside.

"The radio. Translate next time they broadcast."

"Right." Meltzer perched on the base of the ladder.

"Anything I can do to help?" Felix prodded Mohr.

"Yes. Stop interrupting me."

The radio voice repeated, talking longer than before. Meltzer listened. "A policeman hasn't made his regular check-in. The town station dispatcher is asking other patrolmen if they know where he is."

"What are they saying?"

"I can't tell. I think these portable radios are only strong enough to talk back and forth to the station's big transceiver. We won't hear another cop until he's real close."

The dispatcher spoke again. Meltzer translated. "They've asked some other policemen to look for the missing cop."

"And, we know exactly where he is," Felix said dryly.

"Yeah," Meltzer said, fretting.

"Sit tight. Glue your ears to the radio."

Felix turned to watch Mohr, for lack of anything better to do. Mohr's elbows bobbed up and down as he tightened a dozen small nuts one by one with a ratchet wrench. The nuts held a boxy clamping device in position around the trunk cable. Mohr assembled lengths of interconnecting, rigid photon-wave guides, a bridge between the device and one of his modules. He shifted his stance, and began to operate controls on another module. He studied the readouts and didn't look happy.

"Problem?" Felix asked. *Please, no.*

"I have other things to try first. Do not interrupt."

Felix bit his tongue. Mohr was breathing harder and starting to sweat. The work chamber had gotten uncomfortably warm, from all the body heat plus Mohr's equipment running. Felix wondered if Mohr's intent all along had been to damage Israeli systems, not aid them. He remembered Captain Fuller's orders to kill Mohr if the German behaved with deviousness. Felix tried to figure out what a devious Klaus Mohr would look like, as opposed to an absorbed Mohr or a worried Mohr. He drew a blank, having only annoyed Mohr by staring at him.

The radio spoke again. Before Felix could ask, Meltzer said the dispatcher was dealing with other routine business, not the missing cop.

Felix made a face. "There's a point at which they'll announce a town-wide alarm."

"I know," Meltzer said.

Mohr told them both to be quiet. He needed to concentrate.

"Turn off the radio," Felix ordered.

"What?" Meltzer was surprised.

"Turn it off. It isn't helping any of us."

CHAPTER 45

As each minute went by, the heat building up in the work chamber grew more oppressive. Meltzer, with his fiber-optic expertise, would be a better aide for Mohr if he needed assistance. Felix popped his head out at street level to take a breather. The office buildings that had before been his guide to finding this manhole now seemed like vigilant sentries lined up against him. The street itself, his team's route of escape, felt instead like a path that would lead more cops—or soldiers—directly to them. He wondered how much longer it could possibly be before someone looking out a window noticed that something was amiss. *How soon before a patrol car searching for the cop drives by, and then stops?* He worried that one or more of the Kampfschwimmer teams might be compromised somewhere, impairing Pandora but triggering a national alert that would rob Mohr of a chance to finish his job soon enough. These issues, Felix told himself, were beyond his ability to influence, so agonizing further would do no good.

Felix did the most reassuring, visible thing he could think of to delay any curious observers from grabbing a phone to dial 100, the Israeli national police. He left the manhole and sat down on its edge, his legs dangling inside; he stretched his arms, took a deep breath, and relaxed. He forced himself to not glance at his watch. He really didn't want to know what time it was. So long as Mohr succeeded in injecting his quantum-teleportation computer patch, Israel would be protected, and their priority mission goal would be achieved. After that, making it back to *Challenger* was highly desirable, but basically was gravy. A pitched battle against armed Israelis would serve no purpose. It was better in that worst-case scenario to just surrender, and then try to keep mum long enough so the patch, designed to hide itself, couldn't be removed before Germany's worm took effect. The Mossad or Shin Bet would never believe the truth, as Felix understood it. They'd fixate on Mohr's presence right away. Felix had to let Mohr be taken alive if this happened, presuming he still trusted Mohr by then, because Mohr's knowledge was too valuable for him to die unnecessarily on Israel's soil.

Felix asked himself, if it came to that, whether Mohr would be the first one to cave during interrogation or torture, or the last. Mohr was the oldest person on the team, had tremendous strength of character, and had already been tested emotionally in ways far beyond the best-imaginable SEAL training.

Felix sighed. A pleasant evening was coming on. He tried to enjoy what might be his last moments of freedom, or of life. To clear his mind, he gazed up at the sky.

"He's finished."

Felix was startled.

"He's finished," Meltzer repeated from the bottom of the ladder.

Felix flashed Meltzer a grin that, for the first time today, wasn't faked. "Ready to pack up?"

Meltzer nodded. Felix waved to Salih, who'd taken charge of the part of the team that had stayed in the street. Felix helped heft the equipment cases through the manhole opening. Mohr climbed out, tired but satisfied.

Felix went in to do one last inspection. He made sure no

tools were forgotten. The pistol sat on the amplifier; carrying it around, even concealed, would be too risky, too easily noticed or detected. Guile needed to serve from here on, not gunplay. The policeman, well cocooned by duct tape, very thoroughly secured, followed Felix with angry eyes.

"Someone will rescue you soon."

———————

The team made a beeline for the hostel where the dig van had dropped them off. The straight route was much shorter than the zigzag they'd taken in search of a useable manhole. Even so, it was mostly uphill, and the better part of two hours' high tension in Zichron Yaakov had already been as draining as physical labor. Felix told everyone to think and behave as if a keg of cold beer awaited them at the hostel. This way they posed as a private maintenance crew just coming off duty, sweaty from a day in the field, eager for refreshment. Felix repressed the knowledge that soon, if not already, the police in and around the town would sound a full alert for their missing comrade—quickly leaving the cop's assigned town-center patrol area was the only thing that had let the SEALs avoid an unpleasant encounter so far. But if they didn't find the cop quickly, and release him to describe his attackers, they'd conclude he might have been kidnapped by terrorists, and a brutal manhunt would be on; neither scenario favored Felix's team.

Felix also tried to squelch his lingering doubts about what Mohr had done, or failed to do, in the manhole with his quantum equipment.

At the hostel, Meltzer went inside to find a phone and call the van at the dig to come pick them up—American cash used at the hostel desk would buy him telephone tokens or a prepaid card.

We're about to find out if cell phones have already died because of Kampfschwimmer quantum-hacker meddling.

Meltzer came back onto the sidewalk. "The van lady said

she's finishing a run to Haifa. She'll be here in half an hour, maybe."

Felix finally looked at his watch. He shook his head in disgust. "She the only van?"

Meltzer nodded. "The only one working this late on a Sunday."

It was almost 6:43 P.M.; they'd didn't have half an hour to sit around waiting. They had to reach the dig, reclaim their dive gear, suit up, grab a ride out to the underwater work area, swim to a prearranged murky spot to meet the minisub, and then hurry out to sea to dock with *Challenger*.

"What about a local taxi service?"

"With eight of us and all this luggage, I better try a *sherut* company. They're more like minibuses for hire than cabs."

"They take U.S. cash?"

"Oh yes. They'll be very happy to."

Meltzer came out more quickly this time. "When they heard my American accent, they quoted an outrageous price. I told them I'd give the driver a twenty-dollar tip if he could be here in five minutes."

It was closer to ten minutes. There were only seven seats in the minibus, but everybody climbed in with their bags and boxes. Meltzer handed the driver a twenty-dollar bill. He said he'd give him another twenty if he got them the three miles downhill to the beach by 7 P.M.

The driver floored the accelerator. Traffic on the cross roads and the highway continued to be light. The minibus pulled up at the dig. The group found the same two perimeter guards who'd questioned them on the way out from the site encampment, and the women let them pass through the barbed wire. They hustled to reclaim their wet suits and dive gear, then took fresh compressed-air tanks.

Their next problem was getting rafts. Several were pulled up onto the beach—at this late hour, activity underwater was slowing. Meltzer told the woman on duty they'd head out to the wreck site themselves, anchor, then when finished return

on their own. Tired from a long day, she saw no reason to refuse this.

Felix and Costa picked a pair of rafts whose outboard motors had enough gas. They loaded both rafts hastily, revved
up the engines, and headed for the orange buoys. The sun was
very low, in their faces, reminding them that the fixed departure time for *Challenger* was drawing awfully near.

On the beach, sirens grew loud enough to overpower the
sound of the outboard motors. Felix glanced back. Flashing
lights lined the highway outside the site. He saw a man in
blue by the vehicles, with the white of a neck brace around
his throat, pointing out to sea at the rafts, literally jumping up
and down. From the distance, given the circumstances, Felix
recognized the figure too well: the cop from the manhole.
Soldiers near him spoke on radios. The heavy machine gun a
kilometer down the beach opened up like a jackhammer. Red
tracers probed their way toward the rafts. *"Everyone into the
water!"* Felix ordered.

———

The meeting point with the minisub was the wide place of
cloudy water up-current from the dig-support boat Felix's
team had used to get a ride to the beach. Waste silt and mud,
after sifting through screens on the boat, had been dumped
overboard all day, creating an area where visibility would be
obscured.

The team hugged the bottom at thirty feet. Now their
scuba bubbles could ruin everything. Machine-gun bullets
sprayed the surface above, but didn't punch down too near.
The excavation support boat started its main diesel engines.
Clanking and splashes meant it was raising its anchor, and
jettisoning all its hoses. Felix remembered those two soldiers
with the Galils. Fired straight down, their small bullets would
move slowly after thirty feet of water, but the soldiers probably also had hand grenades—and they might call in a naval

craft with full-size depth charges. The dig boat roared at them as they swam at it.

Felix and Chief Costa stirred up sand and silt for camouflage; the whole team froze and held their breaths, halting the bubbles. The dig boat rushed overhead, steering toward where Meltzer had claimed they'd come from earlier—south, by the Crocodile River outlet. Soon there were sharp underwater explosions. The concussions hurt Felix's eardrums and punched at his gut, but the force of the blasts wasn't dangerous.

The team reached their goal, the cloudiest water, which made it even harder to see. Using a low-power homing sonar that Costa wore on his belt, the men and *Challenger*'s minisub found one another. They entered the open bottom hatch. Most of them went in back with Mohr's equipment cases and their other bags.

Meltzer and Costa, still in their damp wet suits, took over from the two *Challenger* crewmen who'd been piloting the minisub. Felix stood behind their seats as they aimed for the pressing rendezvous. Meltzer immediately went to flank speed, making almost twenty knots but guzzling the high-test peroxide fuel left in the German mini's tanks. The mini nosed down as the seafloor fell away. They met *Challenger* where she should be, in 150 feet of water, at 1957—7:57 P.M., three minutes before she'd leave without them. The mini's passive sonars showed increasing naval activity on the surface. Suddenly the mini drifted to a stop. The fuel gauges read empty—they'd reached *Challenger,* but with no propulsion they couldn't make the docking inside her hangar.

"I only have minimal battery power," Meltzer stated. "Captain Fuller will either improvise along with me, or decide it's too late and too risky and leave.... Well, here goes nothing."

He used the digital acoustic link to *Challenger:* Felix watched over his shoulder as he typed a message that appeared, for checking, on a screen. Satisfied, Meltzer sent it. He was asking *Challenger* to maneuver to position her open hangar doors below him. He would have to come inside by Costa flooding variable ballast tanks to make the minisub heavy enough to drift down, while Meltzer depleted the last of his batteries in an attempt to control the docking by using the minisub's small side thrusters alone. Felix thought Meltzer deserved a medal for everything he'd done, and for what he was trying now.

Challenger acknowledged the message. Meltzer flipped on his look-down photonic sensors in short spurts, as the huge submarine turned with her own side thrusters, then held steady underneath the mini, with the open hangar beckoning. Costa worked his control panel. Meltzer's joystick was never still as the minisub descended. He'd switched off as many things as possible, including the environmental systems and internal lights, to conserve the last few amps of available battery power.

They entered the hangar without mishap, but the thrusters stopped responding. The battery charge was almost completely flat. The mini couldn't put itself onto the docking pylons. Felix's watch said 1803.

Captain Fuller's control-room photonic displays must have shown the minisub's plight. The hangar doors started closing around the mini, then *Challenger* began to move. She nosed steeply downward, tilting the mini with her, going deep. From its own inertia the mini, in the water inside the hangar, drifted backward more than Meltzer and Costa could control. The German mini's stern slammed into the rear bulkhead of the hangar with a crunch. Felix realized this was the mini's main screw getting smashed. He hoped the closed hangar doors suppressed the noise enough that it wouldn't be detected by Israeli hydrophones. Meltzer ordered Chief Costa to blow variable ballast, using compressed-air reserves, to make the minisub buoyant. Felix knew at once that this would give them their only chance to get out without flooding the mini or risking being crushed. The inertial navigation system, still operating but its readouts dimming by the second, showed that the mini—and by implication *Challenger*—was accelerating, to twenty-six knots.

No minisub or Axis diesel-AIP could go this fast. Only a nuclear fast-attack sub could. Captain Fuller was clearing the area, racing for outside the circle of possible location of any U-boat that might have picked up a commando team— actually the SEALs—that Israel would be trying to chase and destroy.

Analog gauges showed that the sea pressure in the flooded hangar had been relieved. The mini floated upward until it bumped the hydraulically closed and dogged hangar roof— another mechanical transient Felix prayed would go unnoticed—and lodged there, safe enough for now. Everything went dead except for emergency flashlights. Proper mating to *Challenger*'s air-lock trunk was impossible. The team would need to get back into their scubas, leave through the mini's bottom hatch, and swim down into the air lock. Before they could even start, the minisub tilted sideways as *Challenger* banked into a hard turn southwest.

CHAPTER 46

Late afternoon, local time that Sunday in Norfolk, Ilse was becoming despondent. Captain Johansen, Admiral Hodgkiss's senior aide, had told her she needed to come up with something to prove her innocence. Struggling all week at her console, mostly sleeping on the floor if she slept at all—studying stale data on the Snow Tiger and the odd flow noises, going through on-line references until her vision blurred—she got nowhere. She had a headache and a backache.

The door to the private workroom opened with no one knocking first. Ilse turned around. Johansen stood there, and she braced to attention, but he refused to meet her eyes. Next to him were the two FBI special agents who'd interrogated her many days before. They looked triumphant. Ilse caught a glimpse of a squad of armed marines in the corridor before Johansen swung the door shut.

One of the special agents pulled out a set of handcuffs. Ilse backed up against her console, shaking her head back and forth in fear and disbelief. They grabbed her, spun her around, and cuffed her wrists behind her back. "You are under arrest."

"Captain," Ilse pleaded, "what's going on? I didn't *do* anything."

"They all say that," the more dominant of the two special agents snapped. "Then they try to cut a deal, to cheat the hangman. Then they don't have much to offer. Then they hang."

"Captain."

Johansen finally made eye contact, but his eyes were icy cold. "It was in the open literature all along, and you'll be incommunicado anyway. . . . METOC figured out that the Snow Tiger is almost certainly German. You appear to have not done enough to allow the Allies to track the Snow Tiger, then you misled us into thinking that her flow noise was a natural phenomenon."

"But how could a submarine go so fast and *not make tonals?*"

"An obscure paper by Hong Kong scientists. METOC found it and saw the connection. Sheets of rubber and epoxy with tiny, tuned lead balls."

"What?"

"The indictment against you has been unsealed. A *double* titanium hull? You know how *expensive* that is? Russia doesn't have that kind of money. Russia uses single titanium hulls for better crush depth, and if they use an outer hull for high-explosive torpedo defense, it's always cheap steel. The only reason *anybody* would build submarines with double titanium hulls is if they expected to fight a tactical nuclear war. It takes *years* to build a nuclear submarine. Whoever paid for the Snow Tiger intended years ago to be fighting a tactical nuclear war. . . . It's obvious when you see it. *You* of all people, with where you've been in battle, should have seen it, but you pretended not to."

"You have to warn Captain Fuller!"

"That's no longer your concern. Your clearance is revoked. There's nothing more anyone here can do for you."

"But I didn't *do* anything!"
The FBI special agents dragged Ilse away.

———————

Jeffrey listened to a short debrief from Felix, Costa, Meltzer, Salih, and Mohr after the team's last-minute but safe return from their hair-raising excursion into Israel. Jeffrey chuckled at some parts, but was concerned by others. They'd left a very visible trail behind. This might help, if it warned Israel to be on the lookout for other—Kampfschwimmer—raiding parties. But Israel might realize quickly that one particular raid was American. They could protest to Washington, to extract further aid concessions and in the process make Jeffrey look bad at the Pentagon, or they could say nothing, to save face. In the worst outcome they might begin a hunt for alien code in their computer systems and find Mohr's patch. Even if it was actually benign, and helpful, they might not understand it and could try to remove it, undoing whatever good Felix and Mohr had achieved—assuming they'd beaten every Kampfschwimmer team, which remained to be seen.

Jeffrey ordered Meltzer to get some sleep while he could.

Felix, in private, told Jeffrey that Klaus Mohr seemed to behave well during the mission. But Felix himself admitted he had no way to know for sure what Mohr had done, either for or against Israeli defenses. The big questions hung in the air, more distracting and odious than ever. Should Jeffrey have trusted Klaus Mohr? Was there someone smarter than Mohr in Germany, someone even Mohr himself didn't know about, who'd tricked them all? Was Jeffrey's decision to violate Israeli sovereignty the biggest mistake of his life?

Jeffrey accepted that, for now, things were out of his hands. All he could do in the next few hours was worry obsessively, second-guess himself over and over, and stay ready to respond to whatever did happen. He recognized that he was already in so far, the Allies had little to lose and possibly much to gain by his going one step further: On Jeffrey's orders, Klaus Mohr applied his software patch to *Challenger*'s systems. There were no apparent ill effects, yet. But the worm was designed to hide itself until reaching its activation time. The most skilled conventional searchers might not find it until too late.

———

At midnight, nearing Egypt, Jeffrey went to battle stations. Once again Bell sat next to him as fire-control coordinator. The most experienced people available manned each station in the red-lit, hushed control room. Jeffrey ordered Meltzer, now somewhat refreshed and at the helm, to slow to ten knots.

The tactical plot presented a maze of Egyptian gas-drilling fields. There were dozens of offshore platforms in their path as *Challenger* climbed into shallower water. Some still operated, while others had been damaged in raids by German fighter-bombers, cruise missiles, patrol boats, or Kampfschwimmer. Some of the damaged ones were capped, while others burned unchecked, belching towering, hellish natural-gas flares above the surface.

Jeffrey told Milgrom to switch on the sonar speakers. Bubbling, roaring, clanking, creaking, and grinding sounds filled the air. This background noise, along with the ship's own active acoustic masking, helped conceal *Challenger*. Jeffrey decided to leave the air-circulation fans on: His crew was getting worn out at this late stage in the mission, and despite his best efforts of leadership, they might let down their guards at the thought of starting for home. He wanted the control-room environment to stay nicely crisp and fresh—to keep his people at their sharpest. Just as when he approached Israel, Egypt too might consider an unknown large submerged contact to be hostile.

"Captain, Nav," Sessions called out from the plotting

table, "we are through the twelve-mile limit into Egyptian
territorial waters."

"Very well, Nav."

Jeffrey had respect for the battle-hardened Egyptian Navy.
Coastal defense was their specialty, and Jeffrey was violating
their coastal waters as much as a submarine could: *Challenger* was approaching the designated anchorages at the
northern entrance to the Suez Canal. In water barely 100 feet
deep, even *Challenger*'s innards had enough iron and steel to
get noticed by magnetic-anomaly detection at short range.

Sessions recommended a course for the proper anchorage
area; Jeffrey gave new helm orders to Meltzer, telling him to
reduce speed to five knots. They began to negotiate around
another maze of obstacles—the undersides of floating merchant hulls.

"Our ride should be dead ahead," Bell reported. Passage
through the Suez Canal required five days' prior notice. A
place in the anchorage areas was then assigned by the Suez
Canal Authority, which supervised all canal operations, including toll collection—Egypt's largest source of hard currency came from these tolls; keeping the canal open for neutral
shipping was vital to her economy. This was why Israeli and
Egyptian ships had stopped using the canal soon after the start
of the war—if attacked by the Axis and sunk there, the wreckage would create a long and difficult salvage job.

Ships were assigned where to anchor based on their size,
their speed and maneuverability, their expected mechanical
reliability, and whether they carried dangerous cargo. *Challenger* had picked up last-minute specifics by ELF radio late
the week before. The incoming message had been in a code
that Jeffrey could only read with a one-time-use decryption
key contained in his sealed egress orders.

"Confirmed, sir," Milgrom said. "Master Six-one is operating hull-mounted obstacle-and-mine avoidance sonar intermittently, according to pattern in prearranged instructions." This recognition signal was also in Jeffrey's egress orders, along with the registered name of Master 61.

"Very well, Sonar. Helm, put us beside the *Bunga Azul.*"

The M/V—motor vessel—*Bunga Azul* was a large and modern bulk dry-cargo ship, over six hundred feet long, able to make a sustained speed of twenty-four knots, and with a crew of only eighteen men thanks to automation and computer assists. She'd been constructed by an American firm in a big yard on the Gulf Coast, under security precautions disguised as overdone antiterrorist measures. She was called a motor vessel and not a steamship because she was powered by huge diesel engines, which drove electric generators feeding motors attached to her twin screw shafts—a more efficient arrangement than steam for some merchant ships. She was flagged in neutral Panama, and operated by a neutral Indonesian shipping company. But Jeffrey had been told that, through intermediate dummy corporations, the ship was really controlled by the CIA. Her crew was hand-picked and well paid.

Officially, the *Bunga Azul* was heading to Indonesia with a cargo from Ukraine. In actuality, she had much more in common with the *Glomar Explorer,* the ship built in the 1960s in secret by Howard Hughes, so the CIA could salvage a sunken—and nuclear armed—Soviet *Golf*–class diesel sub that had been lost in the Pacific under suspicious circumstances. The *Glomar Explorer* was designed to float with her bottom open, to lift the Golf off the seafloor and into her hold, all unseen.

From above, the *Bunga Azul* was filled with wheat, but the holds all had false bottoms. Under that was a space large enough to accommodate a submarine the size of USS *Challenger.*

Jeffrey's problem was getting inside. She was anchored

fore and aft to avoid drifting in the breeze or on the current, and her anchor chains created obstacles—plus, there was almost no room under her keel for *Challenger* to fit.

And he did not have a lot of time to enter her. Most of the canal was only one way. Ships here did not have free will. The authority sent them through in groups they called convoys. The standard 0100 convoy, south through the canal, would start forming up into single file very soon. If Jeffrey missed it, this hollowed-out merchie had to wait for the 0700 southbound convoy. The next one after that wasn't until tomorrow, Tuesday—when the Afrika Korps offensive was due to begin, according to Mohr, and the Suez Canal was the last place on earth Jeffrey ever wanted to be trapped.

Meltzer's piloting display showed the underwater part of the *Bunga Azul,* outlined vaguely by *Challenger*'s starboard wide-aperture array using ambient ocean noises bouncing off the hull, highlighted by acoustic hot spots wherever machinery ran within. The constant scraping of her anchor chains' big links against each other gave further sonar clues on how to steer, but all of this wasn't enough.

"Chief of the Watch," Jeffrey ordered, "activate all hull-mounted photonics sensors. Passive image-intensification mode." Stealth now was absolutely paramount; the Egyptian navy would be on guard for enemy subs finding temporary refuge under the convoy before it sailed.

COB acknowledged. Display monitors came on, but their pictures only showed darkness. Scant illumination pierced the dirty water from the quarter moon up in a cloudless sky.

"Use amplification factor one hundred thousand." Now the water by *Challenger* became barely visible. "Helm, put us directly under Master Six-one. Use auxiliary maneuvering units as needed." These were small and quiet propulsors near bow and stern that gave *Challenger* sideways thrust, making her much more nimble in close confines.

Jeffrey studied the display monitors. The *Bunga Azul*'s

bottom seemed to be sitting on *Challenger*'s sail; the space between his own keel and the seafloor was too small for a man to stand upright.

"Helm, engage autopilot in hovering mode."

Meltzer acknowledged. Now, *Challenger*'s computer watched for any drift in the inertial navigation fix. Commands were sent to the auxiliary maneuvering units, as well as to the pump-jet main propulsor, to hold the boat perfectly steady in every dimension except for depth. Depth was maintained by the computer working the variable ballast pumps—which Jeffrey dearly hoped would be mistaken for noises from the *Bunga Azul*.

"Sonar, use look-up obstacle-avoidance array to signal we are ready for bottom doors to open."

Milgrom acknowledged. Jeffrey watched the monitors.

Suddenly a deafening noise came over the sonar speakers.

"Master Six-one is blowing ship's whistle." The foghorn, supposedly stuck, was meant to disguise the mechanical transients about to occur. Radio calls would be made to apologize, explain that it wasn't a sign of distress, and avoid attracting helos and patrol boats. At least, that was the plan.

Jeffrey knew pumps inside the *Bunga Azul* would be moving seawater out of ballast tanks that lined her sides like a floating dry dock, using that water to partly flood the central part of the ship without changing her trim. Next, Jeffrey watched as the bottom doors swung down and open. Their edges cleared both sides of *Challenger*'s sail by inches.

It was time to surface into the *Bunga Azul*'s gigantic secret compartment. Jeffrey double-checked the relative positions of his sub and the merchant ship. COB and Meltzer stood ready to take over in an instant if the autopilot malfunctioned. *Challenger*'s bow dome and her stern parts—rudder, stern planes, pump jet—were delicate, and she could easily be crippled in an upward collision with the *Bunga Azul*. If things went really sour, and the surface ship's rudder or screws were hit by *Challenger* and damaged, Jeffrey's entire egress ahead of the Afrika Korps offensive would be kaput. *Challenger,* her crew, Mohr, and Mohr's computer modules all could go the way of *Ohio.*

Jeffrey swallowed hard. "Chief of the Watch, blow all main ballast tank groups."

There was a hissing sound, accompanying the foghorn that blew loudly on the sonar speakers. *Challenger* rose, inside the *Bunga Azul.* When surfaced, Jeffrey watched the bottom doors close underneath. Rubber blocks came out from both sides of the covert submarine hold, to keep *Challenger* steady inside her host. The foghorn stopped.

CHAPTER 47

COB raised a photonics mast just a few feet, being careful not to hit the top of the hidden compartment *Challenger* sat in. He set the sensor head in omniscope mode; this gave a 360-degree view, all at once, of their confined surroundings. A pair of men appeared on the catwalk beneath the overhead of the compartment. Both of them carried equipment bags. They waved at the photonics mast. Jeffrey and COB walked to a hatch with some enlisted people and a junior officer. By the time they opened the hatch, the men from their host ship had used a winch to lower an aluminum brow onto *Challenger*'s hull.

The ship's master—the formal title for the captain of a merchant ship—and a radioman introduced themselves in heavily accented English; the master's name was Pribadi Siregar. They were citizens of Indonesia who, in addition to their native tongue, Bahasa, said they also spoke good Arabic. Siregar was of average height and build, slightly stoop shouldered, and neither handsome nor ugly. He was someone easily lost in a crowd, which was probably one reason the CIA had picked him.

A fiber-optic connection was made from the *Bunga Azul* down into *Challenger*. Jeffrey ordered COB to wake up Felix and his men and Mohr, and have them inject Mohr's patch into their host's electronics. Jeffrey still didn't know for sure that the patch was harmless, or even if it really worked, but at this point, using it was necessary, a precaution against what might happen any hour now in the environment around the canal.

The radioman, who wore a blue cotton work shirt and jeans, handed Jeffrey a bag of similar clothing, including a red-and-white-checkered kaffiyeh headdress he could use to disguise his face. Jeffrey had studied Arabic in college, enough to get by in casual conversation.

COB went below. Jeffrey followed the master and radioman up through a tangle of secret passageways inside the *Bunga Azul*.

"The canal pilot is aboard," the master whispered. "They are finished with fitting searchlight. I suggest you go directly to special radio room."

The *Bunga Azul* actually had two radio rooms. One was a standard modern merchant-ship arrangement, while the other, with restricted access through what looked like disused maintenance hatches, held high-tech U.S. Navy equipment supplied by the CIA. Among the ship's various radio and radar antennas—some of them inside protective radomes on her mast and superstructure—were antennas that could receive broadcasts and data downloads from the navy's dedicated constellation of submarine communications satellites. These antennas were now linked to *Challenger* through the fiber-optic line. Decryptions of what was received could be passed from *Challenger*'s own radio room up into this special compartment. The compartment had its own receivers and decryption gear, for redundancy—in case something on *Challenger* failed or the connections into the hold broke down or snapped. Display screens here would let Jeffrey observe the theater-wide military situation around him, courtesy of uploads to the satellites from Norfolk or the Pentagon.

The *Bunga Azul*'s antennas also fed raw intercepts to *Challenger*'s electronic support-measures room. Computer interpretations came back for Jeffrey to see and listen to— various radars and radio stations in range of the *Bunga Azul,* with icons that identified the transmitter types and whether they were military, civilian government, or private commercial. The compartment also contained equipment to maintain these feeds if something went wrong on *Challenger.* In this soundproof space, Jeffrey had an intercom to talk to Bell and others in his control room, and one to hear from Master Pribadi on the *Bunga Azul*'s bridge. Instrument readings from the bridge were fed to other displays in the room. These included inertial navigation fixes against a chart of the canal, the *Bunga Azul*'s course and speed, plus copies of readouts from her navigation radar, and forward-looking obstacle-avoidance sonar.

Having a canal pilot on the bridge forced Jeffrey to avoid that area of the ship as much as possible. The pilot was Egyptian, an employee of the Suez Canal Authority, whose presence was required by the authority; he was not in the know about the *Bunga Azul*'s true nature. But in an emergency, from this compartment, Jeffrey could be on the bridge in moments.

This space is like my combat information center, normally buried deep in the bowels of a warship—the position from which a captain fights a naval battle. The only problem is that for all the hours she's cooped up in the hold, Challenger *can't fire a single weapon. No torpedoes, no land-attack or antiship or antiaircraft missiles, no countermeasures, nothing. . . . And the* Bunga Azul *is defenseless but for a handful of machine guns meant to fight off modern pirates striking near Java or Malaysia.*

Jeffrey felt sudden movement and vibrations through the deck, confirmed by the ship's speed and other data he did have. The master had said that because the *Bunga Azul* was fast, maneuverable, and in good condition, she was third in line—one of the very first ships in the convoy of almost fifty. The convoy formed up promptly and headed into the canal.

More displays came alive. Jeffrey began to integrate the images and numbers into a three-dimensional picture within his mind. Ahead and underwater, he could see the sides and bottom of the channel on the *Bunga Azul*'s simple sonar. He knew unarmed Egyptian minesweepers went through the canal far out in front of every convoy, just in case, but was glad he had a mine-avoidance display. *Challenger*'s arrays were of no use enclosed in the secret submarine hold.

Over the years, the bottom had been deepened to more than seventy feet. The canal was six hundred feet wide here, but safety required that the ships stick to the middle and keep a rigid separation distance between each and the next; this was the job of the pilots. The wartime speed limit for canal convoys was twelve knots.

We'll meet Monday's 0500 northbound convoy in the Bitter Lakes, after the halfway point of the canal at Ismailia. We anchor while they keep going, to avoid any chance of a head-on collision.

"Like coffee, Mr. Captain, sir?" The radioman offered Jeffrey a thermos bottle.

"Thanks." Jeffrey needed it. He wouldn't let himself sleep until they went out the other side of the canal, crossed through the 160-mile-long, narrow and shallow Gulf of Suez, then dived from inside the *Bunga Azul* when they reached the Red Sea itself.

Despite the cup of coffee, Jeffrey yawned.

"Why not to go on deck small while? Stretch legs and get fresh air. Once sun up, very hot and you be obvious. . . . Go near stern so pilot not be seeing you."

Jeffrey thought it over, then nodded.

———

Jeffrey stood on deck near the stern. The deck vibrated beneath his feet more strongly here. The air was humid but cool—the desert on either side of the canal got cold at night. He could see glare from the searchlight, fitted to the bow of the supertanker immediately astern, shining toward him and illuminating the landscape to port and starboard. The *Bunga Azul* had a similar searchlight aimed ahead from her bow. The equipment was provided by the canal authority, and served as just what they seemed to be: giant headlights. Each ship in the convoy had one, by law.

Jeffrey kept to the shadows beside the base of a loading crane. Gazing up, once his eyes adjusted to the dark, he could see countless stars. Except for directly overhead, where the *Bunga Azul*'s exhaust fumes and heat distorted the view of the heavens, the desert stars were breathtakingly brilliant and perfectly sharp.

Jeffrey looked around, trying to relax his mind as well as his body. He felt on pins and needles, knowing what he knew about the strategic situation. Yet for a while he was forced into a totally passive role, and he hated it. The *Bunga Azul* and the other ships continued moving south.

Immediately to port he saw big, reddish-brown weathered berms of earth and sand, at least thirty feet tall, with intermittent gaps between and sometimes roads paved up them. On that bank, Jeffrey also saw occasional shacks and patches of scrub brush. This was the west edge of the Sinai Peninsula.

Along the opposite bank, the African side, the narrow strip of land lit by the supertanker's headlight was mostly flat. Sand dunes and more scrub stretched beyond an asphalt road. Along the edges of the canal, where water lapped and splashed from the wakes of the passing ships, Jeffrey could make out the tips of concrete walls that lined the canal to keep the sand and loose soil from caving in.

Jeffrey returned to the secret radio room while it was still night outside. He did feel somewhat refreshed, and had another cup of hot coffee to stay energized. He glanced at a clock: 0430 local time.

As expected from reading his egress orders, a theater-wide operational plot began to be broadcast from the U.S. via satellite—not just for Jeffrey but for all Allied forces in Egypt and Israel and the Central African pocket. The egress orders had said that a spy satellite would be diverted to watch the sailing of the 0100 Monday southbound convoy. Since the *Bunga Azul*'s master had been instructed not to take the canal unless *Challenger* was securely inside, her movement was the signal that Jeffrey was leaving the Med.

He realized that, because of his continued radio silence, his superiors probably had no idea what had happened with his mission. Although the *Bunga Azul* possessed the equipment to send a message burst to Norfolk, doing so now, with Axis electronic warfare surveillance at its peak, might too readily give the host ship and its passenger sub away. That would make them a valid military target to the Axis, and could draw immediate lethal fire while trapped inside the canal.

No, there's nothing useful I have to say to anyone, or to ask them.

The data download did tell Jeffrey several things. German forces of all types were massing in Libya, at what seemed like logical jumping-off points for an assault to the east in North Africa—targeting Alexandria and Cairo, then the Sinai, and then Israel. Other German forces were on high alert in Greece and Italy.

Jeffrey scanned wider parts of the big-picture plot.

Turkey's defenses were strengthening along her western border with German-occupied Bulgaria and Greece, to dissuade the Axis from getting too ambitious there at Turkey's expense.

Egypt and Israel were also on maximum alert. Israeli armor, with Egyptian permission, was moving through the Sinai Peninsula on high-speed tank-transporter tractor-trailers, to add to the tanks already arrayed well west of the Nile to meet any German offensive out of Libya. Jeffrey was still worried that Israel might have tunnel vision: Attacks on them in the past, from the west, always came through the Sinai. And some of their greatest land-battle victories were won in the Sinai, or by penetrating into the main part of Egypt. Those ekranoplans, with their tremendous mobility, might indeed go for the pivotal flank attack at Tel Aviv that Jeffrey feared.

Israel is well aware that the German-owned ekranoplans exist. No warning I could give would tell them something they don't know.

According to the data, so far there were very few air skirmishes, or artillery or cruise-missile duels.

"Sir Captain," the radioman said, "text message coming. Is for you."

"Who's the sender?"

"Not yet...Bad enemy jamming. Garbled. Message repeating." It took several more tries before the message burst with *Challenger*'s classified address came through properly.

The message was decrypted quickly. Jeffrey asked the radioman to look away.

"I smoke now. Yes?" The young Indonesian left.

Jeffrey read. The message was from Admiral Hodgkiss. It told Jeffrey that a new Russian fast-attack sub, the first of the 868U class, code name Snow Tiger, was almost certainly German owned. The message said her propulsion plant was lined with layers of a composite that suppressed her tonals at flank speed.

Jesus.

The Snow Tiger had a double titanium hull, a single cowled pump-jet propulsor, twin liquid-metal-cooled reactors with silent pumps, and a super-slippery hull coating. An acoustic anomaly detected off Somalia confirmed that the Snow Tiger was able to move at sixty-plus knots with only minimal flow noise as her signature—and was heading toward the Arabian Sea.

Hodgkiss warned Jeffrey that the Snow Tiger might have been ordered to lurk near the strategic Bab el Mandeb choke point, to destroy American submarines heading inward to support the defense of Israel and Egypt.

Jeffrey nodded to himself. During the opening phase of Operation Iraqi Freedom in 2003, the U.S. had had twelve fast-attack subs positioned in the Red Sea at once, launching Tomahawks, with overflight permission, at Iraq.

And since the maximum range of the newest Tactical Tomahawks was about 1,500 miles, to reach the threatened Egyptian frontier from the Indian Ocean, any U.S. subs would have to enter the Red Sea again. Then there were the carrier strike groups—with more Tomahawks on their cruisers, destroyers, and frigates—whose air wings, with multiple midair refuelings, might barely reach the active battle front from outside the Red Sea without violating now-neutral Saudi Arabian or Yemeni airspace.

It was a curse on the Allies, which the Axis was making full use of, that the Boers had nuked Diego Garcia early in the year. It was a double curse that now the Allies didn't have one usable land air base in that direction closer than Australia.

The next part of the message, his new ROEs, made Jeffrey almost physically sick. If he encountered the Snow Tiger, he was forbidden to shoot first since its true nationality remained unproven; to sink a genuine Russian-owned sub could start a full-scale World War III. An ELF code was specified as the signal to him that other forces had been shot at, confirming that the Snow Tiger was enemy. Only if he received this code was he allowed to shoot first—unless the Snow Tiger had already opened fire on him.

The last part of the message was the worst: The Germans might be aware that the Allies had ships like the *Bunga Azul*, since, as the Allies knew from experience, the Axis owned such covert sub transporters too. The Snow Tiger, Hodgkiss said, might have orders from Berlin to watch for SSNs heading *out of* the Red Sea.

In the worst case, given everything that's coming, I've got the dirty-bomb problem all over again—spreading radiation from Challenger's *reactor core around the Suez Canal, or right near Saudi Arabia and Yemen, and Africa.*

Jeffrey blanked his message screen when someone

knocked on the innermost door: the radioman, back from his smoke break. "Come in."

Jeffrey devoted part of his mind to the implications of Hodgkiss's new information, and the other part to watching the theater-operational status display. A clock said it would be getting light outside, with full sunrise soon.

"Mr. Captain?"

Jeffrey turned. The radioman, confused, annoyed, then sheepish, pointed at the electronic support-measures console. *Many of the radars and radios plotted on it before had suddenly gone off the air—including the whole canal-authority voice and data net.* Jeffrey grabbed the intercom for *Challenger.* "Get Klaus Mohr on this line."

"He's still sleeping, sir," Bell said.

"Get him on this line."

The radioman, badly puzzled now, was trying to tune to civilian Egyptian stations. The convoy was nearing Ismailia, halfway through the canal. The city had a population of over one million. The news or a morning talk show should be in range. Nothing. A quick self-check showed that his black boxes were working correctly.

The radioman had a computerized list of station frequencies. His digital tuner tried them. He turned on a speaker, making a helpless gesture. Station after station showed zero signal strength on his digital meters; Jeffrey heard nothing but silence or static. Then the radioman's equipment, reset to autosearch, found a radio station that still worked. Jeffrey knew enough Arabic to understand what the anchorman was saying. Parts of Ismailia, in no clear pattern, had lost electrical power. Internet servers in scattered parts of the country had also crashed. The newsman said his producers were getting fragmentary reports of power outages and cell phone failures.

"Captain Fuller? This is Klaus Mohr."

Jeffrey described what was happening. "What have you *done?*"

"It makes sense.... Quantum decoherence would cause the

effects to be somewhat random at this distance from Zichron Yaakov. Some areas would get the patch, but not the worm, intact, while others would get the worm but not the patch."

"In plain English!"

"Pandora has started, Captain. Berlin moved up the attack. And there's no way to know from what we're seeing locally who got into Israel's main systems first, us or the Kampfschwimmer."

Jeffrey slammed down the phone in frustration and horror.

Challenger was right in the Afrika Korps offensive's path, stuck inside the *Bunga Azul,* inside the canal—and Israeli and German tactical nukes could start to detonate soon.

The download from the satellite continued, for now. New display icons appeared as German aircraft and cruise missiles took to the air. Other icons were added or modified as Egyptian and Israeli jets in groups changed course and speed, or left runways and fought for altitude. Allied cruise missiles launched in retaliation for the German ones. The aerial-situation plot quickly became a muddled mess of red and green symbols charging at each other at supersonic speed. They looked bound for a head-on clash, somewhere between the Nile and the Suez Canal.

What if the worm and Mohr's patch each grabbed hold in different places, not just in small cities in southern Egypt but throughout the entire theater? Or what if there was no patch, and Mohr was a liar or had been deceived? What if it was all a worm, one that didn't work everywhere because of strange quantum effects even Mohr couldn't fathom?

What if Germany thinks Israeli command and control is crippled, but Israel thinks enough of it isn't, and both are sure but neither is right—because everything's like Swiss cheese? What happens next? Do they grapple and inadvertently pull each other into the abyss?

Jeffrey scrolled to the situation plot for the Indian Ocean. The nearest supercarrier was more than 3,000 miles away, still placed to help protect the oil-tanker route from the Persian Gulf to the Pacific.

That was six or ten times the combat radius of the carrier's planes. The midair refueling assets needed to make a difference in blunting the Afrika Korps from so far away simply didn't exist. U.S. Air Force heavy bombers, operating at extreme range, couldn't be a factor before tomorrow at the earliest.

The Germans had decisively beaten any Allied spoiling attack. Egypt and Israel were on their own when it mattered most, the vital first twenty-four hours of a multidimensional blitzkreig—and governments in Berlin, Cairo, and Jerusalem all knew it. Jeffrey snatched the phone handset to the *Bunga Azul*'s bridge. He asked in his best Arabic for Siregar.

"Is the pilot able to hear you?" Jeffrey said in English.

"Na'am," the master answered in Arabic. Yes.

"Then listen carefully. The German offensive has started early. We have to get past the suspension bridge at Ismailia before one side or the other blows it and the canal becomes blocked in our face."

"Na'amal E?" What should we do?

"Make radio contact with the ships ahead. If radio doesn't work, fire a flare to get their attention and use a loud hailer. Tell them you accidentally picked up some broadcasts, and get them to go to their maximum speed or get out of our way. Start a rumor, sound panicky. Scream that the new war has started, Egypt is being invaded, atom bombs could detonate any minute."

"Haqiqa?" Is this true?

"Yes, it's true. . . . And tell the pilot that big canal ships will be main targets. Let him have your launch and tell him to head for the bank and run for his life."

"Na'am. Na'am." Picked up by Siregar's open mike, coming from nearby, on land, Jeffrey could hear the mournful howl of air-raid sirens now.

"Call me back, and make all ahead full, the moment the pilot is gone."

CHAPTER 48

I smailia was left behind and the *Bunga Azul* was pounding nearer and nearer the Bitter Lakes. Jeffrey had taken command of the sub-transporter ship on its bridge—Siregar had readily agreed; he knew Jeffrey was a combat-seasoned naval officer. Fiber-optic lines connected to laptops let Jeffrey watch the same displays he'd seen in the hidden radio room. But now he could read the *Bunga Azul*'s radar and sonar directly, and see the world outside through the big tinted windows that wrapped around the bridge atop her island superstructure sixty feet above the water.

Chaos reigned everywhere. The canal authority's radio net was still dead. The ship-to-ship radios, apparently unaffected by the worm, were swamped with demands and questions and pleading. After forcing one ship ahead of him to the side so he could pass, Jeffrey was now charging south a few hundred yards behind another cargo ship with which his speed was very evenly matched. That ship's wake, at twenty-four knots, churned the canal surface into a foaming white, contrasting with the sparkling deep blue of undisturbed water farther ahead.

The cloudless sky was a lighter, harsher shade of blue. It was streaked with high white contrails, and black or white smoke, where fighter jets with air-to-air missiles tangled. The white smoke meant a missile trail. The black smoke meant a jet had been hit. Sometimes Jeffrey could see parachutes bloom, from pilots who'd ejected. Sometimes he saw bright red flashes, then streaming orange flame, as no one got out and the aircraft plunged to the ground. In the distance, on either bank of the canal, there were spots of flame and smoke rising from where other planes had already crashed.

Jeffrey couldn't tell by eye or by the tactical plot who was winning. The aircraft, both Allied and Axis, had twisted and turned and dived and soared to the point that even through borrowed binoculars he didn't know which planes were which. He did have the impression on the tactical plot that Israeli jets were arriving piecemeal, in an uncoordinated fashion, and that Egyptian aircraft were barely arriving at all. Another bad sign was that the center of the swarming dots and confetti of fresh contrails and smoke trails was moving relentlessly east.

A laptop showed that the ekranoplans were on the move too. German fast-missile boats had darted south from Greece to do battle with the Egyptian and Israeli navies. Jeffrey knew they were clearing a path for the ekranoplans, which had already reached the Libyan coast and turned east just as Jeffrey expected. The naval battle was also confused. The defenders were having trouble massing their forces; it seemed that each vessel looked out for itself, with no central coordination or any strategy.

Jeffrey had watched Israeli tank transporters heading across Ismailia's soaring Mubarak Peace Bridge as he'd passed under it before. The tank transporters' tractors belched black smoke from their straining diesels as they worked toward the top, dragging the tanks on flatbeds, then sped like runaway trains on the roadway's downward slope leading west to the land-battle front. There was no other traffic—the bridge must have been closed to fleeing civilians. It tore enough at Jeffrey's heart to see crowds of men, women, and children standing all along the west bank of the canal, gesturing for help to cross the water. Some jumped in and tried to swim, with pieces of wood or cushions as improvised rafts—or not even that. A few of these figures quickly tired and went under and didn't come up. Others were run down by the speeding merchant ships fleeing south, including the *Bunga Azul*. Jeffrey tried not to look.

The master kept blowing the ship's horn as a warning to those onshore, but so many ships were blowing horns that it did no one much good. Finally Jeffrey had to ask him to stop, so he could think straight.

The theater operational-picture download from the geosynchronous satellite kept going blank, and then coming back.

Either the Germans have increased their jamming power, or the platforms doing the jamming are getting closer. Or both.

Jeffrey stepped back involuntarily when a pair of fighter jets at almost zero altitude raced by right in front of his ship—moving faster than the speed of sound, there'd been no noise in advance to betray their approach. Violet-white searing flame came from their afterburners. Sonic booms from the shock waves of their flight rattled the armored glass of the bridge windows. Their engines were deafening. Even so, Jeffrey could briefly hear the rapid-fire *crack crack crack* of an automatic cannon. He saw red flashes and small puffs of smoke from near the nose of the trailing jet. The one in front jinked desperately to avoid the bursts of tracer that were trying to hit it and chew it apart. In an instant both aircraft were out of sight, leaving a minor sandstorm kicked up by the wash of their supersonic passage. The *Bunga Azul* rushed through the cloud of sand and left it behind.

An image that took him a moment to grasp was frozen in Jeffrey's mind. The leading plane, the one in distress, wore a blue Jewish star in a white circle on each wing. The one behind it, the one in its six—the one doing all the shooting—bore a black Iron Cross on its fuselage.

The Israeli Air Force and the modern Luftwaffe are fighting to the death.

The canal banks opened out before Jeffrey, at the start of the kidney-bean-shaped Great Bitter Lake. The lake was twenty miles long and up to ten miles at its widest. It was narrowest at its far end, in what used to be the separate Little Bitter Lake—until dredging and canal-widening projects joined them into one.

The theater operational plot vanished from Jeffrey's screen altogether. He brought up different data to check that the fiber-optic cable connection was still good and that the laptop was working.

He called on the intercom down into *Challenger.*

"XO, Captain. What happened to the satellite feed?"

"Radio room doesn't know, sir. The antenna's good. We can't tell if it's jamming or if the satellite got knocked out."

Jeffrey hung up. Then he remembered the northbound convoy.

Standard canal operating procedure was for the 0100 southbound convoy to anchor to one side in the Great Bitter Lake and let the single daily northbound convoy pass, with those ships doing ten or twelve knots.

The northbound ships will be desperate to reverse their course, but they can't possibly until they get to a deep and wide enough part of the lake. . . . Some of them will be massive, laden oil tankers with huge turning circles.

No sooner had Jeffrey framed this thought than he spotted the first oncoming ships in the distance trying to make their U-turns. Two collided, one skewering the other at high speed. Fires broke out and the embracing wrecks began to drift, out of control.

Jeffrey and Siregar watched their radar and sonar displays.

"Can we get through the wrecks and traffic jam up ahead?"

"If groundings and collisions do not block the whole canal. How long can you wait?"

If the Germans suspected that a southbound cargo ship had an Allied SSN with Mohr inside, once they won air superiority they might start bombing anything big enough to be a candidate as *Challenger*'s host. What Jeffrey had told Siregar to tell the canal pilot before, that ships would be prime targets, was part of a lie to get rid of him. But now Jeffrey thought it might not have been a lie. At least in the Gulf of Suez he'd have room to zigzag and try to avoid dumb iron bombs.

"We can't wait. We must get through immediately."

"It will be risky."

"Take the risks."

The master had the conn. He began to order the helmsman to put on right or left rudder to avoid other ships, and also ordered the *Bunga Azul* to slow down or speed up. Jeffrey thought Siregar had a good eye in judging the other vessels' distances and speeds and even their masters' intentions—the ship-to-ship radio was useless now, there was so much shouting in different languages on every channel.

The southbound ship ahead of Jeffrey made a fatal mistake, and turned just as an approaching big cargo ship moved into its path. Their bows smacked at an angle, at a combined speed of almost fifty knots.

The forward ends of both ships crumpled hideously with a sound like rolling thunder. They recoiled off each other, dead in the water, and both began to settle by the bow. They were sinking, as salty lake water poured in through gashes and fractures in their hull plates; merchant ships lacked a surface warship's numerous watertight compartments; their crews were too small for extensive rapid damage control.

Jeffrey saw, like ants, men rush to the lifeboats.

"Don't do what they did," Jeffrey said to Siregar, pointing to the sinking ships.

Siregar stood there, watching everything, pursing his lips, his eyes very grim.

He barked orders to the helmsman. Jeffrey had to steady himself as the *Bunga Azul* heeled one way as she made a sharp turn the other way.

Siregar blew the ship's whistle in a series of short, sharp blasts. He seemed to be playing chicken with another oncoming vessel. Jeffrey dashed to the *Bunga Azul*'s starboard open-bridge wing. The northbound ship charged up their side on an opposite course with less than ten feet between its hull and theirs. As their two bridges passed, the other ship's master shook his fist at Jeffrey angrily for ignoring the international rules of the road.

Siregar took the wheel himself. The Bitter Lakes were narrowing. They ended and the canal resumed—again only 600 feet wide. But there were more ships in the canal bed, coming north.

Siregar blew his whistle in an endless series of blasts. Bearing down on the other ships at high speed, giving them no choice but to hug the east side of the channel, he forced each small and slow vessel at the tail end of the northbound convoy out of his way.

They were clear. The *Bunga Azul* had the whole canal to herself. At twenty-four knots they should be past Port Suez in less than an hour, out of the canal—but with seven more hours ahead as a sitting target going through the Gulf of Suez until they reached the Strait of Jubal and finally found deep water.

Jeffrey's laptop showed nothing from the satellite downlink.

He went out onto the open-bridge wing, on the shadier port side. He stared back behind the ship, at the water and then at the sky.

Plumes of greasy black smoke were erupting from the Bitter Lakes. Other plumes, some new and strong and others weak and thinning, rose high from the ground where dozens of planes had been shot down. The sky was still crisscrossed with contrails and missile trails, but the air battle was moving eastward.

Over the Sinai Peninsula. Closer and closer to Israel.

What if Mohr's theater-wide Swiss-cheese effect on Egyptian and Israeli command and control was no accident? What if it had nothing to do with quantum-physics uncertainties at all, but was Mohr's way of faking an out for himself?

What if Gerald Parker was right, and Klaus Mohr was a double agent, and Felix and his team had injected the very worm Mohr claimed to be trying to halt?

What if I made the biggest blunder in modern military history, and handed Imperial Germany control of the Middle East?

Jeffrey stood alone on the bridge wing as the *Bunga Azul* ran south. He felt a strong breeze on his back from her speed. He watched the churning and splashing of her screws, and looked at her wake, receding behind them, and his mind began to wander into a state of despair.

He also watched the horizon carefully, to north and east and west. He waited for the thing he dreaded most: a searing flash, a mushroom cloud, as the Israelis, out of desperation, used their nuclear option to halt the Afrika Korps advance— or the Germans used the nuclear option first, to preempt.

The fate of the world is teetering on the edge of a razor blade, and I don't know what's happening beyond what little I can see from here . . . and it's all my fault for disobeying, no, inventing orders.

Jeffrey remembered what Klaus Mohr had said in that message he'd sent from the brothel: "Eternal darkness if we fail."

It was true, that sentence, regardless of Mohr's real motives. Nuclear winter and human extinction—or an unbreakable Axis grip on half the world, with covetous, emboldened glances cast at the other half.

Which is it, Herr Doctor Mohr? What did you do? Was that message really you begging for help, or you luring me into a trap of unimaginable deviousness?

Jeffrey lost track of how long he stood there on the bridge wing, staring back toward Egypt and Israel, as the ship passed Port Suez and Port Taufiq and the empty northbound anchorages, and then buoy after buoy as she went south. Now, from time to time he saw natural-gas platforms. The sand dunes of African Egypt rolled by, on and on to Jeffrey's left as he looked astern. The rugged, more irregular Sinai-peninsula coast on his right was sometimes near and sometimes far.

"Sir!" Siregar called him.

Jeffrey had been gripping the bridge wing rail so tightly for so many hours that his fingers were cramped like claws. He needed to pull his upper body away to get his hands free.

The master offered an intercom handset to Jeffrey. He tried to take it, but dropped it. The cramping in his fingers was horribly painful and they wouldn't respond to his will.

Siregar held the handset to his head for him.

"Captain," Jeffrey said.

"XO," Bell said. "Sir, the ESM room reports that jamming strength is declining. They aren't sure if it's because we're farther away from the battle now, or what."

"And . . . ?"

"They think they'll have the satellite feed in a minute."

"Understood. I'll watch the laptop screen up here." Jeffrey had it sitting on a shelf under one of the bridge windows, beside a pile of thick mariners' reference manuals. He glanced at the *Bunga Azul*'s bridge crew. They all stood very tensely, looking terribly tired and worried. Their fear of intentional Axis air attack, or an errant cruise missile from out of nowhere, was valid, contagious, and thick.

The laptop screen came alive. Red and green icons peppered the map of the eastern Med and the countries around it.

Things did look grim. German tank divisions were racing across Egypt's western desert, toward El Alamein. Israeli and Egyptian tanks were in the wrong place, useless, too far south to stop them, on the other side of the impassable Qattara Depression—150 miles long from east to west.

Aircraft were fighting now over the eastern Sinai; the Israeli Air Force seemed unable to keep the Luftwaffe squadrons from shoving ever forward. The ekranoplans were moving past the Nile Delta now, continuing east. With their speed of three hundred knots, they could be unloading around Tel Aviv in under an hour. It looked like the Germans were going to achieve the unthinkable—air superiority inside Israel's borders, and naval superiority along her coast. With Israel's armored brigades so far away and so slow, the country was in imminent danger of being overrun.

There were no icons denoting tactical nuclear explosions—yet. A counter in a window in one corner of the display showed zero atomic detonations in Germany so far.

How much longer will Israel's top commanders wait? When will the counter in that window start to climb above zero, toward ten, if Israel begins to set off the A-bombs she planted in Germany?

For all the situational awareness the digital displays gave him, Jeffrey loathed his current status as a spectator. He understood much better what senior people like Admiral Hodgkiss, or the president, must be going through, onlookers in war rooms with largely passive roles as distant battle was joined—a battle over which they no longer had any input or influence. Jeffrey too had already done his thing, made his decision and now would live or die by it, his ordering of the SEALs to take Mohr into Israel secretly.

Something strange began to happen on the screen. The Israeli aircraft formations, like scattered pieces of a ruined jigsaw puzzle, started to assemble themselves into a perceivable, rational pattern.

Icons for air-search radars suddenly came alive all over the Sinai and in Israel's Negev Desert. Other icons, for surface-launched supersonic antiaircraft missiles, popped onto the screen as if from out of nowhere.

Another icon joined the crowd, an unmanned aerial reconnaissance and communications-relay drone, out over the Mediterranean.

A dot appeared in the middle of the drone icon. Jeffrey knew this meant it completed a network-centric data linkup between a target and one or more shooter platforms.

Jeffrey observed all this, confused. Was this data phony, inserted into the Allied net by the Germans? Had Jeffrey become delusional from sleep deprivation and guilt, and was he seeing things that weren't there, things he wanted to see more than he wanted to face real life?

More green icons showed on the display, so many now that the computer-generated imagery refreshed itself, and grouped nearby similar icons into one, with a head count beside it. Clumps of Israeli F-16s became one symbol with a number showing the formation size, such as 4 or 12. New icons quickly separating from Israeli corvettes and fast-patrol boats in the Med updated to show they were Gabriel-III advanced naval-attack missiles, with their radio retargeting links in good working order. These too regrouped and the number beside the Gabriel icon grew as waves of cruise missiles tore southwest. First 16, then 32, then 48, then 64. . . . Slowly the Gabriel-III count rose to over 100.

The Egyptian and Israeli armored brigades south of the Qattara Depression split into two groups. One headed west at high speed, and the other turned back east. Their timing was perfect.

They were going to get the Afrika Korps armor caught in an inescapable pincer, with the Med on one side and the huge Qattara Depression on the other—by looping around the depression itself to come at the Germans from in front and behind simultaneously.

Jeffrey felt a mixture of glee and immeasurable relief.

Israel's and Egypt's commanders are geniuses. It was they who set the world's biggest trap! They realized this morning that the Axis had tried a new information-warfare computer attack when it failed except in remote areas—because of Mohr's patch—but they pretended it truly succeeded and acted as if all their major systems were down.

They'd lured the German planes into a killing zone of seemingly paralyzed ground-to-air defenses that were only biding their time. They'd decoyed the German armor into a different sort of killing zone.

To Jeffrey, those commanders' ability to think on their feet at lightning speed, and the discipline of their troops at every level, was astonishing.

And the Germans knew it. They began retreating everywhere.

The counter in the window monitoring Israeli nukes going off in Germany stayed at zero. Jeffrey gave thanks to God.

The ekranoplans had turned back west, but were so heavily loaded their top speed was 150 knots slower than the Gabriel-IIIs. With real-time adjustments for the cruise-missile courses provided by Israeli drones, the Gabriels couldn't miss. Jeffrey looked on as the red and green icons connected.

It all seemed so abstract, like a video game someone else was playing. But he knew that what the icons stood for were real aircraft with real aircrews, real tanks, real passengers— and real, live, powerful cruise-missile warheads. It didn't take long before the ekranoplan-group icon counter dropped from 24 to 12 to 6 to 0, and disappeared from the laptop screen.

Jeffrey, his fingers loosened up now, used the intercom to call Bell.

"Tell Klaus Mohr I could kiss him."

"Sir?"

"Everything worked. Better than we could ever have expected."

"It's wonderful news, Captain. We can see on the theater-status display down here." Jeffrey heard his people cheering, in the background over Bell's mike.

"Wait one." Something had caught Jeffrey's attention out of the corner of his eye. "XO, rig for dive. We're almost in the Red Sea. I should be in the control room very soon."

Jeffrey double-checked the *Bunga Azul*'s nautical chart against her inertial-navigation readout, dead-reckoning plot, and a fix obtained by a crewman making sightings on the relative bearings to different islands in the Strait of Jubal. He eyed the ship's radar and sonar displays. The water beneath the keel was 100 feet deep, but within 6 miles—14 minutes at 24 knots—the bottom dropped to a comfortable 700 feet. The Sinai peninsula ended just ahead, to port. The African coast of Egypt continued endlessly south, to starboard.

His curiosity aroused, Jeffrey, with powerful image-stabilized marine binoculars, went out on the port bridge wing. Movement and black specks he'd noticed before resolved themselves into helicopters that were hovering or circling over a spot in the water on the horizon off the *Bunga Azul*'s port bow.

Above cobalt blue water where wavelets glinted yellowish gold in the afternoon sun, beneath an azure sky, he saw that two of the helos had cables dangling into the water. Two other helos dropped small things that hit the water and made little splashes.

Dipping sonars, and sonobuoys. Antisubmarine helicopters?

He looked higher in the sky and did a systematic search, spotting two twin-engine maritime-patrol aircraft.

He went back inside and used his laptop to scroll down the screen. Up to now he'd only been looking at the theater network-centric status plot farther north—the counter for nukes in Germany read 0; none had gone off in the Middle East.

Scrolling more, he found the Jubal Strait, where the Gulf of Suez let out into the northern Red Sea. He saw the group of icons. Two helos were Israeli. Two were Egyptian. The maritime-patrol planes were American, working at extreme range, from a carrier strike group far southeast in the Arabian Sea.

These icons were all in green. There was one other icon, in amber. Jeffrey felt as if he'd been electrocuted.

The amber icon was a PROBSUB, a probable submarine contact. The amber color meant that its nationality was unconfirmed. But next to the icon was text that gave a tentative identification of the suspected submarine, and the text said "SNOW TIGER."

If the Snow Tiger is so stealthy, how did they even know she was there? As Jeffrey watched, the network data-satellite feed was updated. The PROBSUB became a CERTSUB—a definite submarine contact was localized. Strangely, its color stayed amber.

He wondered why the German wasn't firing. The aircraft practically had him cornered. Surely he had Polyphem anti-aircraft missiles. He could swat the helos and drive off those patrol planes easily.

Oh. Rules of engagement. He isn't stupid. He won't shoot first. Which means the helos and planes can't drop depth charges or antisubmarine torpedoes first.

Either that, or the Snow Tiger is a nosy Russian after all, not German. Maybe Hodgkiss's information was wrong on that one rather crucial detail.

The intercom connection from *Challenger* buzzed. Jeffrey answered; it was Bell. "Sir, Milgrom reports we've been pinged by a sophisticated sonar. Our arrays could hear it right through the *Bunga Azul*'s side ballast tanks and bottom doors."

What the—

That's *how they knew he was here. He's been going active, probing every ship headed south big enough to hold an SSN.*

"XO, Captain, go to battle stations antisubmarine."

"Battle stations, ASW, aye."

Then the planes did drop torpedoes, on white parachutes to ease their impact with the water, just as the CERTSUB turned red and new icons appeared on the screen. Two submarine-launched torpedoes were coming right at the *Bunga Azul.*

CHAPTER 49

On the bridge of the *Bunga Azul*, Jeffrey took the conn and glanced at the nautical chart.

"Helmsman, right hard rudder! Get us over this shoal marked as forty-six feet!"

"But—" Siregar tried to disagree.

"Do it!" If the chart was inaccurate, or the ship drew a couple more feet than she was supposed to—with USS *Challenger* in her hold—they'd run aground.

It would be a tight race as it was. The torpedoes fired by the Snow Tiger were almost certainly Russian export-model Series 65s; with neutral Saudi Arabia less than fifty miles away, Jeffrey doubted the Snow Tiger would go nuclear. But the latest versions sold to Germany boasted a maximum attack speed of seventy-five knots, three times the speed of the *Bunga Azul*. Conventional Series 65s had high-explosive warheads that weighed a ton, three times the size of an ADCAP Mark 48's.

Jeffrey knew that the standard strategy for an antiship torpedo attack wasn't to actually *hit* the hull, but to detonate the warhead *under* the hull. A hole in a ship's side might not be a fatal blow. A blast beneath her would snap her keel, and maybe even break the ship in half instantly.

I can't let one of those weapons get under the Bunga Azul. *I have to force them to go for her side after all.*

There was some extra protection there, because the ballast control tanks, partway empty now since the submarine hold was flooded, made a sort of double hull, or spaced armor. And the false bottoms of the cargo holds were one continuous structural deck, giving the vessel added strength and stiffening.

Jeffrey grabbed the intercom for *Challenger.* "XO, Captain, collision alarm! Rig for depth charge!"

Bell acknowledged.

Jeffrey told Siregar to sound his collision alarm. The master pulled a lever. The ship's whistle began to sound shrill blasts, and gongs came over loudspeakers.

Jeffrey examined the obstacle-avoidance sonar display.

"Helmsman, all stop. All back full until our way comes off, then all stop."

The master stared at Jeffrey. "We sit here and take two torpedoes?"

"They might miss or they might malfunction. If we're stopped right over a shoal next to a coral reef, they might not see us if their guidance wires break."

"Please Allah, let it be so." There were other shoals and reefs, plus a maze of long but narrow islands, and half-exposed rusting wrecks, both ahead of and behind the *Bunga Azul* in this area outside the main shipping channel.

With bone-shattering concussions, and towers of flame and filthy water, first one and then the other Series 65 slammed into the *Bunga Azul*'s port side. Even by following Jeffrey's example—holding on to something with one hand while standing on tiptoes with both knees bent, to absorb the force and avoid a fractured spine—the bridge crew were knocked to the deck. The *Bunga Azul* rolled hard to starboard and was brought up sharply when her flat bottom hit the top of the reef. She rolled heavily to port and her bottom slammed into the rocky shoal. The whole ship vibrated and flexed.

Jeffrey shook off the numbness that gripped his arms and legs, then shook his head to reduce the pain in his ears and get his eyes to refocus. It seemed to be raining. He realized that this was the many tons of water thrown upward by the torpedo blasts, now coming back down. Then he smelled smoke—burning paint, wood, plastic—mixed with the stink of torpedo explosive. Still feeling disembodied, he vaguely registered men shouting and more alarm bells sounding. Armored bridge windows were cracked; manuals and coffee mugs and laptops were strewn on the deck; phone handsets, hanging dislodged, bounced and swayed by their wires.

Jeffrey rushed to the engine-order telegraph, and rang up all ahead full. Someone at the other end of the telegraph acknowledged, and the ship began to vibrate in an ugly new way—but she moved.

The master and helmsman began to revive.

"Steer one-eight-zero!" Jeffrey yelled to the helmsman, who took the wheel. Due south. "Get us behind Shakir Island, into the Shadwan Channel. Then steer one-three-five." Southeast, down the middle of a small side channel between the island and Africa, leading to deep water in the Red Sea.

The *Bunga Azul* was already listing ten degrees to port.

Jeffrey grabbed Siregar by both shoulders and looked right into his eyes. They urgently needed to lighten the ship and keep her from rolling onto her side. "Pump out all your ballast control tanks. Pump the submarine-hold water level down eight feet. Then counterflood the starboard tanks just enough to keep your list to five degrees."

Siregar understood. He issued orders over an intercom. He listened, examined display panels on the bridge, then turned to Jeffrey. "Only half our fire mains can be pressurized. Wheat in the aft-most cargo hold is in flames, with the hatches blown off, and many smaller fires may grow and join between the engine room and the superstructure. Fuel oil leaking near the stern, and fuel bunkers threatened by fires. Injured men reduce our chances of fighting the fires. Our radar and our sonar are knocked out."

Jeffrey called down to Bell. "Do you still have the satellite feed?"

"Affirmative."

"Give me a damage report."

"No significant damage to *Challenger.*" She was very shock hardened, and loose objects had been carefully stowed.

"Status in the hold?"

"Port-side inner bulkhead bulging inward in two places aft. Plates and welds have failed, we're getting heavy spray of seawater into the hold. . . . We can hear the host ship's ballast pumps, they're not keeping up with the flooding into the hold."

"Stand by."

Jeffrey turned to Siregar; the pain in the master's eyes said he knew his ship was going down. "We need that satellite feed to *Challenger* for as long as humanly possible. We need it to target the enemy submarine."

"I understand." There was iron in Siregar's voice.

Jeffrey glanced at the nautical chart. Siregar's navigator stood up, favoring his left arm. He saw Jeffrey erect and determined and ran to the chart, but the man was half dazed. Jeffrey called rudder orders to the helm, to zigzag past shoals and reefs on either side. The bulk of Shakir Island hid the helos and patrol planes from view.

Jeffrey grabbed his laptop off the deck—built to navy ruggedness specs, it hadn't broken. He studied the tactical plot. A pull-down menu gave details about the aircraft battling the CERTSUB: More depth charges and air-dropped torpedoes were attacking the Snow Tiger. It was heading south in water over three thousand feet deep, near the bottom, accelerating. The plot claimed two probable torpedo hits, and six depth-charge near misses. But even the latest U.S. air-dropped torpedoes, the Mark 54s, had a warhead that

weighed only 100 pounds. They could harass a double titanium hull, and shake up the crew—certainly harm the stern
planes or rudder or pump jet if they got lucky—but not by
themselves score a hard kill on the Snow Tiger. Air-dropped
depth charges, which fell but didn't home, also had to be
lightweight; at worst they'd be a nuisance against a target
with such good sensors and such high speed.

*The Snow Tiger's captain knows that. He's gone deep, too
deep to launch his Polyphems because the little missiles have
shallow crush depth. But the latest mod of Mark Fifty-fours
implode before three thousand feet themselves. That's why he
didn't try to shoot down the ASW helos. He's picked sure
self-protection over risky antiaircraft attack.*

*And he's trying to go to flank speed. He's heading south of
Shakir Island, which for now is sheltering me from him on
sonar. He'll block the Shadwan Channel outlet, and fire at me
again.*

Though Jeffrey knew nothing whatsoever about the enemy submarine's captain, and didn't even know his vessel's
real name, to Jeffrey the contest had already become very
personal.

His available information showed the water under the
Bunga Azul was 110 feet deep. *Still too shallow for* Challenger *to escape.*

Challenger's host ship was laboring. The deck vibrations
were heavy, and the highest speed she could manage was
eighteen knots instead of twenty-four.

Jeffrey gave another order. The helmsman turned his
wheel. The *Bunga Azul* turned left and steadied on a course
southeast. The eight-mile-long Shakir Island sat close on the
ship's port side; other islands, and gas-drilling platforms, lay
astern or off the starboard bow. Shakir Island was an arid
reddish-brown hill sticking out of green water. The chart said
its peak rose eight hundred feet high. Jeffrey still couldn't see
the friendly aircraft, but their data continued coming in. With
the naked eye, out the bridge windows, the edge of the
island's coral reef could be seen looming to port. The *Bunga*

Azul was riding visibly deeper in the water. Her subdivided ballast control tanks had helped absorb and contain the blasts, but her wounds were mortal. Thick black smoke was boiling out of the after holds and trailing behind the ship. The smell of burning was stronger in the air, and Jeffrey smelled leaking diesel fuel too. The diesel fuel would catch fire at any moment.

In 2 miles the water would drop suddenly to 650 feet. In 20 miles it would reach past 3,000 feet; the Snow Tiger was still rushing south at that depth, to outflank the island. *He's faster than me but has farther to go.... Will I remain afloat for another two miles?* The *Bunga Azul* had slowed to fifteen knots. Two miles at this speed would take eight minutes.

The water was still too shallow for *Challenger* to leave the hold through the bottom doors. Jeffrey's best place right now was here on the freighter's bridge, doing everything he could to make sure the *Bunga Azul* reached deeper water.

Bell called on the intercom. "Sir, seawater in the hold is rising faster now. We're floating off the support blocks. I'm afraid we'll drift and damage the stern parts or the bow dome. What do you want me to do?"

Jeffrey thought hard. He could have his crew tie the ship to cleats in the sides of the covert hold, but then she'd be trapped inside the *Bunga Azul* as the host ship sank.

"Work the propulsor and auxiliary maneuvering units if you have to."

Again Jeffrey looked at the chart. He watched the inertial-navigation position plot, advancing at a pace that was much too slow. Minute after minute dragged on. The *Bunga Azul* shook harder and settled deeper and handled sluggishly. Jeffrey was afraid her shafts or engines would completely fail, stranding *Challenger* inside so that the cargo ship became her coffin in a horrifying burial at sea. Then more torpedoes would tear in and pound the *Bunga Azul*'s hulk and *Challenger* to pieces.

All at once they were off the shallow shelf, with Shakir Island still to port and a huge coral reef to starboard.

"Master, stand by to open the bottom doors. If you don't hear from me or my crew in five minutes, open the doors regardless." With Siregar's ship in bad shape, once those doors were open, Jeffrey might never make it to *Challenger.* But he needed a fail-safe arrangement now, so *Challenger* could get away even without him.

"Understood," Siregar said.

"Good-bye. Good luck. Thank you. And remember, keep the satellite feed in operation as long as you possibly can."

"I'll do it myself. Go now. Go with God."

"Go with God," Jeffrey responded, knowing how literal this was—Siregar might go down with his ship. He noticed that the master wore a wedding ring, and wondered if he had children.

Jeffrey tore himself away. He hurried through the tunnels down to *Challenger.* In some places lightbulbs had shattered from the torpedo concussions, and he needed to swipe the bigger pieces of glass aside with his forearm so he could keep crawling on hands and knees. In other places AFFF— aqueous fire-fighting foam—dripped from above and made puddles. The slippery white foam was hot. Something up there was busy burning. Using foam suggested a flammable liquid. Jeffrey caught whiffs of gasoline. For deck-mounted winches? He waited for the gas tank somewhere above him to explode. The deeper in the ship he went, the heavier the vibrations from her engines.

When he came out onto the catwalk in the hold, *Challenger* sat there before him, long and sleek and black. Water jetted loudly into the hold through inward-bulging jagged cracks, and the hold was filled with the tangy mist of saltwater spray. Jeffrey tasted it on his lips, he smelled it, and it got in his eyes. He also smelled the acrid, toxic fumes of spent torpedo warheads, and tried not to breathe in too much.

The seawater surrounding *Challenger*'s free-floating hull was choppy, and kept sloshing back and forth and from side to side. This was called free surface during damage control.

It made the *Bunga Azul* much less stable. She could capsize at any moment.

Jeffrey started running down the brow. But the weapons-loading hatch was shut. He saw why: The in-rushing water was washing right over the hull.

Bell shouted from atop the sail. "Up here, sir! We shifted the fiber-optic connect to stay in touch as long as we can as the hold fills!"

Jeffrey noticed that the photonics mast was lowered. There was little headroom now between the overhead of the hold and the top of the sail. He heard throbbing and roaring amid the other sounds, as the master kept trying to pump the water back out of the hold—a losing battle. Jeffrey hit the switch to retract the brow; the remote-control system still worked. The brow's near end raised up, but this robbed him of any handholds.

Warm seawater lapped at Jeffrey's shoes, then a wave of it drenched him up to his knees and almost swept him away. He lunged and grabbed a safety harness and lifeline that crewmen were lowering. He strapped them on, and the crewmen, with Jeffrey helping as much as he could, pulled him up the twenty feet to the top of the sail—there were no ladder rungs outside the sail because they would cause bad flow noise.

Jeffrey ordered the two crewmen to stay in the tiny bridge cockpit, as lookouts of a sort for now. He and Bell slid down the vertical ladders leading below, being careful not to snag the dangling fiber-optic cable. They rushed to the control room and took their seats at the command console; the lighting was red, for battle stations. Meltzer was very busy at the ship controls, trying to keep *Challenger* from damaging herself by hitting the bulkheads in the hold.

At least floating free in the hold helps cushion us from the shaking by our host.

"Fire Control," Jeffrey ordered, "load high-explosive Mark Eighty-eights in torpedo tubes one through seven. Load an off-board probe in tube eight." He wanted this all done immediately, while they were more or less on an even trim.

Bell acknowledged and relayed commands to Lieutenant Torelli, standing in the aisle nearby. He acknowledged, issued more orders, and Torelli's men went to work.

Jeffrey called up data from the helos, masked from the line of sight of the *Bunga Azul* by Shakir Island. The data remained available over the net, through satellites.

"Firing-point procedures, Mark Eighty-eights in tubes one through seven. Target is the Snow Tiger. Load firing solution using target depth and course and speed from the data link."

Bell and then Torelli acknowledged.

This was network-centric warfare at its most extreme. Jeffrey was programming his torpedoes against a target he couldn't detect, while inside a sinking surface ship's hold, using information from helicopters coming to his host's antennas via outer space.

"Make tubes one through seven ready in all respects, including opening outer doors."

Again Jeffrey's crew went to work.

Speaking of doors.

Jeffrey tried to call Siregar, not sure if the intercom inside the master's ship had failed. Siregar answered.

"What's the depth beneath your keel?"

"Six hundred feet now. The seafloor drop-off is steep."

"What's your status?"

"The fuel fires are out of control. We are very low in the water and very difficult to handle. I will not be able to counterflood against the port list without losing too much buoyancy. The main deck will soon be awash regardless."

"Evacuate the covert radio room. In one minute from my mark, open your bottom doors. Then abandon ship. You'll be picked up soon when those helos see you."

"One minute, understood."

"Mark."

"Understood."

Jeffrey grabbed an internal intercom, for *Challenger*'s bridge. "Bridge, Captain, cut the fiber-optic cable. Clear the bridge, smartly. Shut and dog both sail-trunk hatches."

The men on the bridge acknowledged.

The data link was broken.

"Green board, sir," COB reported. *Challenger* was ready to dive.

Jeffrey watched the chronometer on his console. Each remaining second of that minute felt like a lifetime.

Everyone in the control room cringed when they heard the groaning of protesting steel. Some crewmen feared the *Bunga Azul* was breaking up or sinking already. But that groaning had a different cause.

"Bottom doors have not opened!" Bell reported. "Bottom doors appear to be warped and jammed by torpedo hits!"

We're trapped. The Snow Tiger will get in position and shoot at us repeatedly after the Bunga Azul *goes down.... We're defenseless. The German will keep firing until* Challenger *is smashed to pieces.*

Jeffrey grabbed the 1MC. It was noisy, but that was the least of his problems. It was the best way to reach anyone, anywhere in the ship, even if they were asleep. "Lieutenant Estabo to the control room smartly."

There was another groaning noise: Siregar trying again to open the doors.

"Doors have not opened!" Bell yelled.

Challenger jolted. There was a different sound, a metallic scraping.

"Sail roof is hitting hold overhead."

Jeffrey had only one choice. "Chief of the Watch, flood all main ballast-tank groups."

"Flood main ballast, aye!"

COB flipped switches. A new noise started, the roaring of air forced out of the vents in the tops of the ballast tanks, as seawater displaced the air and flooded into the tanks from below.

"Chief of the Watch, flood the negative tank."

"Flood negative, aye."

This would make *Challenger* heavier, giving her negative buoyancy. Jeffrey hoped her weight pressing down on the bottom doors might make them spring open.

Challenger bounced down onto the hold's supporting rubber blocks, landing slightly cockeyed. The control-room deck was tilted a few degrees down and to the right.

It didn't work. The bottom doors stayed shut.

Felix Estabo arrived.

"I'll make this short," Jeffrey told him. "The bottom doors are jammed and we need to break them open with explosive charges planted on each hinge. Take your men and enough equipment, suit up with compressed-air tanks, lock out of *Challenger,* and get it done."

"Are we sinking?"

"We will be very soon."

Felix nodded grimly and ran below.

Jeffrey knew he'd probably just given Felix and Chief Costa and their men death sentences. Once the *Bunga Azul* left the surface, her depth would increase quickly. Men working in scuba would be exposed to ever-greater pressure. At some point, their compressed-air supply would start to become poisonous.

But we don't have mixed-gas rigs that could let them cope at deeper depth. Nobody thought we'd need them.

Then there was decompression sickness, when the men came back into the ship—the bends, agonizing, and fatal if severe enough.

Jeffrey had no choice. All he could do was wait.

COB reported when the SEALs were locking out of *Challenger.* Jeffrey ordered the on-hull photonic sensors activated, in laser line-scan mode for illumination. Control-room monitors let him and his crew observe as the SEALs went to work with practiced skill. From his own SEAL training years before, Jeffrey assumed they'd use as a time delay—to let them get back into his ship—a proper length of fuse cord that would burn slowly even deep underwater, lit by a tiny explosive charge set off manually by a trigger and percussion cap. But the details were up to Felix.

Jeffrey watched in anguish as the men moved in slow motion through the water outside the hull, using small portable floodlights to see in the dark around Jeffrey's blue-green lasers. If they didn't finish fast enough and succeed in blowing open the doors, the *Bunga Azul* would hit the bottom. Then *Challenger* would never escape.

"Hold is fully flooded," Bell reported.

"Very well, Fire Control. . . . Helm, call out your depth as indicated by sea pressure in the hold."

"Fifty-five feet, sir."

Allowing for her deep draft and her freeboard, the *Bunga Azul* would go under any moment.

An explosion from somewhere rocked the ship. Jeffrey thought it was another torpedo hit. He realized it was too soon for that, given the distance and speed of the Snow Tiger and her weapons. He suspected that a hot auxiliary boiler on the host ship, already weakened by mechanical stress, had burst from thermal shock when suddenly covered by much colder water.

The vibrations stopped; the *Bunga Azul*'s engines had gone dead. The sensation was replaced by heavy shuddering, with more metallic groans and eerie crying sounds as the *Bunga Azul* left the surface.

"Depth eighty feet," Meltzer called out.

"Very well, Helm." The deck began to tilt backward. The host ship was sinking by the stern.

Too much angle that way and we'll never get out of this alive.

"One hundred feet amidships," Meltzer said. "One hundred twenty at our stern." *Challenger*'s stern was deeper than her bow because of the way the *Bunga Azul* was going down; the water pressure aft would be higher. The monitors showed that Felix and his men were still working as best they could.

"One hundred fifty amidships."

Here's where breathing compressed air starts getting toxic.
"Depth two hundred feet amidships, two-thirty at our stern."

The ship kept sinking, her rate of descent slowed only by pockets of air in compartments that wouldn't stay unflooded for long. She was also tilting more steeply backward—and so was *Challenger*. Jeffrey watched as Felix and his SEALs frantically laid a main and a backup detcord line, to connect all the charges at the hinges to one central detonator. They moved out of sight of any of the hull's photonic sensors.

"Three hundred feet amidships!" From the nautical charts and Jeffrey's mental estimates, with the forward progress the host ship had made since he'd last spoken to Master Siregar, the bottom at their position should be nearly one thousand feet deep. The carcass of the *Bunga Azul* continued in its death throes. Steel plates tore with screaming noises, bulkheads collapsed with sudden loud booms, air pockets hissed and bubbled away, and major welds failed with thunderclaps. *Challenger* slipped on the blocks and rolled, and was thrown about like a toy weighing thousands of tons.

Jeffrey saw a SEAL float past one photonics sensor, his chest and abdomen squashed, surrounded by a spreading dark cloud that Jeffrey knew had to be blood. A lanyard tangled in what was once his waist trailed off camera. His dive buddy's corpse drifted into view, with a mangled pancake where the man's head should be. They'd been crushed between *Challenger*'s hull and the side of the hold. In the control room, crewmen gasped.

"Depth four hundred feet! . . . Four hundred fifty!"

"SEALs are in escape trunk with upper hatch shut," COB finally said. "Green board, draining escape trunk's water now."

Felix's voice came over the intercom circuit from the lockout trunk. "Fire in the hole in one minute."

"Fire in the hole, one minute, aye," Jeffrey said with immense relief; Felix had at least survived the ordeal so far.

The charges would detonate soon. If they failed, *Challenger* was doomed.

Felix's words had been slurred, more than just from grief at losing two more men. Slurred speech was one of the first signs of decompression sickness.

Jeffrey grabbed the 1MC mike. "Corpsman and all assistants to forward escape trunk. Prepare to receive three decompression-sickness casualties plus two dead. Bring casualties into minisub and use as a recompression chamber."

"Captain," the phone talker said, "corpsman acknowledges, is headed for escape trunk."

The best immediate treatment for the bends was to return the men to a pressurized environment. Then, standard tables told how to decompress in gradual stages so their bodies could adjust with minimum lasting ill effects.

On the monitors Jeffrey saw bright flashes, and through the hull he heard dull thuds and felt new shocks. The SEALs' explosive charges had detonated.

"Bottom doors falling away!" Bell reported.

"Chief of the Watch, shift all variable ballast to forward tanks smartly." COB acknowledged. *Challenger* began to right herself, still half inside the sinking host ship's hold.

"Helm, make your down-angle thirty degrees by the stern planes. Maximum down angle on the fore planes. Ahead one third."

From tilting backward, *Challenger* quickly went to nosing down by the bow. Her pump-jet propulsor kicked in, and drove her out from under the *Bunga Azul*. Jeffrey gave orders and Meltzer made *Challenger* level off. COB's fingers danced on his console, restoring neutral buoyancy and trim. *Challenger* was free, a working warship again—and a powerful enemy was rushing to deliver more killing blows. Jeffrey had to engage his opponent as soon as possible, but Shakir Island still sat between them.

"Fire Control, tubes one through seven, target remains Snow Tiger. Program dogleg course past intervening terrain.

Launch on generated bearings, at ten-second intervals, *shoot.*"

Generated bearings meant the weapon-system computer's best estimate of an updated firing solution, projecting ahead in time from the last stream of data the *Bunga Azul*'s antennas could feed. Bell and Torelli did as ordered; it took a full minute from shooting the first fish until the last weapon was launched.

"All tubes fired electrically!" Torelli said. "Good wires!"

"All units running normally," Milgrom confirmed.

"Helm, put us behind the *Bunga Azul,* follow her down, be careful of our weapon wires." Meltzer acknowledged. This would be a very tricky maneuver. Jeffrey had seven widebody Mark 88 torpedoes dashing through the sea. Their attack speed was seventy knots, and their crush depth was the same as *Challenger*'s—fifteen thousand feet. Jeffrey had fired at a target he couldn't detect, even on active sonar, because of where he and the Snow Tiger were, the island's underwater mass in the way.

Given *Challenger*'s torpedo-tube design, if he reloaded, the control wires to the weapons already fired would be cut. *They'll have to search and home on their own. I need to saturate the Snow Tiger's defenses, to exploit the element of surprise.*

The *Bunga Azul* hit the bottom with a loud thud, and a final screech of tortured metal.

"Fire Control," Jeffrey ordered, "program all units to go to autonomous active search as soon as past Shakir Island." The gravimeter showed that the seafloor a few miles ahead was wide open, and the slope down to past three thousand feet was smooth. Outside the Shadwan Channel, beyond the mouth of the Jubal Strait, there was nowhere for the Snow Tiger to hide. Bell and then Torelli acknowledged Jeffrey's order.

"Fire Control," Jeffrey snapped, "launch the off-board probe in fiber-optic tether mode. Send it around and past the

Bunga Azul's hulk on a course due east at its maximum speed." Twenty knots for short sprints on its batteries. "Reload tubes one through seven, high-explosive Mark Eighty-eights, *smartly*." A rapid second salvo was everything now.

"Torpedoes in the water," Milgrom reported. Outside the host ship, *Challenger*'s sonar arrays could pick up sound acutely well. They'd registered echoes of torpedo-engine sounds, bouncing off the submerged side of Shakir Island— exactly as Jeffrey had intended, knowing that his bow sphere was blocked from directly ahead by the hulk Meltzer hid behind. "Series Sixty-fives, inbound." Milgrom gave their bearings and ranges. There were eight of them.

Had the Snow Tiger's captain detected Jeffrey's first salvo coming at him, and launched a salvo of his own? *Is he guessing, trying to obliterate the* Bunga Azul *whatever her condition, or does he know by my fish that I got out of the host ship intact?*

The wire-guided 65s went active. Sweet, metallic *tings* came over the sonar speakers. Several 65s—their weapons technicians perhaps fooled because of Jeffrey's previous trick of having the *Bunga Azul* sit on top of a shoal—homed on reefs or small islands in the distance back behind *Challenger*. Their engine noises and pinging receded harmlessly up the Shadwan Channel. At least Jeffrey *hoped* they'd be harmless—it seemed less likely that their target seekers would acquire the spindly pylons of a drilling platform; those people had probably shut down and evacuated to shore at the first sign naval combat was brewing.

But two 65s detected the wreck of the *Bunga Azul*, and began to circle around it, as if looking for something hiding there.

Uh-oh. Jeffrey was glad the *Bunga Azul* was much bigger than *Challenger.*

He ordered Meltzer to move *Challenger* around the other way, to keep the wreck between them; Milgrom and Torelli fed steering cues to Meltzer's main display. Jeffrey saw that

Meltzer's hands on the control wheel were white knuckled.

Jeffrey realized how sore his own fingers felt, from hours of gripping the rail out on the bridge wing of the late and much-lamented *Bunga Azul*. He looked at his hands, and prayed that the master and all his men had made it into the lifeboats okay.

It's not too late for her to save Challenger *one more time*.

The torpedoes hit the sunken cargo ship with mighty eruptions. *Challenger* rocked, and her control-room crew were shaken in their seats. Milgrom had known to turn down the sonar speakers, but the big warheads going off so close were intensely loud through *Challenger*'s hull.

Without waiting for the cacophony to die down, Jeffrey shouted, "Sonar, does off-board probe detect propulsion noise from Snow Tiger?" The probe was miles ahead, with a broad view out to deep water.

"Affirmative! Snow Tiger is at high speed, appears unable to achieve sixty knots for effective tonal masking. Hull singing suggests damage to outer hull from air-dropped torpedoes or depth charges."

"V' r' well, Sonar."

He's been banged up by those helos and planes. It's the cost of coming shallow and going active, to attack a host ship before its guest submarine could depart. If he'd opened fire from out in deep water instead, his weapons would've had a twenty-mile run up into the shallows, and his intended victim might have gotten too much warning.... He did exactly what I would've done.

The Snow Tiger's captain paid a price for his tactics, but he was full of fight and acting very aggressively, and his 65s were dangerous—one solid hit would crack *Challenger*'s hull.

"Tubes one through seven reloaded," Bell said.

"Fire Control," Jeffrey rapped out, "firing point procedures, Mark Eighty-eights in tubes one through seven. Target is the Snow Tiger. Make tubes one through seven ready in all respects including opening outer doors.... Tubes one through seven, launch on generated bearings, at ten-second intervals, *shoot*."

When his seven new fish were launched, Jeffrey had Meltzer hover behind the wreckage of the *Bunga Azul,* as an antisonar and antitorpedo shield. The wires to Jeffrey's second salvo, and to his off-board probe, were his front-line eyes and ears. Because of the islands, reefs, shoals, wrecks, and gas-drilling platforms all around, he was in a cluttered environment—and inbound torpedoes ought to have trouble finding him. The wounded Snow Tiger, in contrast, by choosing to go deep to outdive the air-dropped Mark 54s, and by moving fast to reach the Shadwan Channel and use the German's own sonars to locate his prey, had discarded any chance of terrain or acoustic concealment. Jeffrey was trying to overwhelm him with a barrage of fourteen Mark 88 torpedoes coming all at once, each with a warhead twenty times the size of a Mark 54's.

"Sir," Bell said, "I must caution that Snow Tiger captain might adopt more aggressive tactics now that he knows he failed to sink us inside the carrier ship and he is not able to maintain quiet flank speed."

"What do you mean, *more* aggressive? This guy's arrogant, impetuous, impatient as it is. He thought he could outsmart everybody. He didn't allow for our side having smart people too, XO, so our platforms knew what to listen for as he rushed north through the whole Red Sea." The Snow Tiger's flank-speed flow noise that lacked tonals would be distinctive once understood. That had to be how the carrier-based antisubmarine planes knew early enough to head toward this location. It explained why they were ready to help the local helos when the German started pinging southbound merchant ships.

"That's my point, sir. Things haven't gone his way, and he's impetuous. He may feel egged on to score a last-ditch victory if he knows by ELF that the North African offensive collapsed. . . . He might go nuclear here."

"That's why he discarded acoustic stealth? He wants to lull me into a false sense of confidence and then one of his Sixty-fives has a nuke? But we're too close to Saudi Arabia."

"It's my duty to state that he may see things differently, Captain. We do not know his current rules of engagement, or his willingness to violate them if given sufficient cause."

Over the speakers, Jeffrey and his crew heard the echoes and reverb from distant blasts. The Snow Tiger was using its antitorpedo rockets to smash his inbound fish. There were louder blasts when the rocket warheads set off the Mark 88s.

"Assess all units from first salvo intercepted!" Bell said.

This won't be nearly as easy as I thought. And now he's really egged on, because only my ship carries Mark Eighty-eights. He knows that he's up against Challenger.

"Second salvo has acquired the Snow Tiger!"

"Torpedoes in the water! Eight torpedoes, Series Sixty-fives, inbound." The German launched another salvo too.

"Captain," Bell said, "we can't tell if a Sixty-five is nuclear until it detonates. Our only defense is a nuclear countershot to smash his torpedoes at a safe stand-off distance. If we use nukes for defense, we should for offense also."

"It *is* against our own ROEs!"

"Sir, with Mohr and his gear aboard, and his honest intent and his equipment's effectiveness proved now, we dare not let ourselves be destroyed! We're low on high-explosive ammo. We might run out before the Snow Tiger does. We can't be sure with her double titanium hull that our conventional Mark Eighty-eights will have the hitting power to stop her even if any get through!"

"XO, I *can't* go nuclear here!"

"Captain, if we *don't* we could lose *Challenger* and Klaus Mohr and the Allies could lose the war!"

Bell's concerns are valid. The Snow Tiger defeated my first salvo, and I don't have a lot more I can shoot. I need something to give me an edge.

"Sir," Bell pressed, "remember *Ohio*! She succumbed with all hands against a superior force, using every weapon she had and every tactic Captain Parcelli could think of! To us, with the bottom at three thousand feet, the Snow Tiger could represent a superior force *without* going nuclear!"

Jeffrey's next salvo was drawing close to the Snow Tiger.

"He'll just swat them with more antitorpedo rockets, sir! We can't afford to wait any longer."

Was Bell right? Did Jeffrey need to go nuclear, before the German captain had a chance to?

"I have my ROEs! Nukes are forbidden!"

"You disobeyed orders before when you thought it was best!"

"How will Saudi Arabia take it when she sees American mushroom clouds so near her shores? *We can't go nuclear!*"

Jeffrey's high-explosive weapons were very close to the Snow Tiger now.

Jeffrey had an idea, something he'd never thought of before. *Maybe it came to me from being on the* Bunga Azul *in the canal.*

"All right, XO! I want to try one more tactic. If it fails we switch to nuclear Mark Eighty-eights."

"Sir?"

"Put our fish into formation as close as you can to line ahead without loosing the wires." "Line ahead" meant that the units would follow each other, evenly spaced in single file. "Have formation jink in unison each time lead weapon is intercepted."

Bell, surprised, acknowledged. Torelli issued orders and his technicians worked their joysticks. Explosions began, more antitorpedo rocket warheads and Mark 88 warheads.

"Unit from tube one destroyed!"

Jeffrey waited and watched his chronometer. The next fish would be ten seconds behind the first. Ten seconds passed, then fifteen, then twenty. Another blast.

"Unit from tube two destroyed!"

Jeffrey's eyes flitted to his chronometer again.

Ten seconds. Twenty seconds. Thirty. A blast.

"Unit from tube three destroyed!"

Jeffrey's plan was working, so far. Each exploding rocket and torpedo warhead made a giant, persistent disturbance in the water; the Snow Tiger's sonars getting target data for her rockets were blinded by a wall of bubbles and turbulence. They had to wait for the next jinking fish to charge somewhere through that wall, then acquire it, then launch another rocket—which had to cover some distance to reach the latest inbound weapon.

"Unit from tube four destroyed!"

Each time, Jeffrey put a torpedo closer to the German sub. But would the salvo of seven be large enough to get at least one all the way to the Snow Tiger's hull?

"Unit from tube five destroyed!"

Not good. "Weps, obtain the nuclear-weapons arming tool, smartly." Torelli ran to Jeffrey's stateroom; as part of his job he knew the safe's combinations.

Jeffrey's sixth torpedo connected with the Snow Tiger, a direct hit. His seventh hit the German in the same place.

Jeffrey no longer needed wire-guided control on those expended weapons. "Reload tubes one through seven, nuclear Mark Eighty-eights. Preset warhead yields on one and two to maximum." One kiloton, for offense. "Preset yields on three through seven to minimum." One one-hundredth kiloton, for defense.

Bell acknowledged, relieved but still troubled. The phone talker said Torelli had the arming tool, and was in the torpedo room.

"Sonar, assess damage of conventional Mark Eighty-eight hits on Snow Tiger." Sent off to one side and then slowed for a better acoustic-surveillance vantage point, the off-board probe detected a new signature, above the echoes and reverb of all the explosions and the engine noise of the enemy's 65s still inbound.

"Flooding sounds, Captain!" Milgrom called out. "Mechanical transients! Assess as bilge pumps and an emergency blow! ... Propulsion plant noises have ceased!"

The speakers filled *Challenger*'s control room with the high-pitched hissing of a submarine trying to blow its main ballast tanks, combined with the lower-pitched roar as seawater shoved its greedy way into ruptures in the pressure hull.

"It could be fake, sir!" Bell shouted. "That noise could be from their sonar emitters!"

Jeffrey reluctantly acknowledged that Bell was right. It might all be a deception tactic, the German only pretending he'd been sunk. Jeffrey's throat and lungs felt as if they were being seared by the flames of Hell as he issued more orders. "Firing-point procedures, nuclear Mark Eighty-eights in tubes one and two, target is Snow Tiger. Fire Control, enter your arming code." Bell and Jeffrey typed their special-weapon passwords.

"Passwords accepted," Bell shouted. "Warheads preen-abled!"

"Make tubes one and two ready in all respects, including opening outer doors."

"Inbound Series Sixty-fives approaching lethal range if set at maximum yield of one kiloton!" Four thousand yards.

Jeffrey knew he needed to launch defensive nukes very soon.

But what if Bell was wrong? What if those real direct hits by high-explosive Mark 88s in a one-two punch had burst through the Snow Tiger's pressure hull after all? How could Jeffrey tell for sure? His probe was too far away to give him more data in time, even if he sent it on another high-speed dash. Was the Snow Tiger—sitting on the bottom now with no pumps or ballast-blow noises—lying doggo, or was it dead? *We're only fifty miles from neutral Saudi Arabia.*

But what if Bell was right? What if the Snow Tiger was still very much operational or her inbound weapons were nukes?

Jeffrey saw a way to buy his ship a few precious seconds. It meant the end of his career no matter what happened, either death, or court-martial for sure, but other factors vastly outweighed his career. "Tube one, *shoot*. Tube two, *shoot*."

His nuclear fish were on their way to the Snow Tiger. He carefully watched the data on the inbound 65s. Their lethal circles at a kiloton were drawing awfully close. Were they nuclear? Were the weapons technicians on the other end of their wires alive, or drowned? Would they explode them the moment the 65s were in range, or would they let them get closer to *Challenger* to guarantee a score? Were they set on a dead man's switch, with decision rules already programmed in?

The 65s kept coming, as Jeffrey's Mark 88s charged at the Snow Tiger. The off-board probe showed that the German wasn't reacting. That Jeffrey had fired only two fish, not seven, would imply that they might well be nuclear. Time passed, an eternity.

Still the German didn't react. The 65s were now in lethal range of *Challenger* if their warhead yields were only one-tenth kiloton. Was this a clever trick to get Jeffrey to not set off his Mark 88 nukes? . . . Jeffrey's fish were in lethal range of the German at their preset yields of one kiloton. He ordered his warheads to be preset to explode at half their remaining range to the target. Bell acknowledged; from here, if their wires broke for any reason, the weapons would have a mind of their own. Jeffrey was taking a monumental gamble, but at least if both sides used nukes it would be a double kill. Jeffrey intended to absorb the first blow, because the Saudis would know the truth by the relative position and timing of the blasts, and by analyzing the fallout. *Challenger* would be obliterated, but so would the German: a military draw—an even exchange—and a slight diplomatic advantage for Allied relations with the Saudis.

The 65s rushed up the Shadwan Channel, homed on terrain, and detonated; they weren't nuclear. The Snow Tiger sat there, inert.

"*Safe the units, tubes one and two! Shut down their engines!*"

The ocean outside grew much quieter. Now and then,

above his racing heart, Jeffrey heard a *pop* or a *bang* as some item inside the Snow Tiger's hulk succumbed to the merciless squashing by the sea more than a kilometer beneath the surface. There could be no remaining doubt: The German sub was destroyed.

"Overflight!" Milgrom shouted. "Low-flying helos, Israeli!"

The aircraft might not grasp what was happening. This meant serious danger of friendly fire—and it was ten minutes at flank speed to water deeper than a Mark 54's crush depth.

"Fire Control, launch a radio buoy with Allied recognition code, smartly." Bell's face showed he understood the stakes. *Challenger* had to get their nationality into the data net, ASAP.

"Aircraft noises receding," Milgrom said a minute later.

"Nav, relay fire-control position of Snow Tiger wreck, and location of our shut-down nuclear Mark Eighty-eights for recovery. They're in international waters, just barely." Jeffrey told Bell to launch a buoy with this data, encrypted by a deeper code. A U.S. decontamination and intell salvage group was sure to be mobilizing already. "And you realize, XO? This is our first combat mission where not one nuclear weapon went off."

EPILOGUE

Two Weeks Later

USS *Challenger* was staying stealthy, submerged well outside the major naval base at Perth, in southwest Australia. Minisubs, diving from covered piers at the base, shuttled spare parts and provisions to the ship, and brought her crew ashore in batches for liberty.

Jeffrey was pleased by the state of his crew's morale, and the condition of his ship. In this, his fifth combat mission, *Challenger* had taken no significant battle damage. She needed little maintenance because her propulsion plant had almost never gone anywhere near flank speed.

Jeffrey himself had been enjoying some leave on dry land, in a beautiful country where even during wartime the people were very friendly. He'd been able to briefly hold a private chat-room talk with his parents, using U.S. Navy infrastructure, including encryption and decryption at both ends, so they could have a nice typed conversation without fear of enemy eavesdropping. But Michael Fuller had said there were rumors in Washington that Ilse Reebeck had been arrested as a spy. Jeffrey was dismayed, but wasn't sure what to do about it yet.

Klaus Mohr and his equipment, and Gamal Salih and Gerald Parker, were already on their way back to the United States by the safest possible transport: an American nuclear submarine. Felix and his men, including the wounded and the bodies of the dead, flew to the U.S. soon after *Challenger* arrived at Perth.

Now, after a satisfying dinner, Jeffrey was unwinding in the bachelor officers' quarters on the Royal Australian Navy's base at Perth. Much had happened during his covert transit of the Indian Ocean. He was sitting in the lounge of the mess, having beers with some newly made pals in the Royal Australian Navy, and the television was on. Jeffrey was watching a video recording, for the third time in a row.

The broadcast had been copied off Al Jazeera TV. The speaker was the president of Egypt. He'd held a press conference in Cairo over a week ago, while Jeffrey had been busy running silent and deep.

The president spoke in Arabic. The tape had English subtitles added by Allied translators, but Jeffrey just listened to the man's voice.

He said that the Egyptian-Israeli counteroffensive against the Afrika Korps had taken two German generals prisoner, with their headquarter vehicles intact. Analysis of computer files and documents found in those vehicles made it clear that the original German offensive had been intended to roll right through Israel and the Palestinian Territories, and keep going and take the Persian Gulf oil fields by force. Paratroopers and other commando units were tasked to prevent the nations who owned those fields from setting fire to the wells, and death squads would brutally discourage insurgents from trying to damage pipelines or refineries.

The two German generals were paraded before the cameras. Both looked weary, frightened, and humiliated, but not mistreated. The president of Egypt then held up a captured map of the Middle East. The camera zoomed in. The words were all in German, but the intended lines of advance were clearly marked and unmistakable: Germany's goal was to occupy not just Egypt and Israel, but Syria, Jordan, Saudi Arabia, Kuwait, Iraq, and Iran.

The president put down the map, and grew more impassioned. He accused the Germans of being modern Crusaders. He said their botched offensive, and their grandiose goals of conquest, proved that *they* were the true mortal enemies of the Muslim world, not the U.S. or Israel. He called on the leaders and the people, of all the countries marked down as planned German prizes, to join in what Egypt had already done months before—declare war on the Axis, to drive these new Crusaders back where they came from, and wipe out the hostile regime that reigned from Berlin in the name of a trumped-up puppet kaiser.

The video recording ended. "Enough gloating," Jeffrey said. "I think watching that three times in a row is plenty for today."

"More tomorrow," somebody said.

"More beer now," someone else said.

Fresh beers were passed around. Jeffrey, along with the local naval officers—men and women—drank a toast to eventual Allied victory.

The important thing was that the Egyptian president's broadcast had worked, supported by hectic back-channel moves between heads of state and ambassadors and influential clerics. The Muslim and mostly Muslim countries ranging from Turkey and Syria all the way to Pakistan, Afghanistan, and Indonesia—each with their own forms of government and their rivalries and internal ethnic strife—put their differences aside and one by one did join the Allied cause. Though tough negotiations would be needed to create lines of reporting and to agree on effective decision-making hierarchies, vast new quantities of manpower, wealth, and natural resources were arrayed on America's and the British Commonwealth's side. Not wanting to be left out, India joined the Allies too. A wide land route, from the western Pacific through southern Asia and then the Middle East, up Turkey and into Europe's underbelly, was open at last.

"Now we just have to find a way to march on Berlin and Johannesburg without mass destruction on two or three continents," one of the Australians said, a bit less drunk than everyone else.

"And without body counts in the millions," Jeffrey said.

People nodded, as soberly as they could under the circumstances. Jeffrey was worldly wise enough to know that the Muslim states each acted for purely selfish reasons. The ominous vision of an Iron Crescent ascending into the heart of Europe began to encroach on his pleasant buzz of euphoria.

"Russia has to stop selling the Germans arms," someone else blurted out as Jeffrey listened. "Those ekranoplan things were bad enough. That bloody Snow Tiger was simply too over the top. It's the damn Russians we put the pressure on next, I say. Undercut Germany." The man belched. "Make Russia be really neutral, is the key to it all from here. The bloody Boers are a bloody sideshow now. We beat 'em a hundred years ago, we'll beat 'em again, nukes or no nukes."

Jeffrey had to excuse himself when an enlisted messenger found him and gave him an envelope. As he got up from the couch, he was handed another beer by a rather attractive female commander.

"One for the road, you Yanks always say? Take it back to your room. Maybe I'll stop by later and knock, make sure you didn't get bad news from home. Cheer you up."

"Cheers indeed, all," Jeffrey said, holding up the beer bottle and gesturing around the lounge.

Waves of alcohol-lubricated comradeship washed over him in return.

Jeffrey went to his room and put the beer on the desk. The sealed envelope had nothing but his name typed on the outside and a red rubber stamp, PRIVATE AND CONFIDENTIAL. He opened it clumsily, from being tipsy now for several good reasons.

The envelope contained a single sheet of paper in plain text. The sender was Admiral Hodgkiss, Commander, U.S. Atlantic Fleet. Jeffrey swallowed hard. He'd written a formal patrol report while crossing the Indian Ocean, telling everything, trying to explain his reasons for doing what he had done. That report would by now be in Hodgkiss's quite unforgiving hands.

Jeffrey skimmed the page. The gist was simple: Well done, proper judgment and initiative shown at all stages of extremely difficult task-group mission. Medals pending, further details and new operational orders to follow in several days.

Jeffrey felt very happy, and for once also felt at peace with himself. He was sure the beer was part of it—he hadn't had any alcohol for weeks.

That last sentence from Hodgkiss began to tickle his brain. New operational orders? There was still Ernst Beck's *von Scheer* to deal with.

Then Jeffrey began to wonder about something else, what one of the Australians had said in the lounge. That Russia had to be made to stop selling arms to Germany. Jeffrey knew the Snow Tiger—amply confirmed by a salvage survey as having been built in Russia, but commissioned as *Grand Admiral Doenitz* and operated by German officers and crew—set a dangerous precedent. Missiles and torpedoes without their warheads, even ekranoplans, were one thing. Entire state-of-the-art nuclear submarines, with fueled reactor cores, were an entirely separate and very provocative step in support of the Axis while claiming neutrality. Also, Russia's geographic placement let her threaten the flank of the new Allied land route to Europe.

Why can't I do something up in Russia like I did in Istanbul and Zichron Yaakov, with SEALs or other special forces? Make a clandestine penetration that produces results but, in addition, this time, sends a message. Something sneaky and really nasty, *with plausible deniability, yet unmistakable meaning on the receiving end, saying to back off....*

Well, it's not for me to decide.

Jeffrey took another swig of his beer.

There was a knock on the door. "You in there, Yank?" It

was a woman's voice, Australian—the commander with the
bedroom eyes from the lounge.

Jeffrey folded the paper and locked it away in the desk. He
got up and opened the door.

"It's not healthy to drink alone," she told him very assertively. "Much less *fun,* anyway." She held a beer in one
hand. She sidled past Jeffrey into the room, then glanced
back over her shoulder. "I never told you, my first name is
Melanie."

GLOSSARY

Acoustic intercept: A passive (listening only) sonar specifically designed to give warning when the submarine is "pinged" by an enemy active sonar. The latest version is the WLY-1.

Active out-of-phase emissions: A way to weaken the echo that an enemy sonar receives from a submarine's hull, by actively emitting sound waves of the same frequency as the ping but exactly out of phase. The out-of-phase sound waves mix with and cancel those of the echoing ping.

ADCAP: Mark 48 Advanced Capability torpedo. A heavyweight, wire-guided, long-range torpedo used by American nuclear submarines. The Improved ADCAP has an even longer range, and an enhanced (and extremely capable) target-homing sonar and software logic package.

AIP: Air Independent Propulsion. Refers to modern diesel submarines that have an additional power source besides the standard diesel engines and electric storage batteries. The

AIP system allows quiet and long-endurance submerged cruising, without the need to snorkel for air, because oxygen and fuel are carried aboard the vessel in special tanks. For example, the German class 212 design uses fuel cells for air-independent propulsion.

Ambient sonar: A form of active sonar that uses, instead of a submarine's pinging, the ambient noise of the surrounding ocean to catch reflections off a target. Noise sources can include surface wave-action sounds, the propulsion plants of other vessels (such as passing neutral merchant shipping), or biologics (sea life). Ambient sonar gives the advantage of actively pinging but without betraying a submarine's own presence. Advanced signal-processing algorithms and powerful onboard computers are needed to exploit ambient sonar effectively.

Auxiliary maneuvering units: Small propulsors at the bow and stern of a nuclear submarine, used to greatly enhance the vessel's maneuverability. First ordered for the USS *Jimmy Carter*, the third and last of the *Seawolf*-class SSNs (nuclear fast-attack submarines) to be constructed.

Ceramic composite: A multilayered composite foam matrix made from ceramic and metallic ingredients. One formulation, called alumina casing, an extremely strong submarine hull material significantly less dense than steel, was declassified by the U.S. Navy after the Cold War.

Corvette: A type of oceangoing warship smaller than a frigate (see below).

Deep scattering layer: A diffuse layer of biologics (marine life) present in many parts of the world's oceans, which causes scattering and absorption of sound. This can have tactical significance for undersea warfare forces by obscuring passive sonar contacts and causing false active sonar target returns. The layer's local depth, thickness, and scattering strength are known to vary by many factors, including one's location on the globe, the sound frequency being observed, the season of the year, and the hour of the day. The deep scattering layer is typically several hundred feet thick, and lies somewhere between one thousand and two thousand feet of depth during daylight, migrating shallower at night.

Double agent: A spy who works for both sides in a conflict. Often one side believes the spy works exclusively for them, when in fact the spy's loyalty is to the enemy, or only to him- or herself. Double agents in your employ can thus provide valuable information about the other side's intelligence operations. But they might instead (or simultaneously) represent a serious threat to your security by providing good information about you to the other side, or by intentionally misleading your side with false but plausible information.

Ekranoplan: Originally, the name of a very large Soviet military "wing in ground effect" aircraft. More generally, ekranoplans, also known as wiggies, are a hybrid sea-skimmer airplane. They fly just above the sea surface or level ground while obtaining significant extra aerodynamic lift by riding on a cushion of air trapped between the ground and the underside of the wings. Their speed can reach several hundred knots, and their huge cargo capacity can exceed five hundred tons. Smaller civilian wiggies are built in the U.S. for use as water taxis. Military versions can serve as powerful amphibious landing craft because of their excellent mobility and payload, and their ability to fly through marshes or up onto beaches.

ELF: Extremely low frequency. A form of radio that is capable of penetrating seawater; used to communicate (one way only) from a huge shore transmitter installation to submerged submarines. A disadvantage of ELF is that its data rate is extremely slow, only a few bits per minute.

EMCON: Emissions control. Radio silence, except it also applies to radar, sonar, laser, or other emissions that could give away a vessel's presence.

Frequency agile: A means of avoiding enemy interception and jamming, by very rapidly varying the frequency used by a transmitter and receiver. May apply to radio, or to underwater acoustic communications (see Gertrude, below).

Frigate: A type of oceangoing warship smaller than a destroyer.

Gertrude: Underwater telephone. Original systems simply transmitted the voice directly, with the aid of transducers (active sonar emitters, i.e., underwater loudspeakers), and were notorious for their short range and poor intelligibility. Modern undersea acoustic-communication systems translate the message into digital high-frequency active sonar pulses, which can be frequency agile for security (see above). Data rates well over one thousand bits per second, over ranges up to thirty nautical miles, can be achieved routinely.

Hole-in-ocean sonar: A form of passive (listening only) sonar that detects a target by how it blocks ambient ocean sounds from farther off. In effect, hole-in-ocean sonar uses an enemy submarine's own quieting against it.

Instant ranging: A capability of the new wide-aperture-array sonar systems (see below). Because each wide-aperture array is mounted rigidly along one side of the submarine's hull, sophisticated signal processing can be performed to "focus" the hydrophones at different ranges from the ship. The target needs to lie somewhere on the beam of the ship (i.e., to either side) for this to work well.

Kampfschwimmer: German Navy "frogmen" combat swimmers. The equivalent of U.S. Navy SEALs and the

Royal Navy's Special Boat Squadron commandos. (In the German language, the word "Kampfschwimmer" is both singular and plural.)

LASH: Littoral Airborne Sensor Hyperspectral. A new anti-submarine warfare search-and-detection technique, usually deployed from aircraft. LASH utilizes the backscatter of underwater illumination from sunlight, caught via special optical sensors and processed by classified computer software, to locate anomalous color gradations and shapes, even through deep seawater that is murky or dirty.

LIDAR: Light Direction and Ranging. Like radar but uses laser beams instead of radio waves. Undersea LIDAR uses blue-green lasers, because that color penetrates seawater to the greatest distance.

METOC: Meteorology and Oceanography Command. The part of the U.S. Navy that is responsible for providing weather and oceanographic data, and accompanying tactical assessments and recommendations, to the navy's operating fleets. METOC maintains a network of centers around the world to gather, analyze, interpret, and distribute this information.

Naval Submarine League (NSL): A professional association for submariners and submarine supporters. See their Web site, www.navalsubleague.com.

Network-centric warfare: A new approach to war fighting in which all formations and commanders share a common tactical and strategic picture through real-time digital data links. Every platform or node, such as a ship, aircraft, submarine, Marine Corps or army squad, or SEAL team, gathers and shares information on friendly and enemy locations and movements. Weapons, such as a cruise missile, might be fired by one platform, and be redirected in flight toward a fleeting target of opportunity by another platform, using information relayed by yet other platforms—including unmanned reconnaissance drones. Network-centric warfare promises to revolutionize command, control, communications, and intelligence, and greatly leverage the combat power of all friendly units while minimizing collateral damage.

Ocean interface hull module: Part of a submarine's hull that includes large internal "hangar space" for weapons and off-board vehicles, to avoid size limits forced by torpedo-tube diameter. (To carry large objects such as an ASDS mini-sub externally creates serious hydrodynamic drag, reducing a submarine's speed and increasing its flow noise.) The first ocean interface has been installed as part of the design of USS *Jimmy Carter,* the last of the three *Seawolf*-class SSNs to be constructed.

Ocean rover: Any one of a number of designs, either civilian or military, of a small, semiautonomous unmanned submersible vehicle that roves through the ocean collecting data on natural and man-made phenomena. This data is periodically downloaded via radio when the ocean rover comes shallow enough to raise an antenna above the sea surface. Powered by batteries or fuel cells, ocean rovers move slowly but can have an endurance of days or weeks before needing to be recovered for maintenance, reprogramming, refueling, etc. One U.S. Navy ocean rover is called the Seahorse, and is shaped like a very long, very wide torpedo.

Photon decoherence: The tendency for quantum entanglement (see below) to deteriorate with time and distance as the entangled photons interact with matter and energy in their environment.

Photonics mast: The modern replacement for the traditional optical periscope. One of the first was installed in USS *Virginia*. The photonics mast uses electronic imaging sensors, sends the data via thin electrical or fiber-optic cables, and displays the output on large high-definition TV screens in the control room. The photonics mast is "non-hull-penetrating," an important advantage over older 'scopes with their long, straight, thick tubes that must be able to move up and down and rotate.

Pump jet: A main propulsor for nuclear submarines that replaces the traditional screw propeller. A pump jet is a system of stator and rotor turbine blades within a cowling. (The rotors are turned by the main propulsion shaft, the same way the screw propeller's shaft would be turned.) Good pump-jet designs are quieter and more efficient than screw propellers, producing less cavitation noise and less wake turbulence.

Quantum entanglement: An aspect of quantum theory, a fundamental property of the universe first discussed by Albert Einstein. Under the proper conditions, two photons can become entangled, sharing similar properties—such as polarization or "spin"—that remain in lockstep no matter how far apart the two photons become. A change to the properties of one photon causes an instant identical change in the other photon, so long as they remain entangled. Since this instant change at any distance violates Einstein's limit on moving measurable information any faster than the speed of light, special steps are needed to harness photon entanglement practically. Electrons, or atoms, can also become entangled; entangled photons can imprint themselves (and their information) onto electrons.

Quantum teleportation: A complex, emerging method for transmitting information (data) using quantum entanglement (see above). Once referred to by Einstein as "spooky action at a distance," quantum teleportation is real, and has been demonstrated in laboratories.

Seabees: U.S. Navy combat-zone construction personnel, whose motto is "We Build, We Fight." Organized into naval mobile-construction battalions, the "CB" in the acronym NMCB led to their nickname as Seabees when created during World War II. Seabees continue to serve actively during wartime, including in Iraq and Afghanistan, and also provide humanitarian aid worldwide because of their skills at rapidly constructing and repairing roadways, schools, hospitals, housing, etc. after natural disasters. Seabees are armed troops who regularly carry weapons and conduct tactical training exercises. They often work under enemy fire. Commissioned officers in Seabee units are members of the navy's Civil Engineer Corps.

Sonobuoy: A small, active ("pinging") or passive (listening only) sonar detector, usually dropped in patterns (clusters) from a fixed-wing aircraft or a helicopter. The sonobuoys transmit their data to the aircraft by a radio link. The aircraft might have onboard equipment to analyze this data, or it might relay the data to a surface warship for detailed analysis. (The aircraft will also carry torpedoes or depth charges, to be able to attack any enemy submarines that its sonobuoys detect.) Some types of sonobuoy are able to operate down to a depth of sixteen thousand feet.

SSGN: A type of nuclear submarine designed or adapted for the primary purpose of launching cruise missiles, which tend to follow a level flight path through the air to their target. An SSGN is distinct from an SSBN, which launches strategic (hydrogen bomb) ballistic missiles, following a very high "lobbing" trajectory that leaves and then reenters the earth's atmosphere. Because cruise missiles tend to be smaller than ballistic missiles, an SSGN is able to carry a larger number of separate missiles than an SSBN of the same overall size. Note, however, that since ballistic missiles are typically "MIRVed", i.e., equipped with multiple independently targeted reentry vehicles, the total number of warheads on an SSBN and SSGN may be comparable; also, an SSBN's ballistic missiles can be equipped with high-explosive warheads instead of nuclear warheads. (A fast-attack submarine, or SSN, can be thought of as serving as a part-time SSGN, to the extent that some SSN classes have vertical launching systems for cruise missiles, and/or are able to fire cruise missiles through their torpedo tubes.)

Virginia **class:** The latest class of nuclear-propelled fast-attack submarines (SSNs) being constructed for the United States Navy, to follow the *Seawolf* class. The first, USS *Virginia,* was commissioned in 2004. (Post–Cold War, some SSNs have been named for states since the construction of *Ohio*-class Trident missile "boomers" has been halted.)

Wide-aperture array: A sonar system introduced, in the U.S. Navy, with USS *Seawolf* in the mid-1990s. Distinct from and in addition to the bow sphere, towed arrays, and forward hull array of the Cold War's *Los Angeles*–class SSNs. Each submarine so equipped actually has two wide-aperture arrays, one along each side of the hull. Each array consists of three separate rectangular hydrophone complexes. Powerful signal-processing algorithms allow sophisticated analysis of incoming passive sonar data. This includes instant ranging (see above).

ACKNOWLEDGMENTS

To begin, I want to thank my formal manuscript readers: Captain Melville Lyman, U.S. Navy (retired), commanding officer of several SSBN strategic missile submarines, and now director of Special Weapons Safety and Surety at the Johns Hopkins Applied Physics Laboratory; Commander Jonathan Powis, Royal Navy, who was navigator on the fast-attack submarine HMS *Conqueror* during the Falklands crisis, and who subsequently commanded three different British submarines; retired senior chief Bill Begin, veteran of many "boomer" deterrent patrols; and Peter Petersen, who served in the German Navy's *U-518* in World War II. Thanks also go to two navy SEALs, Warrant Officer Bill Pozzi and Commander Jim Ostach, and to Lieutenant Commander Jules Steinhauer, USNR (retired), diesel boat veteran and naval aviation submarine liaison in the early Cold War, for their feedback, support, and friendship.

A number of other navy people gave valuable guidance: George Graveson, Jim Hay, and Ray Woolrich, all retired U.S. Navy captains, former submarine skippers, and active in the Naval Submarine League; Ralph Slane, vice president of the New York Council of the Navy League of the United States, and docent of the *Intrepid* Museum; Ann Hassinger, research librarian at the U.S. Naval Institute; Richard Rosenblatt, M.D., formerly a medical consultant to the U.S. Navy; Commander Rick Dau, USN (retired), former operations director of the Naval Submarine League; Bill Kreher, current operations director; and retired reserve U.S. Navy Seabee chief "Stormin' Normand" Dupuis.

Additional submariners and military contractors deserve acknowledgment. They are too many to name here, but continuing to stand out vividly in my mind are pivotal conversations with Commander (now Captain) Mike Connor, at the time CO of USS *Seawolf*, and with the late Captain Ned Beach, USN (retired), brilliant writer and great submariner. I also want to thank, for the guided tours of their fine submarines, the officers and men of USS *Alexandria*, USS *Connecticut*, USS *Dallas*, USS *Hartford*, USS *Memphis*, USS *Salt Lake City*, USS *Seawolf*, USS *Springfield*, USS *Topeka*, and the modern German diesel submarine *U-15*. I owe "deep" appreciation to everyone aboard USS *Miami*, SSN 755, for four wonderful days on and under the sea.

Similar thanks go to the instructors and students of the New London Submarine School, and the Coronado BUD/SEAL training facilities, and to all the people who demonstrated their weapons, equipment, attack vessels, and aircraft at the amphibious warfare bases in Coronado and Norfolk. Appreciation also goes to the men and women of the aircraft carrier USS *Constellation*, the Aegis guided missile cruiser USS *Vella Gulf*, the fleet-replenishment oiler USNS *Pecos*, the deep-submergence rescue vehicle *Avalon*, and its chartered tender R/V *Kellie Chouest*.

The Current Strategy Forum and publications of the Naval War College were invaluable. The opportunity to fly out to the amphibious warfare helicopter carrier USS *Iwo Jima* during New York City's Fleet Week 2002, and then join her sailors and marines in rendering honors as the ship passed ground zero, the former site of the World Trade Center, was one of the most powerfully emotional experiences of my life.

First among the publishing people deserving acknowledgment is my wife, Sheila Buff, a nonfiction author and coauthor of more than two dozen books on health and wellness, hiking, and nature loving. Then comes my agent, John Talbot, touchstone of seasoned wisdom on the craft and business sides of the writing profession. Equally crucial is my editor at William Morrow, Mike Shohl, always enthusiastic, accessible, and inspiring through his keen insights on how to improve my manuscript drafts.

Turn the page for a preview of the next thrilling
Jeffrey Fuller adventure
from Joe Buff,
SEAS OF CRISIS,
coming soon in hardcover
from William Morrow.

Late June, 2012

War isn't hell, it's worse than hell, Commander Jeffrey Fuller told himself. He sat alone in his captain's stateroom on USS *Challenger*, whose ceramic composite hull helped make her America's most capable nuclear powered fast-attack submarine. But Jeffrey was not a happy camper. Despite his many successes in tactical atomic combat at sea in a war that the Berlin-Boer Axis started a year ago—and despite his repeated brilliant achievements in special operations raids against hostile territory—very recently, for complicated reasons, Jeffrey had felt like a has-been. His two Navy Crosses, his Medal of Honor, his Defense Distinguished Service Medal, and his whole crew's receipt of a Presidential Unit Citation some months ago, all put together couldn't dispel his present dark mood.

Challenger was five days out from Pearl Harbor, deeply submerged and steaming due north, already past the Aleutian Islands chain that stretched between Alaska and Siberia. She was bound for the New London submarine base, on Connecticut's Thames River, having been sent by the shortest but most frigid possible route: through the narrow Bering Strait choke point looming a few hundred miles ahead, separating the easternmost tip of pseudo-neutral Russia from mainland Alaska's desolate Cape Prince of Wales. Jeffrey would sail way up and past Alaska and Arctic Canada. Then he'd sneak through the shallow waters between Canada and Greenland, into the Atlantic, to arrive at home port in two weeks for a reception that he already dreaded.

No one from *Challenger*—including Jeffrey—had even been allowed ashore at Pearl. Taking on minimal supplies and spare parts, and embarking five somber, tight-lipped passengers—an inspection team maybe, or investigators from JAG?—had occurred entirely by minisub. *Challenger* hid underwater, off the coast from Honolulu, frustratingly near its enticing beaches, bars, nightclubs, and more. No fresh fruit or vegetables were provided by the Pearl Harbor Base, to replenish what had already run out since the ship's last port of call. This was supposed to be for security, but Jeffrey thought that was just an excuse; it felt much more like punishment. It was as if, after his most recent mission, despite his major contributions to the Allied cause, he'd become a pariah, shunted out of sight and out of mind by the powers-that-be.

Forget about me, it's an insult to my crew's dedication and courage.

Jeffrey was smart and self-aware. He knew his unpleasant mood wasn't due to exhaustion, usually a chronic problem the way he drove himself. He and his men had had ten days of wonderful leave in Australia, including much consumption of the excellent local beer—cut short by sudden orders to proceed with greatest possible stealth to Hawaii. Also cut short, alas, was his newly made contact with a Royal Australian Navy commander named Melanie, of whom he carried deliciously vivid memories . . . but missing her wasn't the cause of his funk. He'd been gone from her now for a longer stretch than he'd known her.

He wasn't morose either, after the fact, for the adversaries he'd killed; his soul adjusted better than most to this dehumanizing cost of war. Nor was his mood caused by concern for his crew's survival, for the outcome of an impending battle that Jeffrey might well lose—he'd long since mastered these stresses and strains of command through brutal experience. The cruise home should be a milk run.

But there were no new medals awaiting Jeffrey at Pearl Harbor for the latest tremendous things he'd accomplished, despite an earlier message implying there would be. No admirals came to shake his hand, no squadron commodore gave him a pat on the back. And Jeffrey was sure he knew why.

He'd broken too many unwritten rules—too many even for him—on that fateful mission spanning half the globe. He'd stepped on too many toes, made too many new and well-placed political enemies in Washington, while exercising initiative that had seemed to make sense at the time: He'd won a vehement shouting match quashing a civilian expert whose advice he was supposed to respect. On his own accord he'd clandestinely violated a crucial ally's sovereignty, leaving the seeds for what could still become a disastrous diplomatic incident. Worst, while obeying orders he knew he could have chosen to ignore, he and everyone else on *Challenger* had had to listen, horrified, doing nothing but flee while dozens of good men—friends and colleagues—died under Axis attack in the Med.

The real price of that ambivalent inaction under fire only began to show on the transit across the vast Pacific from Australia to Hawaii. *Challenger* should have steered in the opposite direction, toward Boer-controlled South Africa, to engage and eliminate front-line Axis naval units there; eager to clear their names via further mortal combat against a hated foe, the crew grew restive at being banished toward a safe rear area.

It was then that some of Jeffrey's men began to have nightmares so bad that they'd wake up screaming, reliving the deafening battle from which Jeffrey ran. Tragic, yes, but unacceptable on a warship that needed to maintain ultraquiet. There was little that *Challenger*'s medical corpsman, a rotund and normally jolly chief, could do for them. Six of Jeffrey's people were offloaded, also by minisub, at Pearl as psychiatric cases. Not one new crewman transferred on, odd in itself since rotation of U.S. Navy personnel was a common procedure—and in this situation another bad sign.

Jeffrey was working more short-handed even than that. One of his star performers, Lieutenant Kathy Milgrom of the UK's Royal Navy, who'd served as *Challenger*'s sonar officer on the ship's most vital missions, had been summarily detached. Jumped two ranks to Commander, she was now an influential advisor on the Aussie naval staff in Sydney. This was terrific for Milgrom, and Jeffrey was very glad for her, but he'd been miffed that he found out about it only when she got the orders directly and then told him; the way it was handled violated correct protocol. Now, that incident seemed like the first harbinger of Jeffrey's abruptly downgraded status in the eyes of his superiors.

Also during his Australian leave, Jeffrey found out from his father—who'd rocketed from dull bureaucrat to a very senior position in wartime homeland resource conservation at the Department of Energy—that Jeffrey's ex-girlfriend, edgy and self-reliant Boer freedom fighter Ilse Reebeck, was under arrest for treason, an alleged double agent for the Axis. Before deploying to the Med, Jeffrey was grilled about their relationship by the Director of the FBI in front of the President of the United States, with the director slinging rhetoric that made Jeffrey look pretty bad. The president had taken a shining to Jeffrey at the Medal of Honor presentation, followed by a private chat, earlier in the year. He had no idea where he stood with his commander in chief these days. The rumors of Ilse being held in solitary confinement, leaked to him by his dad but neither confirmed nor denied through normal channels, were another contributor to Jeffrey's mounting sense of trouble. His tentative moves intervening on Ilse's behalf had been curtly rebuffed, with sharp instructions for him to stay within his proper sphere—undersea warfare, not domestic counterespionage.

So *Challenger* was back to having an all-male crew, which should have simplified his leadership problems, but the effect on morale wasn't positive when word got around. The men admired Milgrom's talent, and Ilse's as a combat oceanographer, and they believed—with the strength of sailors' superstition—that Ilse's being on board in the past had brought the ship good luck.

Privacy was scarce-to-nonexistent on a sub; scuttlebutt and gossip—and wild speculation, too—traveled fast. His crew, each a hand-picked volunteer who'd passed the toughest imaginable screening, were seeing the same tea leaves that Jeffrey was trying to read. They could sense what he was feeling, no matter how hard he bottled it up to do his duty as their captain and carry on as if all were routine. When he offered quick words of greeting or encouragement, as he moved around his ship that bustled like a snug beehive—with everyone as familiar to him as if they were part of his family—the words rang hollow.

Jeffrey was easy to read; deceit in face-to-face interactions simply wasn't in him. He'd found out the expensive way, early in his Navy career, that he was awful at poker. In stark contrast, the personal anonymity from the opaqueness of the ocean—combined with getting inside an enemy sub captain's mind through a sixth sense that Jeffrey possessed in uncanny abundance—posed the sort of contest, the winner-take-all blood sport, that he excelled at and most craved. The higher the stakes the better, at this type of game, and Jeffrey never felt so alive as when nuclear torpedo engines screamed and their warheads erupted, while he snapped helm orders to maneuver *Challenger* like a fighter jet under the sea.

On his latest missions the stakes had been as high as they could come, possibly shaping the outcome of the whole war. But this last time, it appeared, Jeffrey had gone too far in some ways, and not far enough in others. He suspected there were whispers in the corridors of the Pentagon that he was an uncontrollable cowboy, a loose cannon who second-guessed others too much—and when it mattered most, his jealous rivals would be saying, he'd shown a streak of cowardice. Jeffrey knew he'd done the right thing at every stage of that mind-twisting mission, but what he knew inside didn't count. He was on his way into professional obscurity, dead-ended at the rank of commander, bound for some desk job far from the action. His own worst nightmare was coming true: He was being beached, before the war had even been won.

He listened to the steady rushing sound that came from the air-circulation vents in the overhead of his cabin. The air inside the forward parts of *Challenger* was always cool, to keep the electronics from overheating. Jeffrey was very used to it, but this evening for some strange reason he felt chilled into his marrow. Then he understood.

The cycle of death-defying adrenaline rushes, followed by high-level awards and attention, had for him become addictive. Jeffrey was experiencing the symptoms of withdrawal, leaving him utterly empty inside.

He looked up for a moment at the bluish glare of the fluorescent fixtures, like plant grow-lights to keep submariners healthy while deprived of any sun for weeks on end. He glanced at the grayish flame-proof linoleum squares that covered his stateroom deck, then gazed around at the fake-wood wainscot veneer, and bright stainless steel, lining the four bulkheads of his tiny world. He pulled a standard-issue brown sweater out of a clothing drawer, one made of wool with vertical ribbing, putting it on over the khaki uniform blouse and slacks he always liked to wear while under way. He was still cold.

Outside his shut door, in the narrow passage, he heard crewmen hurrying about now and then, on their way to different stations to perform the myriad tasks that helped the ship run smoothly every second of every minute of every single day. There was no margin for error on a nuclear submarine. Jeffrey dearly loved this endless pressure, much as he'd grown accustomed to the constant, potentially killing squeeze of the ocean surrounding *Challenger*.

He sighed. Too soon another man would sit at this little

fold-down desk, sleep in this austere rack, put up photos of wife and children, and assert his own personality and habits onto the crew. *Challenger* would have a different captain, because Jeffrey's run of luck as captain had finally run out.

Someone knocked.

"Come in!" Jeffrey welcomed any distraction.

His executive officer entered, Lieutenant Commander Jackson Jefferson Bell. A few inches taller than Jeffrey, but less naturally muscular, Bell was happily married and had a six-month-old son to look forward to seeing again, once they arrived in the States. Cautious in his tactical thinking when Jeffrey was super-aggressive, Bell complemented Jeffrey perfectly in the control room during combat. Often he'd played devil's advocate in engagements where split seconds mattered, when the waters thundered outside the hull and *Challenger* shook from stem to stern as if tossed by an angry sea monster—and Jeffrey's crew looked to him to somehow, some way, keep them alive, while an Axis skipper did his damnedest to smash their ship to pieces and slaughter every person aboard.

Right now Bell seemed uncomfortable, as if he could tell that their prior working relationship would end soon. Comings and goings, joinings and separations, were a normal enough part of life in the Navy. This time, though, it was different. Jeffrey and Bell's parting would not be a happy one for Jeffrey, and he knew he'd miss Bell a lot. Their hair's-breadth survival so many times, the shared exhilaration with each added victory, had brought the two men close.

Jeffrey grimaced to himself. *Bell will have a new boss.*

Jeffrey understood Bell's perspective. He needed to attend, first and foremost, to his own future career. Bell had a family to support. If he survived the war and wanted to stay in the Navy, he'd require as much space between himself and Jeffrey's now-tainted reputation as he could get.

Bell had arrived to give his regular evening 2000—8 p.m.—report as XO to his captain. Bell's words held no surprises. He wrapped up crisply and left, pulling the door shut behind him. Toward the end of his verbal update on the status of the ship and her machinery and equipment and personnel, Bell avoided making eye contact. It was as if he was embarrassed for Jeffrey, and tried to hide it, but the more he tried to hide it, the more he made things worse.

Two more weeks of this before they got to New London, Jeffrey told himself. He was a lame duck in every sense of the word. He didn't like the sensation, not one bit.

At least they didn't relieve me of command right there at Pearl. Probably only because nobody with the right credentials was free.

Jeffrey needed something more than meaningless paperwork to keep busy. He refused to start mental rehearsals for the court martial which might be coming—that was just too defeatist, too morbid. There'd be plenty of time for it later if need be, and as a decorated war hero—a national celebrity—such drastic measures were unlikely. No, exile to semi-oblivion in some token land activity was a more probable disposition for a commander who'd become an awkward case to those on high, key officials not just at the Pentagon but in the CIA and the State Department too, coming together at the Cabinet level.

Jeffrey realized his thoughts were going in circles.

To stay occupied, however briefly, and hear the sound of another human voice, Jeffrey picked up his intercom handset for the control room. The messenger of the watch answered, one of the youngest and least experienced crewmen, someone who was still working hard to earn his silver dolphins, the coveted badge of a full-fledged enlisted submariner; officers wore gold. Jeffrey wondered if the messenger, like Bell, would survive this horrendous war or not—assuming civilization and humanity survived.

"Give me the Navigator, please," Jeffrey said, keeping his tone as even as he could.

"Wait one, sir," the still-boyish voice of the teenage messenger said.

"Navigator here, Captain," Jeffrey heard in his earpiece.

Despite himself, he smiled. Lieutenant Richard Sessions was one of the most unflappable people he'd ever met, inside or outside the military. From a small town in Nebraska, Sessions was the type of guy whose hair and clothes were always a little sloppy, no matter what he did. But his indispensable work as head of the ship's navigating department—an extremely technical area—was without fail beautifully organized and precise.

"Nav, when do we pass through fifty-five north, one-hundred-seventy-five west?" In mid-Bering Sea, on the way up to the strait. It was at that point, and only then, that Jeffrey was to open the sealed orders in his safe, containing the recognition signals and other data he'd need to finish his last trip without becoming a victim of friendly fire.

"Hold please, sir," Sessions responded, as earnest as ever.

At her present stealthy speed of twenty knots, and heading due north, *Challenger* would cross one degree of latitude every three hours. Jeffrey had a detailed readout on the computer screen by his desk, so he always knew the ship's exact position to an error usually measured in tens of feet—depth was displayed to the nearest foot. He could have done the calculation easily in his head. Calling Sessions was make-work, for both of them. And it wasn't like anyone would know or care if he opened those orders an hour early or late.

But punctuality was valued—and demanded—in the Navy. It had been thoroughly ingrained in Jeffrey from the time, almost twenty years ago, when he'd done college in Navy ROTC at Purdue, an electrical engineering major. Now, in his late thirties, even in the midst of emotional doldrums, the impulse to stick to a printed schedule died hard.

Sessions had the answer for Jeffrey quickly. "At local time zero-three-twenty tomorrow, sir." The wee hours of the coming morning.

"Okay. Thanks, Nav." Jeffrey hung up.

Aw, what the heck.

As an act of rebellion against those seniors who'd used

him, drained him, and cast him aside when the going got rough, Jeffrey stood and opened his safe.

He withdrew the bulky envelope. It contained a seawater-proof incendiary self-destruct charge, to cremate the classified contents in case of unauthorized tampering. This precaution was normal for submarine captains' order pouches in this war. As Jeffrey knew painfully well, American subs could be sunk in battle. And just as the U.S. had done more than once to derelict Soviet submarines, Axis salvage divers or robotic probes could rifle through *Challenger*'s wreckage if something went wrong, compromising crucial codes and revealing priceless secrets.

Jeffrey very carefully entered the combination on the big envelope's keypad, to disarm the self-destruct. The last thing he wanted was to set it off by accident. Aside from ruining his orders before he could read them, fire on a submerged submarine would be terrible. None was ever considered small until after it was out. When the ship was prevented, because of the need for perpetual stealth, from surfacing or snorkeling to clear the smoke, at best the crew would have to spend long hours in uncomfortable respirator masks, until the air scrubbers removed the toxins and soot. At worst, men would die. No, Jeffrey did not want to further mar this voyage by starting a fire.

The envelope opened safely. Jeffrey emptied its contents on his desk. His heart began to pound.

Among the papers and data disks, and another, inner, sealed envelope, were two metal uniform-collar insignia—silver eagles, which meant the rank of Captain, United States Navy, the next rank above commander. The actual *rank* of captain, not just the courtesy title that every vessel's skipper received. Jeffrey snatched up the hard copy orders and read them as fast as he could, almost desperately.

He realized his mind had been playing nasty tricks, in the vacuum of feedback from above, running toward paranoia that was probably a symptom of his own lingering reactions to his drastic decisions and their traumatic effects in the Med.

Challenger had indeed been ordered to mask her presence at Pearl Harbor because of security. The trip to the U.S. East Coast was a cover story. His five mysterious passengers belonged to a Seabee Engineer Reconnaissance Team; SERTs were elite shadow warriors from among the Navy's mobile combat construction battalions. They gathered unusual intell and did mind-boggling tasks at the forward edge of the battle area. *Interesting.*

Jeffrey was hereby promoted to the rank of Navy captain—the rank immediately below rear admiral. He was also awarded a second Medal of Honor for what he'd done in the Med, though this award was classified. There'd be no bright gold star, for the blue ribbon with small white stars already adorning his dressier uniforms, to denote the second Medal. But selection boards for rear admiral, Jeffrey reminded himself, would certainly know about it when the time came. Plus, *Challenger*'s whole crew had been awarded another Presidential Unit Citation, although this was also top secret outside the ship.

Good. Excellent. Morale will skyrocket.

He skimmed more. Once through the Bering Strait, gateway to the Chukchi Sea, he still would turn toward Canada. Then, in the ice-choked, storm tossed Beaufort Sea, above the Arctic Circle, *Challenger* would rendezvous with USS *Jimmy Carter*. *Carter* was an ultra-fast and deep diving steel-hulled sub of the *Seawolf* class, uniquely modified with an extra hundred feet of hull length—room to support large special operations forces commando raids, plus "garage space" for oversized weapons and off-board probes.

Bell was being promoted to full commander. He'd take over *Challenger* from Jeffrey, who from now on was commanding officer of an undersea strike group consisting of *Challenger* and *Carter*; Bell and *Carter*'s captain would be his subordinates. To avoid confusion between all these different roles and ranks, Jeffrey was granted the courtesy title of commodore.

He was positively delighted. Whatever he'd done, good or

bad, his supporters in upper Navy echelons—and the White House too?—outweighed and overruled his detractors. He wasn't being banished after all. Jeffrey read further into his orders, more slowly now to absorb every detail. Crucial portions of the mission required that two submarines be involved, but there was much more to it than *Challenger* and *Carter* together having more total firepower, while covering each other's back. This piqued Jeffrey's curiosity; no explanation was given of what it meant. Even more cryptically, Jeffrey was told to brush up on the Russian he'd studied in college, and to practice his poker face; the SERT guys would help him on both counts, starting right away. His eyebrows rose, involuntarily, as he took this in.

After the rendezvous and a joint briefing to be held aboard *Carter,* he would lead his two-ship strike group westward, into the East Siberian Sea—Russian home waters. His assignment was to do something that would force Russia once and for all to stop supporting the Axis against America while Moscow outwardly kept claiming legal neutrality. Specifics were inside that inner envelope, to be opened only once the rendezvous was made.

Jeffrey's entire demeanor changed. This was exactly the sort of important and dangerous undertaking he really enjoyed; revealing the whole plan only in stages, for security, was something he'd gotten used to. He couldn't wait to tell Bell the great news about their twinned promotions. Jeffrey was fond of Navy traditions and pomp; he'd been so, almost obsessively, since discovering naval history in a local St. Louis library as a child. He was impatient to hold the formal change of command ceremony, in the enlisted mess—the biggest meeting space on his ship. *No. Correct that. On* Captain Bell's *ship.*

One thing puzzled, disturbed Jeffrey. For this mission, he came under the control of Commander, Strategic Command, a U.S. Air Force four-star general. That general oversaw the readiness and possible use of America's thermonuclear weapons—hydrogen bombs. *Challenger* carried no

H-bombs, and never had. Her nuclear torpedoes bore very low yields, a single kiloton maximum. H-bombs had destructive power a thousand times as large, and vastly greater deadly radioactive fallout that drifted globally.

The Axis, shrewdly, owned no hydrogen bombs and made sure the whole world knew it. This kept America from escalating past tactical atomic fission devices set off only at sea— not that anyone sane in the U.S. would want to further escalate this war.

Jeffrey began to suffer a dreadful unease. *Why am I suddenly reporting to Commander, Strategic Command?*